The
Night
My Friend

The Mystery Makers Series

Francis M. Nevins, Jr.
Martin H. Greenberg

General Editors

The Night My Friend

**Stories Of Crime
and Suspense
by
Edward D. Hoch**

Edited by Francis M. Nevins, Jr.

OHIO UNIVERSITY PRESS → → → → ATHENS

Compilation, Introduction and Checklist
© copyright 1992 by Francis M. Nevins, Jr.
Printed in the United States of America
All rights reserved
Ohio University Press books are printed on acid-free paper ∞

Library of Congress Cataloging-in-Publication Data

Hoch, Edward D., 1930–
    The night, my friend : stories of crime and suspense / by Edward
D. Hoch ; edited by Francis M. Nevins, Jr.
        p.   cm. — (The Mystery makers series)
    Includes bibliographical references.
    ISBN 0-8214-1011-3
    1. Detective and mystery stories, American.   I. Nevins, Francis
M. II. Title. III. Series.
PS3558.0337N5   1992
813'.54—dc20
                                                91-20984
                                                CIP

Contents

Acknowledgments

"Twilight Thunder" (*Alfred Hitchcock's Mystery Magazine*, January 1962). Copyright © 1961 H.S.D. Publications, Inc.; renewal copyright © 1989 Edward D. Hoch.

"The Night My Friend" (*The Saint Mystery Magazine*, British edition, July 1962). Copyright © 1962, 1990 Edward D. Hoch.

"The Suitcase" (*The Saint Mystery Magazine*, September 1962, as by Pat McMahon). Copyright © 1962 Fiction Publishing Co.; renewal copyright © 1990 Edward D. Hoch.

"The Picnic People" (*Alfred Hitchcock's Mystery Magazine*, March 1963). Copyright © 1963 H.S.D. Publications, Inc.; renewal copyright © 1991 Edward D. Hoch.

"Day for a Picnic" (*The Saint Mystery Magazine*, November 1963, as by Pat McMahon). Copyright © 1963 Fiction Publishing Co.; renewal copyright © 1991 Edward D. Hoch.

"Shattered Rainbow" (*Alfred Hitchcock's Mystery Magazine*, January 1964). Copyright © 1963 H.S.D. Publications, Inc.; renewal copyright © 1991 Edward D. Hoch.

"The Patient Waiter" (*Alfred Hitchcock's Mystery Magazine*, May 1964). Copyright © 1964 H.S.D. Publications, Inc.; reprinted by permission of the author.

"Too Long at the Fair" (*Alfred Hitchcock's Mystery Magazine*, October 1964). Copyright © 1964 H.S.D. Publications, Inc.; reprinted by permission of the author.

"Winter Run" (*Alfred Hitchcock's Mystery Magazine*, January 1965). Copyright © 1964 H.S.D. Publications, Inc.; reprinted by permission of the author.

"The Long Way Down" (*Alfred Hitchcock's Mystery Magazine*, February 1965. Copyright © 1965 H.S.D. Publications, Inc.; reprinted by permission of the author.

"Dreaming Is a Lonely Thing" (*Alfred Hitchcock's Mystery Magazine*, March 1965). Copyright © 1965 H.S.D. Publications, Inc.; reprinted by permission of the author.

"In Some Secret Place" (*The Saint Mystery Magazine*, August 1965). Copyright © 1965 Fiction Publishing Co.; reprinted by permission of the author.

"To Slay an Eagle" (*The Award Espionage Reader*, 1965, as by Stephen Dentinger). Copyright © 1965 Universal Publishing and Distributing Corp.; reprinted by permission of the author.

"They Never Come Back" (*Alfred Hitchcock's Mystery Magazine*, February 1966). Copyright © 1966 H.S.D. Publications, Inc.; reprinted by permission of the author.

"The Only Girl in His Life" (*Signature*, February 1966). Copyright © 1965 Diners Club, Inc.; reprinted by permission of the author.

"It Happens, Sometimes" (*The Saint Mystery Magazine*, April 1966, as by Stephen Dentinger). Copyright © 1966 Fiction Publishing Co.; reprinted by permission of the author.

"A Girl Like Cathy" (*Signature*, October 1966). Copyright © 1966 Diners Club, Inc.; reprinted by permission of the author.

Acknowledgments

"What's It All About?" (*The Saint Magazine*, January 1967, as by Stephen Dentinger). Copyright © 1966 Fiction Publishing Co.; reprinted by permission of the author.

"First Offense" (*Ellery Queen's Mystery Magazine*, January 1968, as by Stephen Dentinger). Copyright © 1967 Davis Publications, Inc.; reprinted by permission of the author.

"Hawk in the Valley" (*Alfred Hitchcock's Mystery Magazine*, August 1968). Copyright © 1968 H.S.D. Publications, Inc.; reprinted by permission of the author.

"The Ring with the Velvet Ropes" (*With Malice Toward All*, 1968). Copyright © 1968 Mystery Writers of America, Inc.; reprinted by permission of the author.

"Homecoming" (*Alfred Hitchcock's Mystery Magazine*, April 1969). Copyright © 1969 H.S.D. Publications, Inc.; reprinted by permission of the author.

Introduction

If ever there was a member of an endangered species it's Edward D. Hoch, the only person alive who makes his living writing mystery short stories. To date he has sold almost seven hundred tales, and at his current rate of productivity he should hit the thousand mark in the early 2000s. As if turning out two to three dozen stories a year were not enough, he fills his odd moments with writing a regular column for *The Armchair Detective,* editing the annual *Year's Best Mystery and Suspense Stories* anthologies, and serving tirelessly on various committees of the Mystery Writers of America organization. He's written five novels, plotted a series of mystery-puzzle paperbacks, and is presently working on a book-length whodunit in collaboration with other members of MWA. Not exactly the lightest of work-loads; and yet he never seems harried or overcommitted and comes across in person and correspondence as an amazingly placid and easy-going fellow. His secret? If you are doing precisely what you want to do with your life, and making it pay besides, the distinction between work and play becomes meaningless and every hour is a pleasure.

Edward Dentinger Hoch was a Washington's Birthday boy, born in Rochester, New York on February 22, 1930. His father, Earl G. Hoch, was a banker, but despite the precarious nature of that line of work during the Depression, the family weathered the thirties without serious problems.

From a very early age Ed was fascinated by mystery fiction. "When I was a young child," he said, "I used to draw cartoon strips and have masked villains running around. They were terrible, just stick figures, because I wasn't much of an artist, but I'd try to draw in cloaks and masks to identify the villains so I could have a final unmasking to surprise the reader. Of course, I was the only reader. No one else saw those strips."

In June of 1939, when the sixty-minute *Adventures of Ellery Queen* series debuted on the CBS radio network, nine-year-old Ed Hoch was one of its staunchest fans. Later that year, when Pocket Books, Inc. launched its first 25¢ paperback reprint books, the boy discovered that his hero Ellery Queen had been the protagonist of many novels as well as a radio sleuth. The first adult book he ever read was the Pocket Books edition of Queen's 1934 classic *The Chinese Orange Mystery.* "It was among the first group of paperbacks published, and I recall going down to the corner drugstore and seeing them all lined up with their laminated covers. I debated for some time between James Hilton's *Lost Horizon* and an Agatha Christie title [probably *The Murder of Roger Ackroyd*], and finally settled on Ellery Queen because I had heard the Ellery Queen radio program which was so popular in those days. I bought *The Chinese Orange Mystery* and was completely fascinated by it, sought out all the other Ellery Queen novels I could find in paperback, as Pocket Books published them over the next few years, and from there went on to read other things. I read Sherlock Holmes at about that time too."

It was during the forties that, one by one, Ed Hoch discovered the masters of fair-play detection: Conan Doyle, Chesterton, Christie, John Dickson Carr, Clayton Rawson, and of course the cousins Frederic Dannay and Manfred B. Lee who wrote as Ellery Queen. In 1947, after completing high school, he entered the University of Rochester, but left two years later to take a researcher's job at the local public library. He enlisted in 1950, during the Korean conflict, and once out of basic training he was assigned to Fort Jay, on Governor's Island just off Manhattan, as a military policeman. He took advantage of being stationed near the headquarters of Mystery Writers of America, which was then only five or six years old, to attend the organization's monthly meetings (in uniform) and to mingle with the giants of deductive puzzlement whose books he'd been hooked on since age nine. Discharged from the service in 1952, he went to work in the adjustments department of Pocket Books, the house that had started him reading detective fiction, and continued to write short mysteries as he had since high school. In

1954, back in Rochester, he took a copywriter's job with the Hutchins advertising agency, and late the following year he knew the special pleasure of seeing his first published story on the newsstands. That was the start of Ed Hoch's real career, one that is still going strong thirty-six years and almost seven hundred stories later.

For more than a dozen years after that first sale, he kept his job at the ad agency and saved his fiction writing for evenings, weekends, and vacations. But he was so fertile with story ideas and such a swift writer that editors and readers could easily have mistaken him for a full-timer even in those early years. In 1957 he married Patricia McMahon, with whom he still shares a small neat house in suburban Rochester. (Two of its three bedrooms were long ago converted into his office space, and the basement into a library filled with thousands of mystery novels, short story collections and magazine issues, few of them without at least one Hoch story.) The field's top publications, *Ellery Queen's* and *Alfred Hitchcock's* mystery magazines, began printing his tales in 1962. Six years later, having won the coveted Mystery Writers of America Edgar award for the best short story of 1967, he decided that he could support the family on his writing income and left the advertising agency. He continues to write full-time (many would say more than full-time) today. During 1982–83 he served as president of the organization to whose annual dinners he had first come in military khaki more than thirty years earlier. At age sixty-one he shows no signs of slowing down, and readers around the world hope he'll stay active well beyond his thousandth story.

Why so few novels and so many short stories? It boils down to Hoch's special affinity for the short form. "Writing a novel has always been, to me, a task to be finished as quickly as possible. Writing a short story is a pleasure one can linger over, with delight in the concept and surprise at the finished product." Or, as he put it elsewhere, "I guess ideas just come easily to me. That's why I've always been more attracted to the short story form than the novel. I am more interested in the basic plotting than in the development of various sub-plots. And I think the basic plot, or gimmick—the type of twist you have in detective stories— is the thing I can do best, which explains why so many of my stories tend to be formal detective stories rather than the crime-suspense tales that so many writers are switching to today."

Those words are misleading in one sense: more than two hundred of his published stories are non-series tales of crime and suspense, and some of the best of them are collected here. But most of his energies have gone into the creation of short-story series characters and the chronicling of their exploits. To date he has launched twenty-four separate series, dealing with all sorts of protagonists from an occult detective who claims to be more than two thousand years old to a Western drifter who may be a reincarnation of Billy the Kid to a science-fictional Computer Investigation Bureau. Whatever the concept of a series, whatever its roots, Hoch's tendency is to turn it into a series of miniature detective novels, complete with bizarre crimes, subtle clues, brilliant deductions and of course the ethos of playing fair with the reader that distinguishes the work of Carr, Christie, and Queen. The best introduction to the world of Ed Hoch is a quick tour through each of his series in the order in which they were created.

SIMON ARK, the two-millennia-old Satan-hunter, was the central character in Hoch's first published story, "Village of the Dead" (*Famous Detective Stories*, December 1955), and appeared in many tales that editor Robert A. W. Lowndes bought for the Columbia chain of pulp magazines during the late fifties. The ideas in these apprentice stories are occasionally quite original (e.g. the murder of one of a sect of Penitentes while the cult members are hanging on crucifixes in a dark cellar), but the execution tends at times to be crude and naive and the Roman Catholic viewpoint somewhat obtrusive. Eight of the early Arks were collected in two rare paperback volumes, *The Judges of Hades* and *City of Brass*, both published by Leisure Books in 1971, but the most readily accessible book about this character is *The Quests of Simon Ark* (Mysterious Press, 1984). In the late 1970s Simon was resurrected for new cases in the *Alfred Hitchcock* and *Ellery Queen* magazines, but these tales pare down the occult aspects to a bare minimum and present Ark simply as an eccentric old mastersleuth specializing in impossible crimes.

PROFESSOR DARK, apparently an alter ego of Simon Ark, popped up in two obscure pulp magazine stories of the mid-fifties under Hoch's pseudonym of Stephen Dentinger, but they have never been reprinted and are of interest only to completists.

AL DIAMOND, a private eye character, began life in "Jealous Lover" (*Crime and Justice,* March 1957), which featured a walk-on part by a Captain Leopold, later to become Hoch's most frequently recurring series detective. After two appearances, Diamond's name was changed to AL DARLAN so as to avoid confusion with Blake Edwards' radio and TV private eye Richard Diamond. Although little known and rarely reprinted, Hoch's best Darlan tales, such as "Where There's Smoke" (*Manhunt,* March 1964), are beautiful examples of fair-play detection within the PI framework.

BEN SNOW, the Westerner who may be Billy the Kid redux, was created by Hoch for editor Hans Stefan Santesson, who ran Ben's adventures in *The Saint Mystery Magazine* beginning in 1961. Perhaps the best of the early Snows is "The Ripper of Storyville" (*The Saint Mystery Magazine,* December 1963), a first-rate Western whodunit. With "The Vanished Steamboat" (*Ellery Queen's Mystery Magazine,* May 1984) Hoch launched a new series of frontier puzzles for Ben to solve.

CAPTAIN LEOPOLD, the Maigret of a northeastern city not too different from Hoch's native Rochester, has been the protagonist of close to ninety stories beginning with "Circus" (*The Saint Mystery Magazine,* January 1962). In the best of them, collected in *Leopold's Way* (Southern Illinois University Press, 1985), Hoch fuses the detective gamesmanship stuff of the Ellery Queen tradition with elements derived from Graham Greene and Georges Simenon, burying unexpected nuances of character and emotion beneath the surface of his deceptively simple style.

FATHER DAVID NOONE, parish priest and occasional detective, began life in 1964 as Hoch's version of a clerical sleuth in the manner of G. K. Chesterton's Father Brown. He was dropped after two rather feeble cases but came back to play a major role in "The Sweating Statue" (in *Detectives A to Z,* ed. Frank D. McSherry, Jr., Martin H. Greenberg, and Charles G. Waugh, 1985), which Hoch considers his best Noone story.

RAND, of Britain's Department of Concealed Communications, was created in 1964 for *Ellery Queen's Mystery Magazine* and has since appeared in more than sixty episodes of espionage laced with cryptography and detection. Originally called Randolph, he was renamed because *EQMM* editor Fred Dannay wanted a name subliminally evoking James Bond even though there was nothing Bond-like about the stories. The series began with "The Spy Who Did Nothing" (*Ellery Queen's Mystery Magazine,* May 1965), and most of the Rands retain "The Spy Who" in their titles, reminding us that the greatest espionage novel of the era in which Rand came to life was John LeCarré's *The Spy Who Came in from the Cold.* Rand is now officially in retirement but Hoch still brings him back for an *EQMM* assignment once or twice a year. Seven of his early cases are collected in the paperback volume *The Spy and the Thief* (Davis Publications, 1971).

NICK VELVET is perhaps the best-known Hoch character, a thief who steals only objects of no value and who is usually forced to play detective in the course of his thieving. He debuted in "The Theft of the Clouded Tiger" (*Ellery Queen's Mystery Magazine,* September 1966) and quickly became an international hit. More than sixty short Velvets have been published over the past quarter century. Seven of Nick's early capers are included in *The Spy and the Thief* and a total of fourteen (of which two come from the earlier volume) are collected in *The Thefts of Nick Velvet* (Mysterious Press, 1978). Several books of Velvet stories have been published in Japan and, rechristened Nick Verlaine, our contemporary Raffles has been the star of a French TV mini-series. The character has been under option by 20th Century-Fox for several years and may yet make it to prime time in America.

HARRY PONDER, a short-lived spy-cum-sleuth whose name suggests the Len Deighton-Michael Caine movie spy Harry Palmer, first appeared in "The Magic Bullet" (*Argosy,* January 1969), an excellent mix of espionage and impossible-crime detection, but was dropped after one more case.

BARNEY HAMET, a New York mystery writer, turned amateur sleuth in Hoch's first novel, *The Shattered Raven* (Lancer, 1969), and helped untangle a murder at the Mystery Writers of America annual dinner. In the short story "Murder at the Bouchercon" (*Ellery Queen's Mystery Magazine,* November 1983), Hamet probes another killing among his colleagues and joins the roster of Hoch series characters.

CARL CRADER and EARL JAZINE, who solve crimes for the Federal Computer Investigation Bureau in the early 21st century, were created by Hoch in "Computer Cops," a story he wrote for Hans Stefan Santesson's science fiction-mystery anthology *Crime Prevention in the 30th Century* (Walker, 1969). Later Hoch starred them in his trilogy of futuristic detective novels: *The Transvection Machine* (Walker, 1971), *The Fellowship of the Hand* (Walker, 1972), and *The Frankenstein Factory* (Warner Paperback Library, 1975). They haven't been seen since.

DAVID PIPER, director of the Department of Apprehension and also known as The Manhunter, shows that even when Hoch creates a character with a superficial resemblance to The Executioner, The Butcher, and similar macho action heroes, he converts the man into a mainstream detective. Piper starred in a six-installment serial, "The Will-o'-the-Wisp Mystery," published in *EQMM* between April and September of 1971 under the byline of Mr. X. The entire serial was reprinted under Hoch's own name in *Ellery Queen's Anthology,* Spring-Summer 1982.

ULYSSES S. BIRD was Hoch's attempt to fashion a criminal character who would not turn into a detective-in-spite-of-himself. The first of this con artist's four published exploits was "The Million-Dollar Jewel Caper" (*Ellery Queen's Mystery Magazine,* January 1973), but all of them were negligible except the third, "The Credit Card Caper" (*Ellery Queen's Mystery Magazine,* October 1974), which is a gem.

SEBASTIAN BLUE and LAURA CHARME, investigators for Interpol, vaguely resemble the stars of the classic British TV series *The Avengers,* but as usual when Hoch spins off a series from a preexisting source, he moves it into the domain of fair-play detection. The characters have appeared more than a dozen times in *EQMM,* beginning with "The Case of the Third Apostle" (*Ellery Queen's Mystery Magazine,* February 1973).

PAUL TOWER, who becomes involved in criminal problems while visiting local schools as part of the police department's public relations program, was suggested to Hoch as a character by Fred Dannay. "The Lollipop Cop" (*Ellery Queen's Mystery Magazine,* March 1974) and Tower's two subsequent cases were excellent, and it's a shame the character was retired so quickly.

DR. SAM HAWTHORNE, Hoch's most successful character of the 1970s, narrates his own reminiscences of impossible crime puzzles that he unofficially investigated in the late 1920s and early thirties while serving as a young physician in the New England village of Northmont. To date he has spun yarns and offered "a small libation" to his listeners more than forty times, beginning with "The Problem of the Covered Bridge" (*Ellery Queen's Mystery Magazine,* December 1974), which remains one of the best in the series. Hoch's Northmont long ago surpassed Ellery Queen's Wrightsville as small-town America's Mecca for bizarre crimes.

BARNABUS REX, a humorous sleuth of the future who debuted in "The Homesick Chicken" (*Isaac Asimov's Science Fiction Magazine,* Spring 1977), has since appeared in only one other story. But two cases make a series character even in the world of tomorrow.

TOMMY PRESTON, the young son of a zookeeper, was created by Hoch for the juvenile book market. In *The Monkey's Clue & The Stolen Sapphire* (Grosset & Dunlap, 1978) he solves a pair of mysteries involving animals.

NANCY TRENTINO, an attractive policewoman with a deductive flair, could almost be Connie Trent from the Captain Leopold series under a different name. Which is precisely what she was, until the editors of *Hers* (later *Woman's World*) who bought her first solo case asked Hoch to give her more of an ethnic flavor. Since her debut in "The Dog That Barked All Day" (*Hers,* October 1, 1979), she has solved a handful of puzzles.

CHARLES SPACER, electronics executive and undercover U.S. agent, figures in espionage detective tales, the first of which was "Assignment: Enigma" (*Ellery Queen's Mystery Magazine,* September 10, 1980), published as by Anthony Circus. (Later Spacers are under Hoch's own byline.) The ambience of all these tales and the pseudonym on the first may vaguely suggest John Le Carré, but the leitmotif as usual in Hoch is the game of wits.

SIR GIDEON PARROT, whose name reminds us of two of John Dickson Carr's mastersleuths and one of Agatha Christie's, stars in a series of gently nostalgic parodies of the Golden Age deductive puzzles on which Hoch was weaned. His first appearance was in "Lady of the Impossible" (*Ellery Queen's Mystery Magazine,* May 20, 1981).

Introduction

LIBBY KNOWLES, ex-cop and professional bodyguard, debuted in "Five-Day Forecast," a Hoch story first published in *Ellery Queen's Prime Crimes,* edited by Eleanor Sullivan (Davis, 1984). With her second case, published in *EQMM* later that year, she became an affirmative action recruit in Hoch's small army of series characters.

MATTHEW PRIZE, criminology professor and ex-private eye, is the detective in a pair of paperback mystery puzzles inspired by Thomas Chastain's best-selling *Who Killed the Robins Family?* (1983). Hoch created the plot outlines for these books, just as Fred Dannay did for the Ellery Queen novels, and the writing was done by Ron Goulart. *Prize Meets Murder* (Pocket Books, 1984) and *This Prize Is Dangerous* (London: Star Books, 1985) were published as by R. T. Edwards.

MICHAEL VLADO, farmer, horse trainer, and leader of a gypsy community in Romania, is the latest and perhaps most unlikely of the amateur sleuths in the Hoch gallery. His first appearance was in "The Luck of a Gypsy" (in *The Ethnic Detectives,* ed. Bill Pronzini and Martin H. Greenberg, 1985), and within a few days after the publication of that anthology he became a series character with "Odds on a Gypsy" (*Ellery Queen's Mystery Magazine,* July 1985). Since then he has starred in a handful of *EQMM* tales with East European settings.

That in twenty-four nutshells is the Ed Hoch everyone knows, the master of clues and puzzles whom we encounter in every issue of *EQMM* and almost every mystery anthology of the past twenty years. *The Night My Friend* celebrates the unfamiliar side of his output, bringing together some of the best of his two hundred-odd non-series stories.

Many of Hoch's earliest published stories featured the occult character Simon Ark, but even in his first few years as a writer he diversified quickly and widely. In 1956 and 1957, when his name began popping up regularly in magazines, he published not only Simon Ark exploits but PI stories, westerns, science fiction, horror, and a total of eight non-series crime tales. He first made his presence felt in a major way in the early 1960s when large numbers of his stories were published in the mystery field's top magazines, *Ellery Queen, Alfred Hitchcock,* and *The Saint.* All of the tales collected in *The Night My Friend* date from this decade and all but the last few from its early and middle years, before he gave up his job in advertising to write full time.

If the distinction of almost every Hoch story about a continuing character is its fair-play detective element, no common thread connects his finest non-series tales. There may be an abundance of detection—as in that supreme impossible-crime puzzler "The Long Way Down"—or none at all. There may be a main character who might easily have been put into a series—like songwriter Johnny Nocturne of "The Night My Friend"—or a protagonist who could never return, or no central figure whatever. An occasional touch, such as the use of a picnic or amusement-park setting or of beer as everyone's beverage of choice, may remind the Hoch fan of some of his better-known series work, but most of the building blocks of the tales collected here have no counterparts in his stories about recurring characters. In *The Night My Friend* you will find a boxing story; a juvenile delinquency story; a prep school reunion story; more than one tale about the aftermath of World War II, including "To Slay an Eagle," which is as bleak as the espionage fiction of Greene or LeCarré; a fable about a wandering minstrel and his harmonica; and several thrillers with a *noir* ambience reminiscent of one of the classic TV series of the years when these tales were written, *The Fugitive.* You will find unusually vivid and visual writing, off-trail settings, complex characterizations, emotions that run deep—in short, a side of Ed Hoch's literary personality that has escaped most readers' attention since the early and middle 1960s when he was writing mysteries only as a moonlighter.

Those were the years when I was in my late teens and discovered him. We've known each other for going on a quarter century now, and our collected correspondence would fill a book the size of *War and Peace.* It's been a pleasure to savor these stories again for myself and it's even more of a pleasure to bring them together and share them with Ed Hoch's legion of readers.

Francis M. Nevins, Jr.

Twilight Thunder

Dale Fielding heard the phone ringing from his inner office, and remembered that the girl had gone out to the bank. He pressed the proper button on his phone and picked it up. "Fielding Insurance Agency, Dale Fielding speaking."

"Fielding, this is an old buddy of yours. Harvey Stout." The phone turned to ice in Dale's grip. "I just got in town and thought I'd look you up."

"Hello, Harvey." His mind was racing, tearing through a thousand possibilities.

"That all you've got to say to an old buddy?"

"What's up, Harvey? What do you want?"

"Just to see you again, Fielding. That's all." The voice still had the same bitter edge to it, the same deadly friendliness he remembered.

"I'm pretty busy, Harvey. If you're just passing through town . . ."

"No, boy. I got lots of time. Suppose I run out to your house tonight—meet the wife and kiddies. There are kiddies, aren't there?"

Dale ignored the question with a sigh. "Look, where are you now? Maybe I can meet you for a quick drink or something."

"Fine, fine! That's more like it. I'm over at the hotel. The Riverview. I'll meet you at the bar in ten minutes."

"All right," Dale managed, and hung

up. Harvey Stout, after all these years. He lit a cigarette and tried to calm his jumping nerves and thought about calling his wife. No, that would do no good. The police? What would he tell them?

What would he tell anybody? Certainly not the truth.

The truth was an island in the Pacific called Ie Shima, a tiny hunk of rock just barely large enough for the airfield that made it so important. It was some three miles off Okinawa, and perhaps was destined to be remembered only as the place where a burst of Japanese machine-gun fire cut through the body of war correspondent Ernie Pyle. Certainly no one but his family would remember that Captain Mason died there, in the final bitter moments of a bloody battle.

Mason, Charles F., Captain, U.S.M.C. Age: thirty-one at the time of his death. Married, no children. Born in Dallas, Texas, of an oil-rich family.

Dale Fielding knew all the statistics. He could have written a fairly lengthy biography of Captain Mason, because he'd spent a week in Dallas after the war learning more about this man he'd watched die before his eyes. Mason had been a good man back home, good to his mother and good to his wife, and the news had come as a shock to Dale, bent on justifying one evil with another. But he more than anyone should have known that men change in the service, especially during wartime. The kind, generous, loving man who had been Charles Mason had become the bitter, driving, ruthless officer Captain Mason. Just as Dale Fielding, who'd always hated the bloodshed of a mere hunting trip, had crossed a dozen Pacific islands with flame-thrower and rifle without ever a single doubt.

It had been Harvey Stout who'd first put the thought into words, of course, while they crouched in the bloodied sand of the Ie Shima beach. "Let's kill that so-and-so Mason." Just like that, "let's kill that so-and-so Mason." And Dale's eyes had followed his pointing finger. Further up the beach, in the midst of a fallen forest of young bodies, Captain Mason was indulging in his favorite pastime, slapping the muddy face of a sobbing young private who could go no further. The incident had decided them, after all those months.

Toward twilight on the same day Captain Mason had asked for three men to go with him on a scouting trip. Dale and Harvey had fallen out immediately, along with the third man who'd seen the beach episode, a dark-haired youth named Travello. Mason, suspecting nothing, had led them up the beach a bit, then signalled them to spread out with their rifles and follow him into the underbrush. They knew the Japanese could not be far away, but not one of the three men was thinking of that enemy now.

When Mason was some fifty feet ahead, perfectly outlined in the fading daylight, Dale saw Harvey Stout raise his rifle. Dale and Travello did likewise. The first bullet spun the captain around and perhaps he never knew what hit him but only thought it was a bit of twilight thunder over the water. Stout and Travello kept firing until he went down, his body ripped and violated, the surprise bloodied from his face. At that last instant, for some reason, Dale hadn't squeezed his trigger. And in the noise and flame that followed, the other two never realized it. But that did not make him less a murderer, as he well understood, standing there above the captain's body.

They carried the body back to camp, with a story to go with the blood and the bullets. Luckily they didn't run ballistics tests on Ie Shima.

"Hello, Fielding. You're looking good for a fellow of thirty-five."

"Hello, Harvey." Yes, he still looked the same. Even those long fifteen years hadn't changed him much. A bit heavier, perhaps, with hair that tended just a shade more toward the gray, but he was still the same Harvey Stout. "Can I buy you a drink?"

"Did I ever refuse one, boy? Scotch and water."

"What have you been doing with yourself all these years, Harvey?"

The leer he remembered so well. "Little of this, little of that. You know. Selling, mostly. Always on the road."

"Oh?"

"Gave it up, though. Decided—this is good Scotch, damn good—decided to settle down. Right here in Riverview, maybe."

The chill was back. What did he want? What twisted thoughts were going around that dark mind of his? "Why here, Harvey?"

"Well, my old buddy Fielding is here, for one thing. Thought you might help me get started, with a little money to set up a business."

Dale glanced down the bar to make certain the bartender wasn't listening. "Listen, Harvey, I'll say this once and make it clear. I don't intend to be blackmailed by you!"

"Blackmail! Fielding, I'm your buddy, remember? Don't you think back occasionally to those Pacific days when the three of us were . . ."

"Travello's dead." He'd stepped on a Japanese land mine two days after the murder of Captain Mason.

"Sure, he's dead. Does that mean you've forgotten him, boy? Have you forgotten me too, or what the three of us did out there?"

The Night My Friend

Dale sighed into his drink. "I never told you this, Harvey, but I didn't fire my rifle that day. It was just you and Travello."

Harvey looked at Dale with eyes both deep and curious. It seemed for a moment that he was trying to comprehend something, some great mystery of life. Then the eyes cleared, and Dale saw what he'd known all along—that this admission of his didn't change anything.

"I'm not trying to blackmail you, boy. Get that foolish idea out of your head. What happened to Mason was a long time ago. It's only worth remembering because it made us buddies, and we're just as close buddies whether you helped do it or just watched. Understand?"

"I understand." He felt the other's breath on him like something unclean, sucking the air from his lungs, smothering him. "But I can't help you. I have a family."

"You insurance men got a racket! You're rolling in dough."

Now the bitterness was showing, the battle was joined. "Look, Harvey. If you want a handout I can give you five bucks. Anything more than that you've come to the wrong boy."

"Yeah?"

"Yeah. That's the way it is. I'm sorry." He slid off the bar stool and casually tossed down a five dollar bill for their two drinks, turning purposely away before he could see what became of it.

"You'll be hearing from me, Fielding."

He kept walking without looking back.

Dale Fielding lived in a quiet house on a quiet street where trouble never visited. Even the laughter of children at play had always seemed muted to him, though it never occurred to his preoccupied mind that his very presence might have a quieting effect. At his own home, the last one on a street of nearly identical post-war houses, Marge and his two children would be waiting this evening, as they always were. The boys, eight and ten years old, could be seen from the street, playing at boyish pastimes in the back yard. That was good, because he wanted to speak to Marge alone.

"Home so soon, dear?"

"Yeah. Things were a little slow today, and besides, I have to make a call tonight." He tossed his topcoat over a chair, not feeling just then like hanging it up. "Marge?"

"Yes, dear?" She called him that always, but with the automatic inflection that comes perhaps after too many years of it.

"A man called me at the office today. A man I was in the service with during the war."

"That's nice, dear."

He knew what he wanted to tell her, and yet somehow the words didn't come. Then, before the opportunity came again, the boys were in from their play, clustering about him.

After supper the phone rang, and Marge came back to say it was for him. Somehow he knew it would be Harvey Stout, and he wasn't surprised. "Hello, Fielding. I was wondering if you'd changed your mind."

"I'm . . . very busy. I was just on my way out. Talk to me tomorrow. At the office, not at home."

"Sure, Fielding. I understand."

He hung up, and for a long time Dale just stood there by the phone, looking down at it as if it were a thing alive. Then, in answer to Marge's absent-minded question, he said, "Nothing important. I'll be going out on that call now, I guess. Try to be home early. . . ."

The next morning he was irritable at the office, raising his voice for the first time in months to the girl who typed the fire policies. He sat dully at his desk waiting for the phone to ring, feeling his heart skip a beat every time it did. He'd been foolish to tell Harvey Stout to call today, yet in the panic of the moment it had been the only way to get rid of him. What if he ever came to the house? Or what if he ever told his story to Marge or said something in front of the children?

Dale Fielding, murderer.

The phone rang.

"It's for you, Mr. Fielding."

"Hello. Fielding speaking."

"How are you today, boy?"

"Fine. A little busy."

"What about it?"

"About what?"

"You know."

"I don't."

"Money."

"Oh."

Silence, for the space of a heartbeat. Then, "I can't fool around, boy. I need cash."

Dale cleared his throat. "I'm sorry."

"You'll be a damn lot sorrier."

"Listen—stop calling me. Stop threatening me or I'll get the police after you. Understand?"

"Hell, I'm not threatening you." The old friendly tone was back. "But we were buddies, remember? You and me and Travello? And Captain Mason. Remember?"

"I remember. I had nothing to do with that."

"Sure. But for old times' sake . . ."

Dale hung up.

He tried to light a cigarette and found that his hand was shaking. "Jean, I'm out if anyone else calls."

"Yes, Mr. Fielding."

He leaned back in his chair and thought about it all, about those dark days of war, and its aftermath. He remembered his trip to Dallas and the week he'd spent looking into the past of Charles F. Mason. . . .

The city was still caught up in the excitement of peace, year one. He'd walked among cattle-rich ranchers and oil millionaires, smiling around their thick cigars and thicker fingers. He'd stood in a grassy square and watched workmen putting up a plaque to honor the city's war dead. Captain Charles F. Mason, U.S.M.C.

Killed in action.

Dale wandered about the city, managing finally to catch a glimpse of Mrs. Mason, a slimly beautiful young woman who he thought deserved better. But the more he dug, the more he asked, the deeper the picture seemed to etch itself. Charles Mason hadn't been a really bad man. In fact, there were those who remembered him as a rising young executive, who mourned his death as that of a hero. But surely men changed in the service, men hardened in the face of daily death and uncertain life. Perhaps Mason had been one to crack under the strain. Stout and Travello might even have been doing their duty in some obscure manner when they pumped a dozen bullets into his unexpecting body.

But day by day he became more certain of the facts, more aware of the guilt. On the final evening of his stay in Dallas he sat in his hotel room and thought about the alternatives open to him. He spent three hours debating between confessing everything and killing himself. In the end, because he'd never had a really strong will, he did nothing.

That, in a way, had always been the story of his life, even to the moment in the jungle of Ie Shima. While others acted, he did nothing.

He'd come back east and married Marge and let the bitter, unfriendly memories drift into the further reaches of his mind. War is never won by men who do nothing, but Dale thought that perhaps peace was won that way at times. . . .

On his way back from lunch, Harvey Stout crossed the street and caught up with him as he walked. "I guess we got disconnected this morning."

"Yeah, I guess so, Harvey."

"Let me tell you some more about this business I want to start."

"Don't bother, Harvey. It doesn't mean a thing to me."

He started to turn in at his office, but Harvey put a restraining hand on his shoulder. "I was out looking at your house this morning, boy."

"Stay away from my wife!"

"Nobody's going anywhere near your wife, Fielding. Don't worry, I won't tell her about Mason."

"There's nothing to tell, anyway. I told you I didn't do it."

"Did you tell her?"

Dale was silent. Beyond Stout's shoulder a traffic light turned red. Finally, like a man suddenly collapsing against the wind, he asked, "How much do you want?"

"That's better. That's sounding more like a buddy."

"How much?"

"I think ten thousand would do it."

"Ten thousand!" The light turned green. "Are you out of your mind?"

"You've got a nice house, a business of your own. And I never met a starving insurance man yet."

"That's out of the question. I was thinking of a few hundred, a thousand at the very most."

"Think a little harder, boy." And then, with an expression on his face, a light in his eyes that Dale hadn't seen since the Pacific, he added, too casually, "When I was out at your house I was noticing how close it was to the woods. Must be dangerous this time of the year, with the hunters out. Stray bullet could be dangerous to the kids."

He turned and walked away, leaving Dale staring after him. Within a block he'd been lost in the noonday crowd, and there was nothing but a blur of faces confronting Dale. A blur like a jungle swallowing up the enemies, and for a moment he might have been back there, back on a Pacific island that time forgot, facing the gloom with a rifle in his hands and determination in his mind.

"Marge?"

"Yes, dear?"

"I want to talk."

"Sure. Can you wait till I get the kids off to bed?"

"I suppose so."

"You haven't been looking good, dear. Are you coming down with something?"

"I'm all right. I saw my old buddy, Harvey Stout, again today."

The Night My Friend

"That's nice. You could invite him out for dinner some night if you wanted. Is he going to be in town long?"

"I don't think he really knows. We had a sort of long talk today, and . . ."

"Excuse me, dear. I have to see what they're up to now."

"Sure."

He sat down by the window and looked out across the irregular fields to the blackness of the twilight woods. Even now the hunters were still out—a figure moved, paused, then shattered the silence with a shotgun's roar. Perhaps unseen a partridge had crumpled to earth.

Yes, they were awfully close. A shotgun slug could carry almost to the house. He remembered how it had been in the jungle, then got up and went to the basement. After a time, Marge called.

"Dear, what in heaven's name are you up to?"

"Thinking of doing a little hunting. I was just checking over my shotgun."

"You haven't used that in years."

"This buddy of mine, Harvey Stout, wants to go. Maybe Friday night after work."

Yes, it would be Friday night. He took out his cleaning gear and began polishing the weapon.

For most of the next day he was busy, and there was only a vague awareness of Harvey Stout in his mind. He no longer waited in dread for the phone call he knew would come. Rather, he glowed with an inner expectation, like a schoolboy anxiously waiting to give the correct answer.

Stout, surprisingly, had not yet called at five o'clock. The glow by then was beginning to fade, and replacing it was a sort of uncertainty. Finally, at five-fifteen, he called home to make certain the children were inside, and warned Marge of the possible danger from the hunters. When he hung up his palms were sweating for the first time that day as his mind ran over the score of possibilities. Stout might have given up and already left town. He might be sick, or he might simply have lost interest in Dale. Or, and he had to face this extreme, Stout might be plotting right now some attack on his family.

Finally, just at five-thirty, the phone rang. It was Harvey Stout. "Hi, Fielding. I been thinking. Maybe I could get by with five thousand, if you were still interested in helping a buddy. That's as low as I could go, though."

Dale felt his hand trembling on the receiver, and he steadied his elbow against the desk. "All right, Harvey, on one condition. That you get out of town and don't come back."

"Ah, now, Fielding . . ."

"That's it, Harvey. Take it or leave it."

"Five thousand?"

"I told you all right."

"When can I have it, boy?"

"Tomorrow night, after work."

"I'll come by the office."

"No. My girl will be working late. Look, you know where I live. Just past the house there's a road that leads out toward the woods. Drive out there till you come to a place where cars park. Hunters usually leave their autos there. I'll be there at five sharp."

"You make it sound like a damned TV show or something."

"If you want the money, you'll be there."

"All right," he said finally. "Five o'clock."

Dale hung up and wiped the sweat from his palms. It was done. The deed was as good as done. It was late but he knew the gun shop on the way home would still be open.

"Mr. Fielding! Haven't seen you in years."

"Long time since I've hunted, Joe. I need some shotgun shells. Here, I think this is just the thing."

"What you going to be hunting, Mr. Fielding?"

"Partridge."

"Well, you don't want slugs for partridge. You want shot."

"Oh. I guess you're right."

Dale accepted the box of shells with a firm hand. All right, it just meant he'd have to get a little closer before he pulled the trigger, that was all. The police could say what they wanted, they could accuse him of anything they liked, but they'd never be able to prove it wasn't a hunting accident, pure and simple. It was the easiest way, the only way. He'd gone over the alternatives carefully in his mind. Of course he could have told Marge, but she would never have understood. She would only have seen this uncertain side to his character. Seen it, but not understood. Perhaps no one could understand who hadn't been out there, in the Pacific. Marge would have cried, and told him to call the police. And the police? They couldn't arrest Stout without dragging Dale himself through a drawn-out investigation. And if they believed Stout guilty of that long-ago crime, what would keep them from thinking Dale just as guilty?

He patted the box of shells. This was the only way it could be, the only way to be free of the man.

Friday was a gloomy day, half overcast with the threat of rain, and the dampness was thick in the air. Dale stayed at his desk most of the

The Night My Friend

time, thinking about everything but the date he'd made with Stout. As the afternoon wore on, he became more and more uneasy with the knowledge that the time was nearing. Already he'd reminded Marge that he'd be a little late getting home, storing the shotgun and box of shells in the car when he left that morning. He found himself almost wishing, though, that rain would come—anything to delay or cancel the deed which he must do.

Finally, a bit after four, he told Jean he was going partridge hunting with a friend. He drove slowly toward home, watching the clouds with a careful eye, wondering about a hundred unimportant business details left undone. There would be an inquest, of course, and perhaps he might even have to spend the night in jail. But they couldn't prove a thing. It happened every day.

He reached the point of the meeting, and was pleased to see that only three cars were there before him. With luck they would be undisturbed at the time of the planned accident, but even if someone was nearby it would not greatly change his plan. He opened the car door on the driver's side and placed the shotgun across his lap, its barrels pointed toward the empty space where Harvey Stout's car soon would be. Two shells went into the chambers, and he was ready. In his mind he ran over the details once again. The hunting license was in his pocket—Stout would have neither license nor gun, but the lack of one would explain the lack of the other. He had come along simply to watch. They might suspect differently, but certainly the suspicions would be no worse than those born of Harvey Stout's story of events on Ie Shima.

At five minutes to five a car turned off the highway and headed toward him. From somewhere in the woods came the boom of a shotgun, and the ruffled rushing of birds on the wing. The forest was a living thing, breathing, vibrant.

The last western rays of the orange sun flickered through the enveloping clouds, and the car came silently closer like a great gliding animal breaking into the brush. Up ahead Captain Mason paused to look around, then gave the signal for them to follow. Harvey Stout paused and raised his rifle to his shoulder. Harvey Stout opened the car door and slid across the seat.

"Hello, buddy. You got the money?" Raised his rifle and so did Travello and so did Dale. Three men. The money. "What in hell are you doing with that shotgun?" The first bullet spun the captain around, and Stout and Travello kept firing. The gun was warm in Dale's hands. He sighted at his target. The enemy.

"You damn fool, Fielding! You can't pull it, can you? You couldn't kill Mason and you can't kill me."

Dale heard the voice as if from a distance, and he knew the words were true. The shotgun was limp in his hands. Harvey Stout walked over and lifted it up. Then he slapped Dale twice with his open palm. "The hell with you. I can't fool around any longer. I'll take this gun and be thankful you got off so easy."

He threw the shotgun in the back seat of his car and climbed in behind the wheel. Dale watched the scorn on his face with a mixture of feelings. Somehow it was almost as if he had failed Harvey by not killing him.

After the car pulled away he sat for a long time staring into the dusk, until at last all was darkness around him and the other hunters had departed. Then he drove slowly home to Marge and the boys.

The Night My Friend

His name, they said, was Johnny Nocturne.

Perhaps it was not his real name, but it didn't matter. To the people in Tin Pan Alley, and the disc jockeys, and the lovers who listened dreamily to his songs, he was Johnny Nocturne, creator of mood music for the night people.

He'd never be another Irving Berlin or Cole Porter because his music somehow lacked the universal appeal of true greatness. But for those who liked the ever-changing moods of darkness, he was the master.

And like his music, Johnny Nocturne was a prowler of the night places. He claimed he got his best inspiration riding through the dark places of River City in a police prowl car. The cops of the night beat all knew him, and often they enjoyed having him in the back seat, humming a little tune that might be tomorrow's hit.

Friday night was a good one on the night beat, and Johnny always managed to meet car 52 when it pulled out of Police Headquarters just before midnight. The cops in 52 were good fellows, not the kind who looked for trouble—just good fellows.

On this Friday night, Tom Harper was driving 52. He'd been on the force for some ten years, with the last three spent in a patrol car. It was a lot better than walking a beat, and it had made him feel that he was getting ahead on the force. It gave him an answer when his wife nagged him about the poor pay and long hours.

His partner for the past year had been Harvey Backus, a big, long-legged kid still in his mid-twenties. Harvey could run faster than any man on the force, as any number of young hoodlums had learned to their sorrow.

Together, these two prowled the post-midnight streets of River City. And quite often Johnny Nocturne could be found in the back seat.

"O.K., Johnny, it's been a quiet night," Tom Harper said as he wheeled the car around a corner. "Let's see if we can find some inspiration for you."

Harvey Backus paused in the act of lighting a cigarette to point out the side window. "Look! A light in the back of Blinky's Cigar Store."

Tom Harper pulled the car into the curb. "That means an all-night card game. Come on, let's give 'em a scare."

They hopped out of the car, and Johnny Nocturne slid out of the rear seat to follow. He paused on the sidewalk to shove the pencil and pad into his pocket and then followed them inside.

"What's up?" a short, balding man said from the door to the back room.

"Just checking up, Blinky. Let's have a look."

"There ain't nothin' here, cop, honest!"

"Let's look anyway."

Tom Harper shoved past him and threw open the door. A half-dozen men looked up from around a green felt poker table.

"O.K.," Harper told them. "Everybody out. And make it quick or I'll run the whole lot of you in."

There was some grumbling from the table as the men pocketed their money and moved towards the door. Harvey Backus towered tall and commanding next to it, and they had to edge past his glistening badge to reach the street.

"This is just a warning, Blinky," Harper said. "Next time. . . ."

"Ah, cop, I don't hurt anybody. Here, have a cigar."

Harper accepted the cigar, because that was the kind of cop he was. Then he and Harvey went back to car 52 and Johnny Nocturne trailed along. As they pulled away, Johnny saw that Blinky was dimming his lights and preparing to close up.

"Did that inspire you, Johnny?"

"A little," Johnny Nocturne admitted, scribbling on his piece of paper. "A little . . . *Perhaps in the night, when the cards are all aces . . .*

And the smoke is so thick, you can't see their faces . . . Perhaps that is when. . . ."

"Hold on," Harvey Backus shouted. "What's that up ahead?"

"It's a girl," Harper said, speeding up a bit until they drew alongside. "Are you in trouble, miss?"

The girl lifted her blonde head and looked at them with wide, glazed eyes. She was barely twenty, and Johnny wondered what she was doing alone at this time of night.

"I . . ." she managed to gasp, and then she seemed to collapse in a heap.

Tom Harper jumped out of the car and turned her over. "Damn," he muttered. "She hasn't got a thing on under this coat."

Harvey Backus was already coming around from his side of the car, and Johnny slipped out of the rear seat to join them.

"What happened, miss?" Harper asked her.

She coughed once and opened her eyes, gazing up at them with glazed, unseeing vision. "I . . . it was Cravess . . . Cotton Cravess. . . ."

And then her eyes closed and somehow they knew she was dead.

Cotton Cravess was a big man in River City. Perhaps some day he would be a big man in Washington. Certainly he was trying hard enough, and even Johnny Nocturne's usual casual notice of the political scene had observed Cotton Cravess in action many times.

He was there on the front page of the paper every morning now, touring slum areas, or awarding prizes, or greeting Negro leaders or puttering in the garden with his wife. It was something different every day, but it was always page one news, possibly because Cotton Cravess owned the newspaper.

He'd taken over when his father died some five years before, and now, at the age of forty, he was possibly the most powerful figure in the state. His chain of newspapers could sway at least 10 percent of the public on any occasion, and he'd once proved it by getting out a crowd of 15,000 to hear a poetry reading.

Usually, a man in his position would be content as the power behind the scenes, but not Cotton Cravess. He'd seen his favorite candidates elected to Congress and the State Legislature, and after a time he'd just gotten the bug. So now it was COTTON CRAVESS FOR GOVERNOR, posted on the billboards, shouted from the television screens. Cotton Cravess for Governor. . . .

Johnny Nocturne thought about it as he looked down at the nude girl at their feet. Cotton Cravess was somehow linked to this girl, and now, three weeks before election, that fact could spell his doom at the polls, especially in an ultra-conservative place like River City.

Johnny looked at Harper and Backus, and he wondered what they were thinking. He didn't really know them well, in spite of their nights together in the prowl car. Were they thinking now that the power of Cotton Cravess was suddenly broken, or were they perhaps thinking that here was a chance to make a little money? He didn't know, but long ago he had lost the illusion that all cops were honest.

Now Tom Harper turned to him, as if suddenly remembering he was there, listening with them to the girl's dying words.

"Johnny, you'd better get out of here. This thing is going to be a mess, and you'd only complicate things if you're around."

Johnny Nocturne nodded. He'd heard that before, and he wasn't surprised to hear it now. He was unofficial. He was just a guy who wrote songs—nice to have around when things were dull, but likely to get in the way when there was work to be done.

He nodded again and walked slowly away from the car, hearing Backus as he switched on the two-way radio and called headquarters. Oh well, he could read about it in the newspapers.

As he walked he thought about the dead girl, and slowly, very slowly, the words to a song began to form themselves in his mind. A song for people who lived by night. . . .

With the coming of the dawn he slept. But not for long. Just after ten o'clock the telephone rang, and he rolled out of bed to answer it.

"Johnny Nocturne here."

"Who used to be Johnny Noctorno?" a girl's voice asked.

He'd almost forgotten the name. "Yes . . . Who is this?"

"You probably wouldn't even remember after all these years, but the name is Nancy Stevens."

"Nan! Where are you?"

"Right here in River City. Did you think I was calling from Europe?"

"When did you get back?" Somehow he still couldn't believe it, after all these years.

"Just yesterday. I tried to call you last night but you were out."

"I sort of work by night."

"Can we get together today, Johnny? I've so much to tell you."

"Sure, Nan. I've got a lot to tell you, too. Where are you staying?"

"At the River Arms till I can find an apartment. Suppose I meet you in the lobby at eight?"

"Fine, Nan. Eight o'clock."

He hung up and rolled over in the bed. Nan Stevens! After all these years. . . . Nan Stevens, the girl most likely to succeed. Nan Stevens, a best-selling author at the age of twenty-four. He remembered the first shock of reading her book, a long rambling account of sex and history in fifteenth-century Europe. It wasn't very different from a dozen other books of the times, except possibly that the sex was more sexy and the history more historical. Nan had always liked history, even during her school days.

He remembered trying to reach her after that first novel, only to learn that she'd gone off to Europe to gather material for a new book. That had been—how long?—three years ago. Three long years.

He rolled over on the bed and closed his eyes once more. . . . . *A song for Nancy, whose eyes are like fire; a song for Nancy, after all these years.* . . .

"Nocturne!"

He awoke.

"Get up, Nocturne."

His eyes came open, and he looked up at the stranger standing above his bed. "Who are you?"

"Get up and get dressed. Cotton Cravess wants to see you."

Cotton Cravess. . . . And suddenly the memories of the previous night were back with him again.

Yes, Cotton Cravess would want to see him.

As they drove downtown toward the penthouse office of Cotton Cravess, Johnny wondered which of them it had been. Harper or Backus? Which had tipped off Cravess to the dying girl's words? Because he knew one of them had.

One of them.

"We're here," the man spoke from the driver's seat. "I'll take you up in the elevator."

"Does Cravess always send goons to break into people's apartments when he wants to talk with them?"

"Cut out the talk and come on."

Johnny followed him into the office building that housed the various organizations which made up Cravess Enterprises. He rode on the elevator past the busy editorial rooms of the newspaper, and the silent studios of the radio station. And there were other offices that even he did not know about. It was a long way to the top of Cravess Tower.

But finally he was there.

"This is him, Mister Cravess."

Cotton Cravess turned toward him in his big swivel chair, smiling widely as if he were posing for a campaign poster. "Well, well. Thank you for coming."

"Did I have any choice?"

Cotton Cravess ignored the remark and motioned to another man in the room. "I want you to meet Congressman Yorkman. Jim, this is Johnny Nocturne, the great song writer."

Jim Yorkman stepped forward with an outstretched hand. "Happy to meet you, Johnny."

Cotton Cravess motioned with a big, waving hand. "Find a chair for Johnny, will you, Jim? We've got a lot to talk about."

A Congressman and a candidate for Governor of the state, talking to him as if he were the deciding vote in the election. . . . Maybe he was.

"Cigar?" Cotton Cravess offered.

"Thanks, but I've got some cigarettes."

"I enjoyed your new song. The one about the park at night."

"Thanks."

"Johnny, I understand you were with Officers Harper and Backus last night."

Now it was coming out in the open. "That's right."

"Do you often ride with them?"

"Sometimes. I find the city by night quite stimulating to my song-writing efforts."

Cotton Cravess smiled like a father. "Yes. And we can certainly see from your work that it pays off. The point is, you were present when they found that dead girl."

"She wasn't dead yet when we found her."

"No, of course not. But she died a moment later, as I understand it."

Johnny Nocturne nodded. "You received quite a full report."

The smile stayed on Cotton Cravess as if it were chiselled in stone.

"Ah, yes. But the point is, Johnny, that the election is only days away. You heard what the girl said. You must realize what my political enemies would do with this in the next twenty days."

"What happened to the girl?"

Cotton Cravess waved his arm. "A heart attack. It could have happened to anyone."

"Where were her clothes?"

He noticed Jim Yorkman smile slightly at this question, but Cotton Cravess frowned. "Listen, Johnny, I'll play square with you. I'll tell you the whole thing, right from the beginning, and leave it up to you to judge me. I'll throw myself on your mercy."

Johnny was beginning to feel sick and he averted his eyes. Cotton

The Night My Friend

Cravess was a hard man to take. If he ever won the election, Johnny thought he'd probably move to another state, just on general principles.

Cotton Cravess cleared his throat and continued. "Some of my people got together last night and threw a little party, sort of as a respite from the campaign. Unknown to me, one of my more—well, fun-loving—aides hired some girls to entertain us. Among them was this girl in question, Marie Karling. Apparently she was new in town and didn't realize. . . . Well, anyway she didn't realize what was expected of her."

Jim Yorkman spoke up from the sidelines. "You must understand, Johnny, that none of this was Cotton's idea. It was a stupid thing to do, from any angle, and the man who hired these girls has been fired."

"Correct," Cotton agreed. "But we'd all been drinking pretty heavy, and you know how things get sometimes."

"I know," Johnny said.

"Anyway, somebody ripped the girl's clothes off. She started screaming like the very devil and grabbed a coat and ran out the door. We chased her, but she was too fast for us. I guess the running was too much for her heart. She must have had a heart attack just as you people found her."

Johnny Nocturne frowned and took out a cigarette. The story had just the right ring of truth about it. A more or less innocent affair that had accidentally killed a girl. Innocent, but the rival political party could easily use it to ruin Cotton Cravess.

"Why did she say your name as she died?"

Cotton Cravess waved his arm again. "I was the only one there that she knew. I do have a reputation in this state, you know."

Johnny inhaled deeply on his cigarette. "What do you want me to do about it?"

"Nothing. Simply say nothing about it."

"How about Harper and Backus?"

"They've both agreed that the right thing would be to keep silent."

Johnny frowned. "What did they get for it?"

The smile returned to the face of Cotton Cravess. "Not money, if that's what you think. I don't bribe people. If I offered you money and my political opponents discovered it, I'd really be in a spot."

"Then what are you offering me?"

"I've got a radio station downstairs. One of the best in town as radio goes in these days when everything is television."

"So?"

"Suppose I were to guarantee that my radio station would play Johnny Nocturne records and songs almost exclusively. It would mean a lot to your sales in River City."

Johnny laughed. "How to bribe a songwriter! I suppose if I'd been a novelist you'd have suggested your paper run my novel."

"Take it or leave it."

Johnny rose from the chair. "It was nice meeting you fellows."

"Think about it carefully," the man behind the desk said.

"I will. . . ."

Jim Yorkman joined him at the elevator. "I'll ride down to the street with you."

"It's a free country."

The elevator dropped through its vertical tunnel, and a few moments later they were in the street.

"Tell me something, Congressman," Johnny asked, "how did you ever get involved with a character like Cravess? I don't know much about politics, but from what I hear you've got a pretty fair voting record."

Jim Yorkman thought about it. "Let me buy you a drink and I'll tell you about it."

Johnny nodded agreement and followed him into the cocktail lounge of a nearby hotel. They found a dark corner that would be reserved for lovers at some later hour and settled themselves into the foam rubber upholstery and ordered a couple of drinks.

"It's funny you should ask me that, Johnny," the congressman replied. "People have been asking me that question for years. My wife, my friends. . . . Sometimes, late at night, I even find myself asking the question. The answer is simply that Cotton Cravess got me elected. He put up the money, he gave me the push I needed. And I was just one of these crazy guys who figured the good I could do in Congress would counteract the evil association with Cravess."

"It never works that way."

"No, it never does. But of course I had to learn the hard way. Every time I wanted to vote a certain way, I'd get a long-distance phone call from Cravess. He'd remind me that my first duty was to the people who'd elected me. . . ."

"You still managed to do pretty well."

"Sometimes things work out."

"What about the girl, Marie Karling?"

"It was a heart attack all right. Cravess was just unlucky."

"Did he bribe the two cops?"

"I guess so, somehow. Maybe they're songwriters, too."

Johnny laughed. Then he was serious again. "What would you do in my position?"

Jim Yorkman thought about it. "Just wait and see. You'll make up your mind, one way or the other. These things always work out."

"You're a great believer that things work out, aren't you?"

"They do," he smiled, downing his drink quickly. "I have to be going now, Johnny. Glad to have met you."

Johnny shook his hand. "The pleasure was mine."

He watched Jim Yorkman leave the lounge and after a moment Johnny followed. Outside, he blinked his eyes against the sun and headed back towards his apartment.

But sleep would not come to him now. Back in the apartment, he sat down at the piano and ran over the familiar bars of his first hit song.

It was a lonely kind of song, and now, as the shadows of afternoon began to lengthen, it conveyed to him the feeling it always carried. He closed the blinds and tried to think of the night, and the shadowy places of his mind.

Night . . . his fingers found the keys automatically and gradually the melody began to form itself . . . and surge slowly through his body. . . . *Never*, that would be its name . . . *Never*, a word that did things to you. . . . *Never, when the darkness falls again, never, when we* . . .

The doorbell rang and he was back in the present. He ran his fingers over the keys and went to answer it.

"Hello, Johnny."

"Nan! It's not eight o'clock yet, is it?"

"Hardly," she laughed. "I was just in the neighbourhood and thought I'd drop by to see you. After all these years, who wants to wait till eight o'clock?"

"Well come in, by all means!" He held the door wide for her and she entered, all smiles and silk and satin. If anything she looked even better than he last remembered her, tall and slim and very beautiful.

"A lot's happened in a few years, Johnny."

"It sure has, Nan. Let me get you a drink."

She nodded agreeably and took out a cigarette. "You're a big man now in the music world. They were playing your songs all over Europe."

He smiled a bit as he poured the drinks. "I'm afraid they're more popular over there than they are here. I'm far from being rich off them."

"I know what you mean," she sipped her drink. "Being a best-selling author isn't all it's cracked up to be, either. But this next book of mine will set them all back on their heels."

"Not another sexy historical novel?"

"Not this time. It's non-fiction. I've been gathering material for it for more than a year now."

"The girl writer in Paris! What the devil did you find to write a book about?"

"Joan of Arc."

"Oh, God!"

"I know," she smiled. "There have been thousands of books about Joan of Arc."

"And plays and movies, too."

"But not like mine, Johnny. Not like mine."

"What are you going to do, Nan? Prove that Joan was really a boy?"

"No," she replied quite seriously. "I'm going to prove she was really a witch. . . ."

Johnny threw up his hands and reached quickly for a drink. "Why must young writers—especially girls—be forever so iconoclastic? Can't you even let poor Joan rest in peace?"

Nancy shook her head. "You can't let a lie rest in peace. Joan was a witch, not a saint, and I can prove it."

Johnny smiled. "Some night I'll let you convince me."

The phone buzzed quietly at his elbow and he picked it up. "Johnny Nocturne here."

"This is Jim Yorkman. . . ."

"Oh, yes, Congressman?"

"Have you seen the evening papers?"

"No. . . ."

"What were the names of those two policemen you were with last night?"

"Harper and Backus. Why?"

"Well, a police officer named Harvey Backus was murdered this morning, shot down right in back of Headquarters. . . ."

Harvey Backus, dead.

Johnny spoke into the phone, with a voice he barely recognized. "Who did it?"

"They don't know. Someone was apparently waiting in the garage where they park their squad cars. He got clean away. I've already called Cravess about it, but he denies knowing a thing about it."

"Do you believe him?"

"Who is there to believe in this world, Johnny? All of a sudden things don't seem to be working out any more."

Johnny sighed. "I'll try to talk with Tom Harper, the other officer. Then I'll call you back, probably sometime tonight."

"Right," Jim Yorkman said, and hung up.

Nancy Stevens stretched out on the couch. "What was all that about?"

"It's a long story, Nan. I'm sort of involved in something."

She smiled up at him. "Same old Johnny. You know, sometimes I think we're an awful lot alike. We both have a certain artistic talent, and yet, I wonder if in some ways we ever grew up."

He slid on to the couch next to her. "That's enough of the philosophy for now. Tell me about Joan of Arc."

Nancy forgot about the phone call as her mind switched back to what was apparently her favorite subject. "Well, for the last fifty years or more there's been a concentrated drive to make a saint out of Joan of Arc. The Catholic Church actually canonized her some twenty-five to thirty years ago, and even people like Shaw haven't spared the praise."

"I guess she was a pretty great person."

"She was a witch. I can prove it."

"I think they burned her for being one, but I believe you're a few hundred years behind history if you still believe she really was a witch."

"This is new evidence. Historical evidence that I've uncovered."

Johnny reached over and poured himself a drink. Only half of his mind was with Nancy's tale. The rest of him was back in that police car with Harper and Backus.

"Go on," he told her, aware suddenly that she had paused.

"You're not listening."

"Yes I am."

"Well," she continued, "there are at least four points of evidence supporting the theory that Joan was really a witch. Some authors like Murray and Smith have touched briefly on this evidence, but to my knowledge it has never been the subject of a full-scale study."

"Four points?"

"Four points. First, records show that Joan was the commonest of all names for a witch. Quite often girls were trained in witchcraft by their mothers, who gave them the common witch names. Of course there were others, but Joan was the commonest."

"Not too good as evidence," Johnny pointed out.

"Let me go on. Second, it was quite common for witches to offer themselves in human sacrifice to Satan, and to avoid trouble with the law they sometimes had themselves falsely accused of a crime and put to death by the public executioner. Thus all their cult could gather for the sacrifice and still be perfectly safe from the law. Joan could very well have done this."

"Well, now. . . ."

"Let me finish. Point three: Joan's military commander, Gilles de Rais, a Marshal of France, was actually condemned for sorcery some nine years after she died. The evidence shows that he murdered some two hundred women and children during Satanic rites. And fourth, my dear Johnny, this fact was known to the people and to his servants in Joan's time. Joan *must* have known she was serving under a man who practiced human sacrifice to Satan."

"The prosecution rests?"

"The prosecution rests," she smiled.

"Well, I'll think about it, but I don't know. You intend to make these four points the basis of an entire book?"

"Of course. Johnny, young writers like us—no matter if we write songs or stories—can't get ahead unless we attack some of the old idols. If I write a sexy historical novel, I might make a little money, but what makes it a better book than a dozen others? What makes me a more important author than a dozen others?"

"It's important to be important, isn't it?"

"Now you're making fun of me, Johnny."

"Not really." He glanced at his watch. "Say, it's time for supper. How about it?"

"Fine!" She jumped off the couch and started combing her hair in front of his mirror.

Johnny walked up behind her and stood very close for a moment. She turned half towards him. "Sing me a song, Johnny. One of yours."

"For you I could write them."

"You did once."

"I did always." He kissed her lightly on the mouth.

"Come on now," she broke away. "Let's not behave like a couple of characters in one of my books or one of your songs."

He backed away and sighed. "Same old Nancy. Even after all these years."

They went down to dinner, finding a quiet place not far from his apartment. On the way he bought an evening newspaper and while they waited for their food he read through the article on page one.

"What's so interesting?"

"A cop I knew was murdered this morning."

"Was that what the phone call was about, from the congressman?"

"Yes. It's a crazy thing, all mixed up with this fellow Cotton Cravess who's running for governor."

"I saw his pictures around town. What kind of man is he?"

"I don't know. Newspaper publisher, business tycoon, anything you can name. He got Jim Yorkman elected to Congress, and probably did the same for lots of others. Now he's running for governor, but apparently his associates aren't too careful with their pre-election activities. They caused the death of a girl last night."

It was out now. He'd spoken the words. He'd told someone about it, even if it was only Nancy. He told her the rest of it then, all of it, watching her face for any change of expression that would tell him her thoughts.

"What are you going to do?" she asked him finally.

"Talk to Officer Harper, like I told Yorkman I would."

"Why get involved in it any further, Johnny?"

"I am involved, though. If Cotton Cravess had Backus killed so he wouldn't talk, he might do the same to me."

"Let me go with you, then."

"No. . . ."

"At least to question Harper. There can't be any danger there."

Johnny Nocturne sighed. "All right. I think he goes on duty early tonight. We can probably catch him at Headquarters."

They left the restaurant and headed down the street to the old stone building that served as River City's Police Headquarters. He led Nancy around the back, to the garage, because this was where it had happened.

"Tom Harper around?"

"Yeah, he's around. Who wants to know?"

"Johnny Nocturne. Tell him I'd like to talk to him."

"Hey, Tom! Fellow here to see you!"

From behind a line of gleaming black and red police cars Tom Harper appeared. Johnny was struck at once by the deep, tired lines of his face. He looked as if he hadn't slept in a week.

"Hello, Johnny."

"Hello, Tom. I heard what happened."

Tom Harper frowned at Nancy and then shifted his gaze back to Johnny. "He was so young, so damned young."

"You think Cotton's men did it?"

"I don't know what to think, Johnny. He was shot down right here in this garage, not twelve hours ago. I don't know what to think."

"Of course Cotton Cravess approached you?"

"Of course. As soon as you left us last night one of his men appeared from somewhere. He must have figured the girl had gasped out a dying message."

"They say she died of heart failure."

"She probably did, but in that guy's position he might as well have murdered her. If that story got out he wouldn't have a chance of being governor."

"They tried to bribe you?"

"Offered us a thousand dollars each on the spot. But I must admit that later, when Cravess himself asked to talk to us, he didn't offer money."

"No, he wouldn't."

"But he said we'd be promoted, promised us things like that. He explained it all, too. About the party and how the girl ran away."

Johnny Nocturne sighed. He noticed a spot on the garage floor and wondered if it was grease or possibly the blood of young Backus. "So you believed them and said nothing."

"I said nothing at first, but this morning I went in and told everything."

"You told them about Cotton Cravess and the dying girl's words?"

"Yes. I told them everything."

"What about Backus?"

"He was young. . . ."

Johnny looked hard into Harper's eyes, and then he turned away. "Come on, Nancy. We'd better call Jim Yorkman."

They left the garage and found a pay phone nearby. But no one answered at the congressman's number. Johnny dialled the office of Cotton Cravess and waited.

Presently a gruff voice answered. "Hello?"

"Could I speak to Jim Yorkman, please?"

"Yorkman? I don't know if he's here."

"He's there. Let me speak to him. Tell him it's Johnny Nocturne."

Outside, a truck was dropping off the first copies of the morning newspaper, for the night travellers who could not wait till dawn for their news. Johnny motioned to Nancy. "Get me a copy of that."

From the telephone came the familiar voice of Cotton Cravess. "What do you want, Johnny?"

"Right now I want to speak with Jim Yorkman."

"What about?"

"I told him I'd call. Put him on."

Cotton Cravess snorted into the phone. "The deal's off. You can blab all you want now."

"No songs on your radio station?"

"No songs on my radio station."

Johnny snatched the newspaper from Nancy and propped it up in the phone booth. "Let me read you a few headlines from the morning paper, Cotton."

"What?"

"Cop killing linked to girl's death: police hint political implications."

"What the hell!"

"It's all out, Cotton. I'd suggest you resign from the campaign."

"Go to hell!"

Johnny sighed. "You're already in on the girl's death and the bribery attempts, but I can still keep you out of the cop's murder if you play ball with me."

"What? Are you crazy, Nocturne? Are you trying to blackmail me?"

"Just let me come up and talk to you."

He was silent on the other end of the line for a moment, but finally the voice came over again. "All right. Bring that newspaper with you."

Johnny hung up and left the booth. "Come on, Nan, we've got a date."

"Johnny, would you mind right now telling me what this is all about?" she asked.

"Well, the whole business is a little strange for me. I don't usually get involved in politics or things like that. But what you told me about Joan of Arc started me thinking."

They were walking now through the brisk darkness, passing only occasionally into the pools of light from the street lamps overhead.

"What about Joan of Arc?" Nancy asked.

"I hate to go into it, after you've spent over a year gathering your material, but of course your reasoning about Joan is somewhat in error."

She paused beneath a street light and looked at him. "You should stick to songwriting, Johnny. History is more in my line."

"You're not the first person that's told me that, but I think I have to explain it anyway, so you'll understand this thing."

"Go on."

"Earlier you brought up four points about Joan to prove she was a witch: her name, the manner of her death, her commander's guilt, and her knowledge of this guilt. I'll take the points in order. First, you say Joan was the most common name for witches, but this implies that Joan's parents—or at least her mother—must have also been a witch, and trained her in the black art. If such was the case, though, I'm sure it would have been brought out at her trial, when they tried to uncover all sorts of evidence linking her with witchcraft."

Nancy Stevens started walking again, and he fell into step at her side. "What's all this got to do with Cotton Cravess?"

He ignored the question for the moment and went on. "Your second point—that Joan's death might have been a carefully planned sacrifice to the devil—is hardly possible. Had Joan really been a witch, and really wanted to die, she could simply have told the truth about her Satanic activities. The facts of history show that she certainly didn't want to die. Which leaves you with only two points, Nan, both of which—even if true—prove only that Joan knew her commander was practising witchcraft."

"Isn't that evidence enough against her?"

Johnny gazed up at the night sky, where a thousand glistening diamonds glowed and twinkled. "No, oddly enough it isn't. I met a man today in a somewhat similar situation. Jim Yorkman isn't a saint, but he's that equally rare species, an honest politician. He's honest, but Cotton Cravess got him his job. He feels that he still owes Cravess something. But I think maybe we can get him out from under, and at the same time spike this whole thing before it snowballs into more murders."

"That's not songwriter talk, Johnny."

"No, I guess it's night talk. Talk for when the night is warm and clear like this. And when you're here and I feel I could beat the whole darned world."

Nancy laughed and linked her arm in his. "I guess you and I never did really grow up, did we?"

"You can write a book about us sometime."

"I'll have to, now that you've spoiled my theory of Joan of Arc."

"It's just that sometimes there are so many different ways of looking at the same set of facts. . . ." He turned in at the tall building that housed Cravess Enterprises. "Here we are."

They went up in the familiar elevator, rising into the tower offices of Cotton Cravess. But now all was turmoil there. The followers, campaign managers, aides and speech-writers for the would-be governor were all there, talking on telephones, listening to the news on radios, shouting at each other in utter confusion.

Johnny didn't know many of them, but he recognized Blinky, the man whose card game had been broken up by Harper and Backus the night before. Yes, someone like Blinky would have a place here.

Johnny fought his way through the press of activity, pulling Nancy along behind him. "Blinky," he called out, when the others seemed to ignore him.

"Yeah?"

"Find Cravess and tell him Johnny Nocturne's here to see him."

The gambler gave him a tired look and then retreated behind a thick oak door. He returned after a moment and motioned them in.

Cotton Cravess was there, pleading with some unknown person on the telephone. Finally he threw down the instrument in disgust. "My own newspaper turning against me!" he almost shouted. "What good is it owning a newspaper if they won't print what I tell them to?"

Nancy slipped into an empty chair and Blinky closed the door behind them, staying where he was on the inside. Johnny looked around the room but no one else was there.

"O.K., Nocturne. Start talking," Cotton Cravess said, his mask of goodwill suddenly gone. "What have you got to offer?"

The Night My Friend

Johnny tossed the folded newspaper on the desk. "Judging from the activity outside, you fellows have already seen this."

"It's worse than that now," Blinky said.

Cotton Cravess silenced him with a look. Then he turned his attention back to Johnny. "You might as well know about it," he decided. "The whole story's out now, and the opposition's shouting for my scalp."

Johnny smiled slightly and decided he'd come at the right moment. "Get Congressman Yorkman in here."

"For what?"

Johnny leaned against the wall and took out a cigarette. "If you want to get out of this thing in one piece, you'll do as I say."

"I don't take orders from any hack songwriter."

Johnny Nocturne smiled. "That's not what you were saying about my music a little earlier in the day."

"Get to the point, Nocturne. I'm busy."

"I don't talk until you get Yorkman in here."

Cotton Cravess sighed and pushed a button on his desk. An intercom squeaked into life and he bellowed, "Find Jim Yorkman."

Johnny lit the cigarette. "Thanks."

Cravess studied him for a moment. "When this is all over, I'm going to take special pleasure in running you out of River City."

"We'll see."

The office door opened and Jim Yorkman emerged from the outer bedlam. "Hello, Johnny," he said.

"Hi, Jim. I thought you'd want to be in on this."

"Oh, what?"

Johnny Nocturne walked over to Cotton's desk and ground out his cigarette. "Cravess, I know how you've been running honest politicans like Jim Yorkman here. I know how you got them elected and then thought you could control every vote that they cast."

Cotton Cravess rose from behind his desk. "You seem to forget that you're addressing the next governor of the state."

Johnny Nocturne laughed.

It was then that Blinky moved in behind him and caught him with a rabbit punch to the back of the neck. Johnny felt himself falling forward, unable to catch himself on the desk.

Dimly, he heard Nancy screaming, and then, as he hit the floor and rolled over, he saw Jim Yorkman going into action. The Congressman grabbed Blinky by his shirt and yanked him forward.

"Cravess, we just dissolved our partnership," he said, as he hit Blinky a crushing right to the jaw. The gambler toppled backward and crashed into the desk.

Cotton Cravess groped for buttons on his desk. "I'll see you in hell, Yorkman!"

The door of the office opened and two or three men crowded in "What's up, Cotton?"

Cravess waved his arm. "Throw these bums out."

But Johnny struggled to his feet. "Cravess, call them off if you don't want to face a grand jury on a murder charge."

"I don't know anything about that cop killing."

"But you'll burn for it, Cravess."

Cotton Cravess dropped back into his chair. "Leave us alone for five minutes. Then toss them out."

"Right, Cotton."

Blinky started to get to his feet and Jim Yorkman shoved him into their waiting arms. "Take this with you."

When the door had closed again Johnny walked over and sat on the arm of Nancy's chair. "I can get you out of the murder charge, Cravess, in return for two things. First, you give up all connections with Jim Yorkman and anyone else you helped to elect. And second, you withdraw from the race for governor."

"What? Withdraw?"

"You heard me."

"I'll never withdraw."

"Cravess, I hardly think the people of this state would elect a man under suspicion of killing a policeman and raping a girl."

"I didn't rape any girl and I didn't kill any policeman."

"But try and tell the voters that."

"Damn you."

"You've got your choice. Bow out now and the party still has the better part of three weeks to build up a replacement. Keep fighting and you'll either be tossed out by the party or by the voters."

"And if I agree?"

"If you agree you can still save something of your reputation and also escape a possible murder charge."

Cotton Cravess looked around him like a man suddenly trapped by the press of events. He sought the eyes of Jim Yorkman and asked, "Jim, what do you think?"

Yorkman sighed. "Either way, I'm through with you. You've run my life for too long a time. If it means leaving Congress, I'm ready to do that, too."

"Well?" Johnny Nocturne asked.

The door opened again and the men were back. "Should we throw them out, Cotton?"

The Night My Friend

"No," he answered quietly. "Get out."

They retreated once more, and Johnny, Nancy and Jim Yorkman faced the man behind the desk, now grown suddenly old. After a moment's silence he picked up the telephone and spoke into it.

"Arrange for me to go on radio and television at once. I have a statement to make."

He dropped the phone into its cradle and looked up at Johnny Nocturne. "Now how are you going to clear me of this murder?"

"You're giving up?"

Cotton Cravess nodded. "I'm giving up. . . ."

Twenty minutes later they were grouped together in the studios downstairs, watching as the television camera rolled in for a close-up of Cotton Cravess.

"Friends and supporters," he began, "it is not easy for me to come before you tonight. . . ."

Jim Yorkman tugged at Johnny's arm.

"What's up, Jim?"

"The killer of Harvey Backus just confessed."

Johnny frowned. "Keep it quiet till after the speech. That could ruin everything right now."

And they stood in silence and listened to the words of Cotton Cravess. ". . . and so it is that I feel it to be in the best interests of the party that I withdraw from the race at once, to devote all my time to silencing these false rumors against my name. I feel sure that the party will be able to . . . "

"That's it," Johnny said.

Nancy sighed with relief. "I still don't know just how you did it."

"Come back to the apartment and I'll explain," he said. "Right now I can think better with a piano under me. . . ."

The night shadows had lengthened, conquering the world of glowing neon and blinking lights. Now it was the world of Nocturne, of deep, dreamy mood that slipped across the sleeping city.

And Johnny ran his fingers lightly over the piano keys and thought about how great it was to be alive. Jim Yorkman was gone now, but Nancy was still with him, curled up on the couch as his fingers moved lightly over the keys.

"*Tell me, tell me how it is. . . .*"

"Johnny, the Congressman said someone confessed to the murder."

"Yes. . . ."

"Who?"

"That policeman we saw this afternoon. Tom Harper."

"Tom Harper! But why?"

"Why? . . . The eternal question." His fingers searched among the keys and his gaze was far away, in the night. And in the dimness of the apartment there were only the two of them.

"Why?" he repeated. "Because Tom Harper was a loyal man, so loyal that he couldn't bear to see a young cop being bribed. It was too much for him, and when he confronted Backus in the garage there was nothing left to do but to kill him. Backus had sold out the whole police force, and in Harper's eyes he had to pay for this."

"But how did you know? How did you know it wasn't Cravess?"

The music drifted around them, and the darkness clothed them like a warm friend. "There were many things showing it wasn't Cravess or his men. He was already in enough trouble without chancing a cop killing. And, anyway, Backus had accepted the bribe. They certainly wouldn't have killed him. Besides which, the murder was committed in the police garage, when Backus was going off duty. Why kill him in the very shadow of Police Headquarters when he would have been out in the street on his way home in another minute? The answer of course was that the killer wasn't a hired gunman. He was another policeman."

"Why Tom Harper, though?"

"Because if Backus did accept the bribe and said nothing, only Harper could have known about it. Harper himself didn't report that incident till morning, so only he—and Cotton's men—knew that Backus had accepted the bribe."

"But that's mostly guesswork, Johnny."

"It was guesswork until I talked to Harper in the garage and asked him if Backus had taken the bribe. He just looked at me, and said that Backus had been very young, and I knew. Harper's eyes told me everything."

"Would you have turned him in?"

"I suppose so. Though I knew his confession wouldn't be long in coming. A man who murders for the honor of the police force can't hide his crime for long. The very motivation of the murder told me that Harper would confess the whole thing very soon."

"And you used that knowledge to deal with Cravess. Why, Johnny?"

His fingers moved again over the keys, and a song of the night came drifting to them. "Partly to save my own skin, since I was one of those who heard the girl's dying words. But I guess mostly it was our discussion of Joan of Arc that did it. I saw that if someone like her could rise above the evil around her, possibly people like Jim Yorkman could, too. Why don't you write a book about that?"

She walked over and slid on to the piano bench next to him, and said, very quietly, "Maybe some day I will."

And then the night closed in around them, and there was only the song of the friendly darkness to comfort their thoughts.

The Suitcase

The plane, a silver bird dipping its
wings to the far-off dawn, came in low
over Jason Lean's farmland. Too low,
he remembered thinking, for he'd seen
so many hundreds on the airport approach that he almost at times felt he
could fly one. Too low, with the rising
sun in the pilot's eyes and the double
row of power lines crossing the tip of
the hill. He shouted something, to be
heard only by the field birds and the
indifferent cows, then screwed his face
in a sort of horror as the great plane
touched the unseen wires.

There was a crackle of blue flame,
no more than that of a match lit and
suddenly dying, but it was enough to
spell death to an airliner. The entire
hillside seemed to explode as the plane
twisted into the ground, boring deep
like some hibernating animal, spew-
ing flames that might have told you
the animal was a dragon.

Jason Lean watched until the first
flash of flame had died, and then began the short trek across the valley to
the wreckage on the hillside. Others
would have seen the crash too, he
knew, and already it would be tapping
out on the news tickers of the world.
How many dead—fifty, sixty? Those
big planes carried a lot of people these
days. He shook his head sadly at the
thought, but did not increase his pace.

He already knew he would find nothing alive when he reached the smoldering wreckage.

Now here and there a tree was burning, and there ahead he could see the tail section of the plane itself, a great silver thing that sat silent now as a giant tombstone. Padded seats, so comfortable with their bodies still strapped sitting—grotesque, but all too real. And strewn across the landscape, wreckage, flesh, baggage, mail pouches, fallen trees, dangerously dangling wires. As if a giant hand—a flaming devil's hand—had written its signature on the hillside. All dead, all.

He walked among them, terrified, remembering somewhere deep within the recesses of his mind a time when very young he'd walked through a country graveyard at night. He took in all the details of grief and tragedy, the spilled suitcases, the child's toys, the scorched and splintered packing cases . . . and then his eyes fell on one suitcase, resting apart from the others, its leather hide barely marked by the smoke.

It was a large bag, of pale pebbled pigskin, with two tough straps around it to reinforce the lock. It was the only one he saw that had neither burned nor tumbled open to spread its contents over the landscape. Jason Lean stood for some moments staring at the bag, as if it held some strange sort of fascination for him. Then, in an instant of certainty, he stooped and grasped the plastic handle, lifting the suitcase from the ground. He turned once to look over his shoulder, to make certain that none of the blackened corpses moved in accusation. Then he hurried back down the hillside, through the smoky haze of destruction, carrying his treasure like some traveler only just returned from a world tour.

"A plane crash," Martha said when he returned. "What a terrible thing!"

"Terrible," Jason agreed. He always agreed with his wife. "I was over there, looking at the wreckage. They're all dead." Already, on the distant ridge, they could see men moving like ants. Police, ambulances, morgue wagons, reporters—all converging now on the scene of disaster. Making their way carefully around the fallen wires and the blackened wreckage. Hoping, then feeling hope die as they saw what Jason Lean had seen.

"What's that you've got?" she asked, noticing the suitcase for the first time.

"I found it up by the wreckage. It's not burned or anything. Must have been thrown clear."

"*And you took it?*" She made the words into something terrible, and for the first time he realized just what he had done. "You took it? From the dead?"

"I . . . I thought it might have something valuable in it. They're all dead. It belongs to no one." But even as he spoke the words he knew he would never convince her.

"That's looting! It's like robbing graves, but even worse. Jason, you have to take it back this minute, leave it where you found it."

"Don't be silly—how could I do that when the hill's swarming with people?" It was the first time he had ever raised his voice to her, and he regretted it at once. "I'll get rid of it, just as soon as I open it up and look inside."

"Jason, you're not opening that suitcase! I can't imagine anything more horrible than pawing about in the belongings of some poor dead creature who was so much alive just an hour ago."

"But . . . but there might be something valuable inside, Martha. It's an expensive suitcase, you can see that. Suppose it contains fancy clothes, or an expensive camera, or important papers. Or even money!"

"Jason, either you return that suitcase this minute, or you take it out behind the barn and bury it. I'm not going to have it here. I'm not going to have you opening it and going through it. I don't want the man's ghost coming and haunting us for your awful crime!"

He knew it was useless when she got in one of those moods. And yet his will was torn between her commanding words and the questioning suitcase that rested now on the floor between his feet. "Martha . . ."

"*Bury it! Get it out of my sight, Jason!*"

"All right." He went out with bowed head, carrying the heavy suitcase beyond the faded red barn to the little animal graveyard. While Martha watched from a distance he dug a shallow hole and buried the pigskin bag between the old cow and last year's cat. "All right. It's done."

But as he followed her into the house there was a sort of sadness in his heart.

The following morning a car stopped on the road and a tall young man walked back to the barn where Jason was busy with his daily chores. "Hello there," he called out. "Got a minute?"

Jason set down his milk pails and wiped the sweat from his forehead. "Sure, mister. What can I do for you?"

"We're investigating yesterday's plane crash over on the hill. We thought you might have seen something that could help us." The man had taken out a little notebook. "You're Jason Lean, correct?"

"That's me, and I saw it, all right. Plane came in too low. Hit those power lines. Was just at dawn, and I suppose the sun might have blinded the pilot for a minute. It hit the lines and that was the end of it."

"Did you go over to see the wreckage?"

"I . . . No, I started to, but then turned back. I was afraid of those fallen power lines."

"Just as well," the investigator said, making a brief note in his book. "You couldn't have done anything. They were all killed instantly."

"Yes. Horrible." Jason turned to stare out across the valley, toward the hillside scar which would take many seasons to heal.

"Thanks for your time," the man said. "I may be back to talk to you again."

"Certainly. Anything I can do . . ."

The man nodded a smile and started back to his car. He hadn't asked about the suitcase, Jason thought. They'd never missed it. Burnt to ashes, they probably supposed.

And that night, in bed next to the cold flesh of his wife, Jason imagined it all again. Opening the suitcase, finding a lifetime's treasure nestled there waiting. What would it be? Money? A woman's wardrobe and jewels? A salesman's sample kit of fine furs? Something for Martha, perhaps. Or himself. Even a fine new suit that could be made to fit him.

The next day, in the late afternoon, while Martha was cleaning in the front of the house, his uncertain footsteps took him once more to the animal graveyard beyond the barn. Perhaps, if he could only dig up the suitcase and look—then bury it again before she ever knew the difference. Yes, that was what he would do. Must do.

He retrieved the old spade from the barn and started to dig. After a moment's work he could feel the familiar leather hide as he scraped the dirt from it.

"Jason!"

"Martha. What are you . . . ?"

"Jason, you were going to open it! Cover it up this instant! Don't you realize it will bring us nothing but tragedy? Don't you realize it belongs to a *dead man?*"

"All right, Martha. I was just . . ."

"Cover it up, Jason. And don't do that again."

He covered it up.

But still, as the days passed and the memory of the crash itself drifted further to the back of his conscious mind, there was still the shape of the sealed suitcase to obsess him. He saw it in his waking and sleeping hours, saw it closed as first he'd met it, and open with all its treasures exposed. It became, in various fantasies, a spy's hoard of secret plans, an embezzler's final crime, a businessman's stock of everyday valuables. He imagined all the hundreds of things that might come tumbling out if only he looked. The things he'd never owned; like an electric razor, or a portable radio, or a fine camera.

No, decided Jason with finality, after a week of torment. Whatever was in that suitcase, it was not going to rot in the ground behind the barn. He found Martha in the kitchen and told her of his decision.

"I'm going to dig it up and open it," he said.

"Jason . . ."

"Nothing you can say will stop me, Martha. I have to know what's inside it."

"Jason, there's death in that suitcase. I can feel it in my bones."

"I have to *know!*" he screamed at her. And when she stepped heavily into his path he brushed her aside as he would some animal in the field.

"Stop, Jason!"

He hit her, only to shut that refusing mouth, only to silence her for a few important moments. She fell heavily, her head catching the edge of the old stove. He sucked in his breath and bent over her, chilled now to the bone. She wasn't moving and he knew in some fantastic manner that he'd killed her.

But he didn't stop. He hurried on to the barn, with a speed born now of nameless panic. The spade, digging in the familiar earth, uncovering, revealing.

Yes, the suitcase. Still there like some Pandora's box awaiting him. His hands fumbled with the straps, teeth biting into lips, forehead sweating a chill moisture.

But it was locked.

Into the barn, carrying it gently now, with clods of earth falling from it. Into the barn, and a few careful blows with the pitchfork, prying the lock apart until it snapped under the pressure. Finally.

He opened the suitcase.

The government inspector found them, some time later, when he stopped by the Lean farmhouse to ask some further questions about the airliner crash. He found Martha Lean on the kitchen floor, and she looked so peaceful it was hard to believe she was dead.

And he found Jason Lean in the barn, kneeling in a sort of daze over an open suitcase. It was a salesman's sample case. It was filled with leather-bound Bibles.

The Picnic People

The car radio thundering a Sunday afternoon concert into my ear, the sun bleaching out my hair exposed in the topless auto, I wheeled briskly up the familiar park road searching for them. They always came to the same general area, the same hilltop with its vagrant view of distant beach and specks of suited swimmers, just far enough away to untempt husbands with roving eyes and satisfy wives with children to guard. Today, breeze blowing off the lake, rustling leaves at their summer peakness, was surely a day when the picnic people would be out. All of them.

I spied Fred Dutton's car first, parked with three wheels off the road, sporty and casual like its owner, top up and windows cautiously closed, also like its owner. Surely he could have reached it before any of the less than occasional overhead clouds grouped into a threat of rain, but Fred Dutton was like that. Take no chances. Play it safe. Better safe than sorry. Fred Dutton.

I parked behind him, purposely kissing his bumper a bit harder than necessary, enjoying myself at the thought of the dent I might be leaving in it. Almost I expected him to come running at the sound, but they were just out of sight, down the hill hidden by the willows along the edge of the pond. It was a pleasant place, bringing back half-forgotten memories of days without care and nights when only the happiness mattered. I'd been the one in those days, and I wondered if I still was.

Dora, Fred's wife, saw me first. She was boiling water on the camp stove for her usual cup of tea and she jerked her hand back with such sudden shock that the pan of water clattered to the ground. "Why—Sam!"

"Hello, Dora. Glad to see you remember me." The grass seemed suddenly damp through my shoes, and I was vaguely aware that the children had been splashing here.

"Sam!" She turned her head. "Fred, come here! It's Sam—Sam Waggel." Her voice almost broke as she said it.

Fred came running, and the rest—except for the children—weren't far behind. They came cautiously at first, as if viewing a beast newly escaped from the zoo. Then they crowded around, the foolish false grins on their faces, greeting me. "Sam boy, how the heck you been?" This was a real estate broker named Charlie Thames, who'd never really liked me on my best of days. Charlie hadn't changed much, put on a few pounds maybe, but hadn't we all. His wife Laura startled me a bit with her graying hair, but the rest of them were pretty much the same.

Fred Dutton had his arm around my shoulder almost at once, as if I'd never been away, pressing a sweating can of beer into my hand. "When'd you get out, Sam? Why didn't you let us know? How you feelin'?"

"Well enough, Fred," I said, answering his last question first. "I got out a couple days ago. Called your and Charlie's homes but when nobody answered I figured you were probably out picnicking at the old place."

"Hello, Sam." This was Jean O'Brian—Jean Falconi now, of course— a girl who'd meant a lot to me once. She was wearing white shorts that showed off her legs. She's always had the best legs in the crowd. Her husband, Joe, came into view then too, carrying the youngest of the children in his arms.

"Hi, Jean. Joe. The kids are really growing up."

"Have a hot dog, Sam," Charlie offered. "We got plenty."

Laura, as if to back up the words, went to get one off the grill. "Here, Sam. Just the way you used to like them."

"Used to, Laura? I still do. Nothing's changed that much."

She flushed slightly and turned away, but Dora Dutton was there to take her place. "Do you want to talk about it, Sam? We don't want . . ."

"Sure. What do you want to know? If you've finished eating I can give you some wonderful descriptions of the shock treatments and the aftereffects of the drugs they were feeding me."

"Go play," Charlie said to one of the children who wandered up.

"Go play with your sister." His face was hard and set. Already he was remembering his old Sam-hatred from the days before the trouble.

"Sam," Joe Falconi said, speaking with that sort of almost-accent, "what about the charges? Are you going to have to stand trial now that you're out?" Joe was a contractor, a good guy as guys went.

"No," I told them, taking my time about lighting a cigarette, letting all damned six of them know I was out for good, here to stay, ready for action. "Remember, the court ruled I was insane at the time I did it. But I'm all right now, all cured. All."

"Well," Fred Dutton said, "well, that's damned good. All cured, huh?"

"All cured."

But Jean wasn't quite so convinced. "It's only been two years, Sam. Are you sure? I mean . . ."

I just sort of laughed at her. She did look funny standing there under the willow, thinking about how this guy she once necked with over in West Park might now be a homicidal maniac and what the hell was he doing walking around loose just two years after it happened.

Charlie and Laura sort of drifted off, pretending to hike after the kids, and Dora started the water for her tea again. After all the excitement of my arrival they were acting now as if I'd never been away. Or were they acting as if I'd never come back?

Joe Falconi brought me a beer to go with the hot dog. "It's good to see you again, boy. Come on, let's walk down by the water."

We strolled away from the others, kicking at stones, watching them skip and finally splash in the sparkling pond, stirring here and there an eddy of mud in the tranquil waters. "Your kids are growing." I said. "You and Jean just have the two?"

"No," he answered, a bit embarrassed. "We had another boy last year. I guess you didn't hear."

"Communications weren't too good in there. Especially when none of my old friends ever came to see me."

"Sam . . ."

"What?" I kicked at a loose stone.

"Sam, I don't blame you for being a bit bitter, but you've got to look at it from our point of view."

"Sure," I told him with a smile. "You figured I was locked up in the nut house for the rest of my natural life, so why the hell should anybody bother about me. Right? It was just as if I was dead too, along with her."

"Sam. You don't know what you do to me when you talk like that. Hell, they wouldn't even let anyone see you at first, you know that. We didn't know how bad you were or anything about it. You know the way the newspapers treat a story like that."

"Sure. Frankly, I was surprised they didn't have a gang of reporters waiting for me the other day."

"Look, Sam . . . I know the construction business isn't your line, but if you need a job to tide you over for a while, I could probably fix you up."

"Thanks, Joe. About the only thing I've done for the past two years is make baskets. They have some weird ideas of mental therapy in those places. Maybe I'll take you up on it."

From somewhere behind us we heard Jean calling to him. "I have to get back. She has quite a time with those kids."

I followed him part of the way, but paused a bit by one of the playing children. It was a little girl, unmistakably one of Charlie and Laura's children. "How are you?" I asked her.

"Fine," she answered a bit uncertainly at the question from a stranger.

"You don't remember me. You were just born when I went away." I pulled at a few willow leaves and tickled her nose with them. "What's your name? I forgot it."

But before the child could answer, Laura Thames had appeared from somewhere. "Sam, please leave Katie alone."

"What?" I hadn't quite understood her unexpected words.

"I'm sorry, Sam. Really I am. But I don't want you to get near the children."

"Sure." I stood up and walked back to where the others stood too casually around the charcoal stove. Dora was drinking her tea, while Fred played with a rumpled deck of cards.

"Sam," Charlie Thames said, "what do you plan to do with yourself? Plan to stay around town long?"

"Why not? It's my home." I was conscious of the sun a bit lower in the afternoon sky, the birds not quite as chirping as before.

"Sure. I was just thinking that you might want to go away to some place where people didn't know about the . . . trouble. You know." Charlie was smiling. Keeping it friendly. The smiler with the knife. Chaucer. Charlie Damned Chaucer Thames.

"Thanks for the advice, Charlie."

"New York or someplace. You know, big city. Hell, I was reading the other day that most of the people in Manhattan are nuts anyway."

"Charlie!" This from Laura, warning, rebuking. Charlie glanced at her and heeded the warning. He shut up suddenly and walked over to inspect the dying embers of the charcoal fire.

"Guess I'd better be going," I told them, all of them, not one in particular, because all of them thought alike. Even good old Joe with his offers of a job until I could find something better. Maybe they thought I was going to work on their wives next. Maybe they thought their children weren't safe around a homicidal maniac—even a certified cured homicidal maniac. Maybe, hell.

"It looks a little like rain," Jean was agreeing. "Maybe we'd all better start packing up." I followed her gaze toward the single small black cloud moving fast in the eastern sky and almost laughed in her pretty face. They were all damned scared of old Sam.

I walked vaguely back in the direction of the cars, knowing, feeling that six pairs of eyes were boring holes in my back. "So long," I called out, half turning toward them for a final wave. It hadn't been much of a visit, not much of a one at all.

Fred Dutton ran after me and caught me at the top of the hill. "Sam, look, come over to the house some night, huh?"

"Sure, Fred."

"Don't be bitter."

"I'm not. Guess I just thought everything would be the same, like the old days."

Fred Dutton looked suddenly solemn. "There were eight of us in the old days, Sam. There aren't any more. It can't ever be the same, I guess. You gotta understand that."

"Sure. I'll call you, Fred."

"Do that."

I went on down the hill and opened my car door. I guess I would have gone on home after all if I hadn't seen the kid again just then. Katie Thames, in her red shorts and striped shirt, wandering over the top of the hill. She must have been almost three. I could remember the night she was born, when things were so much better.

"Katie, Katie girl!" I called softly. "Come here, doll."

She came, a bit uncertainly, but remembering me now from our meeting of only moments before. "Hello," she said.

"Come on, Katie, let's run down by the water and play. Let's sneak down real quiet, so mommy and daddy don't hear us." Yes, before I left, before I went out of their lives for good, I'd give them something to remember me by—especially Charlie and Laura.

We made our way through the underbrush and came out suddenly near the point where Joe and I had been walking. I led her around to the other side of the pond, though, until I was sure we would be in view of the picnic people—in view but out of touch. Let them scream and carry on then, damn them. Let them tell me to leave their precious kids alone.

"Here, Katie. We'll play a little game. Up here." I motioned her up on

The Night My Friend

a rock, and watched her running with all the vigor and anticipation of a two-year-old. The rock jutted out a bit over the still, mirrored surface of the pond, and I knew from the old days that the kids often used it as a sort of diving-board for illegal swimming.

Now, my breath coming faster, I waited until she was within reach of my hands. Then I grabbed her up, suddenly, before she could give more than a little grasp. I held her by her tiny ankles and dangled her from the rock, upside down over the stagnant waiting waters.

"Scream now!" I told her. "Scream your head off! I'm going to drop you." And I lowered her a few inches toward the water.

She screamed, a high tiny sound that barely managed to drive the birds from the nearest trees. And I wondered if they would hear. I wondered if they would come running to rescue her. I wondered if I would really let her tiny body drop into the water, perhaps just too soon to be rescued. She was not like the other one, not at all like the other one. She was too helpless, even for the killing, too small for anything like picnics. She needed to grow up, just as cattle must be fattened for market, needed to live.

"Scream! Louder!"

"Sam! You crazy fool!"

It was Joe Falconi in the lead, splashing across the very middle of the shallow pond. Joe Falconi, up to his chest in the dirty water. And Laura, screaming in terror. Charlie, running toward me as he shouted a string of curses. Fred and Dora and Jean. Beautiful Jean. All horrified. Six horrified humans. Let her fall. Let her fall now. Give them a scare.

But already Joe was beneath me, smashing the reflecting surface of the pool, holding out his arms to catch her. Already Charlie and Fred were grappling with me, pulling me back from the edge.

"Somebody call the police!"

"Hold him down! Hold him!"

"He's cracked up—really crazy."

And Laura, screaming. "God, he would have killed her! He wanted to kill her!"

I didn't struggle. I looked up into the fearful eyes of Charlie Thames, sitting on my chest, holding me down. O.K., Charlie, but I gave you a scare, didn't I? Didn't I?

And above me the trees whispered in the wind, the clouds . . . what did the clouds do . . . ?

Day for a Picnic

I suppose I remember it better than the other, countless other, picnics of my childhood, and I suppose the reason for that is the murder. But perhaps this day in mid-July would have stood out in my mind without the violence of sudden death. Perhaps it would have stood out simply because it was the first time I'd ever been out alone without the everwatching eyes of my mother and father to protect me. True, my grandfather was watching over me that month while my parents vacationed in Europe, but he was more a friend than a parent—a great old man with white hair and tobacco-stained teeth who never ceased the relating of fascinating tales of his own youth out west. There were stories of Indians and warfare, tales of violence in the youthful days of our nation, and at that youthful age I was fully content in believing that my grandfather was easily old enough to have fought in all those wars as he so claimed.

It was not the custom in the Thirties, as it is today, for parents to take their children along when making their first tour of Europe, and so as I've said I was left behind in grandfather's care. It was really a month of fun for me, because the life of the rural New York town is far different from the bustle of the city, even for a boy of nine or ten, and I was to spend endless days run-

The Night My Friend

ning barefoot along dusty roads in the company of boys who never—hardly ever—viewed me strangely because of my city background. The days were sunny with warmth, because it had been a warm summer even here on the shores of a cooling lake. Almost from the beginning of the month my grandfather had spoken with obvious relish of the approach of the annual picnic, and by mid-month I was looking forward to it also, thinking that here would be a new opportunity of exploring the byways of the town and meeting other boys as wild and free as I myself felt. Then too, I never seemed to mind at that time the company of adults. They were good people for the most part, and I viewed them with a proper amount of childish wonder.

There were no sidewalks in the town then, and nothing that you'd really call a street. The big touring cars and occasional late model roadsters raised endless clouds of dust as they roared (seemingly to a boy of ten) through the town at fantastic speeds unheard of in the city. This day especially, I remember the cars churning up the dust. I remember grandfather getting ready for the picnic, preparing himself with great care because this was to be a political picnic and grandfather was a very important political figure in the little town.

I remember standing in the doorway of his bedroom (leaning, really, because boys of ten never stood when they could lean), watching him knot the black string tie that made him look so much like that man in the funny movies. For a long time I watched in silence, seeing him scoop up coins for his pockets and the solid gold watch I never tired of seeing, and the little bottle he said was cough medicine even in the summer, and of course his important speech.

"You're goin' to speak, Gramps?"

"Sure am, boy. Every year I speak. Give the town's humanitarian award. It's voted on by secret ballot of all the townspeople."

"Who won it?"

"That's something no one knows but me, boy. And I don't tell till this afternoon."

"Are you like the mayor here, Gramps?"

"Sort of, boy," he said with a chuckle. "I'm what you call a selectman, and since I'm the oldest of them here I guess I have quite a lot to say about the town."

"Are you in charge of the picnic?"

"I'm in charge of the awards."

"Can we get free Coke and hot dogs?"

He chuckled at that. "We'll see, boy. We'll see."

Grandfather didn't drive, and as a result we were picked up for the picnic by Miss Pinkney and Miss Hazel, two old schoolteachers who drove a white Cord with a certain misplaced pride. Since they were already in front, the two of us piled in back, a bit crowded but happy. On the way to the picnic grounds we passed others going on foot, and grandfather waved like a prince might wave.

"What a day for a picnic!" Miss Hazel exclaimed. "Remember how it rained last year?"

The sun was indeed bright and the weather warm, but with the contrariness of the very young I remember wishing that I'd been at the rainy picnic instead. I'd never been at a rainy picnic for the very simple reason that my parents always called them off if it rained.

"It's a good day," my grandfather said. "It'll bring out the voters. They should hold elections in the summer time, and we'd win by a landslide every time."

The Fourth of July was not yet two weeks past, and as we neared the old picnic grounds we could hear the belated occasional crackling of left-over fireworks being set off by the other kids. I was more than ever anxious to join them, though I did wonder vaguely what kind of kids would ever have firecrackers unexploded and left over after the big day.

We travelled down a long and dusty road to the picnic property, running winding down a hillside to a sort of cove by the water where brown sandy bluffs rose on three sides. There was room here for some five hundred people, which is the number that might be attracted by the perfect weather, and already a few cars were parked in the makeshift parking area, disgorging there the loads of children and adults. Miss Pinkney and Miss Hazel parked next to the big touring car that belonged to Doctor Stout, and my grandfather immediately cornered the doctor on some political subject. They stood talking for some minutes about—as I remember—the forthcoming primary election, and all the while I shifted from one foot to the other watching the other kids at play down by the water, watching the waves of the lake whitened by a brisk warming breeze that fanned through the trees and tall uncut grass of the bluffs.

Finally, with a nod of permission from my grandfather, I took off on the run, searching out a few of the boys I'd come to know best in these weeks of my visit. I found them finally, playing in a sort of cave on the hillside. Looking back now I realize it was probably no more than a lovers' trysting place but at the time it held for us all the excitement and mystery of a smuggler's den. I played there with the others for nearly an hour, until I heard my grandfather calling me from down near the speakers' platform.

Already as I ran back down the hill I saw that the campaign posters and patriotic bunting were in place. The picnic crowd was gradually drifting down to the platform, clutching hot dogs and bottles of soda pop and foaming mugs of beer. Over near the cars I could see the men tapping another keg of beer, and I watched as a sudden miscalculation on the part of the men sent the liquid shooting up into a fizzing fountain. "It's raining beer," shouted one of the men, standing beneath the descending stream with his mouth open. "This must be heaven!"

Frank Coons, the town's handyman and occasional black sheep, had cornered my grandfather and was asking him something. "Come on, how about some of your gin cough medicine? I been waitin' all afternoon for it!"

But my grandfather was having none of it. "None today, Frank."

"Why not? Just a drop."

"Have some beer instead. It's just as good." He moved off, away from Frank, and I followed him. There were hands to be shaken, words to be spoken, and in all of it grandfather was a past master.

"When's your speech, Gramps?" I asked him.

"Soon now, boy. Want a soda pop?"

"Sure!"

He picked a bottle of cherry-colored liquid from the red and white cooler and opened it for me. It tasted good after my running and playing in the hot dirt of the hillside. Now grandfather saw someone else he knew, a tall handsome man named Jim Tweller, whom I'd seen at the house on occasion. He had business dealings with my grandfather, and I understood that he owned much of the property in the town.

"Stay close to the platform, Jim," grandfather was saying.

"Don't tell me I won that foolish award!"

"Can't say yet, Jim. Just stay close."

I saw Miss Pinkney and Miss Hazel pass by, casting admiring glances at Jim Tweller. "Doesn't he have such a *mannish* smell about him!" Miss Pinkney whispered loudly. Tweller, I gathered even at that tender age, was much admired by the women of the town.

"Come, boy," grandfather was saying." Bring your soda and I'll find you a seat right up in front. You can listen to my speech."

I saw that the mayor, a Mister Myerton, was already on the platform, flanked by two men and a woman I didn't know. In the very center was a big microphone hooked up to an overhead loudspeaker system borrowed from the sole local radio station. Empty beer mugs stood in front of each place. My grandfather's chair was over on the end, but right now he strode to the speaker's position, between Mayor Myerton and the woman.

"Ladies and gentlemen," he began, speaking in his best political voice. "And children, too, of course. I see a lot of you little ones here today, and that always makes me happy. It makes me aware of the fact that another generation is on the rise, a generation that will carry on the fine principles of our party in the decades to come. As many of you know, I have devoted the years since the death of my wife almost exclusively to party activities. The party has been my life-blood, as I hope it will be the life-blood of other, future generations. But enough of that for the moment. Mayor Myerton and Mrs. Finch of the school board will speak to you in due time about the battle that lies ahead of us this November. Right now, it's my always pleasant duty to announce the annual winner of the party's great humanitarian award, given to the man who has done the most for this community and its people. I should say the man or woman, because we've had a number of charming lady winners in past years. But this year it's a man, a man who has perhaps done more than any other to develop the real estate of our town to its full potential, a man who during this past year donated—yes, I said donated— the land for our new hospital building. You all know who I mean, the winner by popular vote of this year's humanitarian award—Mister Jim Tweller!"

Tweller had stayed near the speakers' stand and now he hopped up, waving to a crowd that was cheering him with some visible restraint. Young as I was, I wondered about this, wondered even as I watched grandfather yield the honored speaker's position to Tweller and take his chair at the end of the platform. Tweller waited until the scattered cheers had played themselves out in the afternoon breeze and then cheerfully cleared his throat. I noticed Frank Coons standing near the platform and saw grandfather call him over. "Get a pitcher of beer for us, Frank," he asked. "Speeches make us thirsty."

While Frank went off on his mission, Jim Tweller adjusted the wobbly microphone and began his speech of thanks and acceptance. I was just then more interested in two boys wrestling along the water's edge, tussling, kicking sand at each other. But Tweller's speech was not altogether lost on me. I remember scattered words and phrases, and even then to me they seemed the words and phrases of a political candidate rather than simply an award winner. ". . . . thank you from the bottom of my heart for this great honor . . . I realize I think more than anyone else the fact that our party needs a rebirth with new blood if it is to win again in November . . . loyal old horses turned out to pasture while the political colts run the race . . ." I saw Mayor Myerton, a man in his sixties, flinch at these words, and I realized that the simple acceptance speech was taking a most unexpected turn.

But now my attention was caught by the sight of Frank Coons returning with the foaming pitcher of beer. He'd been gone some minutes and I figured he'd stopped long enough to have one himself, or perhaps he'd found someone else who carried gin in a cough medicine bottle. Anyway, he passed the pitcher up to the man at the end of the platform, the opposite end from my grandfather. I wondered if this was his revenge for being refused that drink earlier. The man on the end filled his glass with beer and then passed it on to the mayor who did likewise. Jim Tweller interrupted his speech a moment to accept the pitcher and fill his glass, then pass it to Mrs. Finch of the school board who was on his right. She shook her head with a temperant vigor and let it go on to the man I didn't know, sitting next to grandfather at the end of the platform.

Tweller had taken a drink of his beer and shook his head violently as if it were castor oil. "Got a bad barrel here," he told the people with a laugh. "I'm going to stick to the hard stuff after this. Or else drink milk. Anyway, before I finish I want to tell you about my plans for our community. I want to tell you a little about how . . ." He paused for another drink of the beer. ". . . about how we can push back the final remains of the depression and surge ahead into the Forties with a new prosperity, a new ve . . . agh . . ."

Something was wrong. Tweller had suddenly stopped speaking and was gripping the microphone before him. Mayor Myerton put down his own beer and started to get up. "What's wrong, man?" he whispered too near the microphone. "Are you sick?"

"I . . . gnugh . . . can't breathe . . . help me . . ." Then he toppled backward, dragging the microphone with him, upsetting his glass of beer as he fell screaming and gasping to the ground.

Somewhere behind me a woman's voice took up the scream, and I thought it might have been Miss Hazel. Already Doctor Stout had appeared at the platform and was hurrying around to comfort the stricken man. As I ran forward myself I caught a funny odor in the air near the platform, near where the beer had spilled from Jim Tweller's overturned glass. It was a new smell to me, one I couldn't identify.

Behind the platform, Doctor Stout was loosening the collar of the convulsed man as grandfather and the mayor tried to assist him. But after a moment the thrashing of arms and legs ceased, and the doctor straightened up. The bright overhead sun caught his glasses as he did so, reflecting for an instant a glare of brilliance. "There's nothing I can do," he said quietly, almost sadly. "The man is dead."

Suddenly I was bundled off with the other children to play where we would, while the adults moved in to form a solid ring of curiosity about the platform. The children were curious too, of course, but after a few minutes of playing many of the younger ones had forgotten the events with wonder at their newly found freedom. They ran and romped along the water's edge, setting off what few firecrackers still remained, wrestling and chasing each other up the brilliant brown dunes to some imagined summit. But all at once I was too old for their games of childhood, and longed to be back with the adults, back around the body of this man whom I hadn't even known a few weeks earlier.

Finally I did break away, and hurried back to the edges thinning now as women pulled their husbands away. I crept under the wooden crossbeams of the platform, became momentarily entangled in the wires of the loudspeaker system, and finally freed myself to creep even closer to the center of the excitement. A big man wearing a pistol on his belt like a cowboy had joined them now, and he appeared to be the sheriff.

"Just tell me what happened," he was saying. "One at a time, not all at once."

Mayor Myerton grunted. "If you'd been at the picnic, Gene, instead of chasing around town, you'd know what happened."

"Do you pay me to be the sheriff or to drink beer and listen to speeches?" He turned to one of the other men. "What happened, Sam?"

Sam was the man who'd been on the end of the platform, the opposite end from grandfather. "Hell, Gene, you know as much about it as I do. He was talkin' and all of a sudden he just toppled over and died."

At this point Doctor Stout interrupted. "There's no doubt in my mind that the man was poisoned. The odor of bitter almonds was very strong by the body."

"Bitter almonds?" This from Mayor Myerton. He was wiping the sweat from his forehead, though it didn't seem that hot to me.

Doctor Stout nodded. "I think someone put prussic acid in Tweller's beer. Prussic acid solution or maybe bitter almond water."

"That's impossible," the mayor insisted. "I was sitting right next to him."

Grandfather joined in the discussion now, and I ducked low to the ground so he wouldn't see me. "Maybe the whole pitcher was poisoned. I didn't get around to drinking mine."

But the mayor had drunk some of his without ill effects, as had the man on the end named Sam. Someone went for the pitcher of beer, now almost empty, and Doctor Stout sniffed it suspiciously. "Nothing here. But the odor was on the body, and up there where his glass spilled."

"Maybe he killed himself," Frank Coons suggested, and they seemed to notice him for the first time. Frank seemed to be a sort of town char-

The Night My Friend

acter, lacking the stature of the others, an outsider within the party. And—I knew they were thinking it—after all, he was the one who went for the pitcher of beer in the first place.

"Frank," the sheriff said a little too kindly, "did you have any reason to dislike Jim Tweller?"

"Who, me?"

"Don't I remember hearing something a few years back about a house he sold you? A bum deal on a house he sold you?"

Frank Coons waved his hands airily. "That was nothing, a misunderstanding. I've always liked Jim. You don't think I could have killed him, do you?"

The sheriff named Gene said, "I think we'd all better go down to my office. Maybe I can get to the bottom of things there."

Some of them moved off then, and I saw that the undertaker's ambulance had come for Jim Tweller's body. The undertaker discussed the details of the autopsy with the sheriff, and the two of them proceeded to lift the body onto a stretcher. At that time and that place, no one worried about taking pictures of the death scene or measuring critical distances.

But I noticed that the woman from the school board, Mrs. Finch, pulled grandfather back from the rest of the group. They paused just above me, and she said, "You know what he was trying to do as well as I do. He was using the acceptance of the award to launch a political campaign of his own. All this talk about rebirth and new blood meant just one thing—he was getting to the point where he was going to run against Mayor Myerton."

"Perhaps," my grandfather said.

"Do you think it's possible that the mayor slipped the poison into his beer?"

"Let me answer that with another question, Mrs. Finch. Do you think the mayor would be carrying a fatal dose of prussic acid in his pocket for such an occasion?"

"I don't know. He was sitting next to Tweller, that's all I know."

"So were you, though, Mrs. Finch," my grandfather reminded her.

They moved off with that, and separated, and I crawled back out to mingle with the children once more. Over by the beer barrel, the man named Sam was helping himself to a drink, and I saw a couple of others still eating their lunch. But for the most part the picnic had ended with Tweller's death. Even the weather seemed suddenly to have turned coolish, and the breeze blowing off the water had an uncomfortable chill to it. Families were folding up their chairs and loading picnic baskets into the cars, and one group of boys was helpfully ripping down the big colored banners and campaign posters. Nobody stopped them, because it was no longer a very good day for a picnic.

The two remaining weeks of my visit were a blur of comings and goings and frequent phone calls at my grandfather's house. I remember the first few days after the killing, when the excitement of the thing was still on everybody's lips, when one hardly noticed the children of the town and we ran free as birds for hours on end. Frank Coons was jailed by the sheriff when they learned for certain that the beer had been poisoned, but after a few days of questioning they were forced to release him. No one could demonstrate just how he would have been able to poison only the beer poured into Jim Tweller's glass while leaving the mayor and the others unharmed.

I knew that Mrs. Finch still harbored her suspicion of the mayor, and it was very possible that he suspected her as well. All of them came to grandfather's house, and the conversations went on by the hour. The fact that no one much regretted the death of Tweller did little to pacify things in those first two weeks. The man still had his supporters outside of the political high command, all the little people of the town who'd known him not as a rising politician but only as the donor of land for a hospital. These were the people who'd voted him his humanitarian award, and these were the people who publicly mourned him now, while the top-level conferences at grandfather's house continued long into the night.

At the end of two weeks I departed, and grandfather took me down to the railroad station with what seemed a genuine sadness at my going. I stood in the back of the train waving at him as we pulled out of the station, and he seemed at that moment as always to be a man of untried greatness. His white hair caught the afternoon sunlight as he waved, and I felt a tear of genuine feeling trickle down my cheek.

If this had been a detective novel instead of a simple memoir of youth, I would have provided a neat and simple solution to the poisoning of Jim Tweller. But no such solution was ever forthcoming. I heard from my mother and father that the excitement died down within a few weeks and the life of the town went on as it had before. That November, the mayor and my grandfather and the other town officials were re-elected.

I saw my grandfather only briefly after that, at annual family reunions and his occasional visits to our home. When I was sixteen he died, quietly in his sleep, and we went up to the town once more. It hadn't changed much, really, and the people seemed much the same as I remembered them. In the cemetery, I stood between father and Mrs. Finch, who commented on how much I'd grown. The mayor was there, of course, and Doctor Stout, and even Miss Pinkney and Miss Hazel. I understood from the talk that Frank Coons no longer lived in town. He'd moved south shortly after the murder investigation.

So I said goodbye to my grandfather and his town forever, and went back to the city to grow into manhood.

I said a moment ago that this was a memoir and not a mystery and as such would offer no solution to the death of Jim Tweller. And yet—I would not be honest either as a writer or a man if I failed to set down here some thoughts that came to me one evening not long ago, as I sat sipping a cocktail in the company of a particularly boring group of friends.

I suppose it was the sight of cocktails being poured from an icy pitcher that made me remember that other occasion, when the beer had passed down the line of speakers. And remembering it, as the conversation about me droned on, I went over the details of that day once more. I remembered especially that pitcher of beer, and the pouring of Tweller's drink from it. I remembered how he drank from the glass almost immediately, and commented on the bad taste. Certainly no poison was dropped into the glass *after* the beer had been poured. And yet it was just as impossible to believe that the poison had gone into the glass *with* the beer, when others had drunk unharmed from the same pitcher. No, there was only one possibility—the poison had been in the glass *before* the beer was poured in.

I imagined a liquid, colorless as water, lying in the bottom of the glass. Just a few drops perhaps, or half an ounce at most. The chances were that Jim Tweller never noticed it, or if he did he imagined it to be only water left from washing out the glass. He would pour the beer in over the waiting poison, in all likelihood, or at worst empty the glass onto the grass first. In any event, there was no danger for the poisoner, and the odds for success were in his favor.

And I remembered then who had occupied the speaker's position immediately before Tweller. I remembered grandfather with the empty glass before him, the empty beer mug with its thickness of glass to hide the few drops of liquid. I remembered grandfather with his little bottle of cough medicine, clear cough medicine that usually was gin. Remembered his reluctance that day to give Frank Coons a drink from it. Remembered that I hadn't seen the bottle again later. Remembered most of all grandfather's devotion to the party, his friendship with Tweller that must have warned him earlier than most of the man's political ambitions. Remembered, finally, that of all the people at the picnic only grandfather had known that Tweller was the winner of the award, that Tweller would be on the speaker's platform that day. Grandfather, who called out to Coons for the pitcher of beer. Grandfather, the only person with the motive and the knowledge and the opportunity. And the weapon, in a bottle that might have been cough medicine or gin—or prussic acid.

But that was a long time ago, a generation ago. And I remember him best standing at the station, waving goodbye. . . .

Shattered Rainbow

O'Bannion quit his job at three o'clock on a sunny Friday afternoon in April. It happened suddenly, though certainly he had considered the possibility many times in the past. It happened with words, a pounding fist, and then the decision that could not be recalled. It happened, oddly enough, on the same day that a man called Green robbed and killed an armed messenger for the Jewelers' Exchange.

O'Bannion, who had never heard of Green, spent the rest of the afternoon cleaning out his desk, separating the few personal possessions into a home-bound pile. When his secretary returned with her afternoon coffee she asked him what he was doing, though it must have been obvious.

"I finally did it, Shirl," he told her. "I walked out on the old man."

She sat down hard, the coffee forgotten. "You mean you quit?" she asked, still not quite able to grasp it.

"I quit. Walked out while he was still swearing at me. Now if I can just pack my briefcase and make it to the elevator before he comes after me, I really will have quit."

"What will you do?"

"I'm sure I won't sit around the house feeling sorry for myself. This is the best thing that could have happened to me." It sounded properly convincing, even to him.

He zipped shut the briefcase and told her goodbye. There was no sense being emotional about it at that point. "Goodbye, Mr. O'Bannion," she called after him. "Let me know when you get settled."

"Sure. Sure I will."

He rode down in the elevator with an afternoon's assortment of secretaries bound for coffee and businessmen bound for martinis, but he no longer felt a part of them. The cut-off had been too clean, too certain. He was a man without a job, and he wondered how he would tell his wife.

Kate and the kids were still out shopping when he reached home just before five o'clock. He hung his raincoat carefully in the closet and mixed himself a drink. It was the first time he'd drunk before dinner in years, but he felt as if he needed one.

Kate came in as he was pouring the second.

"Dave. What are you doing home so early?"

"I quit my job. Finally walked out on the old guy."

"Oh, Dave—"

"Don't worry, honey. I'll have another one by Monday morning. I've still got a few contacts around town."

"Who? Harry Rider?"

"I might call Harry."

"I wish you hadn't done it. That temper of yours, Dave—"

"We'll make out. We always have." Then, because he'd only just thought of them, "Where are the kids?"

"Outside playing."

"We won't tell them for a few days. They needn't know over the weekend, at least."

"All right, Dave."

"Want a drink?"

"I want you to tell me about it, how it happened."

He told her about it. They talked for the better part of an hour, until the two boys came running in for supper. Then they ate as if nothing at all had happened, as if it were a Friday night just like any other. But it wasn't, and he noticed toward the end of the meal that he was speaking more kindly to the children than he usually did. Perhaps he was beginning to feel a bit guilty.

After supper, when the boys were being tucked into bed by Kate, he phoned Harry Rider.

"Harry? How are you, boy? This is Dave O'Bannion."

The voice that answered him was sleepy with uncertainty. He'd forgotten that Harry Rider always napped after dinner. "Yes, Dave? How've you been?"

"Pretty good. Look, Harry—"

The Night My Friend

"Yes?"

"Harry, I quit my job this afternoon."

"Oh? Kind of sudden, wasn't it?"

"I'd been thinking about it for a while. Anyway, I'm looking, if you know of anything around town."

There was a moment of silence on the other end of the line. Then Harry Rider said, "Gosh, fella, I don't think I could help you right now. Maybe something will turn up though."

"Well, if you hear of anything, Harry—"

"Sure. I'll keep you in mind. Glad you called."

After he hung up, O'Bannion sat for some moments smoking a cigarette. When Kate came back downstairs, he was ready for the expected questioning look. "I heard you talking."

"I phoned Rider."

"Why?"

"Why not? He's got a lot of contacts around this town."

"All the wrong kind."

"Maybe in a few weeks I won't be so fussy."

"Can't you get unemployment insurance or something?"

"Not right away. I wasn't fired, remember. I walked out."

"But Harry Rider! He never did a favor for anybody in his life that didn't have a dozen strings attached."

"You didn't used to think he was so bad, back before we were married."

"That was before we were married. A lot of things were different then, Dave."

He lit a cigarette and started pacing the floor. "Anyway, you don't have to worry. He didn't have anything for me."

She shook her head as if to clear it. "Oh, I'm sorry. I guess the whole thing is just too much for me all at once."

"Just stop worrying. I'll have a job by the end of next week and a better one than I left. You can bet on it!"

She smiled at his words, even though neither of them felt quite that optimistic. They both knew it would be a long weekend.

Monday morning was warm and rainy, with a west wind blowing the drops of rain against the front windows with disturbing force. O'Bannion gazed out at it unhappily. It would not be a pleasant day to be trudging the streets of the city in search of a job. The kids, not yet old enough to attend school, were cross with the prospect of a day indoors, and he could see that Kate was already tense.

"Cheer up, honey. I'll phone you after lunch."

"Where are you going to try?"

"Oh, there are a few offices around town that might have openings, especially for someone who walked out on the old man. I'll hit those today and tomorrow, and if the scent is cold I can always try an employment agency."

He went off in the car because Kate wouldn't be needing it and he wasn't quite up to facing the ride in on the same old commuters' train. It was still too early in the day, and there would be people he knew, people he wasn't yet in the mood to chat with. In the city, he parked the car at the ramp garage he occasionally used, nodding silently in reply to the attendant's cheerful morning greeting.

The first place he tried was an engineering firm where he had contacts. He thought. They listened in friendly agreement to everything he said, and one of them even offered to buy him lunch. But there was no job available and he wasn't yet ready to accept charity. He thanked them and went and bought his lunch from a white-coated sidewalk vendor who sold dry ham sandwiches wrapped in wax paper. He found an empty bench in the park and ate among the damp trees, thankful at least that the rain had stopped and the wind had died to a gentle breeze.

The job he'd left, O'Bannion was beginning to realize, had done little to prepare him for the necessity of stepping quickly into something else. He'd never had any opportunity to build upon some sketchy engineering courses he'd left unfinished at college. The job, for all its nine-thousand-a-year salary, had been little more than an arduous managership of an office full of unmarried and just-married girls more intent on dates and marriage than work.

He called on two other places that afternoon, and the best he came up with was a promise of something "maybe in a month or two." That wasn't good enough. He was already more depressed than he cared to admit to Kate.

Tuesday was much the same, and Wednesday. That afternoon, he swallowed his pride and called the familiar number of his old office. He got by the switchboard operator without being recognized and in a moment he was talking to Shirl.

"This is Dave. How are you?"

"Mr. O'Bannion! I'm fine, how are you? Everyone's been asking about you."

"I'll bet. Who are you working for now?"

"They have me in the pool till they get someone to replace you. Have you found anything yet?"

"Not yet. I've got a couple of leads. What I called for—has there been any mail for me? Anything personal?"

"Just the usual junk, Mr. O'Bannion. Except this morning a letter came for you from California. Los Angeles. It looks as if it might be personal."

"It is." He had some friends in Los Angeles who often misplaced his home address and wrote him at the office.

"Should I forward it?"

"I suppose so," he said, and then had a second thought. "Say, would you like to meet me for a drink after work? I could get the letter from you and you could tell me what's been going on."

She hesitated a moment, but finally agreed. "All right. I guess I'd have time for one."

"Fine. I'll see you at five—a bit after five—over at the Nightcap." He hung up and then phoned Kate to tell her he'd be a bit late for dinner.

By the flickering candlelight of the Nightcap, a quiet little place where it seemed always to be the cocktail hour, he really looked at Shirl Webster for the first time. She'd been his secretary for the better part of the past year, but in that dubious manner of modern business he'd tended to take her mostly for granted. She was nothing more than an impersonal machine to take his letters and dictation, answer his phone, and perhaps suggest a birthday present for his wife. He'd never really thought of Shirl Webster as a woman, though he was aware now that she was surely a woman, and a striking one at that.

"I'm sorry it all happened," she said, seeming to mean it. "I liked working for you."

He noticed for the first time that her eyes were blue, a very light blue in sharp contrast to the dark of her hair. She was a tall girl, perhaps nearing thirty, with a certain regal grace about her. "I'm glad of that, at least," he said with a chuckle. "There were days when I thought the whole place was in league against me, including you."

She shook her head. "Not at all. I was kept busy all day Monday explaining what had happened to you. All the girls miss you."

"Makes me sound like a bluebeard or something." He sipped the martini in front of him. "Do you have that letter?"

She nodded and handed over a flat envelope with a Los Angeles postmark. He pardoned himself and slit it open, just to make sure the news was nothing more urgent than weather and kids and when-are-you-coming-to-visit-us. Then he folded it away in his inside pocket.

"Nothing important?" she asked.

"The usual stuff. They're old friends. I'll have to write them, tell them about my new status."

"Do these leads of yours sound good, Mr. O'Bannion?"

"I'm not your boss any more. Call me Dave."

"All right—Dave."

"To answer your question, no—the leads don't sound good."

"Maybe the old man would take you back. He's having a hard time replacing you."

"I have a little pride left, unfortunately. Want another drink?"

For a moment he thought she'd agree, but then she shook her head reluctantly. "I have to get home."

He realized that in almost a year he'd never even thought where home might be. "God a boy friend, Shirl?"

She blinked at him. "I'm too old to call them boy friends any more."

"Oh, come on! How old are you—twenty-five?" He'd knocked a few years off his real guess.

"You're sweet. Now I really have to go. But keep in touch, let me know how you're doing."

"I will."

He watched her walk to the door, hips tight against the contoured fabric of her skirt, and he wondered why he'd never noticed that walk before.

Thursday was too nice a day to be out of work. It was fine to walk along Main Street on your lunch hour and moan about having to return to a desk on such a beautiful day, but O'Bannion quickly discovered it was only frustrating to be job-hunting on such a day. The trees in the park were already blossoming with spring, and the people he passed were smiling. He would have felt happier in a thunderstorm.

Friday was more of the same. An offer of a job at a thousand dollars a year less than he'd been making, a promise of something "maybe in the summer," a regret for a position just filled. It all added up to a big zero.

On Saturday morning he went to see Harry Rider. He knew the man would be at work on a Saturday because the tracks were racing. Harry's main source of income demanded a six-day week. He was a big man, with a face and hairline that made it difficult for O'Bannion to remember him as Kate's one-time suitor. The years had changed them all, but none more so than Harry Rider.

"What can I do for you, Dave?" he asked, not bothering to rise from behind the wide desk strewn with typewritten sheets, racing forms, and three telephones.

O'Bannion stared at the thinning hair, the wrinkles of tired skin around deep, calculating brown eyes, and said, "I phoned you last week. Maybe you forgot."

"Oh! Sure, I remember now. You're out of a job."

"That's it. I've got some good leads in town, but you know how it is when you just walk out on something. No two weeks' pay or anything like that."

"Need ten bucks?" Harry Rider was already reaching for his pocket. The words, coupled with the motion, made O'Bannion suddenly ill. He was sorry he'd come.

"No, no—nothing like that. I was wondering if you knew of anything around here. Even something temporary. You said once you had a lot of influence in the right places and just to come see you."

"Sure. I can get you a job cleaning out the stables up at Yonkers. How's that?"

O'Bannion's face froze. "I didn't come here for that sort of talk, Rider."

"Just kidding. Never take me serious! Ask Kate. She never took me serious."

"We weren't discussing Kate."

"Sure, sure. She know you came to see me?"

"No."

"Just as well."

"I intend to tell her when I get home. I have no secrets from her."

Harry Rider chuckled. "Maybe it's time you started having a few."

He could see he was getting nowhere with the man. There was no job in the offing, only this opportunity for ridicule. "I'm sorry to take up your time," he told Rider, rising from the chair.

"Wait a minute! Maybe I'll hear of something in your line."

"Thanks. Don't trouble yourself."

He was going out the door when Rider called after him, "I'll be in touch with you, Dave."

O'Bannion didn't bother to answer.

On Sunday he went to church for the first time in a year. Listening to the minister rant about the evils of overabundance, he wondered why he'd bothered. The previous evening he'd told Kate about his visit to Harry Rider. She reacted about as he expected and there had been an unpleasant scene. She hadn't accompanied him to church on Sunday, and when he returned to the house he found her mood had not improved.

"It's a nice day," he said, to make conversation.

"Just great."

"Still upset because I went to Rider?"

"Why shouldn't I be? Dave, there are employment agencies, friends, relatives—why go to Harry Rider for a job?"

"I didn't know you felt that strongly about it."

"You knew—you knew darned well. I have a little pride left, even if you haven't."

Anger growing within him, he spun around and started from the room. Then he paused to face her once more. "Do you happen to know how much we have in the bank? I figure it's just about enough to keep us going for another three weeks. Then we either stop eating or stop paying on the house and car."

Her lips were a thin line of—what? It almost could have been contempt. "Maybe you should have thought about the money before you quit your job," she snapped.

"Sure, sure! Maybe I—" The ringing of the telephone cut into any retort he would have made. He decided it was probably just as well and went to answer it.

"Is this Mr. Dave O'Bannion?" a strange voice asked. Male, perhaps a bit muffled.

"Yes."

"Mr. O'Bannion, I understand you are presently at liberty. I have a position available, temporary work, which I'd like to discuss with you."

"Sure. Who is this calling?"

"My name is Green. Could you meet me tomorrow to talk it over?"

"Certainly. Where are you located?"

"I'll be in Room 344 at the Ames Hotel, anytime after ten. It must be tomorrow, though, as I'm leaving for Canada on Tuesday."

O'Bannion assured him it would be tomorrow. Even this mysterious temporary sort of job was worth looking into. But when Kate questioned him about the call he implied it was from someone he knew, someone he'd contacted the previous week. He had a growing feeling in the pit of his stomach that the strange Mr. Green in his hotel-room office would prove somehow to be an associate of Harry Rider.

Green, if that was really his name, proved to be a tall man in his mid-thirties. He didn't really belong in the hotel room. He seemed more like a man made for the outdoors, a man who might venture inside only for a drink or necessary food. He was obviously ill at ease in the surroundings of impersonal luxury such as one found at the Ames.

"You're O'Bannion?" he asked, frowning as if he might have expected someone older.

"That's right." He held out his hand and Green shook it. Then they both sat down and O'Bannion added, "You have a job open?"

Green leaned back in his chair. "A temporary position. It would involve a trip to Canada."

"For how long a period? I wouldn't want to be away from my family." He said the words because they sounded right. Just at the moment Kate and the boys were far from his thoughts.

"Only a day or two. And the pay would be good."

"How good?"

The man shrugged. "Perhaps five thousand dollars."

His worst fear realized, O'Bannion got suddenly to his feet. "I guess you'd better tell Mr. Rider I'm not interested."

"Who?"

Why had he gone? Why had he gone to Rider when he'd known all along that this would be the only sort of job the man could offer? Across the border for five thousand dollars.

"Harry Rider. I believe that's a name you know."

Green was blocking him at the door, holding him back. "Wait, wait. Look, there's no risk, if that's what's worrying you. It's safe."

"Sure."

"I'll give you something to take with you. All you do is deliver it to an address in Toronto and you'll be paid the money."

"Five thousand dollars for no risk? Why don't you take it yourself?"

Green was nervous now, unsure of himself. "All right," he decided suddenly. "I guess I got the wrong guy. Go!"

O'Bannion went.

The remainder of the day he spent in a sort of twilight, wandering from office to office, filling out applications for jobs he neither wanted nor qualified for, existing in a world of mere minutes adding up slowly to hours. Again and again his thoughts returned to the man in the hotel room, to the five thousand dollars he'd offered for the flight to Canada.

O'Bannion tried to guess what would have been involved. Harry Rider's interests were mainly gambling, horse racing, and the like, although he occasionally dabbled in politics. Perhaps it was nothing more than transporting betting slips or some political material.

The afternoon was sunny, even now when it was almost ended, even with its twilight rays filtered through the blossoming branches of the park trees. He walked with a lengthened, broken shadow behind him, destination undetermined. Then, the random thought just crossing his mind, he started down the street toward his old office. They'd be leaving now, not a minute too early because the old man was always watching, but not a minute too late either. He stood in the shadow of a building, watching faces and figures already receding from memory after only a week's time. Then he saw Shirl Webster, walking very quickly along the curb, head down against the sunset.

O'Bannion crossed the street and intercepted her at the next stoplight. "Hello, Shirl," he called from a few paces behind her.

"Dave! I mean—"

"I told you Dave was all right. How are you?"

"Fine. I was just this minute thinking about you, wondering how you were coming along."

"Got time for a drink?" he asked, and as the words left his mouth he wondered just how accidental this meeting had been. Didn't he subconsciously seek her out rather than return home to Kate?

"Just one. I have to meet my boy friend."

He chuckled. "I thought you were too old to call them that."

"On days like this I feel younger. We going to the Nightcap again?"

"Why not?"

Over a drink, with the candle flickering on the table between them, he suddenly found himself telling her about his interview with Green in the hotel room. It was an odd sort of feeling she gave him and he wondered how he could have worked with her all those months without being affected by the sensuality of her presence.

"So you walked out on him," she summed up, making it a simple statement.

"I walked out on him. Wouldn't you?"

She toyed with the plastic stirring rod from her scotch-and-water. "I don't know. Five thousand dollars is more money than I make in a whole year. I don't know what I'd have done."

"It's obviously something crooked, with Rider involved."

She frowned into the glass. "The Rider you mention—if he *is* such a shady character, why did you go to him in the first place?"

Why? It was the sort of question Kate had asked too. *Why?* Was it purely a spirit of revolt against his wife's wishes, or was there more to it than that? "I don't know why," he answered finally. "Not really."

He lit her cigarette and watched while she settled back in her chair. "I think you're like me, Dave. I think you're sick of working your life away for someone like the old man, who doesn't care about anything but the profit and the overhead."

"You think I should have done it? What Green wanted me to do?"

"I don't know. I think you should have asked a few more questions, thought about it a little more."

"I don't know. I just don't know." He signaled the waiter for another drink.

"Are you going to discuss it with your wife?"

"How can I? She's already barely speaking to me because I went to Rider. Am I going to tell her now that she was right all along about him being a crook?"

"Are you asking me what you should do, Dave?"

He wasn't really. Until that moment he'd been convinced that he'd followed the right course of action. Now she had planted a doubt. "You'd have asked more questions."

"Go back and see him again, Dave. Why not?"

"He's gone. On his way to Canada."

"Maybe not. He might be looking for someone else to make the trip."

"I'm sure he wouldn't be sitting in that hotel room still. How'd he know I wouldn't come back with the police?"

"What could you tell the police? What do you know to tell them?"

"Nothing," he admitted glumly.

"Let me call the hotel for you, see if he's still there."

"I don't know. I'm getting in so deep—"

"It's a great deal of money, Dave. Enough to carry you over till you can find a really good job."

"Well, I suppose you could call. I know he won't be there."

She rose from her chair. "You said it was the Ames Hotel?"

"Yes."

She stepped into a phone booth near the door and he watched her dialing the number. She spoke a few words and then motioned quickly to him. When he joined her at the booth door she covered the receiver with her hand and said, "He's still there. I've got him on the line. You want to go over?"

"I—" He felt suddenly weak in the knees.

"Mr. Green," she said, returning to the phone. "I'm calling for Dave O'Bannion. He was up to see you this morning. Yes—Yes. Well, he'd like to reconsider your offer."

O'Bannion started to protest and then changed his mind. Well, why not? It was five thousand dollars, wasn't it?

He took the phone from her and heard the familiar voice of Green in his ear. "I'm glad you've reconsidered."

"Yes."

"You just caught me as I was checking out."

O'Bannion grunted.

"Can we meet someplace else? How about the park behind the library?"

"All right. What time?"

"It's almost six-thirty now. Make it seven o'clock."

"Fine. I'll be there."

"Alone."

"All right," O'Bannion agreed without hesitation. He hadn't even thought about taking Shirl with him.

He hung up and joined her back at the table. "All set, Dave?"

"All set. But he wants me to come alone."

"Oh." She seemed disappointed.

"I could meet you back here after if you'd like."

His words brought a smile to her lips. "I'd like."

"What about that boy friend?"

"I'll call him."

He tossed a couple of bills on the table. "Get yourself something to eat. I'll be back in an hour or so. Maybe sooner."

He left her and walked across the street to another bar. There he had a quick drink and phoned Kate at home, making some excuse about a possible job that sounded phoney even to his own ears. Then he started for the little park behind the library, his heart beating with growing excitement. He didn't know whether the excitement was caused by Green or Shirl or both. He only knew that Kate had no part in it.

The park was almost dark by seven, lit only by the random lamps in standards twined by ivy. It was a lunchtime spot for summer secretaries, a strolling place for evening couples, a clubhouse for after-dark drifters. Though he was only a hundred feet from the street O'Bannion still had a sense of fear.

He found Green lounging on a bird-specked bench deep in shadow, his eyes caught by a necking couple across the path. "Look at that," he said to O'Bannion. "At seven o'clock."

"Yeah."

"Cigarette?"

"I've got my own, thanks."

"Who was the girl?"

"My secretary."

"I thought you were out of a job."

"She used to be my secretary."

"Oh."

"Now what about this deal?"

Green was grinning in the flare of his match. "You're ready?"

"I'm ready."

"All right. I have a plane ticket here, round trip to Toronto, leaving tomorrow night at six."

"That's pretty short notice. How long will I have to be away?"

"A day. You can fly back Wednesday night if you want."

O'Bannion ground out his cigarette and lit a fresh one. The couple on the opposite bench had unclinched and she was repairing her lipstick. "What's the catch? What do I have to do? What's the deal?"

"Take a box of candy to a friend of mine."

O'Bannion's hands were steady. "What else?"

"That's all. I'll be there myself to pay you the five thousand."

"If you're going up too, why not take the candy yourself?"

Green smiled slightly and in the dim light he looked suddenly younger—no older perhaps than O'Bannion. "We don't need to kid each other. I've had trouble with the police. They might stop me at the border. I'm going up on the Thruway and crossing at Niagara Falls. I don't want them to find anything on me."

"What is it?"

Green looked vague. "That would be telling. You only get the money if the box is delivered intact."

It was now or never. This was the moment to back out, to go no further. But instead he simply asked, "As long as it's not narcotics. I don't want any part of something like that. O.K.?"

"No narcotics. What do you take me for anyway?"

"When do I get the box of candy?"

"Tomorrow afternoon, four o'clock. Right here."

"That doesn't give me much time to catch the plane."

"I don't want you to have much time. The man will be waiting for you at the airport in Toronto. You give him the candy and then get a room for the night. I'll probably pull in Wednesday morning and pay you off."

"How about part of it now?"

Green frowned. "I don't have it. The money's in Toronto. And there's no money unless you produce the box, unopened."

"Why don't you just mail it to him?"

"He's had police trouble too. They might be watching for something in the mails."

"All right," O'Bannion agreed at last. "I'll see you here at four."

Green left first, walking away fast. O'Bannion watched him go, watched him as in a dream, and wondered what he was getting into. He felt, in that moment, like a man trapped in a muddy bog. There was only Kate to save him, Kate and the children, and they were a world away. Then he remembered Shirl Webster waiting back at the bar and his spirits lifted.

"Why don't you come with me?" O'Bannion asked after he'd finished telling Shirl about his conversation with Green.

"What? Go *with* you! That's crazy, Dave. What would people say?"

"Who needs to know?"

It was crazy, but he began to think it might not be too crazy. He'd always been faithful to Kate in the nine years of their marriage—always, that is, except once in Boston with a girl he met in a bar. But now something had changed, something in him, or in Kate, or just in the times.

They talked, debated, argued for the rest of the evening, but he already knew she'd be on the plane with him.

His excuses to Kate in the morning were vague and uncertain. He would be away overnight, up in—Boston seeing about a job, a really good one right in his line. It was a damp, almost rainy day and the hours dragged till four and he met a trenchcoated Green in the park.

"Think the planes will be flying?" he asked.

Green handed over the candy, a great flat box with a ribbon tied around it. "Of course the planes'll be flying. A little rain never stopped them."

"This man will be at the airport?"

"He'll be there."

"How will I know him?"

Green thought for a moment. "His name is Dufaus. He has a little mustache and he's always carrying a briefcase. Looks like a government bigwig."

"All right. What about you?"

"I'll see you sometime before noon. I plan to drive all night. There's a little motel near the airport. Wait there for me."

"How do I know you'll show up?"

Green turned away. "Don't worry. I'm trusting you, you can trust me."

"Will Rider be there too?" O'Bannion asked on an impulse.

"Don't you worry about Rider. He takes care of himself."

Overhead, an unseen jet could be heard through the clouds. The planes were flying.

They held hands all the way.

It reminded O'Bannion of a youthful night on a hayride when he'd dated the most popular girl in the senior class for the first time. He'd held hands that night too, thinking and plotting all the way about how he'd work up to that first kiss, that first hand around her shoulders, on her knee. That night had ended disastrously, with the girl going home in a quarterback's car while O'Bannion sat alone behind the barn and cried for the first time in years. A year later, in college, he'd met Kate and there'd never been anyone else. Not really.

The weather was cooler when they landed, a clear coolness you didn't really mind. Above them the sky was full of stars and ahead he could see the flashing red-neoned MOTEL. The letters fuzzed and flickered irregularly as if the sign were tired. There to meet them at the airport was the mustached man with the briefcase, Mr. Dufaus.

He waited until they'd cleared customs and then he came up smiling. "Ah! O'Bannion?"

"That's right. You must be Dufaus."

"Correct. Quite correct. I have a car waiting. This way."

They followed him to a black foreign-built automobile with low, expensive lines. He motioned O'Bannion into the front seat with him but made no effort to start the car. Instead, he held out his hand. "The candy, please."

"No," O'Bannion said, halfway into the car.

"What?"

"No."

"What do you mean?"

"No candy until I get my money." O'Bannion hadn't really planned it that way, but suddenly he had spoken the words and there was no recalling them.

"You'll get the money tomorrow. Didn't he tell you?"

"He told me. You'll get the candy tomorrow."

Through all of this Shirl had stood behind him on the sidewalk. Now she tried to pull him from the car. "Dave, be careful."

O'Bannion backed out of the car, still clutching the candy box. "I'll be at the motel," he told Dufaus. "See you in the morning."

The man with the mustache was visibly upset. "The money cannot possibly be ready until I've had time to inspect the merchandise."

"Too bad. I'm sure we can work it out in the morning."

O'Bannion slammed the car door and walked quickly away, half pulling Shirl along with him. Dufaus made no attempt to follow.

"Dave, why did you do that? What's the matter with you all of a sudden?"

"Nothing. I just realized that I haven't decided about this thing yet, not really. I want more time to think. A few hours ago we were in New York, a few days ago I was still an honest man, and a few weeks ago I still had a job. Things are moving too fast for me. Too fast."

"Life is fast. We live and die before we know it, much too fast."

"Not by tomorrow morning. It's not over that fast. Let Dufaus sweat about it overnight. If this thing I'm carrying is so valuable, maybe I want to keep it a while."

They'd reached the motel, a low, long building of concrete that seemed about to crumble. The manager gave barely a flicker when they checked into a double room.

"What now?" she asked when they were alone.

"First things first. I'm going to check this candy. They didn't give me a chance before. I suppose that's why Dufaus risked meeting me at the airport—to get the candy before I had an opportunity to exercise my curiosity."

He removed the garish ribbon and lifted the lid, to disclose the regular designs of foil-wrapped chocolates. "Nothing but candy," Shirl observed over his shoulder.

"Maybe."

He unwrapped a piece and studied it. He squeezed with his fingers and broke it open. Inside, darkened and coated by the butterscotch filling, was something sharp and glittering in the light. "It's a—a jewel. Looks like a diamond. Still in its setting." He tried another piece of candy and it yielded up the red of a ruby.

"Dave, what is it?"

After the third one he answered, "It looks like part of a necklace of some sort. It's been broken at the links and separated into individual pieces so it could be hidden in the candy. Come on, help me look inside the others."

Ten minutes later, with all forty-eight pieces of candy broken open on the bed, they had a rainbow-colored collection of gems, each set in a glistening ring of platinum. "Who'd want to wear a thing like that?" Shirl asked, wide-eyed.

O'Bannion half remembered something he'd heard or read. "It's not for wearing, really. It's a necklace called the Rainbow and its gems are supposed to be worth a quarter of a million dollars. It was stolen a week ago from an armed messenger."

"You're sure?"

He nodded. "The messenger was killed. I'm into this a little deeper than I figured." He ran his palm across a forehead suddenly damp with sweat.

Later, sometime in the hours between midnight and dawn, when the only sound to be heard was the gentle buzz of the electric clock on the far wall, Shirl said, "Do you think they'll come for us or something? Because you didn't give them the candy?"

The Night My Friend

He laughed and tried to sound amused. "You've been seeing too many movies, gal. Nothing's going to happen."

"They killed one man. You said so."

"Maybe I was wrong. Maybe these jewels are something else."

"You're not wrong, Dave. If you don't think anything's going to happen, why don't you come to bed?"

He laughed and lit a cigarette. "I don't know, maybe I'm shy." Then, after a moment's silence, "Tell me about this boy friend of yours, Shirl."

"He's just a guy."

"You like him? Well enough to marry him?"

"Would I be here with you if I did?"

"I don't know." He blew smoke in the direction of the window, watching it as it crossed the single bar of dimly filtered light from outside. "What are you going to tell him when you get back?"

"I'll think of something," she said. "More to the point, what are you going to tell Green and Dufaus in the morning?"

He thought about it for a long time before answering. "I think I'll go to the police, Shirl," he said finally.

"The police! But—but why?"

"This is murder. If I don't get out of it now, it may be too late."

"But what about us? What about your wife? Do you want it spread all over the newspapers that we were up here together?"

"No, of course not. But what else can I do?"

"Give them their foolish jewels and be done with it. Take the money and just forget about it. That's what you planned to do originally, isn't it?"

"I suppose so, but things have changed." Suddenly he ground out his cigarette. "All right, let's get out of here then. We'll get the jewels to the police somehow without implicating ourselves and be back in the States by noon."

But she held him back with her hand. "No, Dave. I'm afraid to go out there. I'm afraid they'll be waiting for us."

"I'll take a look around," he said and slipped into his jacket.

Outside, the world was a pale dark landscape sleeping in the full moon's glow. A car was parked at the head of the driveway. A cigarette-tip glowed like a far-off star. O'Bannion sighed and went back inside.

"What is it, Dave?"

"You were right. He's got somebody watching the place." He looked out the back window, but decided against risking it with Shirl. There was a twenty-foot drop to the highway. They could hardly make it without a twisted ankle or worse.

"So?"

"So we stay till morning and see what happens."

The sun was back in the morning, already high in the sky by the time the car drew up outside. O'Bannion had been watching out the window. He saw Dufaus and Green join the man who had been watching the motel throughout the night.

"Here they come," he told Shirl without looking at her. "Green's with them."

She came up to the window and stood just behind O'Bannion, watching. "Give them the jewels, Dave. We don't want trouble."

Then they were at the door, knocking. He opened it and looked into Green's expectant eyes. "Well! I was worried when Mr. Dufaus told me about his troubles. Let's get this settled now."

The two of them crowded into the small room, leaving the third man to wait outside. Green said, "The candy. Where's the candy?"

"We were hungry. We ate it," O'Bannion told them.

Green's mouth twisted into an odd sort of grin. "Look, cut out the wise talk. You'll get your money as soon as Dufaus inspects the candy and gives me the O.K."

"I didn't know I was getting involved in a murder," O'Bannion said. "That wasn't part of the deal."

Dufaus was suddenly agitated. "He knows too much!"

Green's hand dropped to his pocket. "All right, we're finished fooling, O'Bannion. I didn't let you bring this stuff five hundred miles across the border just so you could double-cross me."

His hand was coming out of the pocket when O'Bannion hit him, a glancing blow to the side to the head that tumbled him onto the bed.

Against the wall, Dufaus uttered a gasp of dismay. "No violence— please! I only want to purchase the gems!"

O'Bannion moved again, but this time Green was faster. The gun—a small .32—was out of his pocket, pointed at O'Bannion's middle. "We're through fooling," he growled. "Shirl, where did he hide the stuff?"

Behind him, as in a nightmare, O'Bannion heard her reply, "In the toilet tank. I'll get them." And then, almost as an afterthought, "I'm sorry, Dave. Really I am."

He sat on the bed, unfeeling, as Green and Dufaus counted the gems. And when she came to sit next to him it was as if a stranger had entered, a perplexing intruder.

"In the beginning I thought I was doing you a favor," she said quietly. "You needed the money and my boy friend—how I hate that expression—he needed someone to fly to Canada with the necklace. I talked him into calling you. I never thought it would come to this. I should have risked bringing the thing over myself."

"It wasn't Harry Rider," he said. That was all he could say.

"Not Rider, no. It was me. When you thought I was calling the hotel Monday night I was really calling Greeny's apartment. I was afraid you'd notice that I dialed the number without looking it up. I was afraid you'd notice Dufaus wasn't surprised to see me at the airport."

"I guess I didn't notice anything. Not a thing."

Green came over to the bed. "Dufaus is satisfied. Let's roll."

"A quarter of a million?" She breathed it, like a prayer.

"Not even half, but I can't stay to argue. It'll get us a long way."

"What about him?" Dufaus asked from the door, pointing at O'Bannion.

"That's five grand I saved myself," Green said. He brought the gun into view once more.

Shirl stepped quickly in front of him "No, Greeny. No more killing." She held her position.

"I leave him here to tell the cops everything he knows?"

But Shirl stood firm. "He can't tell them anything without implicating himself, with the police, and with his wife. I don't think he wants to do that. Come on, let's get out of here."

Green faced him with the gun for another moment, uncertain, and then pocketed it as he turned away. "All right, we'll leave him."

She came over to O'Bannion one last time. "Dave?"

"What?"

Her voice dropped to a whisper. "When he gives me my cut I'll see you get something. A thousand or so anyway."

"Don't bother," he said, turning away.

"Dave—"

"Go on. Go!"

He heard them drive away, listened to the sound of traffic reaching him through the still-open door.

After a time he went out and walked until he found the motel manager, who was watering a spring garden by the highway. He asked where there was a telephone he could use and when he found it he dialed the number of the local police.

It would be a long journey back to Kate, and he wondered if he would make it.

The Patient Waiter

"We'll have the check, please, waiter."

"Yes, sir. Right away."

Carley moved off between the tables, back to his station at the service end of the bar where he'd left the check book. He quickly figured the items for table 33, totaled them, and ripped the check from the pad. Another night just about ended.

For Carley, the nights were becoming much the same. He worked the evening shift at the little restaurant a block from city hall, which meant midnight on weekdays and two o'clock on weekends. Then, perhaps, there was a brief stop somewhere else for a drink and always afterward the trek home through deserted streets wet with rain or snow or summer sprinkling. That was the only constant in Carley's world. The streets always seemed wet on his way home.

He'd worked a good many places in his day, the good and the bad, the hotel dining rooms and the private clubs, and even occasionally the cheap beer joints down by the tracks. He was not really a good waiter, which perhaps was the reason he moved so often, but there was never too much problem about making a living. As more than one satisfied owner had remarked on occasion, Carley had a certain touch all his own, a specialty.

Few people over the years had

managed to become his friends, and he lived alone in a little walk-up apartment across downtown from the restaurant. Sometimes, those of his friends who cared would ask him why he'd never married, but the answers he gave to this question were as variable as his places of employment.

The truth of the matter, and perhaps the key to Carley's entire life, was the fact that he was a waiter. He'd watched his life slip by while he waited, waited on tables, waited for the right girl to come along, waited for buses, waited in line, waited. He'd once gotten his picture in the papers waiting all night to be first into a World Series game in New York.

Carley was a waiter, even when it came to his specialty.

He was cleaning up one night near closing time, after a hectic pre-Thanksgiving week that had left him nearly exhausted, when someone called to him from a nearby bar stool. He saw that it was a plump, balding man who'd been in the business for some years.

"Hello, Mister Sykes, how've you been?" He paused in his duties long enough to make the greeting properly polite. He'd never worked at the Sykes place, but he knew other waiters who did.

"I've been fine, Carley, but business is terrible."

"Even with the holidays coming up?"

"Too many people think of my place as a summer spot. Nobody wants to go down to the lake in November. Frankly, ı don't think I can make it through another winter."

Carley muttered something sympathetic and went back to cleaning off his table. The last of the regular customers had departed and the bartender was snapping off the decorative neon tubes behind the rows of amber bottles. Out in back, Carley's boss was checking over the cash. "Well," Carley said finally, when the last of the tables had been cleared away, "maybe I should stop out and see you on my night off. Help your business a little."

"I wish you'd do that, Carley. Maybe next week."

"Fine. I'll be seeing you."

On the following Tuesday evening, Carley took a bus down Third Street to the lake. Sykes had been right about business falling off with the coming of cooler weather. Although winter had not yet set in, the lakefront was all but deserted. The parking lot behind Sykes' Steak House held only seven cars, and Carley knew that most of these belonged to employees.

Sykes himself was behind the bar, mixing a martini for the lone drinker, a bleary-eyed young man who looked as if he'd spent the evening there. "Hello, Carley, good to see you," Sykes greeted him. "What are you drinking?"

"Oh, just a beer, I think. Some of that good imported stuff."

Sykes set it in front of him as Carley turned around on his stool, refreshing his memory of the place. It was a bit garish, but no more so than the usual location geared for the summer people. Wide picture windows overlooked the beach, and outside lights gently bathed the trees in multi-colored hues. It was still summer—or trying to be—at Sykes' Steak House.

Presently Sykes came over to make polite conversation. "Gotten to any football games this season, Carley?"

The little waiter lit a cigarette. "Just one, beginning of the season." He took a sip from his glass. "This is good beer."

"The best. Nothing but the best for somebody in the business."

Carley had a second beer and then gathered up his coat. "Got to be going," he said. The drunken young man was still leaning on the bar with his martini glass empty once more. "I'll stop by again some time when I have the opportunity."

Sykes nodded shortly. "Do that. Oh, if you're going back downtown, could you mail this letter for me? I want it to get out tonight."

"Sure," Carley said, accepting the stamped envelope. It was addressed to him. "Be seeing you."

On the bus he picked a seat far to the rear, and slit open the envelope with his finger, keeping it carefully down out of sight of the driver. There were one hundred ten-dollar bills inside. And a key.

During the remainder of the week, Carley spent his days busily at work in the little apartment. The thing was simple enough, but there was a certain touch to it, a certain technique. He hadn't earned his reputation for nothing. By Saturday night, he was ready.

His boss said nothing when he left early, a few minutes before the two o'clock closing. Carley was just in time for the last bus, but he didn't ride it all the way. The final half mile to Sykes' Steak House was covered on foot, in the event that the bus driver had too good a memory. The parking lot was empty and the place was dark by the time Carley reached it, a few minutes before three. Overhead, the clouds had parted enough to show a scattering of stars. This night even they seemed cold, like drops of ice in a distant landscape.

Carley fitted the key carefully into the front door, but nothing happened. He sighed, removed it, and went around to the back of the place. Here the key worked easily in the oiled lock, and he entered through the dark and forbidding kitchen. All right, he decided, but not here. Through the kitchen, out the swinging door so familiar to all waiters, across the dining room to the bar.

Behind the bar, in that private world he so rarely entered, Carley went quickly to work. He felt along the rear shelf, by the mirror, until he found what he sought—a little opening where the electric cord from the cash register disappeared somewhere to join other cords. In a few moments, with the aid of small crowbar from his pocket, he'd pried away a wall board and located the maze of wiring he sought.

From the pocket of his topcoat he next removed a small newspaper-wrapped package. He peeled back the paper enough to expose a fluffed bit of chemically treated clothesline. With a single match he lit it and watched the spark begin its slow journey down the rope to the match-heads still hidden from view. He checked one or two other refinements and then carefully lowered the whole thing into the wall, resting it on the electric wires. No clocks, no candles, no bottles, nothing left over.

He went out the way he'd entered, through the back room, out the back door. Nothing would happen for an hour, and this was the time to get far away, to establish an alibi. But, because he was Carley, because he was a waiter by profession and by temperament, he never fled from the scene.

Instead, he took up a position some two blocks distant from Sykes' Steak House. And waited. As he had so many times before.

The thing was foolproof, he knew. Even if, sometime, they saw him waiting, they could never prove a thing. There was no law, yet, against waiting on a street corner—even in the middle of the night.

Fifty-five minutes later, he noticed a thin wisp of smoke, and then a tongue of flame suddenly shattered one of the front windows of the steak house. A block down the street, a light went on in one of the houses. Good. It would be about three minutes before the first engine could get there. By that time . . .

He watched through it all, until the roof fell in just after five o'clock. Then he boarded a bus for downtown and his apartment. It had been one of his most successful efforts, really, and he knew Sykes would be pleased with the quick execution.

The next evening at work, MacBanter, his boss, was more talkative than usual. He finished checking the menu for the coming week and glanced around at the sparse Sunday night crowd.

"I hear Sykes' place burned down."

"Yes," Carley answered, going on about his business.

"Tough break."

"It is, just before the holidays like this."

"Still, I guess he had plenty of insurance, and those lake places never do well in the winter. Maybe it's not such a tough break after all."

Carley cleared his throat. "Did you hear what caused it?"

"Something in the wiring."

"Oh."

"Ever stop to think how many restaurants burn up in this town every year? Just take this year, for example. I can think of four places—and in every case they said it was the wiring."

"Old places, I suppose the wiring gets worn."

"I don't know. Some of them weren't so old. You hear stories, being in the business."

Carley began to fill the sugar bowls he'd carefully collected from the tables. "What sort of stories do you hear, Mister MacBanter?"

"Just stories." He started to walk away, then added, "I suppose a guy could make a pile of money if he had the right touch, the way the restaurant business is these days."

The holiday trade at MacBanter's was brisk, and for some weeks the place was filled every night. The nearby city hall offices yielded up the usual assortment of celebrations for Christmas and the New Year, and Carley's only problem during those busy nights was managing to pocket the generous tips while avoiding the drunken young men who staggered after giggling office girls.

But with the coming of January, business at MacBanter's took a sudden, unexpected dive. By the end of the month, the unhappy owner was no longer spending his nights counting the cash. Instead, he was poring over a mounting pile of bills. Early in February, with the outside temperature a business-discouraging three below zero, he came to Carley.

"What am I going to do? January was awful, and February is no better."

"The holidays were good," the little waiter reminded him. "Everyone has bad months. It'll pick up."

"Will it? With these new tax regulations and now this damned weather and the rest of it? Frankly, Carley, I've always had a borderline operation. The holidays saved me for a while, but now I'm close to the end of my rope." He chuckled and turned away. "What I need about now is a good fire."

Carley was silent for a long time. Finally he touched a careful finger to the silverware on the table next to him. "I work here, Mister MacBanter," he said simply.

"So?"

"If you had a fire . . . . a *good* fire . . . . where would I work?"

"I'd take care of you, don't worry."

"But my job . . ."

"I'd get you in with a friend of mine. He's opening a new place out in the suburbs."

"I don't know," Carley said doubtfully.

MacBanter dropped his voice to a whisper. "Twice what you usually get, and I know how much that is."

"I . . . ."

"I'd do it myself, only I don't have the touch. They tell me you're an expert, a specialist."

"Who tells you?" Carley asked.

"Sykes is down in Florida, relaxing on the insurance money."

For the remainder of the week even the daytime temperatures rarely rose above zero, and Carley was happy to be occupied indoors. He worked lovingly on his device, putting an extra bit of care into it.

Saturday nights and early Sunday mornings always seemed to be best for his operations, and this Saturday night seemed especially good to Carley. The place was fairly crowded despite the continued below-zero-cold, and the closing hours had the sort of hectic confusion that the bartender and others would remember and testify to, if necessary.

Carley made certain he was not the last to leave, but he waited in the parking lot across the street until he saw the place darken for the night. It was snowing again, that fine, almost invisible fall which came only with extreme cold, but nevertheless piled up in the streets. He bundled up his collar against the wind and headed back across the street.

Once inside, he worked with precise speed. During these past months, the restaurant had become like a second home to him, and even in the dark he knew every turn. This time there was no need to feel around behind the bar. He went at once to the fuse box, traced a main cable to a likely point within the walls, and went to work. The device had a slightly longer fuse than usual, but that was all right. He lit it with a single match, watched the glowing ember for a moment, and then positioned it as he would place a baby in its crib.

He locked the place carefully behind him and walked quickly away. At first he considered waiting in the empty parking lot, but decided it was too open. He chose instead a street corner a block away, where a pile of plowed snow offered perfect shelter from passing cars. It was cold, and the wind-driven snow stung at his face.

Sometimes, in the past, he'd wondered about this strange obsession to remain at the scene, waiting for the first purple burst of flame through the imprisoning wood and glass. He'd even considered the possibility that he was a firebug—a pyromaniac of some sort. Perhaps he was, but he chose not to think about that possibility. He saw himself instead only as a waiter, standing on a street corner looking at a slice of life he was helping to create. It gave him a sense of power, a sense of belonging, and he could hardly be expected to walk away from it, into the darkness that only led back to his lonely apartment.

So this night he waited again, behind the snowbank, feeling the numbness eating away at his face, running his pocketed hands through the evening's yet uncounted tip money.

He wondered what the temperature was. Below zero, certainly. Possibly ten below. And with this wind . . . It shouldn't be long.

It was foolish of him to stand there freezing. He must get inside, under cover, and then return later. But his watch told him a half hour had already passed. Better to stay here, in case somehow he had misjudged the timing of the fuse.

MacBanter would be pleased. MacBanter would pay him two thousand dollars and get a new job for him. He wondered what the new place would be like.

The wind seemed to have grown colder. One hour. But no purple flame . . . . nothing. He shifted his feet, stamping them, trying to warm them.

At an hour and a quarter, he had a terrible fear that something had gone wrong. He must return to the place and check.

But he was so tired and so cold.

Then, yes—a bit of flame flashed behind the window. It was beginning.

His face had lost all feeling now, and his feet were like things apart. He must move, move . . . .

He saw the flames raging up, out of control, saw a passing motorist screech to a stop and turn in a box alarm, heard then somewhere in the far-off distance the birth of a familiar wailing voice.

Smiling, he toppled forward into the snowbank.

"What do you make of it, Doc?" the policeman asked, rolling the snow-crusted body over on its back.

The doctor's examination was brief. "Exposure," he said. "He froze to death."

Too Long at the Fair

Sam Clinton had traveled nearly a thousand miles to stand here before the empty, snow-blanketed parking lot of the Bayshore Amusement Park, and now, seeing it by fragile moonlight, he wondered if the trip had been worth it. There seemed to be no one about, though he noticed that the double gates in the high wire fence had been left ajar. Perhaps he would find somebody inside, lurking beneath the great snow-covered roller coaster.

The place was strange to him, as such places were even in the summertime. There seemed to his mind no way of explaining the logic of amusement parks with their tinkling gaiety and ten-cent charm, waiting with great open mouths to swallow up the innocents who came hand-in-hand every weekend. Perhaps this was evil—evil as practiced in Twentieth Century New England, where they no longer hanged their witches.

This night, if there were evil, it had been covered by a two-inch fall of sticky snow blowing in off the Atlantic. As Clinton plodded along, leaving his virgin prints in the unmarked white, it seemed to him that even the elements had conspired against him. He passed the shuttered Fun House, the Shooting Gallery, the Airplane Ride, the Dragon Coaster without seeing evidence of another living soul. But then, as he was about to abandon the fruitless quest, a line of tiny, Friday-like footprints crossed his own path. He followed them with a growing sense of elation, knowing now that all was not yet wrong with the world.

Ahead, in the damp, fog-laden night, he saw the lights that told him he was not alone in this place. They were in the oddly circular building which housed the merry-go-round, and the tiny footprints he followed led directly to its door.

"Hello," he said from the doorway by way of warning. "May I come in?"

From somewhere in the maze of resting animals, a girl in jeans and a paint-stained shirt appeared. "I don't know. Who are you?"

"Merry-go-round inspector," he said, stepping in and closing the door firmly behind him.

"What? Look, mister, the park is closed for the winter." She put down her paint brush and hopped to the floor to meet him on equal terms. He guessed her age to be about twenty-five, and he couldn't help admiring the contour of her legs beneath the tight jeans. When he reached her face, he saw an impish upturned nose and deep blue eyes that sparkled with challenge. She wore no makeup, but just then she didn't need any.

"Sorry," he said. "I am here on business. Is there a manager around the place?"

"In the middle of winter? My father owns the park, and he goes south every December for two months. I just came down to touch up a few of the animals. Want to help me paint the stripes on the zebra?"

She had obviously judged him and found him harmless. Many people did, and he'd almost come to expect it. "I'd be happy to," he told her. "I've always wanted to paint stripes on zebras."

She smiled then, and introduced herself. "I'm Jane Boone. Don't let me scare you in this costume."

"I won't. Sam Clinton—I'm a lawyer."

"Really?" She was back on guard at once. "Then this really is a business visit."

"Afraid so. I'll try to make the next one more pleasant. Is there somewhere we can talk?"

"Right here is the best place. It's warm and private, and I can go on with my work while you talk." She pulled herself back onto the merry-go-round, and he was forced to follow. There, in the inner row of prancing animals, was indeed a paint-peeled zebra badly in need of first aid.

"You're pretty skillful with that brush," he said. "Aren't you ever afraid, working here alone nights? Anybody could walk in here."

"The gate's usually locked. Besides, a friend of mine always stops by for me. He should be coming pretty soon, so don't get any ideas."

He felt himself beginning to blush. "I wasn't thinking of myself, believe me."

She daubed a bit at the wounded zebra. "You said you're a lawyer."

"That's right. I've traveled here all the way from Chicago because a man died there with your name in his pocket."

"My name?"

"The name of the amusement park—Bayshore—and the city, and a date."

"A date? What date?"

"Tomorrow's, as a matter of fact. January 14th. What's happening here tomorrow?"

She pursed her lips, and carefully curved a thin black line over the zebra's tired flank. "Same thing that happens every day during the winter. Nothing."

"Nothing?"

"Nothing. Who was the man that died?"

"A client of mine. His name was Felix Waterton."

"I never heard of him. I can't imagine what he would have been doing with our name."

"Might he be a friend of your father?"

"I doubt it. I help out in the office and handle all the correspondence. I never heard the name." She looked up and her eyes were suddenly shaded. "How did this Felix Waterton die?" she asked casually.

"You may have seen it in the papers. He . ." But the door opened behind him at that moment, and Clinton turned to see a tall young man enter, stamping the clinging snow from his feet.

"Hi, Dick. You're early." She started to put down the paint brush, then changed her mind and went on with it. "This is Sam Clinton, Dick Mallow. Mr. Clinton's a lawyer from Chicago on business."

They shook hands and Clinton felt the firmness of the other's grip. "I finished my business early," he explained to the girl. "Two calls and nobody home." Then, by way of explanation to Clinton, "I sell insurance."

"Pleased to meet you," Clinton said, deciding he looked the type.

"What say you knock off on that zebra, and we hop across the street for a drink," Mallow said to the girl.

"Well . . . I was talking to Mr. Clinton . . ."

"He can come too. Heck, man, I'll buy you a beer or something!"

"That's very nice of you. I'll admit I could use a beer."

"Then it's settled. Down with the paint brush, woman."

They left the lights burning in the merry-go-round, perhaps as a reminder to the zebra that they'd be back. Dick Mallow blazed a heavy-footed trail through the snow of the parking lot, while Jane Boone and

Clinton followed behind. The place across the street proved to be an uncertain little neighborhood bar that seemed to lead a double life. The signs of summertime were still visible almost everywhere—in the exhausted blue balloon hanging from the bar mirror, the dusty college pennants tacked to the walls, the faded Polaroid snapshots of clowning teenagers. But now it was winter, and the bar led its other existence—quiet, dim, waiting, catering to the few who made the neighborhood their home, waiting for another summer.

Dick Mallow ordered three beers, and they clustered around a little cigarette-scarred table in one corner. It was obvious to Clinton that he was being allowed to participate in a nightly ritual, and when he noticed Mallow's hand beneath the table he managed to drop a cigarette on the floor so he could retrieve it and confirm the fact that the hand rested in Jane's.

"So you're a lawyer," Mallow said, skimming the foam from his lips with an experienced tongue. "From Chicago."

"That's right. We don't have any snow there. Not this week, anyway."

"You were telling me what brought you here," Jane Boone reminded him.

"A dead man with a note in his pocket. It said simply, *Bayshore Amusement Park, Rhode Island, January 14th.* So I came to find out what's happening here tomorrow."

Dick Mallow scratched an ear with his free hand. "What's happening, Janie? You giving away free kisses or something?"

"Nothing. I told Mr. Clinton that already. I haven't a clue."

Mallow suddenly snapped his fingers. "You forgot the General! It's the second Friday of the month; the General's coming tomorrow night!"

"Of course. The General . . ."

Sam Clinton tensed with interest. "What General? What's he coming for?"

"Major General Tracy Spindler, U.S. Army, Retired," the girl recited. She took a quick swallow of beer and hurried on. "He rents our bingo hall for his meetings, once a month during the winter. My father figures it's income, but I figure it's just a pain."

"What sort of meetings?"

"You wouldn't believe it. They have some crazy club that believes we all came from Mars or some place. I sat in on one of their meetings a few months back, but after ten minutes I'd had enough."

Clinton frowned over his glass. "It doesn't sound like the sort of thing one finds in the depth of New England. It has more a New York or California sound about it. But I'd like to come out tomorrow night, if it's an open meeting."

"They let me in," she said. "I suppose it would be all right."

Dick Mallow downed the rest of his beer with a few quick gulps. "You think this dead guy might have belonged to the General's club, huh? Any good reason?"

"It's a possibility. Right now it seems to be the only possibility."

"What did you say his name was?" Jane Boone asked.

"Felix Waterton." Clinton watched Mallow's face, but his expression was frozen into a bland sort of nothingness that didn't change at the name. "He was a client of mine."

"And what did you say he died of?"

"I guess I didn't say. He was murdered."

Mallow got unsteadily to his feet. "Let's have another round of beers," he called to the sleepy bartender. Then he disappeared into the men's room, leaving Clinton and Jane alone.

"You're some kind of a detective, aren't you?" she asked.

"I told you I was a lawyer."

"I know. I guess I just don't believe you. Maybe it's because I couldn't ever picture you in court, before a jury."

He smiled at that. "You've been watching too much television. There are lawyers and lawyers."

Dick Mallow came back just as the bartender returned with the second round. He slid into the booth next to Jane and his hand disappeared from view once more. "Beer is the staff of life," he said, licking at the foam. "Pretty soon I'll be ready to go back and help you paint zebras all night."

As the second round gradually disappeared from the glasses, Clinton saw quickly enough that he was no longer to be a part of the ritual. He finished his beer and got to his feet. "I have to be going. I would like to stop by tomorrow though, Miss Boone."

"Sure. Come ahead."

Outside, it was beginning to snow. He stood for a moment looking across the street at the deserted amusement park with its monuments of white. The night was very quiet, and he wondered if the zebra would ever get painted.

Felix Waterton had been a strange man in life. Born in the closing days of the First World War, he'd spent his teen years fighting for survival in the streets of a depression-racked Chicago. His father, a minor figure in the vast complex of bootlegging, had come home one Christmas night bleeding to death from three bullet wounds in the side, and the shock of it all had put his frail mother in an institution from which she never returned.

Even in those early pre-war days when Sam Clinton first met him, Waterton spoke almost incessantly of avenging his father's death. He carried a loaded gun with him at all times, a tiny French automatic he'd procured from somewhere, and Sam Clinton was just enough younger than Waterton to be impressed and a bit terrified. The war years had separated them, and after it was over Clinton had returned to Chicago and studied law. He'd set up practice in a one-room office in the Loop, then sat back and slowly starved, until the day Felix Waterton walked through the door.

After that, things had changed in a somewhat oblique manner. Waterton managed a position for him with a leading law firm, and Clinton found himself on the rise. He began to specialize in tax law, at Waterton's suggestion, and the man threw him a good deal of business. This had gone on for better than ten years, through the economic boom of the Fifties and into the Sixties. Felix Waterton grew with the years, and became wealthy while other men, sometimes better men, had sunk into the mire of failure and futility.

Waterton's large holdings were mainly in Chicago real estate, though Sam Clinton had heard frequent rumors of other, less respectable, activities. The man was a known associate of midwest underworld characters, and if he still carried the little French automatic it was no longer to avenge the death of his father. Oddly enough, Clinton's activities on various tax problems for Waterton enterprises had left him with surprisingly little knowledge of the man's sources of income—little knowledge, that is, until he'd spent an evening with a friendly and talkative secretary who told him how he'd been played for a sucker all those years.

Clinton had been carefully groomed by Felix Waterton to fill a specific need in the organization. As a tax lawyer, he'd been used to throw up a smokescreen, while Waterton and his associates systematically diverted funds from their own real estate holding companies. When Clinton accused Waterton of the protracted swindle, the man had merely laughed. And fired his secretary.

That was where things stood on the night Felix Waterton was murdered.

The brief snow of the previous night had given way to rain, and the parking lot of the Bayshore Amusement Park was a shimmering sea of slush by the time the first cars began to pull in. Sam Clinton watched it all from the shelter of the roller coaster, shorn now of its sticky white coat, and he noted with interest that the arrivals for General Spindler's meeting seemed not at all what he had expected. They were neither beat nor bearded, and for the most part seemed to be just ordinary people, men and women, bundled in raincoats against the wind-blown drizzle.

"Here you are," Jane Boone said suddenly, coming up behind Clinton. "I thought I'd find you."

"Well, I said I'd be back. Finish your paint job?"

She nodded. "Finally." Her hair was covered with a pale blue scarf and the wide collar of her coat was turned up against the weather. He could see that she still wore the paint-stained jeans from the previous night.

"Going to the meeting?" he asked.

"I'll sit in with you for a few minutes, near the back. By the way, I've already spoken to the General and told him you'd be around. He said it's all right."

"Just what did you tell him?" he asked, trying to concentrate on her face in the rain. It was a pretty face, and he guessed that it was not at the height of its beauty.

"About this man who was killed in Chicago, and the note he had on him. Of course the General was interested."

"I'll bet." He tried to light a cigarette but it was hopeless in the rain. "By the way, I wanted to ask you something. About your friend, Dick Mallow, if you don't mind."

"Dick?" She wrinkled up her nose in an expression that might have been coy. "You want to know if he's my boy friend."

"Not exactly. I want to know if he's been here every night this week."

She seemed puzzled by the question, and stepped a bit further into the darkened shadows of the sheltering roller coaster. "Why? Why do you ask? Do you think he killed that man in Chicago? Is that it?"

"Not really, but Felix Waterton was connected with someone here. Since you mentioned the killing, though, what about it? Last Monday night, specifically."

"I don't remember. Dick has to work late sometimes. He missed one or two nights early in the week."

"Then he could have hopped a plane to Chicago."

"Sure. And he could have flown to the moon. But he didn't. He never heard of your friend Waterton."

"He seemed awfully quiet last night after the name was mentioned."

Even in the near darkness her eyes sparkled with a touch of fury. "He was probably quiet because he was anxious to be alone with me. Or didn't that thought ever cross your mind, romance still exists?"

"All right, all right. Are you going to take me in to meet the General, or not?" He was growing impatient with her defense of Mallow, who didn't really seem worth all the concern.

"Come on," she replied, "while the rain has let up a bit."

Jane led him through the slush to a long, low building next to the shuttered Fun House. The lights from its glowing windows seemed to cast a bit of unreality across the deserted landscape, which had seemed so natural in the dark. He slid though the partly opened door behind her and found himself in a stark room, filled almost to capacity with people seated at the long makeshift bingo tables. Here and there, on shelves set against the walls, a stuffed animal or packaged blanket remained unclaimed from summer's prizes.

Toward the front of the room, on the little raised platform where the bingo operator usually sat, a tall, slim man with a shock of white hair stood waiting to address his audience. A movie screen was set up behind him, its glass beading catching and reflecting the overhead lights. Clinton knew without being told that he was looking at General Tracy Spindler.

"Ladies and gentlemen," the speaker began, "I'm pleased to see such a good turnout tonight, in view of the nasty weather." Clinton glanced around and figured the audience at nearly a hundred. It was indeed a good turnout, all things considered. He wondered whether Felix Waterton would have been here, had he lived.

"I'm General Spindler, for those few of you who might be new to our little group. Actually, the beliefs of the Noahites are quite simply stated, and we do state them at the beginning of every meeting. We believe that the ark of Noah did not travel the seas of an earthly flood, but rather voyaged here to our planet across a sea of space. We believe that Noah and his family and the creatures that journeyed with them came from a far planet, and brought the first life to this planet earth."

Clinton leaned against the wall and lit a cigarette. He wondered if the General really believed any of what he was saying. The audience, an oddly homogeneous middle-class group, seemed to believe, and they sat in rapt attention through the twenty-minute film that followed. It was a poorly photographed record of archaeological diggings in the region of Mount Ararat, with blurred close-ups of hands holding oddly-shaped pieces of stone and metal, which might have come from another planet, or from the corner junkyard. Clinton, being by nature a disbeliever, was inclined toward the latter.

At the end of the film, General Spindler was joined on the platform by a tall, leggy girl with close-cropped black hair. She was wearing dark leather boots, and they reached almost to her knees. "Thank you, thank you," Spindler said, responding to the scattering of applause at the conclusion of the movie. "Now we'll take a little break before our discussion period, and Zelda will be serving you coffee and doughnuts."

The Night My Friend

Clinton followed Jane Boone through the suddenly active audience. While the dark-haired Zelda began dispensing refreshments, they cornered General Spindler on the platform. "This is Sam Clinton," Jane said. "I told you about him."

"Yes," the General acknowledged, nodding his white mane. "You're the man from Chicago. I read about that killing in the papers."

Clinton shook hands with the man, and felt the dampness of his palm. "I hope you can shed some light on it, General."

The older man's eyes clouded over for a moment. "All I know is what I read. Do you have any further details?"

Clinton glanced around at the crowd lined up for coffee and doughnuts. "Can we go some place and talk?"

"I only have five minutes before the discussion begins."

"Let them linger over their coffee. I won't take long."

"Very well," the General agreed, and Jane Boone led them behind the platform to a little storeroom cluttered with prizes.

Clinton seated himself gingerly on a carton filled with dusty bingo boards. "Well, as you probably know from the papers, Felix Waterton was murdered in Chicago last Monday night. He was shot twice in the head, and his body was dumped by the side of a country road and set afire with gasoline. He was a client of mine, a very good client."

General Spindler shrugged. "Outside of the newspapers, the name means nothing to me. Should it?"

"Waterton was involved in certain financial transactions in Chicago. As near as I've been able to piece together since his death, large quantities of money were being siphoned off and hidden somewhere. I know he often made mysterious trips east, and I believe he was planning to come here tonight."

Spindler nodded. "Miss Boone told me about the note. But that's no connection with me, or with the Noahites."

"What else is happening at the Bayshore Amusement Park today?" Clinton asked. He started to light a cigarette but then thought better of it. The place was a firetrap just waiting for a spark to set it off.

General Spindler glanced at Jane. "Perhaps you should ask Miss Boone."

She seemed to resent the implication of it. "You're the only thing happening here today, General Spindler. And, frankly, I don't think my father would have rented you the place if he knew what he was getting into."

The door of the storeroom swung open and the dark-haired Zelda entered. "They're waiting for you," she said quietly, without changing expression.

General Spindler got to his feet. "You must excuse me. My public awaits. Perhaps later we can continue this."

Clinton and Jane drifted back to their places at the rear of the bingo hall and settled down to witnessing a protracted discussion of the film they'd seen earlier. After a somber young man had risen to ask why the Great Powers conspired to keep the truth of human origin such a closely guarded secret, Jane apparently decided she'd had enough. "I have to go," she said, giving his arm a slight and unexpected squeeze. "Dick's probably looking all over for me."

"I'll see you later," Clinton told her. "I have to talk with the General some more."

He stood, leaned, and finally sat through another hour of questions, answers, and general discussion. The mood of the meeting was a gloomy seriousness that pervaded to the end, when the would-be space people began filing slowly out. Only a few remained grouped around the platform, and those seemed as intent upon the girl, Zelda, as upon anything else.

"Can we continue our discussion?" Clinton asked the General.

"Not here. There's a little bar across the street that's usually open."

"I know the place," Clinton replied, wondering if Mallow would be there with his hand in Jane's.

Spindler turned to the girl. "Zelda, pack up the projector and screen. I'll be back shortly."

As they crossed the rapidly emptying parking lot toward the glow of light from the little bar, Clinton said, "That Zelda is a very attractive girl."

Spindler snorted. "Thank you, she's my daughter. Her looks get her into trouble occasionally."

When they were settled for a drink, Clinton continued, "Do you really believe all this bunk about the ark coming from another planet, General?"

"I see that you are a doubting man. Of course I believe it—publicly. And you'll never get me to say anything else."

"What does the government think of your activities?"

"I'm retired, sir. Have been since just after Korea. While I was an army man, I gave it a full measure of devotion and ability. Now I'm something else."

But Clinton wondered if he was. "Did you start the Noahites?"

"I did. They're all mine."

"Your own private army."

General Spindler smiled, but there was no humor in his eyes. "They are believers, every last one of them. They believe with an intensity that

The Night My Friend

would be hard for someone like yourself to imagine. Some of these people drove all the way from Boston to be here tonight."

The bar was empty except for them, and Clinton wondered vaguely where Mallow and Jane might be. Back at the merry-go-round, probably. "There are always people like that, General, waiting to be found and herded together by someone like you."

"I admit it. Perhaps that is the basis of our civilization."

"Would they do anything for you?"

"I think so."

"Would they kill for you? Did they kill Waterton?"

The General closed his eyes. "You are a devious man, Mr. Clinton. What is it you want?"

"The truth, only that. I worked for Felix Waterton all these years, and I want to know what he was up to. I want to find the money he was stealing from a lot of people."

"I know nothing of any money."

Clinton leaned back against the firm leather of the booth. "I'm a tax lawyer, General. My mind works in devious ways. It took me a long time to tumble to what Waterton was up to, but once I did the rest of it wasn't too tough. I gather your Noahites is incorporated? And it's probably a non-profit institution, a quasi-religious group of sorts. As such, it would pay no income tax on donations. Felix Waterton was looking for such an organization. He could have made donations to you through his various corporations, and achieved a double purpose. He would have avoided tax payments on his sizeable profits, and at the same time he would have removed the money to a perfect hiding place, a place where it would be waiting for him. I think you and the Noahites have a good big chunk of Waterton's money, General."

Spindler's frown deepened. "You'd have a difficult time proving all this, just on the basis of that piece of paper. Perhaps Waterton was delivering the money to Miss Boone, or even to that friend of hers who's always around."

But Sam Clinton shook his head. "First of all, an amusement park wouldn't be in a position to hide large profits in their books. And, more important, if Waterton's contact all these years had been the amusement park itself, he'd hardly have needed to write down its name. I'm sure he'd have remembered it. No, he wrote down the name because he *wasn't* familiar with it, because you've only been holding your monthly meetings here since the park closed in the fall. I suppose he usually sent you the money by check at regular intervals, but this time he decided to visit you for some reason, perhaps because he knew I was starting to uncover the truth about his operations."

"I repeat, prove it!"

"You'll have to open the Noahite books to an investigation. And, of course, the whole set-up makes you the logical suspect in Waterton's killing. You can explain that away too, if you'd like."

"I was in New York last Monday. A dozen people saw me."

"Maybe."

The white-haired man's eyes flicked with an icy fury. "What do you want? Money?"

"*The* money."

He let out his breath, "You asked me if they'd kill for me. They will."

"I don't scare," Clinton said, getting to his feet. The beer was half-finished on the table between them. "Think it over."

He walked out of the bar and back across the street to the towering darkness of the amusement park. It was colder now, and the intermittent drizzle gave hints of turning to snow.

Clinton followed the lights and found Jane Boone cleaning up in the bingo hall after the meeting. Spindler's daughter, Zelda, was still in evidence, talking quietly with two younger members of the departed audience.

"Hello," he said. "Where's Dick tonight?"

"He's working. He said maybe he'd drop by later." She was busy picking up paper cups with coffee dregs and damp cigarette butts in their bottoms. "Did you talk to the General?"

Clinton nodded. "I think we understand each other."

She brushed some gray ashes from the table-top. "You know something? I read mysteries once in a while, and I've got a theory about your murder case."

"Oh?"

"I heard you and the General talking about Waterton's body being burned."

Clinton nodded. "Almost beyond recognition. They weren't sure it was he until Tuesday."

"That's my theory. Maybe it *wasn't* Waterton at all, see!" She faced him with sparkling eyes. "He killed someone else, poured gasoline on the body and set it afire. Now that he's declared dead, he can safely collect this money you say he's hidden."

But Sam Clinton shook his head. "It was Waterton, all right. They got a couple of fingerprints off the body. The Chicago police think it was more an attempt to make the killing look like a gang job, rather than hide the identity."

"Why is it so important to you, all of it?"

He sat on the edge of the table. "I don't know. Maybe just because I was a sucker for so many years. I never tumbled to what he was doing until too late, and now I want to find that money."

Suddenly the dark-haired Zelda had joined them, her booted feet moving silently across the floor. Clinton didn't know if she'd heard their conversation, but she said softly, "I can tell you about my father and Felix Waterton—*all* about them. I'll meet you back here in an hour." Then she was gone, as quickly as she'd come, and they saw her join General Spindler and the two young men outside.

"Well," Jane breathed. "What was all that?"

"The break I'd been hoping for. If she tells me what I think . . ."

"Come on," Jane Boone said. "I'll make you a cup of coffee."

"Thanks. Guess I'll be around for a bit longer tonight."

They sat in the merry-go-round pavilion and drank black coffee, and after a while Jane Boone threw the switch that started it turning. "There's no music," she explained a bit sadly. "The loudspeaker's disconnected. But I left the rest of the power on for when I was working in here."

Clinton watched it turning, slowly at first, but with the inevitable quickening of pace. "That's too bad. It doesn't seem quite real without the music."

"In the winter nothing's quite real around here," she said.

"To me it never seemed real in the summertime, either. I remember going to these places as a boy and, after a few hours of the unreality, crying to go home. I guess I was afraid of staying too long, of losing touch with the real world outside."

She nodded vaguely, her eyes on the prancing, revolving animals. "Some times I think I've been here too long. I think of the whole world as a merry-go-round without music, or a fun house boarded up for the winter."

"Maybe it is, these days. Maybe that's the reality of it."

She hopped aboard the slowing carousel and threw a leg over one of the gaily colored horses. "Zelda will be back soon, if she's coming."

"And Dick?"

"You're a strange guy, Clinton."

The merry-go-round was picking up speed again, and he was about to join her on it when the door slid open to admit Zelda Spindler. "I couldn't find you at first," she said quietly.

Clinton walked over to her. She was shorter, close up, than she appeared. The leggy look was somehow a trick of distance, and the black boots. "I'm here," he said. "What have you got to tell me?"

Zelda shot a glance at Jane Boone, still riding the silent carousel horse. "Can I talk in front of her?"

"Of course."

"All right. What you suspected is true. Felix Waterton met my father during the war. He has been giving my father money for years. I have the financial records of the Noahites in the car. They show assets of more than a half-million dollars."

Clinton's heart pounded a bit faster. "Why are you telling me all this?"

"Because once my father was a good man, a highly respected army officer. I've seen him change since he retired, or maybe not change enough. I've seen him form the Noahites into an army to follow his crazy dreams. These old ladies, and lonely middle-aged men, and insecure kids—they follow him without knowing where they're going. And all the time he's using the Noahites as a front for his schemes with Felix Waterton. I took a lot, but I'm not taking murder. I'm telling all about it, to you and anyone else who wants to listen."

And at that moment the angry, unmistakable voice of General Spindler boomed out from the door. "A very nice speech, Zelda. I'm pleased I arrived in time for it."

Clinton saw the two men moving in behind the General, saw them circling to flank him, and knew that the battle was joined.

In the instant of frozen fear that followed, it was Jane Boone who was the first to act. She swung suddenly off the revolving merry-go-round and yanked Zelda away from her father's menacing approach. Clinton used the distraction to stiff-arm one of the men out of the way, and when the other reached for his pocket, the lawyer hit him hard in the stomach. Then he was outside, running, and he saw that Jane was close behind him. "They've got guns!" she gasped out. "We've got to get the police!"

As if in confirmation of her statement, a dull, flat crack sounded behind them. Clinton dived for cover, pulling the girl with him. They were behind the sheltering entrance to the Fun House, with only a few inches of plywood for protection. "Keep down," he warned. "They mean serious business."

"What about Zelda?"

"She'll have to take care of herself. Right now I'm more interested in getting those records from her car."

In a brief burst of moonlight through the patchwork clouds, they saw the two cars parked near the bingo hall. "The foreign one is Zelda's," Jane confirmed.

"Can you get into this place?" he asked, indicating the padlocked door of the Fun House.

"I've got a key."

"Stay there, out of sight. I'll be back for you." Then he was gone, running bent over across the slushy midway.

He reached the shelter of the bingo hall, and was about to make a dash for the car when he saw Spindler suddenly loom up before him, holding Zelda by the arm in a steely grip. "Stay right there," Spindler commanded. "I have a gun."

Sam Clinton froze. "All right," he answered, trying to keep his voice calm. "Can't we talk this over?"

"The time for talking is past," General Spindler said.

"You can't kill me and get away with it."

"No? You could die the way Felix did. These buildings would make a wonderful funeral pyre."

Clinton was trying to determine where the other two men were, but he wasn't sure of their location. Perhaps they were searching for the girl. But then, out on the highway, he saw a car begin to turn into the parking lot. Dick Mallow was arriving for his belated visit with Jane.

As in slow motion, he saw the General turn toward the approaching car, saw the gun waver only for an instant. But that was the instant he needed. His own gun was out before Spindler's weapon could quite get back, and the road of the two pistols blended simultaneously with Zelda's scream.

Clinton found Jane in the darkened passage of the Fun House, huddled in a corner against some unknown terror. "I heard a shot," she said.

"Two shots. We both fired at once."

"Spindler?"

"I think he's dead. I didn't wait to see. I guess your boy friend's calling the police."

"What's the matter with your voice?"

"His bullet caught me in the side. I'm bleeding a bit." He sat down on the floor next to her.

"We have to get a doctor!" Her hands touched him, but quickly withdrew on contact with the bleeding.

"Stay here! At least till the police come. Those two goons are still prowling around. I'm not hurt badly."

"What about Zelda?"

"She seemed all right. She was screaming when I shot her father."

Somewhere far off, a world away, a siren began its mournful wail. "Where is it all going to end?" Jane Boone asked, her voice almost a sob.

"It's ended."

"Is it?"

In the distance, the sound of the siren was building steadily. She shuddered at the sound. "They're coming," he said simply.

"You wanted the money, didn't you? That's why you came here."

Suddenly he seemed too tired to answer. "What?"

"I have a new theory about Waterton's murder, Sam. Do you want to hear it?"

"No."

But she hurried on anyway, as if the time was growing short. "His body was doused with gasoline and burned almost beyond recognition, and yet you told us about the piece of paper found in his pocket. If there were a paper, Sam, the only one who could have found it was the murderer, before he set the body on fire. I guess you killed him, Sam. I guess you killed him yourself, and then came here after the money." When he didn't answer, she added, "You must really have hated him."

Clinton rolled over, trying to see in the dark, trying to hear beyond the all-powerful siren that filled the night around them. "I hated him," he said, but he didn't really know if she heard.

"They're here now," Jane said as the siren suddenly died to nothing.

"What are you going to do about it?" he asked. "Are you going to tell them?"

For a long time she didn't answer, and it was as if they truly were alone in the world, the only two left in a dark tunnel that led to nowhere. But then there was Mallow's voice outside, calling her name, searching for her.

And she answered. "I don't know what I'm going to do. Does anybody ever know, really?"

Winter Run

Johnny Kendell was first out of the squad car, first into the alley with his gun already drawn. The snow had drifted here, and it was easy to follow the prints of the running feet. He knew the neighborhood, knew that the alley dead-ended at a ten-foot board fence. The man he sought would be trapped there.

"This is the police," he shouted. "Come out with your hands up!"

There was no answer except the whistle of wind through the alley, and something which might have been the desperate breathing of a trapped man. Behind him, Kendell could hear Sergeant Racin following, and knew that he too would have his gun drawn. The man they sought had broken the window of a liquor store down the street and had made off with an armload of gin bottles. Now he'd escaped to nowhere and had left a trail in the snow that couldn't be missed, long running steps.

Overhead, as suddenly as the flick of a light switch, the full moon passed from behind a cloud and bathed the alley in a blue-white glow. Twenty feet ahead of him, Johnny Kendell saw the man he tracked, saw the quick glisten of something in his upraised hand. Johnny squeezed the trigger of his police revolver.

Even after the targeted quarry had staggered backward, dying, into the fence that blocked the alley's end, Kendell kept firing. He didn't stop until Sergeant Racin, aghast, knocked the gun from his hand, kicked it out of reach.

Kendell didn't wait for the departmental investigation. Within forty-eight hours he had resigned from the force and was headed west with a girl named Sandy Brown whom he'd been planning to marry in a month. And it was not until the little car had burned up close to three hundred miles that he felt like talking about it, even to someone as close as Sandy.

"He was a bum, an old guy who just couldn't wait for the next drink. After he broke the window and stole that gin, he just went down the alley to drink it in peace. He was lifting a bottle to his lips when I saw him, and I don't know what I thought it was—a gun, maybe, or a knife. As soon as I fired the first shot I knew it was just a bottle, and I guess maybe in my rage at myself, or at the world, I kept pulling the trigger." He lit a cigarette with shaking hands. "If he hadn't been just a bum I'd probably be up before the grand jury!"

Sandy was a quiet girl who asked little from the man she loved. She was tall and angular, with a boyish cut to her dark brown hair, and a way of laughing that made men want to sell their souls. That laugh, and the subdued twinkle deep within her pale blue eyes, told anyone who cared that Sandy Brown was not always quiet, not really boyish.

Now, sitting beside Johnny Kendell, she said, "He was as good as dead anyway, Johnny. If he'd passed out in that alley they wouldn't have found him until he was frozen stiff."

He swerved the car a bit to avoid a stretch of highway where the snow had drifted over. "But I put three bullets in him, just to make sure. He stole some gin, and I killed him for it."

"You thought he had a weapon."

"I didn't think. I just didn't think about anything. Sergeant Racin had been talking about a cop he knew who was crippled by a holdup man's bullet, and I suppose if I was thinking about anything it was about that."

"I still wish you had stayed until after the hearing."

"So they could fire me nice and official? No thanks!"

Johnny drove and smoked in silence for a time, opening the side window a bit to let the cold air whisper through his blond hair. He was handsome, not yet thirty, and until now there'd always been a ring of certainty about his every action. "I guess I just wasn't cut out to be a cop," he said finally.

The Night My Friend

"What *are* you cut out for, Johnny? Just running across the country like this? Running when nobody's chasing you?"

"We'll find a place to stop and I'll get a job and then we'll get married. You'll see."

"What can you do besides run?"

He stared out through the windshield at the passing banks of soot-stained snow. "I can kill a man," he answered. But deep in his heart he wondered if even this was true any longer.

The town was called Wagon Lake, a name which fitted its past better than its present. The obvious signs of that past were everywhere to be seen, the old cottages that lined the frozen lake front, and the deeply rutted dirt roads which here and there ran parallel to the modern highways. But Wagon Lake, once so far removed from everywhere, had reckoned without the coming of the automobile and the postwar boom which would convert it into a fashionable suburb less than an hour's drive from the largest city in the state.

The place was midwestern to its very roots, and perhaps there was something about the air that convinced Johnny Kendell. That, or perhaps he was only tired of running. "This is the place," he told Sandy while they were stopped at a gas station. "Let's stay awhile."

"The lake's all frozen over," she retorted, looking dubious.

"We're not going swimming."

"No, but summer places like this always seem so cold in the winter, colder than regular cities."

But they could both see that the subdivisions had come to Wagon Lake along with the superhighways, and it was no longer just a summer place. They would stay.

For the time being they settled in adjoining rooms at a nearby motel, because Sandy refused to share an apartment with him until they were married. In the morning, Kendell left her the task of starting the apartment hunt while he went off in search of work. At the third place he tried, the man shook his head sadly. "Nobody around here hires in the winter," he told Kendell, "except maybe the sheriff. You're a husky fellow. Why don't you try him?"

"Thanks. Maybe I will," Johnny Kendell said, but he tried two more local businesses before he found himself at the courthouse and the sheriff's office.

The sheriff's name was Quintin Dade, and he spoke from around a cheap cigar that never left the corner of his mouth. He was a politician but a smart one. Despite the cigar, it was obvious that the newly arrived wealth of Wagon Lake had elected him.

"Sure," he said, settling down behind a desk scattered casually with letters, reports and wanted circulars. "I'm looking for a man. We always hire somebody in the winter, to patrol the lake road and keep an eye on the cottages. People leave some expensive stuff in those old places during the winter months. They expect it to be protected."

"You don't have a man yet?" Kendell asked.

"We had one, up until last week." Sheriff Dade offered no more. Instead, he asked, "Any experience in police work?"

"I was on the force for better than a year back east."

"Why'd you leave?"

"I wanted to travel."

"Married?"

"I will be, as soon as I land a job."

"This one just pays seventy-five a week, and it's nights. If you work out, though, I'll keep you on come summer."

"What do I have to do?"

"Drive a patrol car around the lake every hour, check cottages, make sure the kids aren't busting them up—that sort of thing."

"Have you had much trouble?"

"Oh, nothing serious," the sheriff answered, looking quickly away. "Nothing you couldn't handle, a big guy like you."

"Would I have to carry a gun?"

"Well, sure!"

Johnny Kendell thought about it. "All right," he said finally. "I'll give it a try."

"Good. Here are some applications to fill out. I'll be checking with the people back east, but that needn't delay your starting. I've got a gun here for you. I can show you the car and you can begin tonight."

Kendell accepted the .38 revolver with reluctance. It was a different make from the one he'd carried back east, but they were too similar. The very feel and weight and coldness of it against his palm brought back the memory of that night in the alley.

Later, when he went back to the motel and told Sandy about the job, she only sat cross-legged on her bed staring up at him. "It wasn't even a week ago, Johnny. How can you take another gun in your hand so soon?"

"I won't have it in my hand. I promise you I won't even draw it."

"What if you see some kids breaking into a cottage?"

"Sandy, Sandy, it's a job! It's the only thing I know how to do. On seventy-five a week we can get married."

"We can get married anyway. I found a job for myself down at the supermarket."

The Night My Friend

Kendell stared out the window at a distant hill dotted here and there with snowy spots. "I told him I'd take the job, Sandy. I thought you were on my side."

"I am. I always have been. But you killed a man, Johnny. I don't want it to happen again, for any reason."

"It won't happen again."

He went over to the bed and kissed her, their lips barely brushing. Outside, somewhere, the passing of a nearby train broke the silence of the chill afternoon.

That night Sheriff Dade took him out on the first run around the lake, pausing at a number of deserted cottages while instructing him in the art of checking for intruders. The evening was cold, but there was a moon which reflected brightly off the surface of the frozen lake. Kendell wore his own suit and topcoat, with only the badge and gun to show that he belonged in the sheriff's car. He knew at once that he would like the job, even the boredom of it, and he listened carefully to the sheriff's orders.

"About once an hour you take a swing around the lake. That takes you twenty minutes, plus stops. But don't fall into a pattern with your trips, so someone can predict when you'll be passing any given cottage. Vary it, and, of course, check these bars along here too. Especially on weekends we get a lot of underage drinkers. And they're the ones who usually get loaded and decide to break into a cottage."

"They even come here in the winter?"

"This isn't a summer town any more. But sometimes I have a time convincing the cottagers of that."

They rode in silence for a time, and the weight of the gun was heavy on Johnny Kendell's hip. Finally he decided what had to be done. "Sheriff," he began, "there's something I want to tell you."

"What's that?"

"You'll find out anyway when you check on me back east. I killed a man while I was on duty. Just last week. He was a bum who broke into a liquor store and I thought he had a gun so I shot him. I resigned from the force because they were making a fuss about it."

Sheriff Dade scratched his balding head. "Well, I don't hold that against you. Glad you mentioned it, though. Just remember, out here the most dangerous thing you'll probably face will be a couple of beered-up teenagers. And they don't call for guns."

"I know."

"Right. Drop me back at the courthouse and you're on your own. Good luck."

An hour later, Kendell started his first solo swing around the lake,

concentrating on the line of shuttered cottages which stood like senti-
nels against some invader from the frozen lake. Once he stopped the
car to investigate four figures moving on the ice, but they were only
children gingerly testing skates on the glossy surface.

On the far side of the lake he checked a couple of cottages at random. Then he pulled in and parked beside a bar called the *Blue Zebra*. It
had more cars than the others, and there was a certain Friday night
gaiety about the place even from outside. He went in, letting his topcoat
hang loosely over the badge pinned to his suit lapel. The bar was
crowded and all the tables were occupied, but he couldn't pinpoint any
under-age group. They were the usual representatives of the new
suburbia—white-shirted young men self-consciously trying to please
their dates, beer-drinking groups of men fresh from their weekly bowling, and even the occasional women nearing middle age that one always found sitting alone on bar stools.

Kendell chatted a few moments with the owner and then went back
outside. There was nothing for him here. He'd turned down the inevitable offer of a drink because it was too early in the evening, and too
soon on the job to be relaxing.

As he was climbing into his car, a voice called to him from the
doorway of the *Blue Zebra*. "Hey, Deputy!"

"What's the trouble?"

The man was slim and tall, and not much older than Kendell. He
came down the steps of the bar slowly, not speaking again until he was
standing only inches away. "I just wanted to get a look at you, that's all. I
had that job until last week."

"Oh?" Kendell said, because there was nothing else to say.

"Didn't old Dade tell you he fired me?"

"No."

"Well, he did. Ask him why sometime. Ask him why he fired Milt
Woodman." He laughed and turned away, heading back to the bar.

Kendell shrugged and got into the car. It didn't really matter to him
that a man named Milt Woodman was bitter about losing his job. His
thoughts were on the future, and on Sandy, waiting for him back at the
motel.

She was sleeping when he returned to their rooms. He went in
quietly and sat on the edge of the bed, waiting until she awakened.
Presently her blue eyes opened and she saw him. "Hi, there, handsome.
How'd it go?"

"Fine. I think I'm going to like it. Get up and watch the sunrise with
me."

"I have to go to work at the supermarket."

The Night My Friend

"Nuts to that! I'm never going to see you if we're both working."

"We need the money, Johnny. We can't afford this motel, or these two rooms, much longer."

"Let's talk about it, later, huh?" He suddenly realized that he hadn't heard her laugh in days, and the thought of it made him sad. Sandy's laughter had always been a part of her, and he missed it. He wondered when she would laugh again.

That night passed much as the previous one, with patrols around the lake and frequent checks at the crowded bars. He saw Milt Woodman again, watching him through the haze of cigarette smoke at the *Blue Zebra,* but this time the man did not speak. The following day, though, Kendell remembered to ask Sheriff Dade about him.

"I ran into somebody Friday night—fellow named Milt Woodman," he said.

Dade frowned and looked down at his hands. "He try to give you any trouble?"

"No, not really. He just said to ask you sometime why you fired him."

"*Are* you asking me?"

"No. It doesn't matter to me in the least."

Dade nodded. "You're right, it doesn't. But let me know if he bothers you any more."

"Why should he?" Kendell asked, troubled by the remark.

"No reason. Just keep on your toes."

The following night, Monday, he didn't have to work. He decided to celebrate with Sandy by taking her to a nearby drive-in where the management kept open all winter with the aid of little heaters supplied to each car. The movie was something about young love. They necked in the front seat all during the second feature, like a couple of high school kids.

Tuesday night, just after midnight, Kendell pulled into the parking lot at the *Blue Zebra.* The neoned juke box was playing something plaintive and the bar was almost empty. The owner offered him a drink again, and he decided he could risk it. The night was cold and damp, even in the heated car.

"Hello, Deputy," a voice said at his shoulder. He knew before he turned that it was Milt Woodman.

"The name's Johnny Kendell," he said, keeping it friendly.

"Nice name. You know mine." He chuckled a little. "That's a good-looking wife you've got. Saw you together at the movie last night."

"Oh?" Kendell moved instinctively away. He didn't like the man. He didn't like anything about him.

Milt Woodman kept on smiling. "Did Dade ever tell you why he fired me?"

"I didn't ask him."

The chuckle became a laugh. "Good boy! Keep your nose clean. Protect that seventy-five a week." He turned and went toward the door. "See you around."

Kendell finished his drink and followed him out. There was a hint of snow in the air and tonight no moon could be seen. Ahead, on the road, the twin tail lights of Woodman's car glowed for a moment until they disappeared around a curve. Kendell gunned his car ahead with a sudden urge to follow the man, but when he'd reached the curve himself the road ahead was clear. Woodman had turned off somewhere.

The rest of the week was quiet, but on Friday he had a shock. It had always been difficult for him to sleep days, and he often awakened around noon after only four or five hours' slumber. This day he decided to meet Sandy at her job for lunch, and as he arrived at the supermarket he saw her chatting with someone at the checkout counter. It was Milt Woodman and they were laughing together like old friends.

Kendell walked around the block, trying to tell himself that there was nothing to be concerned about. When he returned to the store, Woodman was gone and Sandy was ready for lunch.

"Who was your friend?" he asked casually.

"What friend?"

"I passed a few minutes ago and you were talking to some guy. Seemed to be having a great time."

"Oh, I don't know, a customer. He comes in a lot, loafs around."

Kendell didn't mention it again. But it struck him over the weekend that Sandy no longer harped on the need for a quick marriage. In fact, she no longer mentioned marriage at all.

And she no longer laughed.

On Monday evening, Kendell's night off, Sheriff Dade invited them for dinner at his house. It was a friendly gesture, and Sandy was eager to accept at once. Mrs. Dade proved to be a handsome blonde woman still in her mid-thirties, and she handled the house and the dinner with the casual air of someone who knew all about living the good life in Wagon Lake.

After dinner, while the women discussed furniture, Kendell followed Dade to his basement workshop. "Just a place to putter around in," the sheriff told him. He picked up a power saw and handled it fondly. "Don't get as much time down here as I'd like."

"You're kept pretty busy at work."

Dade nodded. "Too busy. But I like the job you're doing, Johnny. I really do."

"Thanks." Kendell lit a cigarette and leaned against the workbench. "Sheriff, there's something I want to ask you. I didn't ask it before."

"What's that?"

"Why did you fire Milt Woodman?"

"He been giving you trouble?"

"No. Not really. I guess I'm just curious."

"All right. There's no real reason for not telling you, I suppose. He used to get down at the far end of the lake, beyond the *Blue Zebra*, and park his car in the bushes. Then he'd take some girl into one of the cottages and spend half the night there with her. I couldn't have that sort of thing going on. The fool was supposed to be guarding the cottages, not using them for his private parties."

"He's quite a man with the girls, huh?"

Dade nodded sourly. "He always was. He's just a no-good bum. I should never have hired him in the first place."

They went upstairs to join the ladies. Nothing more was said about Woodman's activities, but the next night while on patrol Kendell spotted him once again in the *Blue Zebra*. He waited down the road until Woodman emerged, then followed him around the curve to the point where he'd vanished the week before. Yes, he'd turned off into one of the steep driveways that led down to the cottages at the water's edge. There was a driveway between each pair of cottages, so Kendell had the spot pretty much narrowed down to one of two places, both big rambling houses built back when Wagon Lake was a summer retreat for the very rich.

He smoked a cigarette and tried to decide what to do. It was his duty to keep people away from the cottages, yet for some reason he wasn't quite ready to challenge Milt Woodman. Perhaps he knew that the man would never submit meekly to his orders. Perhaps he knew he might once again have to use the gun on his hip.

So he did nothing that night about Milt Woodman.

The following day Sheriff Dade handed him a mimeographed list. "I made up a new directory of names and addresses around town. All the houses are listed, along with the phone numbers of the bars and some of the other places you check. Might want to leave it with your wife, in case she has to reach you during the night." Dade always referred to Sandy as Kendell's wife, though he must have known better. "You're still at that motel, aren't you?"

"For a little while longer," Kendell answered vaguely. "It's the off season and their rates are fairly low."

Dade grunted. "Seen Woodman around?"

"Caught a glimpse of him last night. Didn't talk to him."

The sheriff nodded and said no more.

The following evening, when Johnny was getting ready to go on duty, Sandy seemed more distant than ever. Even her kisses had a sort of automatic reflex action about them, and when he gave her the sheriff's list she stuffed it in her purse without looking at it. "What's the matter?" he asked finally.

"Oh, just a hard day at the store, I guess. All the weekend shopping starts on Thursday."

"Has that guy been in again? The one I saw you talking to?"

"I told you he comes in a lot. What of it?"

"Sandy, Sandy—what's happening to us?" He went to her, but she turned away.

"It's not what's happening to us, Johnny. It's what's already happened to you. You're different, changed. Ever since you killed that man you've been like a stranger. I thought you were really sorry about it, but now you've taken this job so you can carry a gun again."

"I haven't had it out of the holster."

"Not yet."

"All right," he said finally. "I'm sorry you feel that way. I'll see you in the morning." He went out, conscious of the revolver's weight against his hip, conscious that the day might come when he'd have to choose between that gun and Sandy.

The night was cold, with a hint of snow again in the air. He drove faster than usual, making one circuit of the lake in fifteen minutes, and barely glanced at the crowded parking lots along the route. The words with Sandy had bothered him, more than he cared to admit. On the second trip around the lake, he tried to pick out Woodman's car, but it was nowhere to be seen. Or was his car hidden off the road down at one of those cottages?

He thought about Sandy some more.

Near midnight, with the moon playing through the clouds and reflecting off the frozen lake, Johnny drove into town between his inspection trips. There wasn't much time, so he went directly to the motel. Sandy's room was empty, the bed smooth and undisturbed.

He drove back to the lake, this time seeking lights in the cottages he knew Woodman used. But all seemed dark and deserted. There were no familiar faces at the *Blue Zebra,* either. He accepted a drink from the manager and stood by the bar sipping it. His mood grew gradually worse, and when a college boy tried to buy a drink for his girl Kendell chased them out for being under age. It was something he had never done before.

Later, around two, while he was checking another couple parked down a side road, he saw Woodman's familiar car shoot past. There was a girl in the front seat with him, a concealing scarf wrapped around her hair. Kendell let out his breath slowly. If it was Sandy, he thought that he would kill her.

"Where were you last night?" he asked her in the morning, trying to keep the question casual. "I stopped by around midnight."

"I went to a late movie."

"How come?"

She lit a cigarette, turning half away from him before she answered. "I just get tired of sitting around here alone every night. Can't you understand that?"

"I understand it all right," he said.

Late that afternoon, when the winter darkness had already descended over the town and the lake, he left his room early and drove out to the big old cottages beyond the *Blue Zebra*. He parked off the road, in the hidden spot he knew Woodman used, and made his way to the nearer of the houses. There seemed nothing unusual about it, no signs of illegal entry, and he turned his attention to the cottage on the other side of the driveway. There, facing the lake, he found an unlatched window and climbed in.

The place was furnished like a country estate house, and great white sheets had been draped over the furniture to protect it from a winter's dust. He'd never seen so elaborate a summer home, but he hadn't come to look at furniture. In the bedroom upstairs he found what he sought. There had been some attempt to collect the beer bottles into a neat pile, but they hadn't bothered to smooth out the sheets.

He looked in the ash tray at the lipsticked butts and saw they were Sandy's brand. All right, he tried to tell himself, that didn't prove it. Not for sure. Then he saw a crumpled ball of paper on the floor, which she'd used to blot her lipstick. He smoothed it out, fearing but already knowing. It was the mimeographed list Sheriff Dade had given him just two days before, the one Sandy had stuffed into her purse.

All right. Now he knew.

He left it all as he'd found it and went back out the window. Even Woodman would not have dared leave such a mess for any length of time. He was planning to come back, and soon—perhaps that night. And he wouldn't dare bring another girl, when he hadn't yet cleaned up the evidence of the last one. No, it would be Sandy again.

Kendell drove to the *Blue Zebra* and had two quick drinks before starting his tour of duty. Then, as he drove around the lake, he tried to keep a special eye out for Woodman's car. At midnight, back at the bar, he asked the manager, "Seen Milt around tonight?"

"Woodman? Yeah, he stopped for a pack of cigarettes and some beer. Had a girl out in the car, I think."

"Thanks."

Kendell stepped into the phone booth and called the motel. Sandy was not in her room. He left the bar and drove down the road, past the cottage. There were no lights, but he caught a glimpse of Woodman's car in the usual spot. They were there, all right.

He parked further down the road, and for a long time just sat in the car, smoking. Presently he took the .38 revolver from his holster and checked to see that it was loaded. Then he drove back to the *Blue Zebra* for two more drinks.

When he returned to the cottage, Woodman's car was still there. Kendell made his way around to the front and silently worked the window open. He heard their muffled, whispering voices as he started up the stairs, and he drew the gun once more. It was easy after the first time. No one could deny that.

The bedroom door was open and he stood for a moment in the hallway, letting his eyes grow accustomed to the dark. They hadn't yet heard his approach.

"Woodman," he said, not too loudly, just enough to be audible.

The man started at the sound of his name, rising from the bed with a curse. "What the hell!"

Kendell fired once at the voice, heard the girl's scream of terror and fired again. He squeezed the trigger and kept squeezing it, because this time there was no Sergeant Racin to knock the pistol from his hand. This time there was nothing to stop him until all six shots had been blasted into the figures on the bed.

Then, letting the pistol fall to the floor, he walked over and struck a match. Milt Woodman was sprawled on the floor, his head in a gathering pool of blood. The girl's body was still under the sheet, and he lifted it carefully to look at her.

It wasn't Sandy.

It was Mrs. Dade, the sheriff's wife.

This time he knew they wouldn't be far behind him. This time he knew there'd be no next town, no new life.

But he had to keep going. Running.

The Long Way Down

Many men have disappeared under unusual circumstances, but perhaps none more unusual than those which befell Billy Calm.

The day began in a routine way for McLove. He left his apartment in midtown Manhattan and walked through the foggy March morning, just as he did on every working day of the year. When he was still several blocks away he could make out the bottom floors of the great glass slab which was the home office of the Jupiter Steel & Brass Corporation. But above the tenth floor the fog had taken over, shrouding everything in a dense coat of moisture that could have been the roof of the world.

Underfoot, the going was slushy. The same warm air mass which had caused the fog was making short work of the previous day's two-inch snowfall. McLove, who didn't really mind Manhattan winters, was thankful that spring was only days away. Finally he turned into the massive marble lobby of the Jupiter Steel Building, thinking for the hundredth time that only the garish little newsstand in one corner kept it from being an exact replica of the interior of an Egyptian tomb. Anyway, it was dry inside, without slush underfoot.

McLove's office on the twenty-first floor had been a point of creeping controversy from the very beginning. It was the executive floor, bulging with the vice-presidents and others who formed the inner core of Billy Calm's little family. The very idea of sharing this exclusive office space with the firm's security chief had repelled many of them, but when Billy Calm spoke there were few who openly dared challenge his mandates.

McLove had moved to the executive floor soon after the forty-year-old boy genius of Wall Street had seized control of Jupiter Steel in a proxy battle that had split stockholders into armed camps. On the day Billy Calm first walked through the marble lobby to take command of his newest acquisition, a disgruntled shareholder named Raimey had shot his hat off, and actually managed to get off a second shot before being overpowered. From that day on, Billy Calm used the private elevator at the rear of the building, and McLove supervised security from the twenty-first floor.

It was a thankless task that amounted to little more than being a sometime bodyguard for Calm. His duties, in the main, consisted of keeping Calm's private elevator in working order, attending directors' meetings with the air of a reluctant outsider, supervising the security forces at the far-flung Jupiter mills, and helping with arrangements for Calm's numerous public appearances. For this he was paid fifteen thousand dollars a year, which was the principal reason he did it.

On the twenty-first floor, this morning, Margaret Mason was already at her desk outside the directors' room. She looked up as McLove stepped into the office and flashed him their private smile. "How are you, McLove?"

"Morning, Margaret. Billy in yet?"

"Mr. Calm? Not yet. He's flying in from Pittsburgh. Should be here anytime now."

McLove glanced at his watch. He knew the directors' meeting was scheduled for ten, and that was only twenty minutes away. "Heard anything?" he asked, knowing that Margaret Mason was the best source of information on the entire floor. She knew everything and would tell you most of it, provided it didn't concern herself.

Now she nodded, and bent forward a bit across the desk. "Mr. Calm phoned from his plane and talked with Jason Greene. The merger is going through. He'll announce it officially at the meeting this morning."

"That'll make some people around here mighty sad." McLove was thinking of W. T. Knox and Sam Hamilton, two directors who had opposed the merger talk from the very beginning. Only twenty-four hours earlier, before Billy Calm's rush flight to Pittsburgh in his private plane, it had appeared that their efforts would be successful.

"They should know better than to buck Mr. Calm," Margaret said.

"I suppose so." McLove glanced at his watch again. For some reason he was getting nervous. "Say, how about lunch, if we get out of the meeting in time?"

"Fine." She gave him the small smile again. "You're the only one I feel safe drinking with at noon."

"Be back in a few minutes."

"I'll buzz you if Mr. Calm gets in."

He glanced at the closed doors of the private elevator and nodded. Then he walked down the hall to his own office once more. He got a pack of cigarettes from his desk and went across the hall to W. T. Knox's office.

"Morning, W. T. What's new?"

The tall man looked up from a file folder he'd been studying. Thirty-seven, a man who had retained most of his youthful good looks and all of his charm, Knox was popular with the girls on 21. He'd probably have been more popular if he hadn't had a pregnant wife and five children of varying ages.

"McLove, look at this weather!" He gestured toward the window, where a curtain of fog still hung. "Every winter I say I'll move to Florida, and every winter the wife talks me into staying."

Jason Greene, balding and ultraefficient, joined them with a sheaf of reports. "Billy should be in at any moment. He phoned me to say the merger had gone through."

Knox dropped his eyes. "I heard."

"When the word gets out, Jupiter stock will jump another ten points."

McLove could almost feel the tension between the two men; one gloating, and the other bitter. He walked to the window and stared out at the fog, trying to see the invisible building across the street. Below, he could not even make out the setback of their own building, though it was only two floors lower. Fog . . . well, at least it meant that spring was on the way.

Then there was a third voice behind him, and he knew without turning that it belonged to Shirley Taggert, the president's personal secretary. "It's almost time for the board meeting," she said, with that hint of a southern drawl that either attracted or repelled but left no middle ground. "You people ready?"

Shirley was grim-faced but far from ugly. She was a bit younger than Margaret Mason's mid-thirties, a bit sharper of dress and mind. But she paid the penalty for being Billy Calm's secretary every time she walked down the halls. Conversations ceased, suspicious glances followed her, and there was always a half-hidden air of tension at her arrival. She ate lunch alone, and one or two fellows who had been brave enough to ask her for a date hadn't bothered to ask a second time.

"We're ready," Jason Greene told her. "Is he here yet?"

She shook her head and glanced at the clock. "He should be in any minute."

McLove left them grouped around Knox's desk and walked back down the hall. Sam Hamilton, the joker, passed him on the way and stopped to tell him a quick gag. He, at least, didn't seem awfully upset about the impending merger, even though he had opposed it. McLove liked Sam better than any of the other directors, probably because at the age of fifty he was still a big kid at heart. You could meet him on even ground, and, at times, feel he was letting you outdo him.

"Anything yet?" McLove asked Margaret, returning to her desk outside the directors' room.

"No sign of Mr. Calm, but he shouldn't be long now. It's just about ten."

McLove glanced at the closed door of Billy Calm's office, next to the directors' room, and then entered the latter. The room was quite plain, with only the one door through which he had entered, and unbroken walls of dull oak paneling on either wall. The far end of the room, with two wide windows looking out at the fog, was only twenty feet away, and the conference table that was the room's only piece of furniture had just the eight necessary chairs grouped around it. Some had been heard to complain that the room lacked the stature of Jupiter Steel, but Billy Calm contended he liked the forced intimacy of it.

Now, as McLove stood looking out the windows, the whole place seemed to reflect the cold mechanization of the modern office building. The windows could not be opened. Even their cleaning had to be done from the outside, on a gondola-like platform that climbed up and down the sheer glass walls. There were no window-sills, and McLove's fingers ran unconsciously along the bottom of the window frame as he stood staring out. The fog might be lifting a little, but he couldn't be certain.

McLove went out to Margaret Mason's desk, saw that she was gathering together her copy books and pencils for the meeting, and decided to take a glance into Billy Calm's office. It was the same size as the directors' room, and almost as plain in its furnishings. Only the desk, cluttered with the trivia of a businessman's lifetime, gave proof of human occupancy. On the left wall still hung the faded portrait of the firm's founder, and on the right, a more recent photograph of Israel Black, former president of Jupiter, and still a director though he never came to the meetings. This was Billy Calm's domain. From here he ruled a vast empire of holdings, and a word from him could send men to their financial ruin.

McLove straightened suddenly on hearing a man's muffled voice at Margaret's desk outside. He heard her ask, "What's the matter?" and then heard the door of the directors' room open. Hurrying back to her desk, he was just in time to see the door closing again.

"Is he finally here?"

Margaret, unaccountably white-faced, opened her mouth to answer, just as there came the tinkling crash of a breaking window from the inner room. They both heard it clearly, and she dropped the cigarette she'd been in the act of lighting. "Billy!" she screamed out. "No, Billy!"

They were at the door together after only an instant's hesitation, pushing it open before them, hurrying into the directors' room. "No," McLove said softly, staring straight ahead at the empty room and the long table and the shattered window in the opposite wall. "He jumped." Already the fog seemed to be filling the room with its damp mists as they hurried to the window and peered out at nothing.

"Billy jumped," Margaret said dully, as if unable to comprehend the fact. "He killed himself."

McLove turned and saw Knox standing in the doorway. Behind him, Greene and Hamilton and Shirley Taggert were coming up fast. "Billy Calm just jumped out of the window," McLove told them.

"No," Margaret Mason said, turning from the window. "No, no, no, no . . ." Then, suddenly overcome with the shock of it, she tumbled to the floor in a dead faint.

"Take care of her," McLove shouted to the others. "I've got to get downstairs."

Knox bent to lift the girl in his arms, while Sam Hamilton hurried to the telephone. Shirley had settled into one of the padded directors' chairs, her face devoid of all expression. And Jason Greene, loyal to the end, actually seemed to be crying.

In the hallway, McLove pushed the button of Billy Calm's private elevator and waited for it to rise from the depths of the building. The little man would have no further use for it now. He rode it down alone, leaning against its padded walls, listening to, but hardly hearing, the dreary hum of its descent. In another two minutes he was on the street, looking for the crowd that would surely be gathered, listening for the sounds of rising sirens.

But there was nothing. Nothing but the usual mid-morning traffic. Nothing but hurrying pedestrians and a gang of workmen drilling at the concrete and a policeman dully directing traffic.

There was no body.

McLove hurried over to the police officer. "A man just jumped out of the Jupiter Steel Building," he said. "What happened to him?"

The policeman wrinkled his brow. "Jumped? From where?"

"Twenty-first floor. Right above us."

They both gazed upward into the gradually lifting fog. The police officer shrugged his shoulders. "Mister, I been standing in this very spot for more than an hour. Nobody jumped from up there."

"But . . ." McLove continued staring into the fog. "But he *did* jump. I practically saw him do it. And if he's not down here, where *is* he?"

Back on 21, McLove found the place in a state somewhere between sheer shock and calm confusion. People were hurrying without purpose in every direction, bent on their own little useless errands. Sam Hamilton was on the phone to his broker's, trying to get the latest quotation on Jupiter stock. "The bottom'll drop out of it when this news hits," he confided to McLove. "With Billy gone, the merger won't go through."

McLove lit a cigarette. "Billy Calm is gone, all right, but he's not down there. He vanished somewhere between the twenty-first floor and the street."

"*What?*"

W. T. Knox joined them, helping a pale but steady Margaret Mason by the arm. "She'll be all right," he said. "It was the shock."

McLove reached out his hand to her. "Tell us exactly what happened. Every word of it."

"Well . . ." She hesitated and then sat down. Behind her, Hamilton and Shirley Taggert were deep in animated conversation, and Jason Greene had appeared from somewhere with a policeman in tow.

"You were at the desk," McLove began, helping her. "And I came out of the directors' room and went into Billy's office. Then what?"

"Well, Mr. Calm came in, and as he passed my desk he mumbled something. I didn't catch it, and I asked him what was the matter. He seemed awfully upset about something. Anyway, he passed my desk and went into the directors' room. He was just closing the door when you came out, and you know the rest."

McLove nodded. He knew the rest, which was nothing but the shattered window and the vanished man. "Well, the body's not down there," he told them again. "It's not anywhere. Billy Calm dived through that window and flew away."

Shirley passed Hamilton a telephone she had just answered. "Yes?" He listened a moment and then hung up. "The news about Billy went out over the stock ticker. Jupiter Steel is selling off fast. It's already down three points."

"Goodbye merger," Knox said, and though his face was grim his voice was not.

A detective arrived on the scene to join the police officer. Quickly summoned workmen were tacking cardboard over the smashed window, carefully removing some of the jagged splinters of glass from the bottom of the frame. Things were settling down a little, and the police were starting to ask questions.

"Mr. McLove, you're in charge of security for the company?"

"That's right."

"Why was it necessary to have a security man sit in on directors' meetings?"

"Some nut tried to kill Billy Calm a while back. He was still nervous. Private elevator and all."

"What was the nut's name?"

"Raimey, I think. Something like that. Don't know where he is now."

"And who was usually present at these meetings? I see eight chairs in there."

"Calm, and three vice-presidents: Greene, Knox, and Hamilton. Also Calm's secretary, Miss Taggert, and Miss Mason, who kept the minutes of the meeting. The seventh chair is mine, and the eighth one is kept for Mr. Black, who never comes down for the meetings any more."

"There was resentment between Calm and Black?"

"A bit. You trying to make a mystery out of this?"

The detective shrugged. "Looks like pretty much of a mystery already."

And McLove had to admit that it did.

He spent an hour with the police, both upstairs and down in the street. When they finally left just before noon, he went looking for Margaret Mason. She was back at her desk, surprisingly, looking as if nothing in the world had happened.

"How about lunch?" he said. "Maybe a martini would calm your nerves."

"I'm all right now, thanks. The offer sounds good, but you've got a date." She passed him an inner-office memo. It was signed by William T. Knox, and it requested McLove's presence in his office at noon.

"I suppose I have to tell them what I know."

"Which is?"

"Nothing. Absolutely nothing. All I know is a dozen different things that couldn't have happened to Calm. I'll try to get out of there as soon as I can. Will you wait for me? Till one, anyway?" he asked.

"Sure. Good luck."

He returned her smile, then went down the long hallway to Knox's office. It wasn't surprising to find Hamilton and Greene already there, and he settled down in the remaining chair feeling himself the center of attraction.

"Well?" Knox asked. "Where is he?"

"Gentlemen, I haven't the faintest idea."

"He's dead, of course," Jason Greene spoke up.

"Probably," McLove agreed. "But where's the body?"

Hamilton rubbed his fingers together in a nervous gesture. "That's what we have to find out. My phone as been ringing for an hour. The brokers are going wild, to say nothing of Pittsburgh!"

McLove nodded. "I gather the merger stands or falls on Billy Calm."

"Right! If he's dead, it's dead."

Jason Greene spoke again. "Billy Calm was a great man, and I'd be the last person in the world to try to sink the merger for which he worked so hard. But he's dead, all right. And there's just one place the body could have gone."

"Where's that?" Knox asked.

"It landed on a passing truck or something like that, of course."

Hamilton's eyes widened. "Sure!" he remarked sarcastically.

But McLove reluctantly shook his head. "That was the first thought the police had. We checked it out and it couldn't have happened. This building is set back from the street; it has to be, on account of this sheer glass wall. I doubt if a falling body could hit the street, and even if it did, the traffic lane on this side is torn up for repairs. And there's been a policeman on duty there all morning. The body didn't land on the sidewalk or the street, and no truck or car passed anywhere near enough."

W. T. Knox blinked and ran a hand through his thinning, but still wavy, hair. "If he didn't go down, where did he go? Up?"

"Maybe he never jumped," Hamilton suggested. "Maybe Margaret made the whole thing up."

McLove wondered at his words, wondered if Margaret had been objecting to some of his jokes again. "You forget that I was out there with her. I saw her face when that window smashed. The best actress in the world couldn't have faked that expression. Besides, I saw him go in—or at least I saw the door closing after him. It couldn't close by itself."

"And the room was empty when you two entered it a moment later," Knox said. "Therefore Billy must have gone through the window. We have to face the fact. He couldn't have been hiding under the table."

"If he didn't go down," Sam Hamilton said, "he went up! By a rope to the roof or another window."

But once more McLove shook his head. "You're forgetting that none of the windows can be opened. And it's a long way up to the roof. The police checked it though. They found nothing but an unmarked sea of melting snow and slush. Not a footprint, just a few pigeon tracks."

Jason Greene frowned across the desk. "But he didn't go down, up or sideways, and he didn't stay in the room."

McLove wondered if he should tell them his idea, or wait until later. He decided now was as good a time as any. "Suppose he did jump, and something caught him on the way down. Suppose he's hanging there now, hidden by the fog."

"A flagpole? Something like that?"

"But there aren't any," Knox protested. "There's nothing but a smooth glass wall."

"There's one thing," McLove reminded them, looking around the desk at their expectant faces. "The thing they use to wash the windows."

Jason Greene walked to the window. "We can find out easily enough. The sun has just about burned the fog away."

They couldn't see from that side of the building, so they rode down in the elevator to the street. As quickly as it had come, the fog seemed to have vanished, leaving a clear and sparkling sky with a brilliant sun seeking out the last remnants of the previous day's snow. The four of them stood in the street, in the midst of digging equipment abandoned for the lunch hour, and stared up at the great glass side of the Jupiter Steel Building.

There was nothing to see. No body dangling in space, no window-washing scaffold. Nothing.

"Maybe he took it back up to the roof," Knox suggested.

"No footprints, remember?" McLove tried to cover his disappointment. "It was a long shot, anyway. The police checked the tenants for several floors beneath the broken window, and none of them saw anything. If Calm had landed on a scaffold, someone would have noticed it."

For a while longer they continued staring up at the building, each of them drawn to the tiny speck on the twenty-first floor where cardboard temporarily covered the shattered glass. "Why," Jason Greene asked suddenly, "didn't the cop down here see the falling glass when it hit? Was the window broken from the outside?"

McLove smiled. "No, the glass all went out, and down. It was the drilling again; the sound covered the glass hitting. And that section of sidewalk was blocked off. The policeman didn't hear it hit, but we were able to find pieces of it. You can see where they were swept up."

W. T. Knox sighed deeply. "I don't know. I guess I'll go to lunch. Maybe we can all think better on a full stomach."

They separated a few moments after that, and McLove went back up to 21 for Margaret Mason. He found her in Billy Calm's office with Shirley Taggert. They were on their knees, running their hands over the oak-paneled wall.

"What's all this?" he asked.

"Just playing detective." Margaret said. "It was Shirley's idea. She mentioned about how Mr. Calm always wanted the office left exactly as it was, and with the directors' room right next door, even though both rooms were really too small. She thought of a secret panel of some sort."

"Margaret!" Shirley got reluctantly to her feet. "You make it sound like something out of a dime novel. Really, though, it was a possibility. It would explain how he left the room without jumping from the window."

"Don't keep me in suspense," McLove said. "Did you find anything?"

"Nothing. And we've been over both sides of the wall."

"They don't build them like they used to in merrie old England. Let's forget it and have lunch."

Shirley Taggert smoothed the wrinkles from her skirt. "You two go ahead. You don't want me along."

She was gone before they could protest, and McLove wasn't about to protest too loudly anyway. He didn't mind Shirley as a co-worker but, like everyone else, he was acutely conscious of her position in the office scheme of things. Even now, with Billy Calm vanished into the blue, she was still a dangerous force not to be shared at social hours.

He went downstairs with Margaret and they found an empty booth at the basement restaurant across the street. It was a place they often went after work for a drink, though lately he'd seen less of her outside of office hours. Thinking back to the first time he'd become aware of Margaret, he had only fuzzy memories of the tricks Sam Hamilton used to play. He loved to walk up behind the secretaries and tickle them—or occasionally even unzip their dresses—and he had quickly discovered that Margaret Mason was a likely candidate for his attentions. She always rewarded his efforts with a lively scream, without ever really getting upset.

It had been a rainy autumn evening some months back that McLove's path crossed hers most violently, linking them with a secret that made them drinking companions if nothing more. He'd been at loose ends that evening, and wandered into a little restaurant over by the East River. Surprisingly enough, Margaret Mason had been there, defending her honor in a back booth against a very drunk escort. McLove had move in, flattened him with one punch, and they left him collapsed against a booth.

After that, on different drinking occasions, she had poured out the sort of lonely story he might have expected. And he'd listened and lingered, and sometimes fruitlessly imagined that he might become one of the men in her life. He knew there was no one for a long time after the bar incident, just as he knew now, by her infrequent free evenings, that there was someone again. Their drinking dates were more often being confined to lunch hours, when even two martinis were risky, and she never talked about being lonely or bored.

This day, over the first drink, she said, "It was terrible, really terrible."

"I know. It's going to get worse, I'm afraid. He's got to turn up somewhere."

"Dead or alive?"

"I wish I knew."

She lit a cigarette. "Will you be blamed for it?"

"I couldn't be expected to guard him from himself. Besides, I wasn't hired as a personal bodyguard. I'm chief of security, and that's all. I'm not a bodyguard or a detective. I don't know the first thing about fingerprints or clues. All I know about is people."

"What do you know about the Jupiter people?"

McLove finished his drink before answering. "Very little, really. Except for you. Hamilton and Knox and Greene and the rest of them are nothing more than names and faces. I've never even had a drink with any of them. I sit around at those meetings, and, frankly, I'm bored stiff. If anybody tries to blame me for this thing, they'll be looking for a new security chief."

Margaret's glass was empty too, and he signaled the waiter for two more. It was that sort of a day. When they came, he noticed that her usually relaxed face was a bit tense, and the familiar sparkle of her blue eyes was no longer in evidence. She'd been through a lot that morning, and even the drinks were failing to relax her.

"Maybe I'll quit with you," she said.

"It's been a long time since we've talked. How have things been?"

"All right." She said it with a little shrug.

"The new boyfriend?"

"Don't call him that, please."

"I hope he's an improvement over the last one."

"So do I. At my age you get involved with some strange ones."

"Do you love him?"

She thought a moment and then answered, "I guess I do."

He lit another cigarette. "When Billy Calm passed your desk this morning, did he seem . . . ?" The sentence stopped in the middle, cut short by a sudden scream from the street. McLove stood up and looked toward the door, where a waiter was already running outside to see what had happened.

"What is it?" Margaret asked.

"I don't know, but there seems to be a crowd gathering. Come on!"

Outside, they crossed the busy street and joined the crowd on the sidewalk of the Jupiter Building. "What happened?" Margaret asked somebody.

"Guy jumped, I guess."

They fought their way through now, and McLove's heart was pounding with anticipation of what they would see. It was Billy Calm, all right, crushed and dead and looking very small. But there was no doubt it was he.

A policeman arrived from somewhere with a blanket and threw it over the thing on the sidewalk. McLove saw Sam Hamilton fighting his way through the crowd to their side. "Who is it?" Hamilton asked, but he too must have known.

"Billy," McLove told him, "It's Billy Calm."

Hamilton stared at the blanket for a moment and then looked at his watch. "Three hours and forty-five minutes since he jumped. I guess he must have taken the long way down."

W. T. Knox was pacing the floor like a caged animal, and Shirley Taggert was sobbing silently in a corner chair. It was over. Billy Calm had been found. The reaction was only beginning to set in. The worst, they all realized, was still ahead.

Jason Greene glared at Hamilton as he came into the office. "Well, the market's closed. Maybe you can stay off that phone for a while now."

Sam Hamilton didn't lose his grim smile. "Right now the price of Jupiter stock happens to be something that's important to all of us. You may be interested to know that it fell fourteen more points before they had to suspend trading in it for the rest of the session. They still don't have a closing price on it."

Knox held up both hands. "All right, all right! Let's everybody calm down and try to think. What do the police say, McLove?"

Feeling as if he were only a messenger boy between the two camps, McLove replied, "Billy was killed by the fall, and he'd been dead only a few minutes when they examined him. Body injuries would indicate that he fell from this height."

"But where was he for nearly four hours?" Greene wanted to know. "Hanging there, invisible, outside the window?"

Shirley Taggert collected herself enough to join in the conversation. "He got out of that room somehow, and then came back and jumped later," she said. "That's how it must have been."

But McLove shook his head. "I hate to throw cold water on logical explanations, but that's how it *couldn't* have been. Remember, the windows in this building can't be opened. No other window has been broken, and the one on this floor is still covered by cardboard."

"The roof!" Knox suggested.

"No. There still aren't any footprints on the roof. We checked."

"Didn't anybody see him falling?"

"Apparently not till just before he hit."

"The thing's impossible," Knox said.

"No."

They were all looking at McLove. "Then what happened?" Greene asked.

"I don't know what happened, except for one thing. Billy Calm didn't hang in space for four hours. He didn't fall off the roof, or out of any other window, which means he could only have fallen from the window in the directors' room"

"But the cardboard . . ."

"Somebody replaced it afterwards. And that means . . ."

"It means Billy was murdered," Knox breathed. "It means he didn't commit suicide."

McLove nodded. "He was murdered, and by somebody on this floor. Probably by somebody in this room." He glanced around.

Night settled cautiously over the city, with a scarlet sunset to the west that clung inordinately long to its reign over the skies. The police had returned, and the questioning went on, concurrently with long distance calls to Pittsburgh and five other cities where Jupiter had mills. There was confusion, somehow more so with the coming of darkness to the outer world. Secretaries and workers from the other floors gradually drifted home, but on 21 life went on.

"All right," Knox breathed finally, as it was nearing eight o'clock. "We'll call a directors' meeting for Monday morning, to elect a new president. That should give the market time to settle down, and let us know just how bad things really are. At the same time we'll issue a statement about the proposed merger. I gather we're in agreement that it's a dead issue for the time being."

Sam Hamilton nodded, and Jason Greene reluctantly shrugged his assent. Shirley Taggert looked up from her pad. "What about old Israel Black? With Mr. Calm dead, he'll be back in the picture."

Jason Greene shrugged. "Let him come. We can keep him in line. I never thought the old guy was so bad anyway, not really."

It went on like this, the talk, the bickering, the occasional flare of temper, until nearly midnight. Finally, McLove felt he could excuse himself and head for home. In the outer office, Margaret was straightening her desk, and he was surprised to realize that she was still around. He hadn't seen her in the past few hours.

"I thought you went home," he said.

"They might have needed me."

"They'll be going all night at this rate. How about a drink?"

"I should get home."

"All right. Let me take you, then. The subways aren't safe at this hour."

She turned her face up to smile at him. "Thanks, McLove. I can use someone like you tonight."

They went down together in the elevator, and out into a night turned decidedly coolish. He skipped the subway and hailed a cab. Settled back on the red leather seat, he asked, "Do you want to tell me about it, Margaret?"

He couldn't see her face in the dark, but after a moment she asked, "Tell you what?"

"What really happened. I've got part of it doped out already, so you might as well tell me the whole thing."

"I don't know what you mean, McLove. Really," she protested.

"All right," he said, and was silent for twenty blocks. Then, as they stopped for a traffic light, he added, "This is murder, you know. This isn't a kid's game or a simple love affair."

"There are some things you can't talk over with anyone. I'm sorry. Here's my place. You can drop me at the corner."

He got out with her and paid the cab driver. "I think I'd like to come up," he said quietly.

"I'm sorry, McLove, I'm awfully tired."

"Want me to wait for him down here?"

She sighed and led the way inside, keeping silent until they were in the little three-room apartment he'd visited only once before. Then she shrugged off her raincoat and asked, "How much do you know?"

"I know he'll come here tonight, of all nights."

"What was it? What told you?"

"A lot of things. The elevator, for one."

She sat down. "What about the elevator?"

"Right after Billy Calm's supposed arrival, and suicide, I ran to his private elevator. It wasn't on 21. It had to come up from below. He never rode any other elevator. When I finally remembered it, I realized he hadn't come up on that one, or it would still have been there."

Margaret sat frozen in the chair, her head cocked a little to one side as if listening. "What does it matter to you? You told me just this noon that none of them meant anything to you."

"They didn't, they don't. But I guess you do, Margaret. I can see what he's doing to you, and I've got to stop it before you get in too deep."

"I'm in about as deep as I can ever be, right now."

"Maybe not."

"You said you believed me. You told them all that I couldn't have been acting when I screamed out his name."

He closed his eyes for a moment, thinking that he'd heard something in the hallway. Then he said, "I did believe you. But then after the elevator bit, I realized that you never called Calm by his first name. It was always Mr. Calm, not Billy, and it would have been the same even in a moment of panic. Because he was still the president of the company. The elevator and the name—I put them together, and I knew it wasn't Billy Calm who had walked into that directors' room."

There was a noise at the door, the sound of a familiar key turning in the lock. "No," she whispered, almost to herself. "No, no, no . . ."

"And that should be our murderer now," McLove said, leaping to his feet.

"Billy!" she screamed. "Billy, run! It's a trap!"

But McLove was already to the door, yanking it open, staring into the startled, frightened face of W. T. Knox.

Sometimes it ends with a flourish, and sometimes only with the dull thud of a collapsing dream. For Knox, the whole thing had been only an extension of some sixteen hours in his life span. The fantastic plot, which had been set in motion by his attempt at suicide that morning at the Jupiter Steel Building, came to an end when he succeeded in leaping to his death from the bathroom window of Margaret's apartment, while they sat waiting for the police to come.

The following morning, with only two hours' sleep behind him, McLove found himself facing Greene and Hamilton and Shirley Taggert once more, telling them the story of how it had been. There was an empty chair in the office too, and he wondered vaguely whether it had been meant for Knox or Margaret.

"He was just a poor guy at the end of his rope," McLove told them. "He was deeply involved in an affair with Margaret Mason, and he'd sunk all his money into a desperate gamble that the merger wouldn't go through. He sold a lot of Jupiter stock short, figuring that when the merger talks collapsed the price would fall sharply. Only Billy Calm called from his plane yesterday morning and said the merger was on. Knox thought about it for an hour or so, and did some figuring. When he realized he'd be wiped out, he went into the directors' room to commit suicide."

"Why?" Shirley Taggert interrupted. "Why couldn't he jump out his own window?"

"Because there's a setback two stories down on his side. He couldn't have cleared it. He wanted a smooth drop to the sidewalk. Billy Calm could hardly have taken a running jump through the window. It was far off the floor even for a tall man, and Billy was short. And remember the slivers of glass at the bottom of the pane? When I remembered them, and remembered the height of the bottom sill from the floor, I knew that no one—especially a short man—could have gone through that window without knocking them out. No, Knox passed Margaret's desk, muttered some sort of farewell, and entered the room just as I came out of Calm's office. He smashed the window with a chair so he wouldn't have to try a dive through the thick glass, head first. And then he got ready to jump."

"Why didn't he?"

"Because he heard Margaret shout his name from the outer office. And with the shouted word *Billy,* a sudden plan came to him in that split second. He recrossed the small office quickly, and stood behind the door as we entered, knowing that I would think it was Billy Calm who had jumped. As soon as we were in the room, he simply stepped out and stood there. I thought he had arrived with the rest of you, and you, of course, thought he had entered the room with Margaret and me. I never gave it a second thought, because I was looking for Calm. But Margaret fainted when she saw he was still alive."

"But she said it was Billy Calm who entered the office," Greene protested.

"Not until later. She was starting to deny it, in fact, when she saw Knox and fainted. Remember, he carried her into the next room, and he was alone with her when she came to. He told her his money would be safe if only people thought Calm dead for a few hours. So she went along with her lover; I needn't remind you he was a handsome fellow, even though he was married. She went along with what we all thought happened, not realizing it would lead to murder."

Sam Hamilton lit a cigar. "The stock did go down."

"But not enough. And Knox knew Calm's arrival would reactivate the merger and ruin everything. I don't think he planned to kill Calm in the beginning, but as the morning wore on it became the only way out. He waited in the private elevator when he knew Billy was due to arrive, slugged him, carried his small body to that window while we were all out to lunch, and threw him out, replacing the cardboard afterwards."

"And the stock went down some more," Hamilton said.

"That's right."

"She called him Billy," Shirley reminded them.

"It was his name. We all called him W. T., but he signed his memo to me *William T. Knox*. I suppose the two of them thought it was a great joke, her calling him Billy when they were together."

"Where is she now?" someone asked.

"The police are still questioning her. I'm going down there now, to be with her. She's been through a lot." He thought probably this would be his final day at Jupiter Steel. Somehow *he* was tired of these faces and their questions.

But as he got to his feet, Sam Hamilton asked, "Why wasn't Billy here for the meeting at ten? Where was he for those missing hours? And how did Knox know when he would really arrive?"

"Knox knew because Billy phoned him, as he had earlier in the morning."

"Phoned him? From where?"

McLove turned to stare out the window, at the clear blue of the morning sky. "From his private plane. Billy Calm was circling the city for nearly three hours. He couldn't land because of the fog."

Dreaming Is a Lonely Thing

"Dave?" Helen queried tentatively.

He rolled over on the bed and stared up at her, surprised to see her awake so early. "What is it?"

"I had a dream, Dave. I dreamed my mother came to live with us."

"No!" He rolled back, burying his head in the pillow. "Go back to sleep and dream me up some fast cash. No dogs or cats or mothers."

"I can't help what I dream, Dave."

"You used to be good, Helen. You used to be damn good. I think you're losing your touch."

He was sorry he'd said it, because he saw at once that she was too upset to return to bed. He watched her move aimlessly about the dingy bedroom, searching for her cigarettes, then curl up in the chair by the window and stare at the dawn coming up over Hudson Street. For a moment, seeing her there with her knees up under her chin, he considered making love to her. But then the desire passed, and he closed his eyes against the brightening square of window.

He'd been with Helen Reston for two years or better, ever since they met during an all-night poker game in Kansas City. She was not the best looking girl he had ever known, and certainly not the most intelligent, but she had one gift that was invaluable to a man like Dave Krown. She had a fantastic imagination, and she always remembered her dreams. He'd realized it the very first night they spent together, back in Kansas City, when she had awakened next to him in the morning. "I dreamed you robbed the poker game," she'd said, as if it was the most natural thing in the world. "Isn't that crazy?"

"Not so crazy," he'd said, thinking about it. He had been a big loser and was just about at the end of his wits. That night, he had purchased a second-hand gun, the blue steel revolver he still used, and had gone back to the game with one of Helen's nylon stockings over his face. They had left Kansas City the next morning seven hundred dollars richer.

Dave needed someone like Helen, someone to come up with ideas, even if they were the stuff of dreams. He was a man utterly without morals or fear, a man to whom brute force and the blue steel revolver under his arm had become the only religion he practiced in a world that rewarded violence with the passing fame of stark headlines and television cameras. With her ideas and his certain skill, they made a team.

The two years had passed like two months, under the sun at Miami Beach, across the continent by jet to California, then to New York, at dog tracks and horse races and poker games. Always where the action was, always where there was a sucker to be rolled or a bankroll to be hijacked. Once before, when Helen's dreams had started running to dogs and cats, he had parked them in a little motel on the Illinois state line and had gone off to hold up a gas station. The thing had been a disaster from start to finish. He'd gotten five dollars for his trouble and been forced to shoot the over-zealous attendant in the bargain. It was the only time he'd been driven to violence in his career, and he brooded about it for weeks afterward as they fled blindly across the country. He never heard if the youth lived or died, though the wound had been serious.

New York had been their last stop, where Helen dreamt of a robbery at the jewelers' exchange after three days of wandering with Dave up and down the side streets of Manhattan. He had pulled it off pretty well, and it wasn't her fault that a fluke of scheduling had made the haul next to worthless.

They'd been living up the Hudson, in the medium-sized city of Seneca, since before Christmas — conserving their money, biding their time, and waiting for the dreams to come again. Some nights Helen worked as a waitress at a nearby lunch counter, and Dave had been doing occasional jobs of auto repair at a garage. It kept them in eating money until their luck changed.

Now, as she sat by the window, Helen asked, "Dave?"

"Huh?"

"Think we'll get to Miami this winter?"

"Not unless we can scrape up some money. The old car would never make it down there with those tires."

"I guess my dreams haven't been so good, honey." She was always aware of her failings, and conscious of the fact that he somehow held her responsible for their plight.

"That's all right." He sat up on the rumpled bed. "I've been thinking maybe we should settle down anyway. Give up this business and get a couple of honest jobs. You know, we'd probably make just as much in a year's time, without half the worry."

She came over to him. "I like to hear you say that, Dave. I like to think maybe someday I'll be dreaming about babies and a house in the suburbs instead of holdups and stuff."

"Got a cigarette?"

"Sure. Before breakfast?"

"I feel like one." She lit it for him and he inhaled deeply. "But we need one more job, Helen. One more big job so we can head south and start a new life."

"In these stories on the TV it's always the last job when the cops catch them."

"That's on TV. I know when to quit while I'm ahead. Anyway, think about it, huh? Think about it and maybe something'll come to you."

"Yeah."

They didn't work that day. Instead, they strolled through the frosty afternoon along the banks of the river, and though the Hudson was no Mississippi, it did bring back memories of their early days together. They stopped at a nearby firehouse to get new license plates for the car, and later, as the city darkened for night, he took her out for a lobster dinner at a restaurant that charged more than they could really afford.

"We'll just relax," he said later, back in the room, "and see what tomorrow brings." The money was running low, and it had been a bit of an added shock to discover that the New York State license plates on his second-hand car were due for replacement.

But he slept well, and didn't awaken until nearly dawn, when he was aware of Helen padding about the room in her bare feet. "I had a dream," she said, seeing his open eye watching her. "I dreamed I was back home at mother's, cleaning the rug, and the vacuum cleaner turned into a snake, and then the snake turned into a lobster and it pinched my foot."

"That's no dream," he mumbled into his pillow. "That's an upset stomach. Go back to bed."

When he awoke again the sun was already high in the morning sky,

The Night My Friend

and he knew it was late. Helen was stretched out on her back next to him, still asleep, half uncovered by the milky sheet. But when he turned over she awakened quickly and sat up, rubbing her eyes. "What time is it, Dave?"

"After ten."

"I had a dream."

"I know. About the lobster."

"No, another one. Just now, I think."

There was something in her voice that excited him. "Tell me about it."

She arranged herself cross-legged on the bed. "Well, remember the line at the firehouse waiting to get license plates yesterday? Remember all those guys plunking down their fifteen or twenty bucks or more for their plates?"

"Sure. What about it?"

"Dave, they have to get them by the end of this week. That firehouse is going to be taking in a lot of money the next few days." She paused for breath. "I dreamed about it. I dreamed you turned in a false alarm, and when all the firemen were gone you just walked in and held up those two foolish women who sell the license plates."

He was silent for a moment when she'd finished, silent just thinking about it. Then his face slowly relaxed into a sort of grin. "You got some imagination, Helen," he told her at last. "You're the only gal I ever knew who could make millions while you're sleeping."

"You think it'll work, Dave?"

"Of course it'll work. And I'll see you get a new dress out of it. Or better still, a good winter coat." He'd been noticing the shabbiness of her old green one.

"When, Dave?" she asked, her eyes sparkling with growing excitement, as they always did. "When will you try it?"

"Tonight's as good as any," he told her. And he went to the closet and took the blue steel revolver from its hiding place.

At exactly ten minutes to nine, Helen telephoned a report of a fire from a booth at the nearby drug store. Dave was waiting in the shadows across from the firehouse, watching as the massive red engines went shrilling off into the bleak winter night. When they were out of sight, leaving only the dying echo of their sirens like a scent to be followed, he walked quickly across the street, hoping there was no last-minute straggler buying his plates.

But the two women were alone, counting out the money into neat banded stacks as their day neared its end. The younger of them, a handsome brunette with deep, pale eyes, looked up as he entered. "Our last customer," she said.

He raised the wool scarf over his mouth and nose, and showed them the gun with his other hand. "I'm taking the money," he said, making it simple

The older woman started to rise. "Oh, no!" she gasped, and then fell back onto the padded metal chair.

He took a paper bag from his overcoat pocket. "In here. All of it. Skip the silver."

The brunette held the bag open, sliding the bills in with professional ease. When she had finished, she said, "You won't get away with this."

"I'll take my chances." The bag was brimming with bills, and he wished he had brought a larger one. He backed slowly from the building, keeping the gun pointed in their general direction. "Just sit there and you won't get hurt, ladies."

Somewhere in the distance he heard the slow clanging of a bell, and he knew the first of the engines was on its way back from the false alarm. He closed the door behind him and broke into a trot, letting the woolen scarf flap away from his face.

Beneath his arm, the soft weight of the money felt good.

"Almost nine thousand dollars," Helen said as she finished counting it. "Who'd have thought there would be that much?"

"It was there, just waiting for me," he told her. "The thing went off like clockwork."

"Do we head south now, Dave? For that new life?"

"We sure do! But not for a week or so. Somebody might get suspicious if we blew town right away. Look—we cool it for about a week, then drive down to New York and trade in this car on something that will get us to Florida. After that, we're in the park." He took four twenties from the stack. "Here. Get yourself that new coat, but nothing too flashy, understand. No fur or anything."

She clutched at the bills with a grateful smile. "We still make a good team, Dave."

He was reading a newspaper account of the robbery when she returned the following evening with the new coat, a fuzzy red thing with black speckles that matched her hair. "That's not supposed to be flashy?" he asked with a laugh.

"It didn't cost much, honey. Only seventy dollars. You like it?"

The Night My Friend

"I like it."

"Dave, why did I buy a new winter coat if we're goin' to Florida next week?"

"You need one, don't you? Maybe we won't be spending our lives down there."

"You're not going to give it up, are you?"

He sighed and reached for a cigarette. "This one went so smooth, doll."

"Don't call me that."

"All right. But be sensible, Helen. You don't quit when you're ahead."

"No! You wait till you're lying with your face in the gutter and some cop's bullets in your back! Then you'll decide to quit!"

"All right, calm down." He slipped into his fleece-lined jacket. "I'm going out for a walk."

"So they can find you easier?"

"We agreed to stay here a week, didn't we? So how is it going to seem if I never show up at the garage? I'll just look in on them, and I'll be back in an hour or so. Here." He gave her another twenty. "Think nice thoughts while I'm gone."

"Sure. I'll have myself a dream or two about a castle in Spain."

Outside, a January wind had come up, cutting through Dave's jacket like a knife and driving him quickly to the shelter of a nearby bar. He ordered a beer, although he could have afforded whiskey, and carried it, foaming, to a damp cigarette-scarred table because he didn't like to stand at bars.

He had been sitting alone for only a moment when a vaguely familiar woman with dark hair and pale eyes entered the place, and headed unhesitatingly for his table. "You're Dave Krown, aren't you?" she asked in a low voice he barely heard.

"I guess I am. You look familiar."

"May I sit down?"

"Sure." He half rose to pull out the opposite chair for her. But the first beginnings of something like fear were building within his stomach.

"I'm surprised you don't remember me. You robbed me of nine thousand dollars just last night."

He kept his hand steady on the beer, hoping his face didn't reflect the sudden emotion that shot through him. "I guess you must have the wrong guy. I don't know what you mean."

She glanced around to make sure no one was within earshot. "Look, you can drop the act. I'm not going to yell for the police — not right now, anyway. I recognized you, even with the scarf over your face. I remember faces, and I remembered yours. I remembered you had been in for your plate the night before, and I remembered you had an odd name. I looked through the forms I had turned in, and I found yours. Dave Krown, with address. I was waiting outside, wondering what to do next, when I saw you come in here."

She had fixed him with the intenseness of her deep pale eyes, and the fascination of it was enough to keep him from running. She was serious, and she had no intention of calling the police. Maybe she was just a girl out after kicks. Well, he'd see that she got them. "What's your name?" he asked suddenly.

"Susan Brogare," she answered.

"What do you want?"

"Just to know you, to know what kind of a man you are."

"Come on," Dave said, suddenly deciding on a course of action. He led her through the beaded curtains at the rear of the room, into a dim dining area of high-partitioned booths. In one booth a couple was kissing, leaving their beer untouched.

"Why back here?" she asked.

"It's better for talking." He slid into the booth opposite her. "You're not afraid of me, are you?"

The pale eyes blinked. "You probably should know that I've left a very detailed letter with a friend at the office. In it I give your name, address, and description, as well as the license number and description of your car. I identify you as the holdup man, and I say that I'm going to confront you with the fact. I end up by saying that you'll be responsible for my death if I'm killed." She paused for breath and then hurried on. "That letter goes to the police if I die or disappear for more than a day."

"Are you some kind of a nut or something?" he asked, baffled now by this strange woman. "Look, lady, if . . ."

"I said my name was Susan."

"Look, Susan, if you think I'm some sort of criminal, you should call the police. If not, just let me alone." He didn't know if the part about the letter was true or not, but the cool brazenness of her approach made him willing to bet that it was.

"I'm sorry if I frightened you. Would you buy me a drink?"

"Sure. Beer?"

She shook her head slightly. "Vodka martini."

While he was getting the drinks he considered the obvious solution —leave her sitting there, and be ten miles away with Helen before she caught on. But that was just the point. He wouldn't be more than ten miles away before she had the police on his tail. He could lure her to the apartment and tie her up (or kill her?) but there still was the problem of the letter. Dave was not a man to spend the rest of his life hiding in alleys.

So he carried the drinks back to the booth as if the whole thing were the most natural situation in the world. Just a girl and a guy on a date. "Are you married?" he asked, because another thought had just crossed his mind. He'd read about women like that.

"I was. For a bit over a year. My husband was killed in a plane crash." She played with her drink. "I know what you're thinking—maybe I'm lonely. And I guess maybe I am. You're the most exciting thing that's happened to me in two years."

By the dim indirect lighting of the back room, she might have been on either side of thirty. He guessed the far side, closer to his own age. She was about the same size and coloring as Helen, but there was a world of difference between them. "Isn't it usually exciting on your job?" he asked, just making conversation while he continued to size her up.

"At the Motor Vehicle Bureau? Are you kidding? A job's a job."

"So now that you've met me, you're looking for more excitement. Is that it?"

"I told you, I just wanted to see what sort of man you were. I've known lots of people, but never an armed robber. And the way you went about it was quite experienced. The police are properly baffled."

"Thanks. But I'm still not admitting anything." He had read somewhere about miniature tape recorders hidden in women's purses.

"Are you going to run away now?"

"Maybe."

"Alone, or with a girl?"

"There's a girl," he admitted, thinking this might discourage her seeming advances.

"Do you love her?"

"How do I answer that? I've lived with her for two years now."

"I suppose she's waiting across the street."

"Yes."

Presently they ordered another drink, and the talk drifted almost imperceptibly to their past lives. He found himself (fantastically) listening to her account of college days with all the interest of a fellow on a first date, and it was only with an effort that he managed to pull himself back to the fuzzy reality of the situation.

It was almost midnight when he returned to the apartment, and he did not mention the encounter to Helen, though his exact reasons for not doing so were unclear even to himself. She was already in bed, not yet asleep, and as he entered she said, "I called the garage. You weren't there."

"I stopped for a drink and got talking to a guy."

Helen seemed to accept the explanation. She rolled over on her wrinkled pillow and said, "I was afraid the police had picked you up."

"Not a chance."

"We've got to get out of it, Dave. I can't take the worrying any more. I think that's why the dreams are coming harder."

"That last one was a beauty. Come up with a few more like that one."

"What about Florida, Dave?"

"I'm remembering."

"I hope you are."

The following night he met Susan Brogare again in the dim room behind the bar. This time they left quite early and drove out along the river in her car, because he feared that Helen might discover them at the bar.

"You're a strange woman," he told Susan once, while they parked by the river watching fat white snowflakes drift aimlessly down from the darkened sky.

"I just want to get something out of life, that's all."

"By blackmailing me into making love to you?"

"I'm not blackmailing you. You're free to leave any time you want."

"But you know I won't," he said quietly, wondering in that moment where it was all going to end.

They never spoke of the holdup after that first night; not directly, though it often intruded onto the fringes of their thought and conversation. He learned more about this strange girl with the pale eyes than he had ever known about Helen, and found himself at the same time telling her things he had never spoken of to another person.

By the end of their third night together, he knew he was going to leave Helen.

"Do you know what today is?" Helen asked him in bed the next morning.

"Sunday, isn't it?"

"But it's Groundhog Day too! And the sun is shining. What does that mean?"

He rolled over and tried to go back to sleep, but it was useless. "All right," he said finally, "I'm awake. And the sun is shining."

"Dave?"

"What now?"

"When are we going to Florida?"

He was silent for a long time as he puttered about the bedroom in his bare feet and pajamas. Finally he said, "I've been meaning to talk to you about that, Helen."

"About what?"

"Florida and all. I've been thinking maybe it's time we split up. You know, went our own ways for a while." He saw the expression on her face and hurried on. "I'd give you your cut from the job, of course. I'd even give you an extra thousand just to get settled."

Her face was frozen into a pale mask. "Two years, Dave? Is this all I get after two years?"

"Just for a while, that's all. Maybe we could get together again in six months or so."

"You'd leave me, just like that?"

"Don't make it sound like something—dirty. We've had two good years together."

"Where do you think you'd be without me, Dave? Without my dreams?"

"Maybe I've got to find out. At least you've got those dreams. They're always with you."

She looked away suddenly. "Dreaming is a pretty lonely thing when there's nobody to tell them to."

"You'll find somebody."

"No I won't." She seemed suddenly decided. "Dave, I won't let you leave me like this. I won't let you."

He fumbled for a pack of cigarettes and wondered why the thing was suddenly being so difficult. For two years of wanderings, she had been nothing but a woman, a paid companion who ate with him and slept with him and remembered her dreams. He had always been the boss of the situation, always knowing in the back of his mind that the day of their parting would sometime come. He had needed her, but only because there was no one else for him to need.

"What will you do about it?" he asked, suddenly angered at her resistance.

"I think I'd turn you in to the police before I'd let you go, Dave. I really mean it."

And he could see by her eyes that she did.

The next two nights were difficult ones for Dave. He was still meeting Susan Brogare secretly, but there was a feeling about the thing that made him think of a water-soaked log being pulled slowly into the vortex of a whirlpool. He knew now that this girl—this woman—would accompany him anywhere, to Florida or the moon. And he knew, just as certainly, that Helen Reston would not simply pack up and leave. He was involved, deeply involved, with two women, and both of them had the knowledge to destroy him.

But he'd known, almost from their first meeting, that the strangeness of Susan would attract and entrap him. She was fascinating and mysterious, with a sense of reckless adventure that matched his own. And it was to Susan that he brought his problem on that fifth night. "I can't shake her," he said. "She's threatening to tell the police."

But the dark-haired girl only looked at him through half-closed eyes, and blew smoke from her nose like some dragon of old. "You ought to be able to think of something," she said quietly, and he wondered what she might have been implying. Neither of them dared to put the thought into words, but that night in bed, Dave Krown dreamed about the service station attendant he had shot back in Illinois.

The next day Helen was calmed down a bit, and, for the first time, made no mention of their long-delayed journey to Florida. She left for work early, and he didn't see her the rest of the day. He began to feel good, so good that he even ventured a stroll past the firehouse for the first time since the holdup. An unusual February warmth was in the air, and a few of the firemen sat outside talking and waiting, as firemen do. Dave nodded to them as he went by.

And later that night, in his car, he told Susan, "She's better today."

"Do you think she'll let you go?"

"Well . . . no."

"Then something has to be done."

"We could just leave."

"And have her tell the police?"

"She would be implicating herself if she did," he argued, but he knew deep within himself that such a possibility would not deter Helen. In the two years they'd traveled together, he'd come to know the streak of unreasoning vengeance that slept just beneath the surface of her personality. She was not always the simple, stupid girl she seemed.

Susan stubbed out her cigarette. "I want you, Dave. All my life I've had the things I really wanted taken away from me. I knew I wanted you from that first moment in the firehouse, and I'm not going to lose you."

"You won't," he said. "I'll think of something."

Helen was quiet that night, preoccupied. And the following day was much the same. She puttered about the apartment for a time, and once asked him if he had decided what to do. He replied that they would be moving on soon, and left it at that. But he found himself watching her when her back was turned, watching and nurturing the growing hatred within him.

"Dave," she said to him suddenly, "I'm tired of sitting around this apartment alone every night. I want you to take me out to dinner."

"Dinner? When?"

"Tomorrow night. And at some nice place out in the country. The Willow Grove, maybe."

"I don't even know if they're open in the winter."

"They're open."

"O.K. We'll see."

He told Susan that night, explaining his commitment for the following evening. They were at a little neighborhood bar on the far side of town, a place she had introduced him to a few nights before. She was impatient, constantly lighting cigarettes and stubbing them out only half-smoked.

"You've got to do something, Dave. I can't stand this town any longer."

"Just be patient, will you? We've hardly known each other a week."

"I've known you for a lifetime," she said, and lit another cigarette.

After a time a thought crossed his mind, and he asked her, "Did you ever destroy that letter? The one you left in the office?" It was the first time he had referred to it since she'd told him about it.

"I'll bring it along when we leave this town," she told him. "Don't worry."

"I'm not."

She rested her hand on his. "Dave—if it has to be done, please do it. For me."

He knew what she meant, and somehow the cold calculation of her voice did not surprise him. He was in so deep already that nothing surprised him any longer.

When he awakened in the morning, one sandy eyeball pressed against the wrinkled white of the sheet, he saw that Helen was already up. She was standing at the window smoking a cigarette, and he could see at once that she was upset.

"What's the trouble?" he asked.

"I had a dream, Dave. A terrible dream!"

He propped himself up on an elbow, looked around for his cigarettes, and then decided he didn't need one. "Tell me about it."

"I don't know how to—it was so awful! We were—we were at a bar someplace. Up in the mountains, I think. Just the two of us. After a while I went to the ladies' room, and when I came out you were gone, just gone! You had left me there, all by myself! I was frantic and I ran outside. A car came from somewhere and hit me. That's when I woke up, just as the car hit me."

"Crazy dream," he said.

"It was awful."

"Well, forget about it now."

She had put down the cigarette and was twisting her hands together. "Dave—"

"What?"

"Dave, it was you driving the car."

"Helen, pull yourself together. It was only a dream."

He showered, shaved, and dressed in silence, trying to keep his hands from shaking, trying not to think about the black shape forming, growing, in his mind. It was a full hour before he could bring himself to ask her about their plans for the evening. "Still want to go out to dinner?"

"Of course. I'm counting on it."

"Good," he said. "I think it will help us both."

Neither of them mentioned the dream again. There was no need.

The Willow Grove was, in the off-season, a dark and almost deserted place that stood by itself next to a seldom-traveled country road. The willows, that had given the place its name in some far distant past, were almost gone now, felled by blight and age and an ever-expanding parking lot. Dave imagined that the summer customers on a Saturday night would crowd the walls to bursting, but in February there were only a few tables of scattered diners, and a dimness of illumination that unintentionally directed the eye to the glowing cigarette machine that was the brightest single spot in view.

Dave had parked far back in the nearly deserted lot, and inside he led Helen to a table a bit out of the way. They chatted through dinner with a rapport that was almost like the old days, though he was not completely unaware of the occasional strain between them.

"The food is always good here," he said once, when the conversation threatened to lag.

"We've only been here once before."

"Still, it's good. Want another drink?"

"I guess not. What time is it?"

"A little before nine. Why? Got a late date?" He said it with a chuckle, but she did seem edgy about something. She had kept her coat over her shoulders, the new red one with the black speckles that matched her hair, but he thought still that he detected a shiver. "Are you getting a cold?"

"I don't think so, honey. I'm just nervous, I guess. I'd like to get out of here, head south."

The Night My Friend

"Then you couldn't wear the coat."

"No kidding, Dave, when are we going?"

"I don't know."

"Are you still thinking of leaving me?"

"Let's talk about it on the way home," he said, postponing the conversation.

Coffee came, and an after-dinner drink. Finally, Helen excused herself while he motioned for the check. He watched her go off in the direction of the ladies' room, and sat for some moments wondering whether he could really go through with it. Then, almost reluctantly, he rose from the table and started for the door. It was just five minutes after nine, by the clock in the checkroom.

Outside, his breath white against the night air, he climbed behind the wheel of the car and started the motor. He turned the car a bit, into position, aiming it down the driveway like a torpedo.

He waited, the motor purring, ready for a touch of his foot on the pedal. Waited for Helen to come running out.

As in the dream.

But then perhaps all of life was but a dream, and Dave Krown, sitting in the dark, was only a vision conjured up by nightmare. Perhaps all this would pass, as it had the night he'd shot the man in the gas station, halfway across the country.

Had he ever died, finally? Don't we all die, finally?

Helen, Helen . . . forgive me.

And there she was, running out of the doorway, her new red coat bundled against the cold, black hair barely visible over the fuzzy collar. His foot went down and the car shot ahead.

Forgive me, Helen.

He closed his eyes at the last instant, feeling rather than seeing the thud and crunch of metal against flesh.

"It was an accident," he kept saying over and over. "I didn't see her. It was an accident!"

Someone had covered the body with a tablecloth from inside, and far in the distance he could hear the beginnings of an approaching siren. One of the bartenders stepped forward through the sparse crowd of onlookers. "He's right. I saw the whole thing through the window. This dame came tearing out and ran right out in front of him, He couldn't have stopped for her."

One or two others mumbled in agreement, and Dave began to relax for the first time. He still averted his eyes from the sprawled, broken body, though, even after the first police car pulled into the parking lot.

"She dead?" the officer asked, reaching for the clipboard he kept on the dash.

"She's dead."

"Anybody here know her?" he asked, his voice reflecting the professional's only half-concealed boredom with death.

"I knew her," Dave started to reply. "Her name was Helen . . ."

He stopped, the words frozen in his throat like a lump of suddenly congealed sweat. There in the doorway, not twenty feet away, stood Helen Reston. There was a slight smile playing about her lips, and of course she wasn't wearing her coat.

"This the woman you know?" the officer asked, lifting the tablecloth and turning the head for a better view in the sparse lighting of the parking lot.

Dave didn't answer. He knew without looking that the dead woman at his feet had become, fantastically, not Helen, but his Susan.

"Driver's license in her purse says her name is Susan Brogare. Looks like she worked at the Motor Vehicle Bureau. She the one you knew?" the officer queried.

"I knew her," Dave answered mechanically.

"Well, you'll have to come along with me for questioning. Just routine, you know."

He nodded, then asked, "Can I speak to a friend over there for a moment?"

"Sure. I got all the time in the world."

Dave pushed his way through the people and walked over to Helen in the doorway. "What did you do? God help us, what did you do?"

The smile, if it was a smile, still played about her lips. "I called her, told her I had to see her. I said I knew all about you two and had reached a decision. She met me in the ladies' room at nine o'clock. I told her she could have you, told her you were waiting in the parking lot to take her away. I even gave her the coat, because I said you wanted her to have it. She ran out there to meet you."

"But—but you knew I'd be waiting to—"

"I knew, Dave."

"There never was a dream, was there? You made it all up. You knew just what I would do."

"I've always known what you would do, Dave. And there have never been any dreams, not really."

"No dreams," he repeated, not understanding. Understanding only that this woman before him had depths of which he had never dreamed—depths of wisdom, and hate.

"You'll get off," she said, "It was an accident."

"Sure." But he was remembering the letter, the damning letter, Susan had written on that day so long ago, a week ago. The letter that would send him to the electric chair.

"I couldn't let you go, Dave. I couldn't."

"How did you know about her?"

"I said I didn't dream, Dave. I never have. But you talk in your sleep. You've talked in your sleep every night for two years."

Behind him, like a voice from a dream, the police officer said, "Come on, mister. We'd better get going."

In Some Secret Place

I was almost too young to remember it, and certainly too young to understand it all, but that July weekend of Uncle Ben's funeral has stayed with me through all these years. Perhaps, by putting the words down on paper, I can expel the demon from my memory. At the very least I may be able to clarify my own thinking on those awful events.

The farm that Uncle Ben had worked alone since his wife's death was a great sprawling sort of place, stretching out on both sides of the dusty road that bisected it. He'd planted crops on only a small portion of the land closest to the house, preferring to leave the rest for grazing or for timberlands that might prove valuable in his old age. Thus it was that Uncle Ben rarely visited some parts of the vast farmlands.

That summer, that July, we'd seen very little of him. My mother and father were busy with other things and I'd reached the mid-grammar school age when a trip to the beach twenty miles away was much more exciting than a journey over the hill to Uncle Ben's farm. So it was with a special sense of shock that the midnight phone call reached my father. I remember even then the deep dread I felt at the unknown, and I remember the next morning when my mother dressed me in my only Sunday suit with a lecture that I was to act like a perfect gentleman for the next few days. Then we waited on the front porch in the shade until my father came by for us with the car.

I could see at once, even with my youthful eyes, that the death of his brother had greatly upset my father. He barely spoke during the brief trip up to the farm, and he handled the old Packard as if he'd never driven it before.

"How did it happen?" my mother asked him once.

"Fell off the tractor and hit his head on a rock. Mike Simpson found him out in the field after dark, when he heard the tractor still running."

That was as much as he said, and the rest of the trip was completed in silence. Overhead, the sun had retreated behind a vast grey cloud that stretched beyond the horizon.

I'd never seen so many people at Uncle Ben's farm before. The driveway that led past the house and back to the barn was lined with cars and a few wagons. Even the county's dirt road out front was almost blocked by the vehicles. I recognized only a few of them, and decided at once that I wouldn't enjoy myself here today.

A group of the men were standing in a circle near the barn, listening to Mike Simpson. He was probably telling them how he'd found Uncle Ben out by the tractor and I wanted to hear it, but my mother hustled me inside. There the women were gathered, somber already in black, speaking in whispers about the tragedy.

My Aunt Mary, a large woman married to a balding banker from a nearby town, came over to take mother's hand. "A terrible shock, Barbara. He was so young!"

"Are they having the wake here, Mary?" my mother asked.

Aunt Mary nodded. "The undertaker will have him back tonight, and the funeral will be on Monday."

My mother sighed deeply. "It will be a hard weekend for us all. Tom told us on the way over that he fell off the tractor and hit his head on a rock."

Aunt Mary dropped her voice to a whisper I could barely hear. "That's what they say, but my God! Ben never fell off a tractor in his life. He was only forty-three, still in the prime of life."

"What do you think did happen then?"

"Ever since his wife died he'd taken to drink. That's no secret. I think he'd had too much, and then out there in that sun . . ."

"He was your brother, Mary," my mother admonished.

"I'd say the same thing about anyone, if it was true. Ben was a good man, but he drank."

My mother seemed suddenly to remember my presence at her side. "Run out and play, David," she told me. "But don't get dirty and stay away from the animals."

I let the screen door bang behind me, happy to be out of that house with its blanket of whisper and gloom. As I ran across the barnyard toward the freedom of the open fields beyond, one or two of the men called out to me, but I kept on going. My father was with Mike Simpson and the others, and if he noticed my going he didn't seem to mind. The Simpson farm was right next to Uncle Ben's, and as I ran across the field I saw the deserted tractor still parked where it had stopped, near the wire fence that was the property line.

I started toward the tractor, to investigate it with the curiosity of childhood, but then turned quickly away. A tall lean figure had risen from the shadows behind it, and I recognized the familiar tanned face of Sheriff Yates. I wondered what he was looking for, but I knew better than to go any closer. Sheriff Yates was a terrifying figure at any time, and there was something about him just then—rising from behind Uncle Ben's tractor—that sent a special chill down my spine.

They brought Uncle Ben's body back that night, and I watched the arrival of the distant hearse with a feeling of unreality that only distance could achieve. It was a hot night, although the sun was low in the western sky, and even on the hill that was my vantage point only a little breeze was stirring.

I stayed up there until my mother called, and returned there early the next morning—after a hurried embarrassed prayer before the open coffin. I was too young to have a full sense of death, and the man in the coffin was not the Uncle Ben I'd known for all of my brief life. He was not really a man at all, but only a thing to be buried in the ground like so much waste.

But from the hill, all was different. I could see the entire stretch of Uncle Ben's property, all the way to the tin-roofed sugar shack in the distant corner, where maple syrup was brewed each spring. I could see the rolling hills and the lush farmlands, the wooded patches and even the swampy stretch where industrious beavers had dammed a meandering stream. To me just then, it seemed like the world.

I'd been playing on the hill most of that afternoon, watching the distant comings and goings with detached interest, when I spotted a vaguely familiar figure coming out of the farmhouse. The first thing I recognized was the great waving bush of red hair, flaming in the afternoon sunlight, and then the swift-paced gait, almost like a horse moving at a trot. It was my Uncle Charlie, up from New Orleans, and in that instant I hated to admit that I'd completely forgotten about the logic of his coming for his brother's funeral.

Uncle Charlie was one of those rare figures that appears all too briefly in every boy's life. He was the youngest of the three brothers, and younger than my Aunt Mary too. In my earlier days I'd often thought of him in dashing pirate garb, sailing out of New Orleans to plunder the vast Spanish Main—which was down there somewhere. Now, vaguely aware that he was only some sort of warehouse supervisor, I still treasured my ideal. After all, perhaps he was only a pirate on weekends.

"David! David, my boy! Where are you?"

He was calling to me, searching the landscape for some sign of me. And all at once I didn't want to hide any more. Here was Uncle Charlie, my one friend in all the world, filling the void left by Uncle Ben's going, the void that even my own father had never quite been able to comprehend.

"Here, Uncle Charlie," I called out, standing up and brushing the bits of dead grass from my knees.

"Were you hiding from your old Uncle?" he asked when he'd joined me atop the hill. He was puffing with the uncommon exertion, but his wild red hair was as dashing and youthful as I remembered.

"No. I was just sick of it."

"You shouldn't be," he said, gripping me about the shoulders with his bear-like arms. "I know it's not much fun for a ten-year-old boy, but your Uncle Ben only dies once and he's entitled to a little respect."

"I liked him," I admitted. "But not as much as you, Uncle Charlie. Why don't you come more often?"

"New Orleans is a good distance away, boy, I can't be coming up here every month, much as I'd like to. Come on now—tell me what you've been doing with yourself."

"Not much," I admitted a bit guiltily. With Uncle Charlie you always had to be doing something, because he was. "I flew my kite a bit."

"Ah, there's a sport." He was down on the grass and pulled me with him. "Did I ever tell you about kite-flying down in Trinidad? No? Well, they sure do take it serious down there. Grown men fly them, and they try to cut the strings on other kites and capture them. Sometimes they put slivers of glass in the tails of their kites, or glue ground glass to the kite string itself, so it cuts through the other strings. Men have been killed flying kites in Trinidad. I even hear that it's illegal now, but then all the really great sports are illegal now."

"You know everything, Uncle Charlie."

"I get around a lot, boy. And I keep my eyes and ears open. That's how you learn in this here world. Ben and Mary and your Dad stayed here, close to home, but I went south to see a little of this world. I guess that's really been the difference between us all these years."

"Did you like Uncle Ben?" I asked, for no special reason.

Uncle Charlie shrugged. "He was my brother." He lit a cigarette and stared out at the changing sky for a time. Then, all at once, he was on his feet. "Come on, kid. Let's go back to the house."

"What for?"

"What for? Well, because your Mom and Dad will be wondering about you, that's what for. Come on."

He took my hand and pulled me along, and I went because it was Uncle Charlie.

But at the base of the hill we were met by a tall, slender woman of about Uncle Charlie's age. It was Thelma Brook, a landmark in the town, editor of its weekly newspaper, keeper of its conscience. She'd always been around, and though she couldn't have been over forty she seemed to me like a hundred. "Hello, Charlie," she said, ignoring me as she did all children.

"Hello, Thelma. Still at the old grind?"

"Yes, if you mean the paper. And I've got a deadline Monday noon."

"So?"

"Sheriff Yates just told me your brother was murdered, Charlie. Have you got anything to say about it? For publication?"

We found the sheriff holding court under an apple tree, a broad hat brim shielding his face from the sun. My father was already there, and so was Aunt Mary. They were listening to the lawman's words with expressions of disbelief mingled with fear. Suddenly the day seemed very hot.

"Murdered," Sheriff Yates repeated. "I'm sure of it. I was at a political dinner in the next county Thursday night, so I didn't get to see the body or the area till yesterday. But a couple of things struck me as awfully odd right away. Ben was a good man with a tractor, not likely to fall off. Besides, what would a stone that size be doing in a plowed field? Ben would have carted it off before he started working with the tractor. Another thing—the cows were all milked, so he must have gone out in the field after supper. Did you ever know Ben to do his plowing after supper?"

They had to admit they didn't. "He couldn't have finished the field before dark," David's father said.

"That's right," Yates agreed, warming to his role of sleuth. "He never believed in plowing by his headlights. Besides, go out and look over the field. Part of it's already plowed, but nothing's been done where the tractor is. In fact the plow isn't even hooked up to the tractor. Why would he take the tractor out in the middle of the field just before dark? The answer is that he wouldn't. It was moved there by the killer to make the thing look like an accident."

"I don't know," my father mumbled. "Who'd want to kill him?"

"I have my ideas about that too," the sheriff said. "But I need a little more evidence."

Thelma Brook had joined the little group with pencil poised, and there was a general movement to break up. Uncle Charlie steered me into the house behind my father and Aunt Mary, before I could break away for the safety of the hills. Mother was in the kitchen with some of the other ladies, preparing a light supper for those who had stayed through the day, and Aunt Mary clucked a few words to indicate her willingness to assist at the task. The men wandered together into the sitting room to continue their discussion.

I stayed in the kitchen, because the food was there and I was beginning to get hungry. Nibbling on a plate of cold sandwiches when nobody was looking, I heard my Aunt Mary say, "You know where that boy of yours was all afternoon? Up on the hill with Charlie."

My mother frowned at me from across the kitchen. "Were you, David?"

Before I could reply, Aunt Mary was talking again. "It hardly seems to me that Charlie is fit company for a growing boy. He's my own brother, but heaven knows I've never missed him since he went South. You know that wild talk of his. It's bad for a growing boy."

"I like Uncle Charlie," I answered defensively. "I like him better than anyone else in the world."

"What's going on here?" my father asked, coming into the room behind me.

"Charlie," my mother said with a sigh, as if that explained everything.

"Haven't we got enough trouble without getting into a fight over Charlie, for God's sake? Ben was his brother too, and he has every right to be here."

I saw my opportunity and I took it, running through the open screen door to the freedom of the fields once more. My father called to me but I kept running until I saw Uncle Charlie ahead, strolling toward the line of cars with Mike Simpson from the next farm.

"I never enter a dry county without coming prepared," Uncle Charlie was saying. "I've got a bottle in my car."

"Moonshine?" Simpson asked.

"You fooling?" Uncle Charlie seemed insulted at the suggestion. "It's bonded rye whiskey, up from New Orleans. The stuff they serve in the finest clubs."

They sat in the car with the door open and I saw Uncle Charlie pass him the bottle. "It's good stuff, all right," Mike Simpson admitted reluctantly. "You know how to live, Charlie. You always did."

"I knew enough to get out of this town, at least. But tell me—what's the story on my brother?"

"How do you mean?"

"Did someone really kill him?"

"No. That Yates is crazy. Ben didn't have an enemy in the world, and no money to speak of. Why would anyone kill him?"

"Was anybody else around the farm Thursday night?"

"Not a soul! I seen him working around, plowing in the afternoon, milking the cows—like he always did ever since his wife died. After supper he took the tractor out in the field for something."

"To plow?"

"The plow wasn't attached."

"Why else would he go out there in the evening with the tractor?"

"How should I know? Anyway, he went, and a lot later—after dark— I heard the motor of the tractor still running. Naturally I was worried, because he didn't have the tractor lights on or anything. I climbed over the fence and walked out to it and I found him dead. He'd fallen off and hit his head on that big rock."

"What did you do then?"

"I turned off the tractor and ran back to the house to phone. I called the sheriff first but he was out of town."

"Why'd you stop to turn off the tractor?"

"I don't know. I just did." He took another drink from the bottle. "What difference does it make?"

"None, I suppose," Uncle Charlie said. He brushed a hand through his long red hair and beckoned to me. "David, my boy, let's us walk a bit."

We left Mike Simpson in the car with the bottle. He was happy there.

"It might rain before morning," my uncle told me as we walked. "See those clouds in the west?"

I saw them, but I had other things on my mind. "You think Uncle Ben was really murdered like the sheriff said?"

"I don't know, boy." There was a breeze coming up, and he cupped his hands to light a cigarette. "Let's take a look at that tractor ourselves."

The Night My Friend

It sat where I'd last seen it, next to the fatal rock, a great smooth thing that seemed almost the size of a man. The rock had been there for many years, but Uncle Ben had never before plowed over that far. Perhaps he hadn't planned to this year either. "Can you start the tractor?" I asked.

He turned the switch and ground the starter into life, but it died almost immediately. "Out of gas." Hopping from the driver's seat, he noticed some stains on the earth and bent to investigate.

"What is it?" I asked. "Sheriff Yates was out looking at it yesterday too."

"Gasoline, I think. Soaked into the earth, but there are still traces left."

"Why?"

"A good question. Always a good question, my boy. Granting that Ben would have no reason for letting the gas out of his tank, that means someone else did. A murderer, perhaps?"

"I don't like it here, Uncle Charlie. Let's walk."

It was getting toward dusk, but we walked a long way, back across fields I hadn't visited that summer, through woods that were only vague playgrounds in my memory. We talked of many things as we strolled, of the time when Uncle Charlie had been running rum across the waters from Cuba, of the time when he'd flown a battered biplane for revolutionary forces in Central America. I think I believed him then, every word he said. I think I still believe him.

"There's the sugar shack," he said at last. "We've walked a long way."

I remembered the sugar shack, with its tin roof and corrugated walls. In my summers on the farm it had always been my secret place. "Let's go in, Uncle Charlie."

"It's getting dark."

"Just for a minute."

"All right."

But even the secret place was not as I remembered it. The great metal tubs had given way to a maze of serpentine tubes I'd never seen before. "It's all changed!" I told Uncle Charlie.

"I see that it is. Were you up here for the syrup season in the spring?" He was inspecting the new arrangements with a great deal of care.

"Sure. That was the last time. In April before Easter."

There was a crinkling sound behind us, and I whirled in frightened anticipation of a bear or some other beast. But it was Sheriff Yates, ducking his head to enter through the low doorway. The revolver on his hip caught the last reflections of the dying sun and then he was with us in the gloom. "What have we here?" he asked, not really addressing either of us.

"I don't know," Uncle Charlie said in reply, trying to look casual. "Sugar shack, I guess."

"But not for maple syrup," the sheriff observed. He reached under a table and pulled a battered kerosene lantern into view. After a moment's fumbling to light the wick, he held it up for a better view of the sugar shack. "It's a still—for moonshine. And I think that gives us our motive for the murder."

The next day was Sunday, and I was bundled off to church before I'd had time to fully digest the events of the preceding day. When I'd been taken home, Uncle Charlie and Sheriff Yates were deep in conversation about the discovery of the still, but I had no idea just what it all meant. Did they think that Uncle Ben had been a moonshiner? My mother was tired and father was cross so I mentioned nothing to either of them about the discovery. There'd be time enough for that tomorrow.

But after church and a hurried breakfast I was lectured about staying away from Uncle Charlie. Then we all hustled back to the wake with a guilty air of tardy school kids. Already the house was crowded with local farm families who'd been unwilling or unable to come on a weekday, and over everything hung an air of mourning mixed with muffled merriment. Old friends greeted each other, children were shown off to half-forgotten relatives, and reminiscences were exchanged amidst only slightly suppressed gaiety.

Aunt Mary cornered my father almost immediately, pinning him in the corner with her bulk. "Sheriff Yates wants us all to stay around tonight. He says his investigation's just about complete and he wants to talk to us."

"More about Ben being murdered? I'm still not convinced. All Yates is doing is giving a couple of pages of gossip to Thelma Brook's newspaper."

As if on cue, Thelma Brook materialized above me, notebook in hand. "Did I hear my name mentioned?" she asked sweetly.

I glanced around for Uncle Charlie, but he was nowhere to be seen. I knew he'd been staying at the weather-beaten old building that served as a hotel in town, and perhaps he'd overslept. Or perhaps he was off somewhere with Sheriff Yates again.

It was not until mid-afternoon that he appeared, driving the familiar car up the long rutted driveway. "How are you, boy?" he shouted, and I dropped the stick I'd been playing with to run and greet him.

"I missed you, Uncle Charlie. Where've you been?"

"Around. Talking to people."

"To the sheriff?"

"Some. I have to drive into town. Want to come along?"

"Sure." I piled into the car next to him, pleased at the horrified expression glimpsed on Aunt Mary's face as we pulled out of the drive. That was worth the whole three days to me. That, and the exhilarating feeling of sitting next to him as we bumped over the dirt roads at a speed my father would never attempt.

The town was sleepy on a Sunday afternoon, and the dust raised by our arrival seemed to hang unmoving in the muggy air. "I think it's going to rain," Uncle Charlie observed, though there wasn't yet a cloud in the sky.

We parked before the old hotel, and I waited while Uncle Charlie chatted a bit with the balding desk clerk. They seemed to be talking about something to drink, about moonshine, and after a time the desk clerk accepted a folded bill from Uncle Charlie and disappeared into the office. When he returned he carried a brown paper bag. My uncle thanked him and we left.

"Is it moonshine?" I asked when we were back in the car, full of the thrill of illicit excitement.

He opened the bag and showed me a mason jar full of an almost colorless liquid. "It's moonshine, boy."

"Is your own stuff all gone?"

"No, I just wanted to see how easy I could buy some of this. Come on, we'll go back now."

"Was Uncle Ben making moonshine?"

He chuckled at that. "Your Uncle Ben wouldn't even take a drink except on Christmas and his birthday."

I had so many questions to ask that I finally decided to just keep quiet. Back at the farm, Sheriff Yates had reappeared, chewing on a damp cigar that seemed somehow out of place. The crowd had dwindled a bit, except for a group of close and near relatives that clustered about the undertaker making plans for the following morning's funeral procession. Who was coming, who was driving, who was riding with whom. The ritual for the dead.

In the evening, when it became obvious that no other mourners would journey up the hill to pay their respects, Sheriff Yates called everyone inside. I was not included, but it was easy to take up a position outside the open sitting room window, where the night breeze ruffled the old lace curtains with irregular persistence.

"All right," Sheriff Yates began, clearing his throat and glancing about the room. "Is everybody here?"

Everybody was there. My mother and father, Aunt Mary, Uncle Charlie, Thelma Brook with her pad and pencil, and a couple of others. The only one missing seemed to be Mike Simpson from the next farm. I wondered about that, since he'd been the one who found the body.

"Get on with it," Uncle Charlie said, leaning against the wall.

"Well, I've already talked to some of you about this thing, and about the reasons why I think Ben was murdered. He wasn't plowing—there was no reason for his tractor to be where it was, especially at that time of night. And the presence of that big rock was just too much of a coincidence for me to swallow. I discovered something else yesterday—the old sugar shack at the rear of Ben's property had been converted into a still. Somebody was making moonshine back there."

I heard my mother gasp at the news, and Aunt Mary started to say something, but Sheriff Yates hurried on. "There were two possibilities, of course. Either Ben was making the stuff, or someone else was. I think you'll all agree that it's not the sort of thing a man like Ben would do. Besides, everyone knows he never goes back that way except in the spring. It would be easy for someone else to set up the still and work it without being discovered. Easy, that is, for someone who lived nearby and knew Ben's comings and goings. Someone who could be discovered on Ben's land without arousing undue suspicion."

It was Thelma Brook who spoke the name that must have been on all their lips. "Mike Simpson!"

Sheriff Yates nodded. "Mike Simpson. He could sneak over from his farm any time and get back to the sugar shack. Only I guess Ben must have discovered it at last and threatened to expose him. So Mike Simpson killed Ben and made it look like an accident."

"I can't believe it," Aunt Mary whispered.

"There was one piece of evidence that convinced me his story of finding the body was a lie," Sheriff Yates went on. "He said he was attracted by the sound of the tractor's motor, and that he turned it off after finding the body. But the tractor couldn't be moved because it was out of gas. He couldn't have heard the motor, because there was no gas in the tank to run it!"

There was a mumble of assent at that. "Maybe we'd better ask him some questions about that still," my father said.

The sheriff seemed to agree. "His lights are on. I'm going over now and confront him with the evidence. If he won't come back and answer some questions, I'm going to arrest him on suspicion."

The Night My Friend

I watched the sheriff's lean figure move through the dark toward the farmhouse some hundred yards away. The others were waiting inside, and I was surprised to see Uncle Charlie suddenly appear at my side. "Damn it, boy," he muttered.

"What's the matter, Uncle Charlie?"

"I've been a fool, that's what's the matter. Stay here!"

But of course I didn't. I sprinted after him across the yard, seeing at once that he was following the sheriff toward the lights of Mike Simpson's farmhouse. Suddenly they were the only lights in a night of darkness, and there was something terribly urgent about reaching them.

But Sheriff Yates was there first, just inside the doorway, and as Uncle Charlie hurled himself up the porch steps the dull crack of a single shot split the quiet of the night. I reached the doorway an instant behind Uncle Charlie, just as the sheriff whirled around from Mike Simpson's crumpled body to cover us with his revolver.

"You damned murderer!" my uncle shouted. "A second sooner and I'd have stopped your devilish scheme!"

Sheriff Yates was sweating, but the gun in his hand was steady as a rock. "He was resisting arrest. I had to kill him."

"Resisting arrest without a weapon? You didn't have time to plant one on him."

"Why would I want to kill him?" the sheriff asked.

"Because he was your partner in that illegal still, and you saw this as a good chance to get him out of the way. A perfect crime—the victim shot by the sheriff while resisting arrest for murder."

"He was a murderer. He killed Ben."

But my uncle only shook his head. "Nobody killed Ben. He fell off the tractor accidentally, just like everybody thought. With all your flowery theories, everybody missed the most obvious explanation. He was out in the field with the tractor after supper simply because he was trying to move that very rock on which he fell. I suppose he wanted to clear it out for the next day's plowing, but somehow he lost his footing and hit his head on it. A simple accident and nothing more, until you heard of it and decided to twist it into a killing so you could murder Mike Simpson."

"What about the empty gas tank on the tractor?"

"A foolish thing, really. David here even saw you letting out the gasoline Friday, but of course he didn't realize what you were doing. It became a clue only to an illogical mind like your own, Yates. You wanted to prove that Simpson couldn't have heard the motor running—but if Simpson was really the killer he'd hardly have made up the story. And he certainly wouldn't have gone so far as to say he turned off the motor. He could have easily explained the empty tank by saying he left it running. No, he told the truth. You were the one who emptied the tank onto the ground to try and disprove his story."

The gun came up an inch. "You think they'll believe you?"

"They'll believe that the still couldn't have existed without your knowledge. When I—a stranger in town—could walk up to the hotel desk clerk and buy a jar of moonshine with no questions asked, the thing is pretty much out in the open. You must have known it, and you certainly knew about the still in the sugar shack."

"Who says so? I just followed you two back there yesterday."

"You walked into that dim shack and immediately reached under a table for a lantern none of us could see. You knew it was there because you'd been working the still with Simpson."

From somewhere in the night there was a shout. It sounded like my father, and I prayed they'd come soon to investigate the shot they must have heard.

Sheriff Yates must have had the same thought. "That's enough talk," he said. "You're both goin' to have to die too. I'll say Simpson shot you both."

"With your gun? Don't be a fool!"

"I'm no fool. Simpson was, to think he could double-cross me on the take. I'm not goin' to prison for killing that swine."

I think he would have shot us then. His eyes were suddenly hard and cold and decided, and I knew I was looking at death. Then, faster than my eye could follow, Uncle Charlie's hand moved. One instant it was empty and then there was the silver flash of a knife blade. Sheriff Yates stumbled backward, startled, and I saw that the weapon had found its mark in his throat.

"They killed each other," Uncle Charlie told the others later, while I stood silently in the corner. "Mike Simpson must have hurled his knife a second before the sheriff fired."

Thelma Brook's pencil was busy. "The sheriff died a brave man," she said, already composing the lead for her front-page story. Nobody disputed her, least of all Uncle Charlie.

My father wondered vaguely how Mike Simpson had ever obtained a knife that was made in Trinidad, but nobody wanted to ask too many questions. Uncle Charlie went away after the funeral, back to his job in New Orleans, and things began to settle into their familiar patterns.

I guess I was the only one in town who knew just what happened that night, but nobody ever asked me.

To Slay an Eagle

Augsheim that autumn was still a place only beginning to recover from the destructions of war. Coming in low on the airport approach, Emerson gazed out over the ruins and remembered how it had been. He remembered his first sight of the city, flare-lit at midnight as he streaked in over it in the lead bomber. He remembered especially the blaze from the fire bombs, destroying everything in its path. Circling that night and heading back for home, over the burning city, he never imagined he'd see it again, never imagined he'd want to return there to the wounded land whose scars he'd caused.

He didn't want to return now, but he had a job to do. A dirty job.

"November is a bad month anywhere," the girl said.

"Especially in Germany. Drizzle and fog and mist." Emerson lit an American cigarette and settled back in his chair.

"You've been here before?"

"To Augsheim? Only once, from the air. But I've seen Berlin and Munich. And Bonn, of course."

She was young and almost beautiful and her name was Mona Kirst. They'd met by careful prearrangement in a back street bar that catered to prostitutes.

"Augsheim used to be beautiful,"

she said, "before the war. I remember when I was only a child how I used to play in the park. Now it's only a mud hole, without flowers or even grass."

"It'll come back," he assured her. Then, glancing at his watch, he said, "Hadn't we better . . . ?"

"Yes." She finished her drink and rose to leave. Emerson followed. It was the most natural thing in the world in the place, at that time. Nobody even looked up.

Mona Kirst lived on the third floor of a sagging apartment house overlooking the mud hole she'd mentioned. Further down the block the steel skeleton of a new building was rising—the first visible sign of the phoenix which would come from this fire. "You were lucky," he remarked, following her up the stairs. "Not many buildings survived."

"Were any of us lucky? Really?"

They passed an old woman on the stairs, and a British soldier who seemed embarrassed. Both of them looked away as they passed. Then Mona unlocked the door at the top of the landing and they entered a dingy, dank room with a double bed and a battered kitchen set as its only furniture.

There was a man stretched out on the bed, fully clothed. His name was Visor, and Emerson had journeyed four thousand miles to meet him.

"Ah! You must be Emerson!" He rose to shake hands. "Do you have a word from Washington?"

Emerson had always thought passwords were foolish, but he said it anyway. "*The Sphinx is drowsy, her wings are furled.*"

Visor nodded. "*Her ear is heavy, she broods on the world.*" He motioned Emerson to sit on the bed. "A fitting quotation for someone with your name. How much did they tell you of the mission?"

Emerson looked at the girl. "What about her?"

Visor shrugged. He was a big man, and he did it well. "She was necessary for the meeting. In this neighborhood, no one pays any attention to a prostitute's customers. Not even if there are two at a time."

"I mean, can she be trusted?"

"She is my sister," Visor replied.

Emerson stared at the two of them, not knowing whether to believe it. Finally Visor motioned her into the bathroom. Emerson nodded to show his approval and started talking. "I was sent because of Eagle. That's all I know."

The big man nodded. He was close to fifty, more likely the girl's father than her brother. But it was obvious he'd been in the business a long time, and when he spoke he chose his words carefully. "As you may know, Eagle is the code name for an American army colonel. His name is Roger China, and he must be dead within forty-eight hours."

"All right."

"Washington tells me you're a good man, a killer. Have you ever worked in this area before?"

Emerson gazed out the window at the mud hole. "Yes. Once."

"Have you ever killed a fellow countryman before?"

"No."

"Then perhaps I should tell you something about Colonel China. Since the beginning of the occupation, he has looted German art treasures valued at something like two million dollars. The proceeds from this looting have gone to set up a neo-Nazi movement of highly dangerous potential. Unfortunately, and ironically, his fame as a war hero and his influence in Congress made his removal and court-martial extremely difficult. For urgent reasons of national security which even I do not fully understand, the verdict of Washington is that Colonel China must be removed."

Emerson nodded. "You don't need to tell me any more."

They shook hands. Then Visor added, "There's one other thing."

"Yes?"

"It must look like an accident."

Emerson was staying at a small hotel a mile across town from Mona Kirst's room. When he returned there, the sky to the west had taken on a sort of glow, diffusing the pale light of the full moon through a layer of mist. He'd flown many missions under a moon like that, skimming over the ice-blue clouds with a sense of power he couldn't put into words. All was silent in his world above the clouds, and even the bomber's roar muffled by the sands of night. It was a world he hoped to recapture someday, somewhere.

"This is a man to see you," the balding little desk clerk told him. "Over there."

Emerson turned to see a stocky, middle-aged German standing by the side of the desk. He had a folded newspaper stuffed into one pocket of his topcoat. "Mister Emerson? I've been waiting for you." He spoke English well, but with a strong accent.

"Yes?" Emerson's muscles tensed. Had Colonel China somehow heard of his mission?

"My name is Burkherdt, and I'm with the *Augsheim Zeitung.* I would like an interview."

Emerson raised an eyebrow. "Do all American businessmen rate newspaper interviews?"

The stocky man squinted and shook his head. He needed a shave. "All, no. But you are something special, are you not? You led the bombing raid in Augsheim in the final days of the war."

"Oh?"

"Now can we talk in private?"

Emerson glanced at the room clerk still hovering behind his desk and motioned toward a little bar off the lobby. "How about in there?"

The bartender frowned as they entered. "It's late," he said. "We close in ten minutes."

Emerson laid a bill on the bar. "That's all right. One drink and then leave us alone. We just want to talk."

The reporter slipped off his topcoat and tossed it over a chair. Underneath, his suit was rumpled and stained. He gave the appearance of a man without a woman's care, a man no longer interested in his appearance. "So you came back to see the city, Mr. Emerson."

"The reporters on the *Augsheim Zeitung* are very alert. How did you know about me?" There was no sense denying it at this point, and the web of a plan was beginning to form in Emerson's mind. Perhaps he could use this reporter's story to reach Colonel China.

"I researched an article on the bombing raid last year. Your name appears in the Air Force's official history. I was checking airport arrivals this morning and I recognized your name on the passenger list. Simple, no?"

"I suppose so. What do you want, Burkherdt?"

"A story. What does any newspaperman ever want? Why did you come back—to see the place?"

"Perhaps you might say that, I suppose. I had an interest in it, and I heard they were rebuilding here."

"Rebuilding, yes. All Europe is rebuilding this November. Have you seen the ruins?"

"I've seen them."

"Like Rome, no? Or ancient Greece?"

"Not exactly."

"You are out of the Air Force now?"

Emerson nodded. "I've been out for almost two years."

The stocky man was making notes on the back of an old envelope. "I was in it, you know—in the bombing. My wife, too. She was horribly burned."

"I'm sorry."

"She was a Catholic. Religion never meant much to me, but that night she died . . . She was begging me to kill her at the end, to put her out of her pain. I knew it was against her religion. I sat there for two hours holding her hand, just talking to her, making her want to live again. When finally she overcame the pain enough to say she still wanted to live, only then did I give her the release of death. The sin, if there was a sin, would be on my soul, not hers."

Emerson looked at his hands. "A lot of innocent people died in the war."

Burkherdt nodded sadly. "But you helped to end the war. They say Hitler himself flew over the city on the morning after the bombing, looking down at the fires that still were burning. Perhaps it was then that he knew it was hopeless."

"Look, what do you want of me?"

"Only your observations on the city, Mr. Emerson. What do you see of Augsheim now, three years after you destroyed it?"

"I see a city trying to rebuild itself, trying and seeming to succeed. I see a city far from dead. I see. . . . hell, what do you want me to see? If I hadn't led that bombing raid, someone else would have!"

Burkherdt scratched his bristled face. "Of course, of course. Tell me, do you ever dream about them? About the people who burned to death in Augsheim?"

"No. I never dream."

"They say that killing people from ten thousand feet is different from killing them face-to-face. They say it's an impersonal thing, with no feeling afterward. Did you find it so?"

"There are feelings," Emerson said, aware that his palms were sweating. "There were for me, anyway."

"Feelings, but no dreams."

"I think you've got enough," Emerson said, getting to his feet. "They're closing now."

"You haven't finished your drink. Just one or two more questions, please. Are you married?"

"No."

"What is your job?"

"I'm a buyer for a chain of specialty shops. I'm looking for possible gift items to import."

"There is nothing for you in Augsheim."

Emerson got to his feet. "Nothing but memories. Thank you, Mr. Burkherdt, but I really must be going now. I've had a long day."

"Certainly." The German studied him through drooping eyes. "I appreciate the interview."

Emerson went upstairs to his room and undressed for bed. He fell asleep almost immediately. It was a trick he'd learned during the war.

Burkherdt's interview was not in the morning paper, and so he waited till afternoon. He found it on page one of the *Zeitung*, complete with a candid photograph of himself emerging from the hotel on the previous day. He wondered if Burkherdt had followed him on his journey to Mona's room, but then decided against it. The reporter surely would have mentioned something.

Toward evening he went again to the bar where he'd met Mona. This time they dispensed with the preliminaries and went at once to her room. Visor was not there.

"He didn't think it would be safe two nights in a row," she explained. "But here is the information you wanted. China's picture and a schedule of his usual movements."

Emerson studied the face in the photograph, an ordinary enough face, set between officer's cap and eagled shoulders. "All right," he told her.

"Stay a bit," she cautioned, "in case someone is watching. My customers are always good for at least a half-hour."

He sat down on the bed. "Why do you do this, anyway?"

She smiled sadly, staring at the darkened square of window. "An odd question for you to ask. Why do you do it? Why do you kill?"

"You know about it?"

"Enough. He tells me. He trusts me. You should, too."

"Did you see the story about me in the *Zeitung*?"

"Yes."

"I destroyed your park, your buildings, your lives."

"Yes."

"And this was only one of the cities. There were many others. It's no different up there. It's exactly the same as killing a man with your bare hands—or at least it was for me. When the war ended, I had to go on. Now I work unofficially for a government agency that would throw me to the wolves in a minute. Why do I do it? Because if I didn't I think I'd go mad."

"Are you so sure of your sanity now?" she asked.

"Is anybody?"

She lit a cigarette, waving the wooden match afterwards to put it out. It might have been a signal to some watcher outside the window, but he knew it wasn't. He trusted her, just as Visor did. "Do you want to make love to me?" she asked casually.

His mouth seemed suddenly dry. "I'm sorry. I have to be going."

"It's the killing, isn't it? It's that instead of sex."

"I have a job to do."

"Get out of it," she said. "Get out of it before it destroys you."

He paused at the door. "I guess it destroyed me the first time I flew over a burning city."

Then, more serious than he'd seen her before, she came to him at the door. "Emerson," she whispered, "be careful. You came back too soon."

He left her in the doorway and hurried down to the street.

Emerson waited in the shadow of a ruined building until he saw Colonel Roger China enter the Allied Officers' Club on schedule. Then he walked several blocks until he found a telephone. It took them several minutes to page Colonel China and get him to the phone, but finally his voice came on the other end of the line.

"China here."

"Colonel, you don't know me, but as a fellow officer I thought I might appeal to you. My name is Emerson. You may have read about me in the newspaper."

"Emerson. Yes, you're the one who led the bombing raid."

"I must talk to somebody. Could I come to see you?"

"When?"

"Tonight. Now."

A snort from the other end. "I'm afraid that's impossible."

"Please, sir. It's an important matter."

There was a moment's hesitation, and then China said, "Very well. I can give you ten minutes. No more. Ask for me at the desk."

"Thank you, sir."

Emerson waited a half-hour before putting in his appearance. He saw Colonel China at once, standing with a group of English and French officers near the entrance to the club dining room. Playing out the charade, he asked at the desk, and waited while the colonel was summoned.

"You're Emerson?"

"That's right, sir. Pleased to meet you." The harsh lights of the club anteroom played down on China's balding head, giving it momentarily the appearance of a grinning skull. His eyes were dark and deep-set, and the weathered skin of his slim face was stretched taut. He was an ugly man, but he had the bearing of a leader.

"We can talk in here," China said, leading him into a smoking room hung heavily with the male trappings of the military.

"You have a nice club here."

The colonel nodded. "It's a nice retreat from the rest of Augsheim. If I may say so, you did a thorough job with your bombs, Emerson."

"I'd like to forget about that, sir. It's one of the reasons I came to you."

"And why me?"

"You're the ranking officer in Augsheim. After that newspaper interview, I felt I had to talk to someone—a countryman."

"What's your trouble, man?"

"I. . . . I feel I did the wrong thing. I feel that the whole war was wrong and I was wrong to kill all those people. I suppose that's really why I came back here. I need somebody like you to tell me, sir."

Colonel China regarded him with something like distaste. "War is never wrong to a soldier. If you think so, it's just as well you're out. I won't say I agree with every aspect of our government's policy, but I fought for it. Now, after the war, is the time to work for changes in that policy."

"I do want to change it, though!" Emerson insisted. "War is nothing but burning and looting and killing!"

China smiled slightly. "But you see, even to change it, to achieve an end to war, would necessitate more of the same. This old world will never be free of war until the Russians and the English—and, yes, the Americans too—are as defeated as Germany is today. Perhaps that will be the only true communism this planet will ever know—the communism of destruction and defeat."

"Who would rule a world like that?"

"The strong will survive. There are always rulers. Hitler was one, until he went mad." Then suddenly he got to his feet, ending the conversation. "I've given you more than ten minutes already. Come see me tomorrow at my office."

"Thank you, sir. You've helped me."

Colonel China paused. "I did it for a fellow officer. Have all the doubts you want, but remember one thing. Don't ever forget how to kill."

Emerson found a nearby bar from which he could observe the club parking lot. He kept his eye on the big black car in which China had arrived. The Allied Officers' Club had been carefully chosen as the one place where China would probably drive himself. An enlisted man who might be his regular driver would not be allowed inside, and colonels weren't usually important enough to keep drivers waiting outside a bar all night. No, China had arrived alone and would leave alone—unless he decided to drive another officer home. In that event, Emerson had two alternate plans.

It was two in the morning before China appeared, but he was alone. Though he'd obviously been drinking, he walked hurriedly to his car and got in. Emerson stepped out of his hiding place and ran across the street.

"Please, sir," he said, pulling open the door on the passenger side. "I've been drinking. Could you drop me at my hotel?"

Colonel China stared at him with surprised distaste. "What's the matter with you, Emerson? Get out of this car!"

Emerson gave a last glance to make sure the parking lot was empty. Then he leaned over and delivered a short judo blow to the colonel's throat. The man coughed once and started to sag, and Emerson broke his neck with a second blow.

He slid over the body into the driver's seat and edged the car quickly out of the lot. The highway to Colonel China's rented house had been carefully covered, and Emerson knew exactly the right place for the accident. He aimed the car for the guard rail and jumped.

It started burning at the bottom of the gully, and he had to keep low to avoid being silhouetted by the flames.

Emerson had killed a great many men in the brief years since the war. It didn't bother him any more, if it ever had. He reported to a quiet man behind a desk in Washington and went where he was sent, to contact people like Visor and Mona in dingy back rooms. Sometimes he wondered how much official Washington ever knew of his activities, if they knew anything. Perhaps, in the bureaucratic confusion of the postwar world, he was a lost segment simply serving the whims of some minor department head. But the truth of Emerson was that he didn't really care.

He walked back into town, thinking abstractly that he would like to see Mona again before he left Augsheim. The city was sleeping, and he strolled for a long while among the ruins, seeing them for the first time bathed in a silvery moonglow. The mists of the previous night had dissipated, and the air was clear with November coolness.

Piles of brick, blackened timbers. Still, after all this time. Perhaps some bodies, too, undiscovered yet in their unmarked tombs. The city would come back, but not the same. Not ever the same.

He paused on the street where Mona Kirst had her apartment, and pressed his face against the damp bark of a tree to stare up at the rectangle of curtained light that was her window. She would not be alone, not even at three in the morning. He wondered vaguely where Visor was that night, and turning to walk back to his hotel caught the distant shrill pitch of sirens heading out of town. Perhaps the burning car had only now been discovered, and Roger China had spent this hour alone in his death.

Ahead, finally, the hotel glowed like a beacon on the dim street. He hurried toward it, suddenly tired, not hearing the voices until they were almost upon him.

"Emerson!"

"That's him. Get him!" The words were German, but he understood. He turned to see a half-dozen men emerging from the shadows. Some carried clubs, and at least one had a knife.

"We've been waiting for you, Emerson. This is for the city. For Augsheim. And for our families."

He thought he saw the reporter, Burkherdt, watching from across the street. Then he closed his eyes against their hatred as the first blows fell. In that final moment he was once more skimming over the ice-blue clouds in the lead bomber, free and powerful as an eagle.

They Never Come Back

Harry Gordon swung the car out of the driveway, belatedly switched on his lights, and began the long drive home. It had been a late party, later than he'd planned, and Lois was already half dozing beside him on the seat. Near the river, the road plunged suddenly into scattered patches of post-midnight fog, and he cursed to himself as he slowed the car to a crawl.

"What's the matter?" Lois asked, rousing herself from near slumber. "You slowed down."

"Little fog. Don't worry about it. Only slowed as a precaution."

"I told you we should have left earlier. But you had to have one more drink."

"Go back to sleep. We'll be home soon."

She was silent, and he glanced sideways at her. Curled up on the seat with her long blonde hair falling over one eye, she might have been a little girl on the way home from a birthday party. There were times during the past six years when he'd regretted marrying her, but this was not one of them.

He turned back to the fog-patched road, a half-instant too late. The car was headed straight for the steel guard rail on the river side. He twisted hard on the steering wheel and felt the wheels skidding wildly beneath him.

There was a grinding, tearing crash, and then a sheet of flame that might have been a dream. And then nothing.

His vision came swimming out of an amber pool, into a tropic oasis where the only sounds were the rustle of white-skirted legs and the tonal beeping of some far-off chimes. The place might almost have been a hospital.

"Harry?"

He started to turn his head and then the pain stopped him. The pain and the bandages. "Is that you, Les?"

Lester Shaw stepped into his vision and bent over the bed. "Thank God you're all right, Harry."

"I don't feel all right. Where am I?" He asked it even though he knew.

"In the hospital. There was an accident, Harry." Lester's face was a somber mask that looked like molded putty.

"Lois . . . ?"

"I'm sorry, Harry. She didn't make it."

"Lois!" He started out of bed, and had one wobbling foot on the cool floor when the nurse grabbed him and pulled him back. Then his head began to spin and someone plunged a needle into his arm.

Harry was in the hospital only three days. He came out with a slight concussion, two cracked ribs and numerous bruises, in time to attend his wife's funeral at the little church where they'd worshipped on infrequent occasions. Lester and Muriel Shaw were at his side during the whole service, and the painful, eternal drive to the cemetery afterwards.

It was Muriel who had explained, a bit too bluntly, about the closed coffin at the funeral parlor. ("There was nothing left of her, Harry. She was burned to a cinder.") And it was Lester who had filled in the details of the accident itself. ("We were about a half-mile behind you, Harry. We saw the car turn over and burst into flames, and we got there in time to pull you clear. But she was a goner from the start.")

After the funeral they'd driven in silence back to Harry's house—the rambling ranch on the hill that now seemed too big, too dank, too empty. While Muriel fixed coffee and Lester helped settle things, Harry dug out the folded newspapers from the last few days and read all about it in the clipped jargon of the newsman.

Mrs. Lois Gordon, 33, prominent socialite and wife of insurance man Harry G. Gordon, died early this morning in the flaming crash of their car on Route 17. Mr. & Mrs. Gordon were returning home after a party at the home of Joseph Angora when the accident occurred. Gordon, who was driving, was hospitalized with undetermined injuries, and is listed in fair condition.

The Night My Friend

There was a picture of her too, a recent one with her long blonde hair in all its glory. Some anxious photographer had flopped the negative, though, so that the familiar little mole was on her right cheek instead of the left. It was almost as if he were seeing her in a mirror, and somehow it made her seem still alive.

"I suppose it's a good thing there aren't any children," Muriel said with her usual tact. "It would be terribly hard on them."

"It's hard on me," Harry told her, sipping the coffee that was a poor imitation of Lois' brew.

"Would you rather be alone tonight?" Lester asked.

"I think so, Les. Why don't you two run along? Thanks for everything. Thanks for saving my life." He didn't add that they might better have let him burn along with her.

Later, when he was alone, he got out the bankbooks and stock certificates, and tried to figure out the financial meaning of Lois dead. Much of the money had been in her name, but there were two joint bank accounts and some other things like the house and car. Her mother had died a year after their marriage, leaving her close to a quarter of a million dollars.

Staring at the figures until they started to blur before his eyes, Harry Gordon wondered if it had been Lois or only the money that he'd loved. Now Lois was gone and the money remained, and he was afraid of what he might be learning about himself.

He went back to the office the next day, with his head still bandaged and his ribs taped. The injuries didn't bother him, but the smothering air of careful solicitude drove him from the office after only an hour. Joseph Angora phoned him for lunch, and he used it as an excuse to say he'd be gone the remainder of the day.

Angora was a middle-aged balding man who ran an export business of vague dimensions and hovered at the fringes of Long Island society. Since his wife Betty was crippled and confined to a wheel chair, Angora did more than his share of party-giving at the big old house out beyond Garden City. Harry and Lois had been returning from one of Angora's parties when the accident occurred.

"Sorry I couldn't get to the funeral," he said with a somber shake of Harry's hand. "Betty and I just couldn't believe it."

"Thanks for the flowers," Harry said.

They ordered drinks and talked about it, in the matter-of-fact manner of mature men. To Harry it was a relief, after the solicitude of the office. But then, over the second drink, Angora suddenly looked away. "You know, Betty doesn't think she's dead."

"What?"

"Well, you know how Betty is, stuck in that chair all the time. Sometimes she gets some pretty strange ideas. She doesn't think Lois is dead."

"Who does she think we buried?" Harry asked, somehow becoming angry at this sudden turn in the conversation.

Angora tried hard to chuckle, apparently sorry he'd mentioned the subject. "Forget it, Harry. Forget it! It's getting late. We'd better order our food."

But though no more was said, the seed of thought had been planted. All that afternoon, Harry tried to remember Lois as she had been, tried to summon up in his mind a picture of Lois alive, not Lois dead. It was foolish, of course. She was dead and buried, and Betty Angora's ramblings would never bring her back.

On the weekend, Harry bought a new car and drove into Manhattan. The city had never seemed quite so lonely to him as it did that Saturday night, and when he finally parked in an all-night ramp to walk the streets for a while he found that a light spring drizzle had deprived him of even the companionship of the sidewalk.

He finally settled for two beers in a Greenwich Village bar, but even there he could not be free of the memory of Lois. They'd come here once or twice, and over the second drink he found himself sneaking a look at the folded newspaper clipping that told about her death. He tried to tell himself that such feelings were only natural just a week after her death, but somehow rationalization didn't help. He left the bar and found that the drizzle had stopped. The streets of the Village were beginning to fill once more.

And then he saw her—Lois.

His heart seemed to stop beating, and a cold sweat covered every inch of his body. Lois, her blonde hair hanging free, dressed in a shabby raincoat and slacks, carrying a paper bag from an all night delicatessen.

He started after her, hurrying as she threaded a rapid passage through the suddenly crowded sidewalk. She's not dead, Betty Angora had said. She's not dead.

"Lois!"

She didn't turn, only kept going. At the south end of Washington Square she turned suddenly and entered the dimly lit hallway of an apartment house. It was there that he caught her by the arm. "Lois— you're alive!"

She turned to him in the harsh light of the overhead bulb. "Take your hand off me, mister, or you'll be dead."

"I . . ." There was still an amazing resemblance, but now, up close, he could see his mistake. The eyes were different, harder, and there was no mole. Even the long hair was not exactly the right shade. It was not Lois. "I'm sorry," he mumbled.

"You thought I was somebody else. That's an old line, mister."

"I thought you were my wife. She died last week."

"Well! That's the first time I've ever been mistaken for a ghost!"

"I—I'm sorry," he repeated. "Could I make up for it by buying you a drink?"

"I've got a whole bagful of beer right here, and a party going upstairs." He started to turn away and she stopped him. "Let me drop the beer and I'll come out for a quick one, mister. I guess you owe me something after scaring me half to death. Be right back."

She was back down in a few moments, with a drunken male voice calling after her, "Don't be long, Rosie."

He took her back to the same bar and introduced himself over a beer. She smiled and said, "I'm Rosie Yates. Rosemary, but nobody calls me that. I'm an actress, I guess. Been in some off-Broadway stuff by Albee and Beckett. Now tell me about this wife of yours."

"She was killed in an auto accident last week." He touched the bruise on his forehead where the bandage had been. "From a distance, in the street, you looked like her. Besides that, some crazy woman I know thinks Lois is still alive."

"Well, if she is, I'm sure not her."

"I know that now. I also know that Lois is dead."

"Do you want to come back to my party?"

"I don't think so, thanks."

They had another beer, and talked, and it was almost the way it used to be. It had been a long time since he'd spoken to a girl like this. "Come see me in a play some time," she said.

"I'd like to. I hope it's up in Times Square."

"I'm getting old for the big time. Almost thirty. Playwrights don't write leads for women my age any more."

Harry shrugged. "Not unless they're Tennessee Williams or Edward Albee."

"I think I'd like to do comedy somehow. Life is tragic every day. It's tragic when the bills come in and you're out of a job, and you've got a big choice of sleeping with your producer or starving."

He shook his head sadly. "And I thought the insurance business was bad."

He walked back to the apartment with her and left her at the bottom of the stairs. "Goodnight, Rosie."

She smiled, just for a second. "Goodnight, Harry."

Outside, it was starting to drizzle again.

Harry spent Sunday with Lester and Muriel, and was thankful for their company. The day dragged toward evening, with all of them too conscious of Lois. Dead, she contributed more of a presence than she ever had in life.

Monday morning he went to the office early for the first time. The daily routine had taken hold, and no one gave him more than a passing glance. He flipped through his mail, noting the return addresses, and opened a few. There were sympathy notes from business associates, and one or two letters from friends. A square white envelope finally attracted his attention and he opened it.

The message was brief and typewritten: *Harry—Please help me. I didn't die in the accident, but I'm in terrible trouble. I'll try to reach you later today.* It was signed *Lois,* but in a shaky handwriting he barely recognized.

His first thought was that the thing was some sort of horrible joke. He sat staring at the letter for a long time, wondering which of his friends could have been guilty of such a thing. It certainly wasn't from Lois. She rarely typed her letters, and the signature wasn't much like hers at all. And besides, she was dead.

Besides, she was dead.

But for a moment he'd almost forgotten that fact. For a moment, while checking off the reasons why the letter couldn't be from Lois, he'd almost imagined she was still alive!

He turned over the envelope and studied the inky black postmark. Early Sunday morning from New York. Grand Central Station. It could have been mailed Saturday night or Sunday morning.

Terrible trouble.

He picked up the telephone and called Lester Shaw at his office across town. "Les, something's come up. Can I meet you for lunch?"

"Sure, Harry. Noon all right?"

They met at the same place he'd lunched with Angora a few days earlier. There was never much of a crowd on Monday noons, and he sometimes wondered what people did on Mondays instead of eating lunch.

"Thanks for coming, Les."

Lester Shaw ran a nervous hand through his thinning blond hair. "What's the trouble, Harry?"

Toying with the tapered base of his water glass, Harry began to talk. "I think I mentioned to you and Muriel yesterday about this crazy thing

Angora told me, how his wife didn't believe Lois was dead. Well, I didn't tell you something else. Saturday night I went into New York and almost assaulted a girl down in the Village that looked something like Lois."

"Harry!"

He held up his hand. "There's more. Luckily, this girl was very understanding. I bought her a drink and everything was fine. But the point is, what Angora told me has lit some sort of a spark in my own mind. Call it anything you like, but I suppose it's all traced to the shock of the accident and the fact that I never saw her body."

"There was nothing much to see, Harry. Believe me."

"I know. I know. But I didn't see it, and for all I know, maybe she is still alive." He took the folded letter from his pocket and passed it across the table to Lester. "I received this in the morning mail."

Lester Shaw read it through quickly. "Do you believe this?"

"No, of course not. And yet I . . . ."

Lester put the note on the table between them. "Harry, you've got to come to your senses about this thing. You can't accept the responsibility for Lois' death, so you're building up a fantasy that she's still alive."

"What about this note? Who sent it?"

Lester Shaw bit his lip before answering. "Is it possible that you could have sent it to yourself, Harry, without remembering you did it?"

"What? Do you think I've cracked up completely?"

"You said you mistook somebody for Lois the other night."

"That was different."

"Well, you'll know soon enough if the note's on the level. She says she'll contact you today."

"Yes," Harry said quietly, thinking about it. "And right now I don't know which would be worse—to have her dead or alive."

The second message came at four that afternoon. It was a telegram addressed to Harry at his office. He ripped it open with an unsteady hand and read the brief words. *Harry, need money desperately. Have Lester Shaw meet me Sherman Park fountain tomorrow morning at seven. Trust me. Lois.*

He stuffed the telegram into his pocket and left the office. But he didn't immediately phone Lester. Instead, he drove out beyond Garden City to Joseph Angora's old house. As he pulled into the driveway he remembered it was his first visit since the night of the accident. The place looked different now, gloomy and alone in the uncertain light of dusk. It didn't look at all like a place for parties.

"I just got home," Angora said, answering the door. "How are you, Harry?"

"Not so good, I guess. I was wondering if I could see Betty."

"Sure. What about?"

"About Lois."

Angora nodded and led the way through the familiar rooms. There was a maid at times, and a cook, but Harry saw neither of them now. Betty was alone in her chair on the rear sun porch, staring out toward the west where there was nothing now but a faint remembered glow low in the evening sky.

"How are you, Harry?" she said, holding out her hand to him. "We don't often have this pleasure on a weeknight." She was a small woman of perhaps forty-five, who looked just a little the way Queen Victoria must have looked.

"Hello, Betty."

"So sorry about your wife."

"That's what I wanted to talk to you about." Behind him, he was aware that Angora had joined them on the enclosed porch. "Joe told me something last week. Something you said."

She looked up at him with steady eyes. "About Lois. I said she was still alive."

"Why do you think so?"

"I've seen her," Betty Angora answered, quite simply. "I saw her the day after the accident, walking out there in the garden."

A sort of shiver ran down Harry's spine at the words. "I think you'd better tell me about it," he said, in a voice he might have used to comfort a deranged person. Until now he'd always considered Betty to be sound of mind, even though her body was crippled.

"I was dozing in the afternoon," she said, "and as I came awake I saw her, right down there among the rose bushes. She almost seemed to be looking for buds, but of course it's still too early for them."

"Couldn't it have been a dream?" Harry asked. "A dream brought on by the news of her death in the accident?"

"Perhaps it was a dream," Betty admitted, "but that really doesn't matter. What matters was that I had a vision of her alive, and therefore she really *is* alive."

Angora spoke softly from behind Harry. "Betty's been right about these things before," he said. "Remember that little boy who was lost in the desert a few years back? Betty said right from the start he was still alive, and sure enough, pretty soon they found him."

Harry sighed and reached into his pocket for a cigarette. "I received a letter and a telegram signed with her name," he said. "Did you send them, Betty?"

"Of course not! Why do you fight it like this, Harry? Accept the fact that she's still alive. I didn't send you any letters."

The Night My Friend

He stared at the deep brown pools of Betty's eyes, trying to decide if she were lying. But all he saw there was a strangeness he could never understand, a borderland of shadow he could never hope to reach. He did not envy Joseph Angora.

"Thank you," he said finally. "Thank you for talking to me."

As he rose to leave, Angora took his arm. "Keep in touch, Harry. If there's anything we can do . . ."

"Thanks," Harry said.

He drove back to his own place and phoned Lester Shaw. In brief, clipped phrases he told him about the latest message, and the visit to the Angora home. "What do you think, Les?"

On the other end of the line Lester Shaw's voice was uncertain. "I think somebody's got a pretty mad sense of humor," he said, but there was a questioning tone in his words. "Do you think Betty Angora sent the messages?"

"Why should she?"

"Why would anybody? Any sane person, at least."

"Could Lois still be alive, Les?" Harry asked. It seemed he'd been asking that question ever since the accident, if only to himself.

"We got there right after the crash, Harry."

"But did you actually *see* her in the car?"

"Harry, Harry! There was a body in the car. It *had* to be Lois."

"I suppose so. And yet, suppose she really is alive, somehow, and in need of help? This isn't just some nut that sent the telegram. It's someone who knew your name, for one thing."

Lester Shaw sighed. "What do you want me to do now, Harry?"

"I think you should meet her in the morning—whoever she is. I'll give you a little money, maybe a hundred dollars. And I'll be waiting nearby. We'll find out about this, once and for all."

"All right, Harry. If that's what you want."

"I'll come for you in the morning. At six-thirty."

On these spring mornings there was a sort of mist off the ocean that often clung till almost noon, obscuring vision and casting a fog-like gloom over all like a smothering blanket. It was like that at Sherman Park, at five minutes to seven.

"She picked this place because she knew about the mist," Harry said at once.

"She wouldn't have known yesterday what the weather would be like," Lester said. "It doesn't happen every day."

The park, covering only a few square blocks near the center of the village, was a strange place in the dawn's half-light. They could barely make out the fountain at its center, and the still bare trees hung damp with droplets of clinging vapor.

"I'll wait here," Harry said. "Give you a few minutes alone with whoever it is."

Lester Shaw nodded. "I won't give her the money till you show up anyway." Then he left Harry's side and hurried toward the fountain.

For some moments Harry strained his eyes, trying to make out something in the brightening landscape. There was no sound but the distant traffic of work-bound motorists and the steady splashing of the fountain water.

He waited until his watch showed five minutes after seven. Then he started walking into the park. Ahead, he thought he heard someone cough. But there was nothing to be seen, nothing but the wetness of the trees and the first beginnings of springtime buds.

"Les?"

There was no one at the fountain, not Lester Shaw or Lois or anyone. He walked all the way around it and was about to start back when he saw something in the fountain, something almost hidden by the rippling, foaming water.

It was Lester Shaw, and he was dead.

After a time a detective came who seemed to be in charge. He had a bulky look about him and constantly jingled the coins in his pants pocket as he spoke. Harry Gordon didn't like him.

"Name is Kater. Sergeant Kater. Want to tell me what happened?"

"I—I was to meet somebody here," Harry began. "I told the officer all about it."

"Suppose you tell me, too. Start with the dead man."

"Lester Shaw. He was a close friend of mine."

"Did you shoot him?"

"No! Of course I didn't!"

"Somebody did. You must have seen who."

"I didn't see a thing."

"Did you hear the shot?"

"No. I heard something like a cough. I suppose that was it."

Kater held a whispered conversation with another detective, and then came back to where Harry sat on the damp park bench. "Small caliber gun pressed against his jacket. I suppose it could have sounded like a cough. Who did you come here to meet?"

"My wife. Lois Gordon."

"Did she come?"

"I didn't see her."

"Where is she now?"

"She's been dead for over a week."

The detective nodded his head and stopped jingling the coins. "You'd better come down to headquarters, Mr. Gordon. This is going to take a while."

It took quite a while. Harry found himself, before the day was over, recounting to Kater every incident since the night of the accident. Conversations and movements and messages and meetings were gone over in detail, and toward the end of the day, when Harry was ready for even a jail cell cot, the detective seemed to be just warming up. He excused himself for a half-hour, and when he returned he was jingling the coins again.

"Just been talking to the victim's wife," he said.

"Muriel. How's she taking it?"

"As well as could be expected. She's a good-looking girl."

Harry sighed and wished he had a cigarette. "What's that supposed to mean?"

"Men have been killed for lots less. Is there anything between you and Muriel Shaw?"

"Not a thing. I told you everything I know. Why can't you believe it?"

"The story is a bit hard to take, Mr. Gordon. From where I stand, you're the best suspect I've got."

"Are you arresting me?"

"Not quite yet."

He went out again, and Harry spent the next hour staring through the heavy wire window grating, watching home-bound traffic in the street below. He tried to remember what it had been like just two short weeks ago, when Lois was alive and the world was right.

When Lois was alive. Had she ever been really alive?

"I'd like you to talk with a witness," Sergeant Kater said behind him.

"A witness? To the murder?"

"A man who may have seen your wife."

Harry's heart began to thud as he followed the detective into the next room. Kater offered him a cigarette, and then introduced him to an elderly man with white hair who sat uncertainly on a long wooden bench. The man's name, it appeared, was Otto Carry, and he sold newspapers to the early morning commuters at the Long Island railroad station down the street from Sherman Park.

"A woman," he said, peering at Harry through thick glasses. "Long blonde hair and a mole on her right cheek. She got off the train from New York around a quarter to seven. I noticed her because not many people come out from the city at that hour."

"A lot of women have blonde hair and moles," Harry said uncertainly.

Kater cleared his throat. "He's already identified the picture in the newspaper."

"The picture of Lois?"

The detective nodded. "That's right," he then confirmed aloud.

"Then she is alive."

Kater showed Otto Carry to the door. "Thank you, sir. We'll be in touch." Then he came back and sat down opposite Harry. "She might be," he conceded.

"Back from the dead?"

The detective shook his head. "They never come back. But then, perhaps she never went away."

Greenwich Village that night was alive with the warmth of spring. The streets around Washington Square were crowded to overflowing with the heady mixture of artists and tourists and students and would-be beats who seemed always to come out when the air was clear and inviting. Harry Gordon threaded his way among them, seeking and finally finding a half-remembered doorway.

He was in luck. She was home, and she came to the door after his second knock. "Hello, there. Remember me?"

She frowned for only an instant. "You're the fellow from the other night! Harry!"

"Right the first time. May I come in?"

Rosie Yates stood aside and let him enter. She'd been washing her hair and it was a mass of brightly colored plastic curlers. "If you don't mind my appearance," she told him. "I don't usually get visitors on Tuesday evenings."

"It's such a nice night. I thought you might be out."

She gestured toward her hair.

"Weekly chore. This and cleaning the apartment. I used to do it Mondays, but now I have a class at the New School."

The apartment was a confusion of vacuum cleaner and dust cloths, and he saw at once that he had indeed interrupted a weekly chore. "I'm sorry. I should have called first."

"Not at all! Good to see you again so soon. Want a beer? I don't have anything stronger right now. That party Saturday night pretty much cleaned me out."

"A beer will be fine."

He sat down somewhat uncertainly on the edge of a faded and shabby divan that quite possibly opened into a bed. He heard her rummaging around in the kitchen, and she returned in a minute with two cans of cold beer. "So what's been new with you?"

He found himself filling her in briefly on the events of the past few days, telling her of the strange messages, and his visit to the Angora home, and finally the murder of Lester Shaw.

"It's like a nightmare," she said. "Aren't there any definite clues?"

"None that point to anyone but me. The detective, Kater, thinks I killed him because I was having an affair with his wife, Muriel."

"Were you?"

"Hardly!"

She flung back her head in a gesture he'd seen her use before. "Still, this part about your wife being alive is so ridiculous. Couldn't someone have set up the whole plan, the messages and everything, just to murder this man Shaw?"

"Somebody like Muriel?"

"Or that Angora you mentioned."

"But why?"

She puzzled over it a moment and then went back to her beer. "I wish there was some way I could help you, Harry."

"If you mean that, I think there is."

"How?"

"I noticed you Saturday night because at a quick glance you looked something like Lois. I want to take you to see a couple of people in the morning. I want to see if they react the same way."

"What people?"

"The newspaper vendor, Otto Carry. And perhaps Mrs. Angora, too."

"But why?"

"These people think they saw someone; someone who might have been Lois. I want to visit them with you and try to get some reaction out of them. If they really did see her, they'll probably notice your resemblance to her. Carry should, at least, since he never saw her alive."

"Harry, do you want her to be alive? Or dead?"

He tried to think about that, but whatever the answer was, he wasn't yet ready to face it. "I don't know. I guess I'll have to wait and see."

"You're an odd guy."

"Will you come with me in the morning?"

"Sure. I guess so." She hesitated a moment and then said, "Lois was a very beautiful woman. I found a picture of her in this magazine." She reached over to the coffee table and picked up a three-month-old copy of a fashion magazine. There were some color shots taken at Newport last summer, and one of them showed him with Lois on the beach. He remembered how they'd kidded about it when the magazine appeared.

"Yes," he answered simply.

Later that night, alone at home, he cried for the first time since the accident. But he cried for himself rather than Lois.

In the morning he picked up Rosie Yates early, and they reached the area of Sherman Park before eight. It was another sunny day, with train-bound crowds moving perhaps a little slower than they did in the chill months of winter. Harry parked the car and they waited till a dull period between trains before approaching Otto Carry at his post.

"Hello, there," Harry said.

The old man looked up from his stack of papers, peering through the thick glasses with uncertain recognition. "You—you're the fellow from yesterday, at the police station."

"That's right."

"Want a paper?"

"Sure. Give me a *Times*. This girl is a friend of mine. Miss Yates."

Otto Carry's eyes swept over her. "Mornin'," he said without interest.

"I was wondering . . . This woman you saw yesterday—did she look anything like Miss Yates here?"

The old man peered again. "Not much. Hair's the wrong color for one thing. And no mole. The one yesterday, she had a lot more makeup on, too."

Harry brought out the newspaper photo and the picture from the magazine. "Was this the girl?"

"I seen the one picture yesterday. Yeah, that's the girl."

"Thanks. Thank you very much."

He started to turn away with Rosie Yates when a familiar voice said, "Playing detective, Mr. Gordon?" It was Sergeant Kater, looking sleepy in a topcoat he didn't need.

"Hello. No, just buying a paper."

Kater stepped up close. "Mind introducing me to the girl, Mr. Gordon?"

"Rosie Yates, Sergeant Kater."

The detective nodded. "He told me about you. It's a pleasure."

"Look," Harry began, "are you following me or something?"

"No. I was looking around over at the park and I saw you come in here. I was just curious." He took out a cigarette. "I'm especially curious about your social life, Mr. Gordon."

Harry was annoyed. "Look, I told you I just met Miss Yates last Saturday. Right, Rosie?"

The girl flushed a bit and nodded. "That's right."

Kater nodded. "I'll see you around, Mr. Gordon." He drifted out of the station, leaving them alone with the newsdealer.

The Night My Friend

"I don't like that man," Rosie said. "He thinks you're hiding something."

Harry was reminded of Lester Shaw's words. Was it possible after all that he was hiding something? Was it possible he'd sent those messages to himself, and even murdered Shaw without knowing it? He remembered the head injury he'd suffered in the accident.

"I gotta go," Otto Carry said suddenly. "Train due in three minutes."

"Now what?" Rosie asked. "That woman? Betty Angora?"

"I guess not today," Harry decided. "She'll keep. Besides, I've got some other things to do."

"That detective upset you."

"I suppose so. He might still be following us, and I don't want to go up to Angora's now. I'll take you home."

They made the trip back to the Village apartment mostly in silence. He dropped her with a promise to call again, and then turned the car back toward Long Island. On the way he remembered an unpleasant duty. Lester Shaw's body would be at the funeral parlor, and he would have to pay his respects. Somehow the thought of seeing Lester dead, and Muriel alive, was something he couldn't yet face. The death of Lester had been almost more of a shock than the death of his wife, and there was no chance of Lester's returning.

He parked across the street from the funeral parlor and went in. It was too early for regular visiting hours, but Muriel was already there, dressed in somber shadows that rustled when she walked. "Hello, Harry. It looks like a bad year for us both."

"I'm awfully sorry, Muriel."

"Who would want to kill him, Harry? Who would want to kill a big dope like Les?"

"He was an old friend, Muriel. I'd rather it had been me." Harry walked into the dim sanctum where the casket rested among dripping baskets of flowers. He knelt for a momentary prayer, then went back to Muriel's side. "Harry," she said softly, "do you think he was killed because he saw something that night? At the accident?"

"I don't know, Muriel. Look, I'll be back tonight. OK?"

"Sure." She tried to smile as he left.

Across the street, Sergeant Kater was waiting in his car. "Get in," he said simply.

"You've been following me." Harry slid into the seat next to him. "Why?"

"Because I wanted to talk some more."

"About Muriel and me?"

"And other things."

"Like what?"

"I want to hear everything you've been up to since the last time we talked," he said curtly.

Harry gave a sort of growl. "Is that going to help find out if Lois is dead or alive?"

The detective stared straight ahead. "If I were you, Mr. Gordon, I wouldn't be so anxious to find that out."

"Why not?"

"Because if your wife is still alive, she's a murderess. She killed Lester Shaw, and very possibly the person who burned to death in your car. If she's alive, she might try to kill you next."

The night came with uncertainty, the reflected glow in the western sky lingering far beyond its appointed time. Harry had spent a few hours at the office, shuffling papers into vague piles for a future date, and when he returned home it was with a feeling of emptiness that seemed worse than the day of the funeral. Lois dead was a body lost, but Lois alive might be a soul lost as well. He wondered if he could face her alive, the strange wild thing she might have become.

The telephone rang at ten minutes to ten, and he picked it up to hear a whisper that was tantalizingly familiar. "Harry?"

"Who is this?"

"Try to listen. I can't speak any louder. This is Lois."

Suddenly his body seemed to be sweating from every pore. A cold knot began to grow in the pit of his stomach. "Lois? Are you alive?" he asked, realizing at once how foolish the question must sound.

"Of course I'm alive. Didn't you get my messages?"

"I can hardly hear you."

"I'm alive. But I'm in awful trouble. I need money, Harry. I have to get out of town."

"Where are you?"

"I'm hiding. It doesn't matter where."

"Les is dead."

"I know it. I didn't kill him, Harry. You have to believe that."

"You were seen near the park."

"I was there, but I didn't kill him."

"Who did? And whose body was that in the car?"

"I'll explain it all when I see you, Harry. Can't you trust me?"

Something, something."Is this really Lois?"

"Harry! Do I have to come there?"

"Maybe you'd better."

"I need money. Ten thousand dollars."

"Where am I supposed to get it?"

"There's money. And it's really mine anyway."

Really hers. Maybe that had been the trouble for all those years. "I can't raise it in the middle of the night."

"Don't you have any around the house?"

"How much did I ever have around the house? Fifty, sixty dollars."

"Tomorrow? Can you get it tomorrow? In cash?"

"You come here tonight and we'll talk about it. I have to get to the bottom of a few things first."

She gave a resigned sigh. "I'll come, Harry. But it'll be dangerous. There are people who want to kill me."

"I'll call the police."

"No! They'd send me to prison, Harry. They'd say I killed Lester Shaw, and that woman in the car."

"All right. Come out here now. Tell me what happened, the truth, and we'll see what we can work out about the money."

"I'll be there in an hour," she whispered, and hung up.

He sat for a long time at the telephone, wondering if he should call Kater. If it weren't Lois, if it were someone else, then his life was in great danger. Even if it were Lois, he couldn't be sure of handling her. If it were Lois . . . If she'd come back.

The doorbell buzzed at five minutes after eleven, and he knew it would be her. He walked to answer it, trying to keep his emotions under control, wondering what he would see when he swung open the door. He was ready for almost anything, but he was not ready for Lois.

She stood there, wearing dark glasses and a scarf that partly covered her hair. She was more beautiful than he remembered her, more mysterious, more feminine.

"Come in," he said quietly.

"Hello, Harry," She still spoke in a whisper, as if unsure of herself.

"You can speak up. We're alone."

"I . . ."

For a moment, for just a moment, he felt like forgetting the whole crazy business. He felt like taking this woman in his arms and making love to her, as he had with Lois so many countless times in the past.

"She would have used her key," he said simply.

"What?"

"Lois wouldn't have rung the doorbell. She would have used her key."

The gun appeared in her hand by magic, and he knew she must have been holding it out of sight all the time. It was a tiny weapon, just enough of a one to make a muffled cough against a man's chest. "What do you want?" he asked her.

"Money. Ten thousand dollars."

Then it was her natural voice, and it no longer went with this vision of Lois alive. He took a step toward the gun and saw it explode in a flash of anger. As the bullet ripped into his side he saw Kater leap from somewhere and tackle the girl with a bound of fury.

"I didn't think she'd shoot," Harry said stupidly, feeling the blood trickling through his shirt.

Kater had the gun now, and he held her on the floor in a viselike grip as he tried to get handcuffs on her. "She shot Shaw, didn't she? Why not you, too?" Finally he had her on her feet and was calling an ambulance. "I told you," he said to Harry. "I told you they never come back. Not from the grave."

Rosie Yates looked at them both and spat.

Harry was back in the hospital for a few days, and it seemed somehow, awakening the next morning, that none of it had really happened. Perhaps it had all been a long, long nightmare. After a time, Sergeant Kater was standing by his bed, and he knew it was all too true.

"The girl is just plain nuts," Kater was saying. "Imagine thinking she could get away with something like that!"

"I helped her get the idea," Harry said. "I mistook her for Lois the first time I saw her, and then I told her all about it. Since Betty Angora had already come up with the idea that Lois was still alive, this Rosie Yates decided to follow through on it."

Kater nodded from beside the bed. "She looked it up in the papers and learned that Lois had been fairly wealthy. I suppose that's when she decided to try a shakedown by pretending Lois was still alive. From her point of view the scheme was pretty good. She'd send you a couple of messages and get you to send her some money, and that would be the end of it. She figured Lester Shaw for the go-between, because she thought she could fool him with her makeup."

"How did she know Shaw's name? She had it in the telegram."

"That part was simple. She followed you Monday to see your reaction to the letter. She was probably wearing a wig. Remember, she was an actress. Anyway, in that restaurant she saw you show Shaw the letter. You said it was on the table between you for some time. She figured Shaw must be a friend, the kind you'd trust to deliver money to Lois. She simply followed Shaw and found out his name, and then sent the telegram. The real Lois probably wouldn't have used his full name in the telegram, but she did, of course."

"And like a fool I sent Les to meet her."

"Don't blame yourself. With her makeup on and her hair dyed to match that color photo in the magazine, she probably thought she could fool Shaw and get the money from him. Of course she couldn't, especially since he'd seen Lois' body in the car and was convinced she was really dead. He grabbed Rosie and she shot him in a panic."

"How did she ever expect to fool me last night when she wasn't able to fool Les?"

"She hoped you'd be enough in doubt that you'd have some money around for her anyway. Then she could take it, and it wouldn't matter what you believed. She'd have left you dead. I guess the second murder always comes easy after the first one."

"The makeup was good," Harry admitted. "But of course she couldn't possibly imitate a voice she'd never heard."

"You gave her a bad start, visiting her apartment Tuesday, just after she'd washed the coloring out of her hair. And then she had to mention the magazine with Lois' picture in it, because she was afraid you'd already spotted it."

"You knew it wasn't Lois," Harry said.

"I knew. I had a pretty good idea of the whole caper, in fact. The news vender, Otto Carry, described the woman he saw as having a mole on her right cheek. That matched the newspaper photo, but you told me it had been mistakenly flopped, that the mole was really on her left cheek. That told me two things: it wasn't really Lois, but somebody who tried to make up as her; more important, it wasn't anybody who had known Lois in life, or she wouldn't have made that mistake with the false mole. That eliminated most of your friends, and immediately turned my suspicions to the one woman in the case, who by your own admission looked something like Lois to begin with, and was an actress besides."

"And Otto Carry didn't recognize her without the hair coloring and the mole."

"Would you expect him to, after one quick glimpse?"

"But Rosie Yates worked from two pictures for her makeup. Didn't she notice the correct position of the mole in the color shot?"

The detective shrugged. "She guessed which was the right one, and guessed wrong."

Harry had one more question. "But who was it Betty Angora saw in her garden, the day after the accident? It couldn't have been Rosie then."

"I don't answer questions like that, Mr. Gordon," Kater said. "I'm only a detective. Maybe she just saw what she wanted to see, some dream or other. It started everything in motion, though, that vision of hers."

Harry didn't get to Lester Shaw's funeral. He was a day late getting out of the hospital, and when he went to visit Muriel she wasn't at home. He thought of calling on the Angoras, but decided to wait a while. Lois was really dead, and now he had his whole lifetime to get used to the idea.

The Only Girl in His Life

George Granger hadn't seen Beach since he'd gotten out of the hospital and so this first meeting was something of a shock. The months of mental and physical torment had aged Howard Beach in a way that Granger wouldn't have believed possible. He was an old man now, though not yet 50, and his white hair, wrinkled skin and tired eyes produced a sad and sorrowful sight.

"How's the construction business?" Granger asked, shaking the damp, bony hand.

"I wouldn't know. I've been away." Howard Beach's eyes stared through him, as if focused on something far away. "Have you heard anything from Linda?"

Linda Beach, Howard's young bride, had walked out on him on her 27th birthday. Two months later, Howard had received a letter from a San Francisco address asking for a divorce. He'd brooded about that letter for three weeks, while trying to reach Linda by phone and by wire. Finally, one rainy night, he'd gone out to his garage, closed the door behind him and turned on the car motor. A neighbor had found him just in time and Howard Beach had been in the hospital ever since. Granger had heard rumors of shock treatments and psychiatrists, but he hadn't tried too hard to learn the details. Beach was no more than a casual business associate.

"Linda? No, I wouldn't expect to, really. I just met her once, Howard. At a builders' dinner with you." Granger spoke with the careful solicitude one uses for the ill.

"I've written her, but the letters just come back." He stared down at his hands as he spoke. "She's moved, but her lawyer says she's still in the San Francisco area."

"Lawyer? She still wants a divorce?"

Howard Beach nodded. "I suppose when you get to my age . . . Maybe I'm too old for her. Maybe if we'd had children, things would have been different."

"Don't blame yourself," Granger said, trying to make it sound sympathetic.

Howard Beach brightened a bit. "I don't, really. Anyway, I phoned you because I wanted to ask a favor, George. It's a big favor and I'll understand if you say no."

"What is it?"

"I heard you were driving out to California with your wife. Will you be visiting San Francisco?"

Granger nodded. "For a few days. I'm only taking two weeks' vacation. We'll spend most of it driving."

"I was wondering . . ." He went over to a chair and picked up a full-length fur coat. To Granger's inexperienced eye, it looked like beaver. "She left some things here—this coat and her jewelry box—that I'd like her to have. I was wondering if you'd take them to her, since you're going to be out there anyway."

"But you don't know her address."

"I'm sure someone could tell you where she's staying. If nobody at the old address knows, call her lawyer."

"Couldn't you send these things to the lawyer?"

Howard Beach seemed suddenly very tired. "George—don't you understand? I want to hear about *her*. I want you to come back and tell me you actually saw her, tell me she's all right, that she's happy. God, George—sometimes I lie awake all night thinking of the awful things that might be happening to her out there, all alone."

There was nothing Granger could say, nothing but, "Of course I'll do it for you. I'll take the stuff out and try to find her. I can't promise anything, but I'll try."

Howard Beach smiled for the first time. "I'll put the coat in a box. I don't know how to thank you, George."

Granger didn't tell his wife about it till they were loading the car for their trip. She picked up the large, gray cardboard suit-box, with its girdings of tape and twine, and asked, "What's this?"

The Night My Friend

"Don't get excited. You remember Howard Beach. He asked me to deliver some things to his wife in San Francisco—her fur coat and some jewelry."

"Why couldn't he mail them?"

"He's not sure of her address. Besides, he wants to hear how she is."

Sue Granger snorted. "But you hardly know them!"

"I just couldn't say no, honey. It won't take long. If I don't find her right away, I'll dump the box at her lawyer's and forget about it."

"I'll bet! George, sometimes you're just too . . . too . . ."

He kissed her lightly on the lips and took the box out to the car. He loved his wife and always would, but he was still young enough to remember Linda Beach as a beautiful young woman who'd smiled at him once across a dinner table.

They entered San Francisco from the north, coming down Highway 101 from Santa Rosa, crossing the magnificence of the Golden Gate and swooping down into the Presidio Drive. It was a May-like day, even though it was still early April, and there was not a trace of the fog and mist they'd expected. The temperature was just under 60 degrees.

"I won't be long," Granger told Sue at the hotel. "I'm just going to drive out to the address Beach gave me."

"I'll be back from shopping by 5," she said. "And I don't want to spend my first night alone in a hotel room."

"Don't worry."

The address Howard had given him proved to be in the North Beach section, not far from Fisherman's Wharf. It was an area full of restaurants and shops, with a noisy life of its own that even at noon reminded him a little of Greenwich Village. He parked the car on a narrow side street and found the number he was looking for, a three-story brick building over an Italian restaurant.

A girl in tight pants and long hair passed him on the narrow stairs. "Pardon me," he asked, "but does Linda Beach live here?"

She paused, eyed him up and down, and then said, "Linda's been gone for months. You her husband?"

"No, just a friend. Where could I reach her?"

The girl shrugged. "Ask the landlady. Mrs. Cossa. She's downstairs."

He found Mrs. Cossa behind the nearly deserted bar in the restaurant. She was a big woman with an indifferent expression. "Beer?" she asked.

"Information. I'm looking for Linda Beach."

"You a detective or something?"

"No, just an old friend from back east."

"You look like a detective."

"I'm not. Could you give me Linda's address?"

"She didn't leave one. I kicked her out for not paying her rent. That's the last I saw her."

"How long ago was that?"

"After Christmas. I let her stay over Christmas. Then I kicked her out. This neighborhood—we used to be decent around here, before the artists and the girls moved in. Now they have parties and all sorts of carrying-on."

"Did she have any close friends in the building?"

"Girl on the top floor. Myra White."

He wondered if that was the girl he'd spoken to. "Long blond hair?"

"That's Myra. Pretty soon I'll kick her out, too, if she don't get rid of that guy she lives with."

He went back into the street and started walking. He knew Myra was out and there was probably nothing more to be gained from her, anyway.

Well, he'd tried, hadn't he? Maybe he'd just call the lawyer and forget about it. He found a pay telephone and dialed the number. In a moment he was speaking to Jay Tearbon, a brisk man who spoke in clipped phrases.

"Busy day. What can I do for you, Mr. Granger?"

"I'm looking for a client of yours. Linda Beach."

"Beach. Oh, yes."

"Could you give me her address?"

"Just why do you want to see her?"

"I have some things from her husband."

"Ah—I'm sorry. Mrs. Beach wants no contact at all with her husband."

That was fine with Granger. "Could I drop this package off at your office for her?"

"Certainly, certainly. Leave it with my secretary." Tearbon hung up and that was all.

Granger stared hard at the telephone, wondering what to do next. The lawyer hadn't impressed him, but there seemed no place to turn. He started walking back to where he'd parked the car, suddenly conscious of the city sounds around him. Down the block, construction workers were blasting rock for a building foundation, and that reminded him of Howard Beach. The man had been through a lot—a runaway wife, attempted suicide, months of mental care. Perhaps he owed it to Howard to try once more, to bring the man some news of Linda, if only that she was living happily with a bearded artist in some dingy loft.

The Night My Friend

He looked up and saw a girl with familiar blond hair hanging down her back. "Pardon me—Myra White?"

She turned and eyed him once more, cradling a package of groceries in one arm. "Didn't I just see you at the apartment?"

"That's right. I asked you about Linda Beach."

"So what do you want now?" She wore no makeup and, oddly enough, didn't need any. He guessed her age at just over 20, several years younger than Linda Beach. And yet they could have been friends.

"Mrs. Cossa says you were her friend. You must know where she is."

"I don't know. I haven't seen her in months."

"It's important that I find her. I have a package from her husband."

This caught her interest for a moment, but then she glanced up at the apartment windows across the street. "Look," she said, "my boyfriend doesn't like me talking to strangers. He might be watching. You don't want to find Linda, really you don't."

"Why not?"

"She's been sick."

"Perhaps her husband could help her."

"Nobody could help her. I've got to go now."

"Look, call her. Tell her I have some of her things—her fur coat and jewelry box. I'm sure she'll want them. Tell her it's George Granger. I think she'll remember me." He only had time to add the name of his hotel and then she was gone, hurrying across the street with her groceries.

He was back at the hotel long before Sue and he went downstairs for a haircut while he waited for her return. She finally got back, burdened down with two shopping bags, anxious to try on the dress she'd purchased.

"Been back long?" she asked.

"An hour or so."

"Did you deliver the box?"

"Not yet. I talked to a friend of Linda's, who's going to contact her. If I don't hear anything by tomorrow morning, I'll take it down to the lawyer's office."

Sue Granger started to make a face, but then thought better of it.

They dined at an expensive restaurant near the hotel and spent the rest of the evening strolling through the downtown area like a couple of kids. For a little while, George forgot about his search for Linda Beach. But when they got back to the hotel, he found a message waiting for him. *Phone Myra White*, it said.

"You're going to call her *now*?" Sue asked irritably.

"I'll take a chance. She's not the type who's in bed before 12."

Myra answered on the third ring. Her voice was familiar but a bit out of focus, as if she'd been drinking. "It's too late now. But she'll see you in the morning."

"Where?"

"You come here. We'll take you."

He couldn't argue. "All right. I'll be there at 10."

"Now what?" Sue wanted to know.

"Tomorrow morning will end it. I'll see her and that'll be it."

"I hope so," Sue said, settling into her side of the bed.

Myra White was waiting for him when he arrived, standing on the sidewalk next to a thin youth whose hair was just a bit too long. She introduced him as Charlie and never mentioned his last name. They climbed into Granger's car, with the girl in front and Charlie in the back. As he followed their directions, he wondered for the first time about his own safety. He had mentioned the fur coat to Myra. People had been robbed and even killed for far less.

"Nothing but hills in this city," he said, making conversation.

"Some say there are 42 of them," Charlie supplied, as if quoting a fact from a guided tour.

"How far are we going?"

Myra lit a cigarette. "Not far. Down by the docks."

"You said she was sick."

"She's sick."

Another thought crossed his mind. "Is she alive?"

Charlie laughed a little and they drove on in silence for a time. Finally, Myra signalled for him to stop. They were in front of a shabby brick building facing the waterfront. George grabbed Howard Beach's box and followed them into the building.

The stairs were lit by a single dim bulb. Granger followed Myra up the staircase, watching the lithe movement of her hips beneath the tight slacks, aware that Charlie was bringing up the rear. Suddenly he was afraid. He wanted to tell them to take the damn coat and the jewelry and leave him alone. He silently cursed Howard Beach and Linda and everything that had led him to this place.

"In here," Myra said, unlocking the door with a key.

Granger stepped through the doorway, knowing that Linda Beach would not be there.

She was.

She was not the Linda Beach he had known, not the beautiful young woman who'd smiled at him once across a dinner table. Her hair was rumpled and she wore a faded housecoat stained with the dregs of coffee and life, but this was Linda. How many years later?

"Hello, Linda," he said softly. "Do you remember me?" The fear had dropped away, to be replaced by another emotion akin to pity.

"I remember you. George . . ."

"Granger. George Granger."

"Yes." Her eyes seemed to fade and drift away.

He turned to Myra. "What's the matter with her?" he whispered.

"Heroin," Charlie said, and laughed.

"God!" Granger put down the box and went to her. "Linda, what's happened to you?" But he knew, without her answer. It was the same thing he'd seen happen to Howard. They'd chosen different paths, but they'd arrived at the same hell.

"Now you found her," Charlie said. "How about some money?"

Granger turned on them angrily. "Get out of here! Get out of here before I call the police!" Myra backed out of the door, but Charlie took a step forward. He was going toward the box when Granger hit him, a glancing blow on the side of the head.

Charlie cursed and doubled his fist, but Myra grabbed his arm. "Come on, Charlie. We don't want any trouble."

He cursed again and then they were gone. Granger listened to the clatter of their footsteps on the stairs, then went to the window to be sure they didn't think of his car.

When he turned back, Linda Beach was on her feet, swaying. "Thank you," she said. "They . . ."

"Never mind. You should have medical care."

"It's not as bad as it looks. How is Howard?"

"He was in the hospital. He tried to kill himself."

"I heard that. I'm sorry."

"He sent your fur coat and some jewelry." Granger placed the box next to her on the rumpled bed. She touched the twine and tape uncertainly and he knew what thought was going through her mind. "Will you sell them to buy more drugs?"

She tried to smile. "I've sold everything else."

"Howard was wondering how you were. Perhaps if I tell him, he could come out here and help you."

"Do you really think he still cares? He hates me."

"I think he loves you."

She stared down at her shaking hands. "It's too late for love now."

"I don't think so. Promise me you won't sell these things, at least for a day or so. Let me phone Howard and see what he says."

"What he says!" She made it a curse. "What has he said till now?"

"He cares about you."

"He hates me. He always has."

Granger sighed and turned to leave. "Let me at least call him."

She picked up the box and began slowly to untie the knotted twine. "Go. It doesn't matter what you do."

He watched her for a moment, wondering what tomorrow might bring. He remembered the woman who'd smiled at him across a dinner table, but he knew that whatever happened, she was gone forever. There was nothing left to do, nothing but to carry a message without hope back to Howard Beach.

"Good-by, Linda," he said very quietly, looking back at her. As he closed the door, she was pulling the last of the twine from the box.

Granger was halfway down the stairs when the explosion came, blasting the door of the apartment from its hinges and nearly pitching him down the stairs. He looked back in horror at the smoke and flame and knew in a blinding instant what Howard Beach had sent his wife— out of madness or hate. Or desperate love.

It Happens, Sometimes

Craidy woke early that morning, as was his habit. He'd never slept well in a strange bed, and with the approach of middle age he'd found himself to be sleeping poorly even in familiar surroundings. Perhaps he needed a woman, or perhaps he only needed a life to live.

His window was at the back of the building, facing on this May morning a snowy field of dead dandelions that ran down the slight hill to Arnie's Amusement Arcade where he worked. It wasn't much of a job, but it paid the rent and it allowed him to spend eight to ten hours a day tinkering with the electrical gadgets which had become the most important thing in life to him.

Craidy ate breakfast downstairs in the little lunch counter which would open its fringed front later in the day to transform itself into a hotdog stand for the beach-bound crowds. He never ate there late in the day. It was bad enough in the mornings. After breakfast he strolled slowly down the hill to work, kicking occasionally at the puffy whiteness of the dandelion heads, watching with a sort of pleasure as they disintegrated into tiny windblown snowflakes. It was one of the pleasures in life that was not dependent upon the little room over Arnie's Arcade, or upon the memory of better days past.

"Morning, Craidy," someone said, and he saw that it was Arnie himself, just opening for the sprinkling of morning business.

"Hi. Expecting much today?"

Arnie was a big man with a quick leer and shifty eyes. "Getting close to Memorial Day. It'll be picking up. You almost done rewiring those bowling machines?"

"Yeah. I'll finish them today." He went down the long aisle between rows of colorful machines, standing ready for nickels and dimes. There were machines for bowling and baseball and ice hockey play, and even a machine which simulated the flying of a jet plane. Over against one wall, near the back, was a line of pinball machines demoted by reason of age and obsolescence to their present inferior location. The age of the pinball had passed, Craidy decided. It had passed almost unnoticed, in those post-war years when even the sentiments of Saroyan's play *The Time of Your Life* seemed vaguely old-fashioned. The kids today wanted something else—rayguns to shoot at monster targets, or six-shooters to gun down outlaws who talked back, or driving machines if they were a bit older, or bowling, over by the Coke machine.

He went up the narrow flight of wooden steps and entered the little room above the great arcade. It was the closest thing to home, much closer than the place where he spent his nights. Here, looking out on the activity below while he repaired and rewired the complex electrical systems of the three hundred-odd machines, Craidy felt a peace of mind which was rare. He was never disturbed while working up there, and sometimes he felt himself a sort of god as he watched the teenagers at the machines, the girls lined up at the little fortune-telling booth which was Arnie's latest innovation.

For a long time, through all the chill of spring, Arnie and Craidy had worked alone in the big arcade, getting ready for the summer crowds that would overflow from the nearby beach. Though he didn't really respect Arnie, he couldn't help liking the man, and he'd felt a twinge of regret when Arnie had taken on the pale blonde girl who told fortunes. Her name was Rita O'Blanc, and she was twenty-two years old. While she was working she wore a gray wig to make her look older, but most of the guys who hung around the place in the evening were wise to that, and a few had even gotten to taking her out on dates.

But until that morning, her relationship with Craidy had been confined to a single nod when they passed each other downstairs. It was as if she sensed his feeling and stayed clear of him because of this. Now, as he worked over the intricacies of wiring removed from the back of the bowling machine, she appeared suddenly in the doorway.

"Good morning!"

He looked up, hiding his surprise. "How are you today?"

"Fine. I wondered if you might like a cup of coffee."

"From that machine downstairs? No thanks."

"I know, it's pretty bad. I was thinking of walking up to the hotdog stand. I won't have any customers for a while yet."

"Sure, I'll go for a cup. But let me pay for yours, too." He handed her two greasy dimes.

She returned some ten minutes later, carrying two steaming paper cups. "It's longer up there than I thought."

"Thanks a lot, but you shouldn't have bothered." He put down his wire strippers and leaned back against the workbench. She wasn't bad to look at, really, in the good light.

"You live in that building, don't you? Over the stand?"

"Yeah. Beautiful view of all the dead dandelions."

"I like them, alive or dead." She sipped her coffee. "I don't think of them as a weed at all. Not really." Another sip, then, "What are you doing?"

"Fixing up these bowling machines. Damn wiring is like a maze."

"Is there really enough repair work to keep you busy all summer?"

He'd often thought about that himself. "Well, most of that stuff is pretty old. Arnie bought a lot of it second-hand. It'll take me another month to have everything working, and after that he thinks maybe he can get me some work from the other concessions."

"Were you always an electrician, Craidy?"

He smiled, somehow liking her. "Were you always a fortune teller?"

"Yes, as a matter of fact. I can read people's minds."

"That must be handy when you're out on a date."

"You're a crazy guy." She walked over to the window and peered down at the arcade, where she could see a couple of boys playing pinball machines. They were wearing swimming trunks and knitted shirts. "Look at those kids down there! Swimming this early in the season! That water must be freezing."

"Maybe that's why they came here instead." He lit a cigarette and offered her one. "Do you swim?"

"Not till after June first, I don't."

"What do you do with yourself evenings? When these guys around here aren't dating you?"

She laughed and blew out some smoke. "I'm going to the fight tonight. You going?"

The weekly fights were held in a little arena a half-mile down the beach. The fighters were mostly one-punch nobodies on their way up, or more often on their way down. Many of them progressed no further than the Beach Arena. "Well, I drop by occasionally," he admitted.

"Would you take me? I feel funny going alone."

"So that's why you came up this morning." He had to laugh about it. She wasn't the sort of girl anyone could dislike, and he wondered how he'd avoided her charms for so long. "Isn't Arnie going?"

"Sure, but I don't want to go with the boss."

"What's so special about tonight, anyway?"

"Frank Wayne's fighting. The fellow that hangs out here all the time."

Frank Wayne was an old friend of Arnie's, a down-and-out boxer with a glass jaw. The only thing that kept him going was a solid right that managed to connect once in a while. For a time he was known as Tiger Wayne, but somewhere along the downward path he'd reverted to just plain Frank.

"I'll take you," Craidy said, "if you don't mind being seen with someone old enough to be your father."

"Come *on!* You're only thirty-seven."

"How'd you find that out?"

"I told you I could read minds," she answered with a laugh. "It comes in handy sometimes."

There was some noise from below and they looked down to see Frank Wayne strolling in, calling out a greeting to Arnie. "Let's go down and see him," Craidy said, surprised at his own sudden interest in the fight. During the past weeks, the Beach Arena had been nothing more than a destination that need not be reached. Now he was actually taking an interest in this man who would be fighting.

Arnie was talking with Wayne when they reached the arcade, and the two boys in bathing trunks stood watching from a distance, trying to decide on the correct attitude toward this almost-hero. "What kind of shape you in, Tiger?" Arnie asked him.

"I'm not Tiger any more, just Frank. But I'll take that punk tonight! I'll flatten him in one round. A cheap punk kid on his way up!"

Arnie smiled. "You're talking big, Tiger. Here, you know Rita already. This guy's Craidy—he sits up there like God in his little room and fixes the wires. He keeps the whole damn joint running."

They shook hands, and Wayne gave it a little extra squeeze to show he was in condition. "Glad to meet you. Coming to see me tonight?"

Craidy nodded. "I'll be there. We'll both be there."

Wayne nodded like a small boy. "Good! After the fight I'll come back here and beat these machines."

The Night My Friend

After he'd gone, Arnie started opening the big overhead doors that lined one side of the arcade. "Going to be a warm one," he said. "If the rain holds off we'll have a good crowd today."

Craidy breathed in some fresh air and took out his cigarettes. "Think Wayne'll win tonight?"

"He should, but don't make any bets. That manager of his—Sam Seffer—isn't above a little hanky-panky. And when you get to Wayne's age you can't really do much but go along with it."

"You mean he might have to throw the fight?" Rita asked, unbelieving.

"He might. This young punk is just getting started. If there's money behind him, they might be trying to give him the big buildup. You know, fifteen straight knockouts, that sort of thing."

"Would Wayne do it?"

"What choice has he got?"

Craidy climbed back up the stairs to his little room, feeling suddenly depressed. Frank Wayne was no longer a Tiger, but there was still about his chiseled features and metallic hair the look of an almost-champion, a man of integrity in a world that had too few. He hoped that Arnie was wrong about the fight.

The day clouded up around noon, which turned out to be good for the arcade's business. The early swimmers were driven inside by the threat of rain, and a good many of them drifted into the aisles of glistening, neoned machines. Craidy watched them come and go from his room, occasionally pausing in his work to give a special bit of attention to a girl in a bathing suit or a boy who looked as if he might cause trouble. Arnie was busy giving change and keeping order and generally running things, and Craidy noted a steady stream of customers—exclusively girls—for Rita O'Blanc's fortune telling booth. He watched a couple of them giggling in a corner after a session with Rita and decided she must have a pretty good act.

The rain, when it came, was brief and cooling with a sudden wind that churned up little eddies of sand along the length of the beach until the moisture darkened and dampened it. Arnie worked hard, and when the returning sun scattered his customers he relaxed with a cold bottle of beer. "Want one?" he called up to Craidy. "Tastes good."

Craidy came down to join him, and after the beer he finished rewiring the last of the bowling machines. He played a game to be certain it was working properly, and Rita came out of her booth to watch. "You're pretty good at this," she said.

"It's all a trick. After working on them for a solid week I know just where you have to hit those pins to trip the scoring mechanism."

"Life is pretty much of a trick to you, isn't it?"

"I guess maybe you can read minds. Mine, at least."

The evening was cool, and after supper he met Rita back at the arcade, wondering vaguely where she lived. He supposed that she had an apartment nearby much like his own, but he'd never really had occasion to think about it before. They walked the short distance to the arena, under a sky turning dark as clouds once more obscured the setting sun.

"It'll rain tomorrow," Rita said. "Not good for the holiday weekend."

"Is that a guess or a prediction?"

"We'll see tomorrow," she answered with a laugh.

He was surprised at the crowd in the Beach Arena. Generally, the promoters considered it a good night when they could fill half the seats, but tonight the little place was loaded almost to capacity and a cloud of blue cigarette smoke was already visible near the ceiling lights.

They sat in bored relaxation through the first two bouts, watching a boy not yet twenty flatten a colored youth in the second round, then two older fighters who went the limit as if the whole thing were a dull spring dance. They were earning their money, but just barely. During this last bout Craidy went outside for a smoke and some popcorn, unable to gear his body to the hour of uneventful sitting. He amused himself by studying the lights and wiring of the place for a time, and then returned to Rita with the box of popcorn.

"Did I miss anything?"

She shook her head. "Wayne's fighting next, though. That's the other guy, just getting into the ring."

Frank Wayne's opponent was a youth in his early twenties who carried himself already as if the television cameras were on him. He had sandy, wavy hair, and a body like a Greek god, and his name was Blaze Dungan. "He looks good," Craidy commented.

Rita munched her popcorn. "He's got six knockouts."

"Think it'll be like Arnie said?"

"I hope to hell not."

The smoke had grown thicker during the first two bouts, and now the fighters in the ring appeared as if in a dream—a half-remembered fog of action that lacked the hard sharp outlines of waking truth. They came out at the bell, clashing like iron-chested gladiators, and Wayne's first punch was only a glancing blow to the neck. Blaze Dungan danced back, bobbed and weaved with professional stance, and landed a neat right to Wayne's jaw. To Craidy the two seemed evenly matched, though even this early in the bout Dungan's youth was beginning to show. What he lacked in experience he more than made up for in sheer guts.

At ringside, Craidy could see a fuzzy little man with a damp cigar urging Wayne on, wringing a towel between his hands. This would be Sam Seffer, the manager, a man obviously acclimated to the shoddy, smoky squalor of the Beach Arena. At the end of the first round he was up there, massaging Wayne's shoulders, whispering words of battle into his ear. They might have been the same words spoken by every manager to every fighter, and Craidy wondered if Wayne even heard them, in spite of the nodding of his head.

They came out for the second round a bit more slowly, a bit more respectfully. In the center of the ring, almost lost in the smoke and overhead lights, they traded punches to the gradually rising throb of the crowd. Then, suddenly, Blaze Dungan landed a solid left to the body, a right to the jaw, and Wayne began to cave in, all at once.

"Craidy! He's down!" Rita gripped his arm in sudden alarm.

They left their seats and ran down to ringside as the referee counted Wayne out. Rita clawed at the canvas floor of the ring and shouted his name over the roar of the crowd, but he only lifted his head a bit and stared at her through bloodshot eyes. They were not the glazed eyes of a semi-conscious man, but rather the sad eyes of a lost man, lost in a world he never made.

As the referee held Blaze Dungan's right arm high in victory, Rita turned away and brushed past Craidy. There were tears in her eyes.

"He threw it! He threw the fight!" she said later, as they walked back along the beach in the darkness.

"You don't know that."

"I know it."

"I suppose you read his mind," Craidy said. He was beginning to get just a little annoyed with Rita O'Blanc.

"Yes, I did! But you don't have to believe that if you don't want to. All you had to do was look into his eyes to know the truth."

"I looked into his eyes." He lit a cigarette, blinking as the flare of the match blinded him for a moment. "So maybe he did throw the fight. So what? That's life—it happens every day."

"Not to a man like Frank Wayne."

Craidy kicked at a floundering piece of driftwood, sending it splashing into the surf. "What's with you, anyway? Do you really believe this bit about reading people's minds?"

"I learned that I could quite early in life, actually. When I was twelve mother took me to a doctor who'd studied such matters. He gave us a long speech about every human mind being different, about some minds being below normal and some being above normal. He said what I had was a great gift. My mother didn't look at it that way. She just wanted a normal daughter, without any gifts. I remember she kept asking the doctor how I'd gotten that way—as if the thing was some sort of disease. And all he answered was that it happens, sometimes."

Somehow he believed her. He couldn't help believing her. "How did you end up telling fortunes at Arnie's, of all places?"

"I left home when I was seventeen, and went to New York. Some friends I met there told me about the experiments in extrasensory perception going on at Duke University, and I went down there for a time. They were quite impressed, actually—Doctor Rhine and the others— but I guess I wasn't really as unique as I'd supposed. They ran me through a series of tests with a special deck of cards, and I scored high—but not perfect. This ESP of mine seems only a sometimes thing. After a while I left Duke and went back to New York. I tried to get a job using this talent, but it—or I—wasn't good enough for a nightclub act or anything like that. I drifted for a couple of years, through a few jobs as a secretary, a waitress, just about anything. It was hell, though, having this thing—like taking dictation from your boss and *knowing* what he was thinking about when he looked at you. Finally I just decided I was safer and happier just telling fortunes at a place like Arnie's. He gave me a job and I like it."

"Does he know you can read minds?"

"I told him, but of course he doesn't much believe it."

Craidy flipped his dying cigarette into the water. "You been reading my mind much?"

"Not much, really. I guess you interested me, up there in your little room. That's one of the reasons I wanted you to bring me tonight. I was able to tell your age by ESP, though. That's easy, once I get you thinking about it."

"And Wayne?"

She was suddenly somber. "I knew he threw the fight, knew it was tearing at his insides as he was being counted out. I guess that's why I started to cry."

Ahead of them, the lights of Arnie's Arcade came into view. Arnie had gotten one of the beach hangers-on to look after the place while he went to the fight, but now they saw he was back already, standing in the wide entrance with the neon shimmering around him like a giant halo.

"You two took forever," he said as they came up off the beach.

"We were talking," Craidy explained, a bit weakly.

"Have you seen Wayne since the fight?"

"No, why?"

Arnie's face was hard in the neon light. "The cops were just here. Blaze Dungan was beaten to death in an alley right after the fight, and it looks like Wayne did it."

Arnie pulled down the big overhead doors and closed the place a half-hour before midnight. The three of them sat in his office drinking beer by the light of his little desk lamp. For Craidy, it was an unreal experience—a dream night of dark fantastic conversation. He felt once like leaping up and telling them both he wanted no part of people, telling them both he wanted only the safety of his little upstairs room. Where he could be merely an observer.

"*Murder?*" Rita O'Blanc was saying. "Who could possibly call it murder?"

"If it was just a fight, it couldn't be more than manslaughter," Craidy said, his mind growing thick with beer and sleep and frustration.

But Arnie waved a hand in disagreement. "In the eyes of the law, a boxer's fists constitute a deadly weapon. Assault with a deadly weapon is a felony, and murder during commission of a felony is first-degree murder, even if it was unintentional. It would depend a lot on the District Attorney, but they could throw the book at him if they wanted to."

Rita shook her head as if to clear it. "But they were fighting in the ring only minutes before! If Wayne had killed him there it would have been nothing—nothing but an unfortunate accident!"

"That's right. But they weren't in the ring. I think we all know what happened. Sam Seffer forced Wayne to throw the fight. But afterwards, something got to Wayne. He sought out Blaze in that alley just to prove to both of them who was the better man. I suppose he just kept on hitting him, maybe waiting for the referee to stop it." He took a sip of beer. "Only there wasn't any referee out in that alley."

Craidy looked at Rita, and saw that she was as uneasy as he was. "It's late," he managed to say finally. "We'd better be going." He wanted no more talk of murder and beatings and the dark things of the world. He wanted only to be alone.

Rita set her glass carefully on the table. "Will you walk me home, Craidy? I have a room just a few blocks away."

"Sure." He shot a glance at Arnie. "You coming?"

"No. I . . ." He hesitated, then said, "I think he might come by here, if he needs help. I'm going to stay awhile."

Rita put a hand on his shoulder. "I know he's a friend of yours, but don't get yourself in a jam."

"Never fear," Arnie said, and he unlocked the side door to let them out. "See you both bright and early for the holiday. We'll be getting busy right after the parade. I might even need you down on the floor, Craidy."

"Yeah," Craidy answered, not too happy at the prospect.

When they were a block away, Rita broke the unnatural silence between them. "I caused it all," she said quietly. "Running up to the ringside like that. When he saw me, and knew that I knew—I think it was too much for his pride."

"Don't be silly. He probably didn't even see you there."

"He saw me."

They parted a few moments later at the door of her apartment, a place much like Craidy's own, a place for lone and lonely people. He thought of kissing her goodnight, but there was no real reason for it. "Good night," he said simply.

"Good night. And thanks."

"For what?"

"For not doing it. It wouldn't be right, tonight."

He went out into the street without another word, and walked quickly back to his own apartment. For the first time in years he was afraid, and he felt the fear knotting his stomach. He was afraid of this girl who read minds, afraid of the fighter named Wayne, afraid of people. He wanted to be alone again.

Alone.

Memorial Day. And the sun was already too high in the morning sky when he opened his eyes and sat up in the rumpled bed. Distantly, muffled by a mile or more of space, he felt rather than clearly heard the throbbing of the drums from the parade. Everyone would be there, watching, and when it broke up they'd head as always for the beach and the swimming and Arnie's. It was his first summer there, but he knew what to expect.

Arnie gave him only the briefest nod when he arrived, and he didn't see Rita at all, though the drapes of her little booth were pulled shut. He climbed the stairs to his room, thankful for at least a brief time alone. By noon the parade was finished, and below he could see the occasional uniforms beginning their mingle with the crowd. A girl in the brief, spangled costume of a drum majorette, and a limping veteran—obviously drunk—for whom the day was his big excuse for dusting off the row of medals across his chest. All of them came to Arnie's.

Finally he saw Rita come out of her booth and walk across the crowded floor to the tiny ladies' room. He could tell from up there that she was warm. The wig she wore wasn't made for sitting by the hour in a stuffy little booth. He went back to his job, wiring an electric fox-and-geese game that Arnie had picked up somewhere, and was intent on it when Rita entered his room a few moments later.

"Good morning," she said.

"Hi, but it's after noon. How are you?'

"Fine, I guess."

He glanced out his window. "Shouldn't you be down there? You've got a line."

"They can wait. Craidy . ."

"What? What's the trouble?"

"Wayne is here."

"*Here?*" He glanced to the corners of the room, as if expecting the fighter to be lurking there.

She nodded. "In Arnie's office."

"Did you see him?"

"I don't have to. He's there."

"All right," Craidy said, annoyed at being drawn once more into the web of circumstance. "What do you want me to do about it?"

"Go down and see if I'm right."

"I thought you were always right," he told her. Then, seeing the look of hurt in her eyes, he added, "I'll take a look."

He left her there and went down the steps to the arcade, dodging between two groups of giggling girls intent on attracting the attention of some nearby sailors. Through the open doorways he could see the beach already crowded with afternoon swimmers brave enough to tackle the still-chilled water. It was a holiday time.

The door to Arnie's office was locked, and when he tapped his fist to the wood he heard Arnie mumble something from inside. After a moment the door opened a crack. "What do you want?" he asked.

"Is Wayne in there?" Craidy asked quietly.

Arnie sighed and stepped aside. "Who else knows?"

"Just Rita."

"Get her in here. I've got one of the bums covering the floor. Tell her to put the out-to-lunch sign on her booth."

Craidy nodded and went back to the girl with his message. A few moments later they were gathered in the tiny, sweaty office where Arnie conducted his business affairs, talked to popcorn salesmen, and slept on lazy afternoons. "Where is he?" Rita asked.

"Come out, Frank," Arnie said, and Wayne appeared suddenly from a battered wardrobe that stood against the outside wall. He was unshaven and looked tired, and his eyes still held that beaten expression Craidy had seen the night before on the canvas of the ring.

Rita O'Blanc went to him, and held out a hand to touch him tentatively. "You did it," she said, as if she hadn't really believed it till that moment. "You killed him."

Wayne nodded his shabby head. "I did it. Every cop in town is looking for me."

"How long have you been here?" Craidy asked.

"Since early this morning, when Arnie opened up. I slept on the beach last night, under one of the piers, but I was afraid to stay there in the light." Then he added, as if feeling it necessary, "Listen, I didn't mean to kill him. You know that. When Sam told me I had to take a dive in the second round I thought he was kidding at first. I never had to do anything like that before."

Arnie nodded sadly. "I told you it would come to that. I know these operators like Sam Seffer. Always out for the fast buck."

"But why did you do it?" Rita asked. "Why did you take the dive?"

Wayne ran a bruised fist over his growth of gray stubble. "Up until the minute I did it I wasn't sure I could go through with it. And then, after it was over, I opened my eyes and saw your face only a couple of feet away, looking at me like you could read my mind. It was too late then to change things in the ring, but I wanted to make damned sure that punk kid didn't get the idea into his head that he could really floor me. I waited for him outside and caught him on the way to his car. He couldn't figure out what the hell I wanted. Even after I hit him, he just seemed to stand there. Finally he started to fight back, and I just got him into a corner and kept punching. I was waiting for him to go down but he couldn't, with the wall behind him. When I stopped punching and let him fall, I saw that he was . . ."

Arnie ran a hand over his sweating forehead. "Maybe you shoulda gone after your manager instead."

"Sam? He owes me too much money. If I had my pay from the fight I could get out of town."

"We'll get it for you," Rita said suddenly, and Craidy shot her a startled look. "You stay here, under cover."

"And how do you intend to get any money out of Seffer?" Craidy asked.

"I'll go to see him. He must know Wayne's in a bad jam."

"Sure. And he knows he can be in one too, when it comes out in court that he forced Wayne to take a dive."

"That's just why he won't want Wayne around. He'll give him the money just to get rid of him."

"Maybe," Craidy said doubtfully. He wasn't inclined to trust Sam Seffer very far. Then, because he'd already been carried along so far, he heard himself saying, "But if anyone goes to see Seffer it'll be me. I can handle myself a bit better than a girl."

"He doesn't even know you," she objected.

"He knows me as well as he knows you. Besides, Wayne can give me a note or something."

"Sure," the fighter agreed at once. "Give me a pencil and some paper and I'll write it now."

"I'm going too," Rita insisted. "We'll go together."

Arnie was quick to agree. "Don't worry about the place. I'll take care of things. Just get the money."

"How much does he owe you?" Craidy asked.

"Five hundred," the fighter replied, licking his dry lips. "He promised me the extra hundred for taking the dive."

"You did it for a hundred dollars?" Craidy asked, and then was sorry he'd said anything.

"Sometimes that seems like a lot of money. Sometimes, at my age."

From outside there came the familiar clamor of youthful roughhouse. Some boys were vigorously attacking one of the machines, claiming they'd lost a dime. "I better get out there," Arnie said. "You two get going. Wayne, you get back under cover."

Craidy and Rita left a few minutes later. He was unhappy about having the girl along, just as he was unhappy about the whole mission. He couldn't imagine how he would get the five hundred dollars out of Sam Seffer, but he knew the task would be no easier with her along. He thought about his room, and the dead dandelions, but he didn't say anything.

"I know where we can find him," Rita said as they walked quickly along the boardwalk. The beach was crowded, and they were constantly dodging the onslaught of screaming children bound for ice cream or balloons.

"Where? We're heading for the arena."

"There's a bar in the next block where the fight crowd hangs out. I've seen him in there before in the afternoon."

"You reading minds again?"

"No, just guessing."

"Then maybe you'll be wrong for once."

She smiled "Maybe."

But when they reached the place, the bartender motioned toward the dim back room. "In there," he said.

The place was a windowless cell large enough for just six booths, where a dim ceiling light cast its pinkish glow over a world where night and day blended into one. It was a place to bring a girl or meet one, not a place for a man who drank alone in the middle of the afternoon.

Sam Seffer, seeming smaller than ever alone in the booth, looked up as Rita spoke his name. "Yeah? What'd you want?" There were four empty beer bottles on the table.

"Frank Wayne sent us," she said, getting right to the point.

"That damned fool! He deserves whatever happens to him!" Seffer lifted his glass and drained the last of the beer.

Craidy slid into the booth opposite him. "Look, Seffer, we didn't come to kid around. We want the money you owe Wayne. Five hundred."

"Who the hell are you? I don't know you."

Craidy reached across the table and wrinkled a handful of sweat-stained shirt. "We're meeting right now. Either you help Wayne get out of town or he spills everything to the cops, including your part in the fix."

"Get your hands offa me! I don't know about any fix."

"Think a jury will believe that? Or the State Athletic Commission?"

Seffer pulled away as Craidy relaxed his grip. "Anyway, I don't owe him no five hundred!"

"He thinks so," Rita joined in. "Four hundred for the fight and another hundred for taking the dive."

Sam Seffer snorted into his empty glass. "Hell, the guy's gone nutty! Nobody on this earth ever got four hundred at the Beach Arena."

"Five hundred better be the figure, anyway," Craidy said softly. "Have you got it?"

"You think you're tough, don't you? Ha!"

"Have you got it?" Craidy repeated.

Seffer's hand went for one of the beer bottles, but Craidy was faster. He smashed it on the edge of the table and held out the jagged edges toward the little man. Behind him, Rita gasped.

"All right," Seffer said. "I don't have it with me, but I can get it."

"By tonight."

"By tonight."

"Bring it to Arnie's before nine. Understand?"

"I understand," he gulped.

Craidy tossed the broken bottle on the table. "We'll be looking for you."

As they walked out the bartender looked up from his task of refilling an empty scotch bottle. "What was all the noise?"

"Dropped a bottle," Craidy said.

"I don't like noise. We got a respectable place."

"Sure. I'll remember that."

Outside, the day seemed suddenly chilled, and he walked along for a time without speaking to the girl at his side. He was back in it, back in the mess once more.

"I was scared in there," Rita said finally, after they'd covered half the distance back to Arnie's arcade. "I thought for a moment you were going to kill him."

"For a moment, I was."

"You're awful mixed up, aren't you, Craidy? More than me, even."

"Let's go someplace and talk," he said suddenly. "I don't want to go back there yet."

"They'll be waiting to hear."

"We'll phone them." He found a glassed-in booth along the board-walk and dialed Arnie's number, explaining that Sam Seffer had prom-ised to bring the money that evening. Then, when he hung up, he saw that Rita had moved to a nearby ice cream stand. A police patrol car was parked nearby, with two uniformed officers out of it, asking questions of the white-shirted ice cream man.

When Craidy came over, Rita handed him a chocolate cone. "I hope you like this brand," she said.

"What's with the cops?"

"Looking for Wayne. Still."

"Let's get out of here. I told Arnie we'd be back in an hour."

"How're things there?"

"Rough. Police all over the place. They seem convinced he's still around the beach somewhere."

Perhaps to escape from the threat of police, or perhaps only to leave the salt-air beach behind for a time, they walked a few blocks inland, to where great old mansions still stood silently on treelined streets.

"This was a classy section once," Rita said. "Now they're mostly cut up for apartments."

"I know. I used to live in a house like that myself, a long time ago."

"Tell me about it, Craidy," she said.

"What is there to tell?"

"You would have killed Sam Seffer. Did that ever happen before?"

"Not really. I seem to have spent most of my life getting involved with people, pulling myself out of messes. I guess that's why I came here, for some sort of peace. Fooling with electrical things is the only sort of peace I get any more"

"You must have had lots of girls."

"That was a long time ago, when I was a kid. I'm a middle-aged man now."

"Were you ever married?"

"Engaged. She was killed in an auto accident."

"You were driving?"

"The mind-reading's a bit hazy this afternoon. She was with another guy. They were going like hell and the crash killed both of them. Good thing. If he'd lived, I'd have killed him myself, I suppose."

"Then what?"

"Oh, my family had a little money which they promptly lost to some schemer. He was one of the people I almost killed. I guess that's why I can feel sorry for Wayne. I guess he only did what I would have done."

"You wouldn't have thrown the fight in the first place, Craidy."

"No," he agreed. "I suppose not."

The air was suddenly filled with breeze-blown white fuzz."It comes off the trees," Rita explained, brushing some from her dress.

"Fluffy and white, just like the dead dandelions." He glanced at his watch. "We'd better be getting back."

"Craidy."

"What?"

"You know, we're both a couple of misfits, in our own way. You can't communicate with people, or don't want to. And I communicate with them too well. I read their minds. Maybe we'd make a good team."

But Craidy only shook his head. "I'm too much of a loner for you or anybody."

"You weren't a loner today, helping out Wayne."

"I told you, it might have been me."

The arcade was there ahead of them again, great and gross and ugly, yet somehow handsome in the afternoon sun. A fun place, and there were so few of them left.

Arnie was sweating over his coin-changing machine when they entered. "Damn thing's busted! Busiest day of the year and the damn thing's busted! Can you fix it, Craidy?"

"I'll see." He was thankful for something to do, something to take his mind from the day and its too-pressing events. He quickly dismantled the machine and carried the guts of it upstairs to his little room with the window.

Toward evening, the teenagers seemed to gravitate toward the beach for a final swim. Craidy had repaired the coin-changer, and during a lull in things they gathered once more in Arnie's tiny office.

Wayne came out of hiding, looking sick and sweaty with a renewed growth of beard.

"Have you had anything to eat?" Rita asked him.

"Just candy bars out of the machine," he said.

Arnie wiped the sweat from his brow. "How could I risk getting him food with cops all over the place? I don't even know how he's goin' to get outa here tonight."

"When it's dark I'll make it, don't worry. All I need is money."

"He'll be here before nine with the money," Craidy said.

"You hope. I might have to go after old Sam with my fists."

Craidy took out a cigarette. "Like you did with Blaze?"

"I can still floor any man in the state with this right. Don't you forget it."

"Come on," Rita said, stepping between them. "Let's calm down. It's after eight already. Seffer should be on his way."

Arnie walked over to the window. "We're goin' to have a damn nice sunset. So nice the kids'll be lovin' it up on the beach instead of playing the machines."

"Don't complain," Rita said. "You've had a good day."

Outside, a car pulled up with a screeching of cinders. Then another, and a third. They stood for a split second frozen to the floor, and then Craidy ran to the other window. "Cops!"

"Seffer sent them," Wayne growled. "I'm getting out of here."

"Wait!" Rita tried to hold back, but already he'd sprung for the office door, letting in the garish light and the jukebox noises. Then it was happening too fast for any of them to stop.

Wayne hit the first two cops with his bull-like shoulders, on the run, knocking one of them into the glass top of the hockey machine. But already there were others outside, blocking the only routes of possible escape. He stood like a trapped animal as kids and onlookers scattered, as Rita and Arnie and Craidy tried to fight their way through to his side.

Then he ran back, toward the bowling machines and the stairway to Craidy's room, thinking perhaps in some mad moment that the only escape was up those steps. One of the policemen was unsnapping his holster, and a plainclothes detective already had his gun out.

"Stop, Wayne!" one of them shouted. "We'll shoot!"

The fighter turned at the bottom step and yelled back, "Shoot then damn it!" But as the nearest cop brought up his gun Rita O'Blanc suddenly hurled herself at him.

"No don't, don't shoot," she screamed, as the gun seemed to explode at her touch. She straightened, turned, half propelled by the force of the bullet, and toppled across the line of bowling machines.

Wayne put a hand to his face, staring at the blood that welled from her bosom, and didn't move, even when the nearest detective snapped a handcuff on his wrist. "She's dead," one of the officers said simply.

"God I didn't mean to shoot her. She jumped in front of me. You all saw it. I didn't mean to shoot her." The cop was very young, and he held the gun now loosely, forgetting it was there.

Arnie walked over and stared down at her, unspeaking, and a detective came up to him. "We're sorry. Who was she?"

"Just a girl," Arnie answered.

And a policeman near Craidy said, "She shouldn't have tried to save him. Who was she, his girlfriend?"

Craidy shook his head, remembering suddenly the unlit cigarette still between his fingers. "No, she was just . . . involved with people."

"We're sorry," the cop said. "It happens sometimes."

"Yeah. I guess that's the only epitaph she'll get."

Craidy left them there, and went up the steps to his little room and closed the door behind him. He pressed his forehead against the cooling glass of the window and stared down at them for a long time, unseeing.

A Girl Like Cathy

She was a girl like Cathy, and I suppose that was why I noticed her in the first place.

She was browsing among the remaindered books in a little Greenwich Village shop, her long, dark hair falling in twin columns around her slim, pale face. I could see even from a distance that she had a good figure and showed it—with black stockings, a tight skirt, sweater and a faded leather shoulder bag that would have been out of place anywhere but in the Village.

I watched casually while she purchased a copy of *Art Treasures of the World* and a book of O'Hara short stories, then followed her into the evening turmoil of Eighth Street. "Pardon me," I said, catching up with her at the corner, "but don't I know you?"

She turned her pale face toward me with a wise smile, as if she'd heard that line many times before. "I don't believe so."

"You don't have a sister named Cathy?"

"No."

"I used to know a girl who looked a great deal like you. I thought it might have been your sister."

She shifted the package of books to her other arm. "I don't have a sister. Sorry."

"Well. . . . Could I perhaps buy you a drink anyway?"

She almost seemed to relax at my words, as if knowing how to cope with a familiar situation. "I guess I'm never one to refuse a drink. But I am in a hurry. How about right in here?"

It was a gloomy little bar, but once inside she seemed to relax even more. She propped her elbow on the package of books and smiled at me across the table. "Would you mind telling me your name—I mean now that you've picked me up?"

"Tony," I told her. "Tony Gunther. And you're. . . ?"

"Not Cathy. Or her sister. My name's Laura Ring."

"You live here in the Village, Laura?"

She nodded. "I have an apartment nearby." Careful not to give me the address. Not quite yet.

"I've always thought I'd like to live in the Village."

"You're not from New York. I can tell that from your accent."

"Chicago. I'm just here bumming around for a while. You go to college?"

She chuckled. "Thanks for the compliment. I've been out of college more than five years. No, I paint a little, work in the department stores at Christmastime, that sort of thing. I was even in an Off Broadway show last year."

"I'll bet you were good."

She sipped her beer and eyed me from under the hair. "I'm good at anything I try. But I do have to be going. Big date tonight."

"Just when we've met?"

"Oh, all right, then. Phone me, Tony. My number's in the book."

"Tomorrow?"

The eyes studied me. "If you'd like." Then she was gone, leaving only an empty beer glass and two half-finished cigarette butts. That was the beginning of it.

The following day was Sunday—one of those playful November days when you almost think summer might be returning to Manhattan. I called Laura Ring just after noon. If she was the kind of girl to go to church, she was already home, and she accepted my invitation for an afternoon stroll without hesitation.

"Pick me up here," she told me. "At 2 or so."

I was there on the dot, finding her on the third floor of a dim and dismal building just around the corner from Eighth Street. But the apartment itself surprised me. It was furnished in a simple but modern style that showed a good deal of taste, with framed reproductions of Klee and Picasso on one wall and a bookcase full of art volumes and modern authors on the other.

"You live here alone?" I asked. "It's very nice."

"I had a roommate till a few months ago. Do you want a drink? In return for the one you bought me last night?"

I accepted a Scotch on the rocks and settled down to enjoy myself. "You know, I wasn't kidding last night. You do remind me of a girl I used to know."

"Yes. Tell me about this Cathy."

"Oh, she looked a lot like you. Remarkably so. Enough to be your sister."

"This was in Chicago?"

I nodded, sipping my drink. It was expensive Scotch.

"I was still under 25 at the time, and something of a kid, I suppose. Cathy was the kind of a girl I dreamed of meeting, and I fell for her, hard. That was a mistake."

"Why?"

I didn't really want to tell her any more. "Oh, we got involved in a sort of business deal and I came out on the short end." Then, "Say, how about that walk?"

"All right. Over to Washington Square?"

We walked through the park, kicking leaves from our path, talking about the latest books and about art. She was way ahead of me on that subject.

"You said you painted a little?"

"Very little. But right now I'm involved in something quite interesting, Tony. A man—a sort of dealer—has commissioned me to obtain certain works of art."

She talked vaguely about her work, and I talked vaguely about the reasons I'd left Chicago. Things didn't get definite until we returned to her apartment toward evening.

I saw a lot of Laura Ring after that. We took in a few shows uptown, and a greater number of colorful Village bars, but mostly we just stayed around her apartment because I liked it there. It was perhaps three weeks after I'd first met her that she asked me the question.

"Tony?"

"Yes?"

"Were you ever in trouble with the police?"

"What kind of a question is that?"

"I don't know. There are always a lot of police on patrol in the Village. Sometimes when we pass them, you seem to tense up."

I lit a cigarette and pondered what to tell her. Finally I decided on the truth, since she'd guessed it anyway.

"It was that thing I mentioned, back in Chicago with Cathy. She was a wild sort of girl, and one night after a few drinks we stole a car. We were going to head west with it. We got as far as a motel in Iowa. I woke up in the morning to find that Cathy had skipped out with my money and left me with the hot car. The police found it in the motel parking lot. Since we'd crossed the state line, it was a Federal offense, and I ended up with a year and a day in jail. They let me out early, but it was still a bit of a blow. I'd never been in trouble before."

She asked me how old I was when this had happened.

"Twenty-four. Old enough to know better."

"What ever happened to Cathy?"

"I heard from her once, after I got out of jail. She was living in San Francisco, married to an insurance man. I don't know why she even bothered to write to me. I never answered her."

She patted my knee. "I'm sorry."

"Oh, I guess I'm over it now. Except for the nerves when I see a cop."

Laura said nothing more about it that night, but the next time I saw her, a few days later, she began the conversation with a question. "Tony, could I trust you? Could I talk to you about a business deal and rely on your silence?"

"I guess so," I answered with a smile. "But our relationship at this point is hardly a business one."

"I told you a while back that I was commissioned by a man to obtain certain works of art. There's something coming up that needs a man— someone like you."

Her voice was dead serious, and I tried to read something in the deep luster of her eyes. "What do you mean by that?"

"Tony—would you be willing to risk another run-in with the police? What I have in mind could be dangerous."

I shook my head. "No, thanks. I'd be a second offender. I could get 20 years."

She sighed and leaned back in her chair. "It would be worth $10,000 for a single night's work."

I stopped shaking my head. "Tell me about it. I'm not promising a thing, but tell me about it."

She walked to the bookcase and brought back an oversize volume of color plates. The one she opened to showed a sort of cup or chalice encrusted with jewels. "Have you ever heard of the Institute for Medieval Studies?"

"Can't say that I have."

"They maintain a sort of museum in North Jersey, filled to overflowing with priceless art objects imported from Europe. This particular piece is the chalice of Salisbury Cathedral. Those jewels along the side are worth a fortune in themselves."

"Don't talk about fortunes. How many dollars?"

"Who knows? Maybe it's priceless. In any event, the man who hired me will pay $70,000 for it. Out of that, I'll pay you 10."

I looked at her steadily. "You're planning to steal this thing from the museum, right?"

"Tony, you can get out now if you want."

"Was this all you wanted me for? From the beginning?"

"Of course not! But you're here and I need someone. I can't do it alone."

"All right," I said. "Tell me."

It's hard to explain why I went along with her at that moment. Perhaps it was only because the alternative—to walk out of her apartment and her life—had very little appeal for me.

Laura got up and walked back to the bookcase. This time she produced a rolled-up map of the North Jersey countryside. I'd driven over there once or twice since coming east, but I didn't really know the area.

"Here," she said, pointing to a junction of two roads. "This is the state highway, and over in this section is the Institute. You'll notice I've drawn in a large building with a smaller one some distance behind it. The smaller one is our goal—where the chalice is."

As she talked, her long hair fell occasionally over her face. She brushed it back with a quick, impatient gesture that I liked. At that point I think I would have followed her into hell itself. "What is it?" I asked.

"A rebuilt chapel, transported here from Spain. They use it as a showcase for some of their special treasures."

"And you're going to rob it?"

She lifted her eyes to mine. "*We* are."

I got up and lit a cigarette and started stalking about the room. "Even if I agreed to it, the thing's probably impossible. Don't they have guards, alarms?"

"They have guards *and* alarms *and* spotlights. But it can be done, by two people."

"How?"

"The alarms are on the doors and bottom windows only. There's one window around the back, maybe 20 feet above the ground, that has only a metal screen over it—no alarm. The screen can easily be cut."

"Is the window kept locked?"

"It doesn't open. It's stained glass, from this church in Spain. But the windows are all leaded into place. With a small torch you can melt the leading and lift the whole thing out."

"Lot simpler to break it."

"Not the way I have things worked out, Tony. The place is closed to the public on Mondays, and the guards only patrol the outside. If we pull the job on a Sunday night, get the chalice and replace the window, the theft won't even be discovered till Tuesday!"

"How often do the guards check the building?"

"Once an hour. Plenty of time for fast workers."

"How do I reach the window in the first place?"

"Did you ever see these trucks Con Ed uses to change street lights?"

Just about then I knew I was hooked. She had the thing worked out with a clockwork precision that amazed me. Whatever the risks, whatever the gain, I was in it with her right up to the end.

On Saturday night I dreamed about Cathy. It was the first time in nearly a year that she'd intruded on my sleep, and I didn't like it. She was standing in the doorway of that motel, looking the way I remembered her. She was laughing.

I rolled out of bed a little before noon, glanced out at the sunny street where churchgoers strolled briskly against the autumn breeze, and opened a can of beer. It tasted terrible before breakfast.

By midafternoon I was at Laura's apartment, ready for the big adventure. She greeted me through the closed door, then opened it carefully to reveal herself in an unflattering male uniform.

"Come on in," she urged. "I've got yours, too."

"Where'd you get them?"

"Same place as the truck. I know a fellow with the New Jersey power company. This one's off duty on Sundays."

"How much did you tell him?"

She smiled her wise smile. She seemed very wise just then. "Nothing. The poor boy thought he loved me once. He'd do anything I asked. It's good to have a few like that around. They come in so handy."

I sat down and lit a cigarette. "I'm learning new things about you every day."

"You've only scratched the surface, Tony. Now take off your clothes. I've got the other uniform in here."

It fit me better than I'd expected. "I guess it's all right. The pants are a bit tight."

She frowned at that. "You think you'll be able to climb down the rope? And back up again?"

"Sure," I said, hoping silently that I was still in condition. "Tell me something, though. This guy who's buying the chalice—how's he going to get rid of something as famous as that?"

"He doesn't intend to get rid of it. He'll just keep it to look at, and maybe someday sell it secretly to another collector. There are men like that. They buy paintings, statues, rare books, anything that could be considered an art treasure."

I didn't understand it, but I went along with it. For Laura and $10,000, I'd have gone along with just about anything. Once during that long afternoon I questioned her about my small share of the proceeds, but she had an answer for that, too. After all, she'd done the groundwork, scouted the place, thought up the plan, gotten the truck and uniforms. Besides, she reasoned convincingly, what difference would it make when we were both together, afterwards? The money would all be *ours*.

She drove the truck like a professional, the peaked cap hiding her dark hair and shadowing her feminine features. We headed north in the early darkness and crossed the Hudson at the George Washington Bridge. From there it was another hour's ride to the museum.

Once in New Jersey, we stopped to uncover the Jersey Power Company signs she'd kept covered in the Village. Then it was straight ahead till we were only a mile or so from the museum itself. I got out of the truck and walked over to a manhole she'd indicated. As the heavy cover rolled away and I slid into the depths, she said, "It should be the cable on the right."

"I know. You've told me the whole thing enough times." It took me only a moment to burn through it with my torch. Up above, along the highway, the lights blinked out as though it was the end of the world.

"That's it. Come on."

I climbed back out, guided by her flashlight. "This won't knock out the lights and alarms around the museum?"

She shook her head. "No such luck. They have their own generator on the grounds. But it'll give us an excuse for being around."

"The real power truck will arrive soon, looking for the trouble."

"All the better. It'll help us if there's more than one truck in the area."

We drove on through the darkness until our lights picked out the high wire fence surrounding the grounds of the museum. There were two uniformed Pinkerton men in a car by the side of the road, and they waved us to a stop. "What's the trouble?" one of them asked.

Laura let me do the talking, for obvious reasons. "That's what we're trying to find out. The road's dark for a couple of miles back. Probably a wire down somewhere."

The guard nodded and waved us on. In the rearview mirror I saw him get back in his car and light a cigarette. "We're all right now," Laura said. "They won't check the other building till 9:45. That gives us a good 45 minutes."

"Not long."

"Long enough."

We turned a bend in the road and came to stop beside a locked gate.

"Now what?"

"I told you, Tony. The electric wires on the top have to be disconnected so we can get the gate open."

I climbed into the plastic basket on the back of the truck and waited patiently while she raised me into position. The thing was sometimes called a "cherry picker," and when you weren't picking cherries with it, you could change street lights, repair rockets and replace power lines. The plastic basket would not conduct electricity and, thus ungrounded, I could handle live wires as harmlessly as a bird sits upon them. It took me only a moment to pull the wire free from the gate. Down below, Laura was already working on the lock.

The rebuilt chapel that was our goal sat about 200 yards behind the main building, connected to it by a gently winding road. Four spotlights played upon it from the ground. They'd have been easy to black out, but of course that would have been a dead giveaway to the Pinkerton men. Instead, we approached the chapel from the rear, keeping it between us and the other building.

"There's the window! Hurry!"

I felt the basket going up once more, and I was suddenly only inches away from a vast stained-glass scene depicting an armored knight in final combat with a grinning, flame-breathing dragon. The window was more than six feet high and perhaps four feet across. It was covered by a screen of fine wire mesh that might have kept out insects, but little else. I cut through it in two minutes flat. With the screen out of the way, I tackled the leading that held the window in place.

First, I attached a suction device such as window installers use, which in turn was attached to a rope and pulley. As soon as the window was free of its frame, the whole thing could be carefully swung down to the bed of the truck, then raised again and leaded into position after I returned. Laura had explained that a couple of spots of lead would hold it well enough till Tuesday—just enough so the window would be in place when the guards passed.

Our time was down to 25 minutes, but I worked quickly. The leading softened swiftly under the heat, and some of it merely fell away when I ran my knife along the edges. The window swung safely away, with Laura working the pulley, and I tossed my knotted rope down the inside wall. She waved me a final okay as I started down.

The interior of the chapel was black with gloom, and the tiny flashlight I allowed myself could pick out only an occasional glint of a reflected glow from the rows of display cases. I found the case Laura had described easily enough, but then something went wrong with our careful planning. The case held only a few ancient coins and a battered cup that might have been made of tin. This was certainly not the jeweled chalice of the photograph.

I hesitated a moment and then decided to follow the plan anyway. I was about to cut through the glass when I heard Laura start the truck. Something had happened. Someone was coming!

I sprinted for the wall where the rope still hung, and climbed hand over hand to the window opening. The Jersey Power truck was just disappearing through the gate. I didn't wait to spot the Pinkerton men. Pulling up the rope, I made certain it was still secured to the metal window frame and then dropped it down the outside wall. When I was 10 feet from the ground, I let myself fall the rest of the way and took off, running.

We'd worked out a plan for just such an emergency, and I made my way by foot to the prearranged pickup point. She was nowhere in sight. That meant they were on her tail and she'd have to meet me back at the apartment. I set off walking, keeping to the deeper shadows of the darkened highway, hoping at least that she'd made it safely back.

I took a bus the last part of the way into the city, and reached the apartment sometime after 2 in the morning. The duplicate key was still in my pocket. Inside, I saw the change at once. Her books and most of her clothes were gone. So was a large painting that had hung over the sofa. She'd been here ahead of me and taken those things and left. Could they have been that close to catching her? Could they have been so close she hadn't even had time to leave me a note?

I couldn't stay there. I took a chance on returning to my own place, where everything seemed normal enough. My sleep was light and troubled, waiting for the phone call that didn't come.

In the morning I went down to the corner for a late edition of the *Times*. The story was on the front page, near the bottom, with a three-column picture. They always liked museum robberies; there was something cultural about them.

WINDOW OF ST. GEORGE
STOLEN IN DARING
MUSEUM ROBBERY

The Window of St. George, a stained-glass masterpiece created in the early 16th century by Guglielmo de Marcillat, was stolen last night in a daring museum robbery at the Institute for Medieval Studies near Lyntown, N.J. The window, transported here from Italy in 1926, is valued by collectors at more than $50,000.

I folded the paper and dropped it into a trash basket. There was no need to read any further. I already knew I wouldn't be seeing Laura Ring again. As I said in the beginning, she was a girl like Cathy.

What's It All About?

The engine coughed once and then caught, throbbing to life as I eased down on the accelerator. Then I was traveling, heading across town to the expressway where I could really open her up. The dark came late on these summer nights, and even now at past nine-thirty a sort of red-orange glow lingered in the western sky, as if reluctant to vanish completely.

I had all the windows open and the breeze felt good, and I wondered where I was going. Not that it mattered. It never mattered when I was behind the wheel, feeling the power of the engine as we tore through the night—just it and me. Maybe that was the only taste of power—real power—I got in an otherwise dull life. Five days a week I could work away like all the other jerks, and walk the streets during the lunch hour with that set expression of pleasant boredom, but when Friday nights came I was master of myself, driving two tons of steel along a gray ribbon of highway.

It was at times like this that I knew what the air aces of the First World War must have felt when they took to the sky in their Spads and Fokkers and Sopwith Camels. This, right here now, speeding along the expressway at seventy miles an hour, was what life is all about. I flipped on the radio but then turned it off again. I didn't need it. I didn't need anything but the speed and the power and the certainty that I was going somewhere.

But where tonight? I jacked up the speed to eighty-five, taking a long low hill as if it didn't exist, roaring down the other side with all the fury of the night around me. I passed a little sports car with a girl at the wheel, turned sharply in front of her and debated having some fun. But no, I had other things on my mind. She might remember me, or the license number, and report it to the cops later. I couldn't take a chance on anything like that.

Further along, pressing ninety, I caught an animal in the road—a rabbit, probably—and pinned him to the pavement before he knew what hit him. All right, all right. No faster, or they might pick me up. I slowed it back gradually, seeing the lights of the city off on my right.

And turned off into downtown. The city reminded me of the resort season in Florida. Flowering sport shirts, girls in shorts, open-topped convertibles prowling the streets. Friday, Friday night, the beat beat beat of the rock place as I passed. "Hey, cat." Sure. I remembered Florida, and the old man I'd caught on the crosswalk there.

Friday night was alive, with the blood of the city throbbing in its veins, and I was its master, as long as I stayed behind the wheel, as long as I saw it all only through the windshield speckled with the guts of a dozen dead bugs.

I cruised some more, thinking about where to go. Maybe down to the Negro section. I could hit a kid in the street and keep on going. They'd see a white man driving away and that would be enough for a nice riot on a hot Friday night. Or maybe down to the beach, where there'd be a crowd even after dark. They were never individual people when I had them in my sights, never men or women or children when I gunned the car forward in that final second. They were only objects like bags of sand.

Some kids in a pickup truck yelled at me as they went by, and I followed them for a while until I got tired of it. Then I swung around to follow the circling red flasher of an ambulance as it roared through the night. I figured it would be an accident and I was right. A couple of hot rodders piled into each other on a turn. The one kid was screaming when they lifted him out, and I watched it for a long time through my windshield.

Pretty soon I was heading back toward the expressway, hungry for another taste of the speed. A few big drops of rain glanced off the glass in front of me, and I rolled up the windows as the full fury of a brief downpour hit the road ahead. It was good, and I liked driving in the rain. I remembered the first car I'd ever owned—a supercharged French job with an eight cylinder engine. My father had bought it for my eighteenth birthday, back when the family had money, and it had rained the first day I drove it. They'd taken it away from me soon after that, because of the accident and my father's death, but I always had the memory of that first drive in the rain.

Now my tastes ran to American cars, because the foreign ones were too distinctive. Someone might remember, reports might be compared. I was very, very careful—always.

Two girls loomed up in my headlights as the rain abated. They had a flat tire and they huddled under a single black raincoat while they debated what to do. I sped past them, then cut back to the exit lane and left the expressway at the next feeder. It took me only a few minutes to double back and get on again where I had before. This time I turned off my headlights.

The rain had stopped and they were trying to do something with the tire. I could see them clearly in the reflected glow from the distant lights, but they didn't see me. The car hummed along like a silent bat swooping through the night. I pushed it to the speed limit and held it there—no faster, because they might be able to tell later. No faster . . . careful. . . .

The girl in the raincoat glanced up at the last instant, her dim face a mixture of surprise and then terror. As I felt the car crunch against them, I slammed on the brakes and switched on my headlights. It would look good, even if they searched for skid marks on the wet pavement. It would look fine.

I got out then and looked at them. It was the first time I'd ever tried two at once.

The police came finally, with their spotlights cutting little arcs in the night. There was no need for the ambulance that came along too. "God, officer, I never saw them. Not till it was too late. That black raincoat, and they didn't have any lights. ."

"It wasn't your fault, buddy. It was just one of those things."

I turned away, covering my face, feeling the exhilaration flood through my veins. All right, all right for now. In a few months, in another state, with a different name and a different car, I'd be ready again.

That's what life is all about. . . .

First Offense

Davy Knowles had spent most of the summer hanging around the Star Drug Store, playing the pinball machine and talking to the new blonde behind the lunch counter. He had one more year of high school, one more year of dozing in class and smoking during the lunch hour and chasing around town in Tom Hasker's convertible. Sometimes he wondered if it was worth it. He wondered especially if it was worth the nightly battles with his father and the crying scenes with his mother.

"How are things, Davy?"

He looked up from the pinball machine and nodded to Tom, who had taken to arriving at the Star Drug earlier in the day since the blonde had started to work there. "What say?"

It was a dull Saturday morning, and both had had dates the night before with high school girls they didn't particularly care about. For Davy, without a car, it had ended with the familiar stroll home from the movie, with a few unsatisfactory kisses in the doorway of the girl's home.

"Date last night?" Tom Hasker asked him, his eyes already on the blonde as she bent over for a jug of soft-drink syrup.

"Yeah." Davy stuck another coin into the machine, not wanting to hear about Tom's conquests.

"Me too. With Barb. We parked

down by the lake. Man, she's really something!" He lit a cigarette and lounged against the lunch counter. "What you need is a car, Davy. You're missing all the action."

"Yeah."

"Folks still won't let you have one?"

Davy didn't answer. The subject had come up again the previous evening, with the usual results. His father had shouted and his mother had wept. It had been like that ever since his older brother had stepped on a land mine halfway around the world and died in a war that Davy didn't understand. That had happened a year ago, and his parents hadn't been the same since.

Tom Hasker ordered a Coke from the blonde girl, giving her a special look. "Ever think about just taking off, Davy?"

"If I had the money I damn well would."

"Even before you finished school?"

"Tomorrow, if I had the money." And he meant it.

"Come on, let's go for a ride."

Davy finished his game and followed Tom Hasker out to the street. He was only seventeen, a year younger than Tom, and he knew he lacked the other's assured swagger and casual manner with girls. His face had too many pimples still, and his dark brown hair never seemed to fall quite the right way. It was only in Tom's company that he began to feel the sense of wild freedom that he was certain went along with adulthood.

The top was down on Tom's car, and they pulled out of the parking lot with a roaring surge of power that caused bystanders to turn and stare. This was the part Davy always liked—the feeling of motion, of the wind in your hair and maybe a girl at your side. It was what life was all about.

"How'd you like to make some money?" Tom asked after a while, driving easily with one hand on the wheel. "Enough so's you could leave this town and not bother with finishing school or that jazz."

"You mean stealing hub caps?" Davy asked with a snort.

"This is no hub-cap deal. Does twenty-five thousand bucks sound like hub caps?"

"Twenty-five—"

"You heard me. Twenty-five thousand, split down the middle. With that much you could get yourself a car and take off for New York."

Davy's heart was pounding with excitement. "What do we have to do—rob a bank?"

"That's it, exactly."

"You're nuts!"

Tom slowed the car to a stop at the curb. "If you think so, you'd better get out here."

"Rob a *bank?*"

"Not really a bank. Not inside, anyway. Sort of outside. It's the easiest job in the world. We just walk away with the dough. No tools, no alarms, no guards, no nothing."

"That's a Federal rap, Tom. Hell, I'm not getting mixed up in that!"

Tom Hasker lit another cigarette. "Think it over, Davy. Think it over till tomorrow. Maybe you'll change your mind."

All the way home Davy thought it over—not really seriously, because he still doubted that Tom was serious, but with that half a mind reserved for daydreams and impossible quests.

To get away, to be gone from that house where only the gloomy memory of a brother's death lived now among the everyday treasures of a lifetime. To get away . . .

After supper he walked down to the drug store and waited for the blonde girl to finish work. If only he could offer her a ride home, drive down to the lake and neck with her under the stars . . . But he had no car, and someone else was there waiting. A neighborhood fellow with a fancy sports car.

What was it? Was his father afraid he'd smash the thing up and be dead like his only brother? Did they think they could keep him alive and innocent by keeping him on foot? He thought some more about Tom's scheme. Maybe he could just listen to it, and then decide. Just listening to it wouldn't commit him to anything . . .

Sunday morning he told his parents he was going to church, but instead he went over to Tom's house, where he found the older boy washing his car.

"Hi, Davy. Change your mind?"

"Not really. Just tell me some more about it."

"I'll do better than that. I'll show you. Hop in."

They drove over to a shopping center about three miles away, and Tom parked in the large empty lot.

"Is this it?" Davy asked.

"Take a look. What do you see?"

"Nothing. Just an empty lot."

"Look again. See that branch bank?"

Davy stared through the spotless windshield at the low Colonial brick building near the street. "That one?"

"That one. I've got everything planned to the split second, just like we were in the army."

Davy nodded. He knew he'd never be in the real army. There was

The Night My Friend

some sort of regulation about sole surviving sons being exempt from the draft. Sometimes his father reminded him of that, as if his brother's death had been partly Davy's doing. "Tell me about it," he heard himself say.

"This broad I've been taking out—Barb. She works in the bank and she got talking one night. She told me all about it. See that little auto teller unit over the other side of the parking lot? That's so people can do their banking without leaving their car. Two girl tellers are in that thing all day long."

"But they're protected, Tom. They got thick glass and everything."

"Sure they have! And there's even a pneumatic tube connecting the auto teller unit with the bank, so they can shoot money back and forth."

"Then how—?"

"Listen, will you? Every morning the two girl tellers come out the back door of the bank and walk across the parking lot to the auto teller. Nine o'clock sharp! We'll come out tomorrow and I'll show you. The money they'll need for the day is sent to them through the tubes—except on Friday mornings."

"What happens on Fridays?"

"They need lots of cash for payroll checks. And most of it's bundled for easy handling. The bundles are too big to fit in the tubes, so the girls carry it to the unit in sacks. No guards, no guns, no nothing. Just two girls with sacks full of money. Barb says they take twenty-five thousand out every Friday morning for the payroll checks."

"Doesn't one of the men watch them?"

Tom shook his head. "They used to have a guard go along with them, but nothing ever happened, so they stopped. If they only knew! The whole thing'll take about ten seconds and we'll be gone." Then, "How about it?"

Davy looked down at his hands. "I—I don't know."

"We'll pack some clothes and leave them in the car. We'll just take off."

"The cops'll be watching for the car."

"So maybe we'll use another one. I'll rent one, and then we'll switch to mine later. They won't get us—not before we reach New York with all the money in the world."

"I don't know, Tom. We've never done anything like this."

"You want to waste your life away in this hick town playing that lousy pinball machine? Or you want to get out and live—have girls like that blonde at Star Drug?"

"I—" All right, he decided suddenly. *All right!* "I'll do it, Tom."

"Good. We'll drive out tomorrow morning and take a look at the girls."

On Monday morning it rained, a light drizzle driven by a stiff westerly wind into an unpleasant downpour that emptied the streets. Tom drove the car slowly down Maple Street and turned into the big parking lot, bringing the car to rest by the supermarket at the far end.

"There are the girls," Davy said after a moment. The rear door of the bank had opened and two girls with raincoats over their heads ran out to a waiting car.

"One of the men is driving them over," Tom said. "But usually they walk. They'll be walking on Friday."

"If it doesn't rain."

"It won't. I already checked the weather bureau's five-day forecast. No more rain in sight the rest of this week."

Davy glanced at him. "You think of everything."

"You gotta think of everything. You gotta be watching for the big chance all the time. You know what cops look like—detectives?"

"Big guys with big feet."

"Sometimes. Sometimes not. The F.B.I. agents are usually younger and more ordinary-looking. And the secret service, when they're walking with the President, always have their coats open so they can draw their guns."

"Yeah?" Davy knew that Tom could teach him a great deal. He thought of how things would be for them in New York, with all that money. They'd get girls right away, and move into some swell apartment, and maybe after a while get jobs somewhere. But not right away.

"That's enough for today," Tom said. "We'll check it again on Thursday and run through the whole plan."

"Is one of those girls Barb?" Davy asked suddenly, because he'd just thought of it.

"No. She works inside. Neither of these ever laid eyes on us. Anyway, we'll have handkerchiefs over the bottom of our faces, like in the Western movies."

"Everything but guns, huh?" Davy said with a laugh.

Tom Hasker didn't reply.

The blonde in the drug store called herself Candy, and by Wednesday afternoon Davy had worked up the courage to ask her for a date. "A movie, maybe? Tonight?"

She eyed him uncertainly while washing glasses. "You don't have a car, do you?"

"We could go close by. Maybe tonight, after you finish work."

"Tonight! Heavens, no! I only date on week-ends."

"Oh." He didn't know where he'd be on Friday night. "Well, I'll ask you again."

She smiled and went back to the glasses. He strolled over to the pinball machine but decided he didn't really want to play it. He didn't want to do much of anything, except get away, far away.

On Thursday morning they parked on the street and watched the two young girls—one blonde, the other a lively redhead—prancing across the asphalt lot to the auto teller unit. "I like that redhead," Tom remarked. "Maybe when we hold them up we should just say, 'Your money or your honor!' and let them choose."

He laughed, then noticed that Davy was frowning. Davy asked, "What do you mean, hold them up? I thought we were just going to grab the dough and scram."

Tom reached over to open the glove compartment. "You grab the dough. I'll just show them this to give them a little scare."

"Tom!"

It was a blue-steel revolver with worn grips and a look of hard usage. "Don't worry. It's not loaded," Tom said, trying to reassure him.

"But—where did you get it?"

"I found it. With my father's things." Tom's father, a plant guard at a local factory, had died of a heart attack the previous year.

"You didn't tell me anything about a gun!"

"So I'm telling you now. It's just to scare them."

Davy could feel his heart pounding, feel the empty yawning of his stomach. Somehow the fact of the robbery hadn't seemed real until that moment. "No," he said.

"What difference does an empty gun make? Maybe I won't even use it."

"Promise you won't. Promise, or I'm out."

Tom looked at him steadily. "You're in, Davy. It's too late to be out now."

"All right, I'm in! But no gun!"

"I'll have it with me. I promise I won't use it unless I have to."

Davy had to be content with that. He stared grimly through the windshield, watching the girls as they unlocked the auto teller unit and went inside.

Tomorrow. So soon—tomorrow.

Davy didn't sleep well that night. He tossed in the humid darkness and thought about it—his last time in this bed, in this house. What would New York be like? What would the girls be like there? Were they all like in the magazines, with short skirts and big smiles, posing against traffic signs in the latest fashions?

He got out of bed early, at the first hint of daylight, and took a shower. He went over again in his mind the plan that Tom had outlined the night before, picturing the details as they would take place. It was a good plan—foolproof.

Tom would use a rented car and park it near the exit. Then he would follow the girls from the bank, while Davy approached from the other direction. The whole thing would take less than a minute. He wondered abstractedly, as he had before, whether Tom had told the girl, Barb, what he planned. But that didn't really matter. They'd be far away before she or anyone could spread the alarm.

He mumbled something to his mother at breakfast, trying to avoid a conversation. "Really, Davy, the summer's almost gone and you don't have a job or anything. I wouldn't mind so much if you were going to summer school and learning something."

"I'm learning," he answered, his mouth full of toast.

"Where? At the Star Drug? And I want you staying away from those girls around there, you hear? They're nothing but—"

He got up and left the table, not hearing any more of it. After today he'd never have to listen to any more of it.

Already the day was warming, and he knew as he hurried along the sidewalk that by noon the temperature would hit ninety. There'd be one more visit home, to pick up the overnight bag he'd carefully packed the night before and hidden in his room. Then, away. Tom would abandon the rented car somewhere and they'd meet again at the convertible, which would be parked near the high school stadium.

Easy. A cinch. Foolproof.

But his heart was beating fast when he neared the bank. He felt in his pocket for the handkerchief he'd use as a mask, glanced around for a sign of Tom and the rented car.

Did they rent cars to eighteen-year-olds that easily? And this early in the morning? And wouldn't Tom have to make a deposit on it?

As he turned it over in his mind, Davy knew suddenly and clearly that Tom had no intention of renting a car. The car would be stolen, as would the money. He wondered why the sudden realization bothered him somehow.

A horn honked, and he turned to see Tom at the wheel of a green sedan, passing him and pulling into the parking area behind the bank. The time was 8:46.

Davy walked past the car and nodded slightly to Tom. There was no need to speak—they both knew what had to be done.

The Night My Friend

At exactly five minutes to nine Tom left the car by the lot exit and walked around to the front of the bank. He was wearing a jacket despite the heat, and Davy could see the sagging of the gun in its righthand pocket.

Then Tom disappeared around the back of the bank and Davy started walking across the parking lot, very slowly, with plenty of room between himself and the auto teller unit. The rear door of the bank opened, and the same two girls appeared, each carrying a white canvas sack.

Davy's legs were beginning to tremble, but he kept on walking, gauging his speed by the girls'. He saw Tom round the corner of the bank building and start after them, pulling a handkerchief from his pocket.

It was the lively redheaded girl who happened to turn and see Tom, when they'd covered half the distance to the auto teller unit. She gasped something and put a sudden hand to her mouth.

His face already masked by the handkerchief, Tom pulled the blue-steel revolver from his jacket pocket and pointed it at the two girls. "The money!" he barked out.

Davy started to run toward them, forgetting his own handkerchief in the excitement. The two girls stood as if petrified, still holding their bags of currency as they faced the gun in Tom's hand.

Then came the sudden crack of a pistol shot, and for a split second Davy thought that Tom had fired at the girls. He thought it until he saw Tom start to fold and crumple like an autumn leaf. Then he saw the bank manager in the doorway the girls had just left; the manager was holding a smoking gun in his hand.

Tom Hasker was dead by the time the ambulance arrived. He died without speaking, though in the final instant of life his eyelids might have flickered toward Davy, who stood above him with the others, trying not to see the bloody pool forming on the asphalt.

"Just a kid," the bank manager said, his voice barely a whisper. "Just a kid and I killed him."

"He was trying to rob you, wasn't he?" one of the officers said. "Don't let it worry you." Then he turned to Davy once more. "What about this kid?"

"He was trying to help us," the redhaired girl volunteered. "He came running up when the other one drew his gun."

They questioned Davy for a time and then released him. He looked around for the girl, to thank her, but both girls had already been sent home by the manager.

Davy headed for home, walking quickly in the heat but not even noticing it, thinking only of Tom dying there in the parking lot for a crazy dream that could never come true. He wondered what would happen when the police found out that Tom had been a friend of his.

He remembered Tom's car parked at the high school stadium and headed for it, not knowing exactly what he intended to do. When he reached it, standing alone in the noonday heat, he found that it was locked. Tom had a small suitcase in the back seat, and there was another suitcase on the floor, almost out of sight. It looked like a girl's week-end bag.

"Hello," a voice said behind him very softly.

He turned, startled, the fear building in him once more, and saw that it was the redhaired girl from the bank, the one who had gotten him off. "I—What are you doing here?"

She smiled at him, at his confusion, perhaps at his fear. "I'm Barb. I was Tom's girl. That didn't work out so well this morning. But don't worry, we'll do better next time. Won't we?"

Hawk in the Valley

Perhaps you've passed this way before. The valley is sleepy in the summertime, but very beautiful, with lush fields of corn and oats rising against a backdrop of wooded hills that stretch for miles toward the horizon. Sometimes, especially in the late afternoons, a hawk or two will come circling overhead, looking for the evening meal or perhaps only for a place to light.

Tucker Baines passed this way, and sometimes on a summer's night they still tell his story in the valley.

June is the warmest month, even warmer than July for some reason, maybe because on a July afternoon the heat is often broken by a blowing thunderstorm that comes in low over the hills. June, especially late June, is something else again; hot and humid without a chance of relief, when the big flies buzz around over the fields and roads, and even the hawks are listless in their circling. It was on such a day that Tucker Baines came into the valley.

He was, first of all, a wanderer. Born in the swampy Everglades of Florida to parents who ran a roadside alligator farm with a marked indifference to his upbringing, Tuck had learned early to shift for himself. He'd left them to their reptiles and each other at the age of sixteen, and headed nebulously north toward a world he knew only from comic books and movies which he saw infrequently.

Tucker was also a musician of sorts, always had been since the age of seven when a drunken uncle made him a present of a shiny silver-plated harmonica. It had grown up with him, serving at times as his only link to the more settled joys of boyhood in the dismal swamp-side house.

So he wandered north with his harmonica, working by day in dusty gas stations that sat by the side of the highways like bulbous tumors, waiting to pump new life into the pipeline; life, and sometimes death. He remembered the time a tractor trailer had jackknifed on a curve down the highway, and taken a carload of vacationers with it down a grassy slope.

In many ways he hated the highways, hated especially the odor and clang of the gas stations where he worked. Perhaps that was why he started working nights with his harmonica, playing for his supper at the little greasy truck stops on the road north. When he was eighteen he was playing for drinks, even though he was still under age by most state laws, but he was not really a drinking man. One night he'd had too much and ran his jackknife into a man's gut outside a roadhouse in North Carolina. He didn't like to drink or fight or get into trouble, but sometimes it happened. Sometimes he moved out in a hurry, carrying only his harmonica and a few meager articles of clothing.

Gradually the harmonica became the center of his life. The tavern owners liked him, because he was a clean-shaven young man who could play *Night Train* as easily as *Greensleeves,* and because he worked cheap and always showed up. The customers liked him, too, liked the sounds which he coaxed from the instrument, hunched over it on a plain wooden stool with the single spotlight riveting their attention. Perhaps he could have made it all the way to Nashville or New York with that sound, but he was too much of a wanderer to be happy in the city. There was always a dirt road to be followed off the main highway, and that was how he happened into the sleepy valley so far from home.

The first person to see Tucker Baines as he wandered down the center of the road with his harmonica and jackknife and paperboard suitcase was Mariam Coty, the postmaster's daughter. She had lived all of her life in the valley, venturing out only on occasional shopping trips to the big plaza beyond the river. Some spoke of her as a strange, shy girl, but in fact she was only lonely, bored with the sameness of the tassel-haired farm boys who were her only acquaintances. This boy coming down the road now, who surely was no more than nineteen or twenty, was a new face, a new interest.

The Night My Friend

"Lookin' for somebody?" she asked, coming out of the mowed field to intercept him. "This is the Coty place."

"I . . . no, not really." He paused to rest his suitcase, and she saw that he was indeed handsome, with a firm, suntanned face and deep blue eyes that sparkled when he spoke. "I'm looking for a place to stay, I guess." He glanced uncertainly toward the western horizon, as if calculating the remaining hours of daylight.

"A hotel? We don't have any in the valley."

"No, maybe just a drinking place, where they got a cot in back." He pulled something from his pocket. "I play the harmonica, see? People pay me to play."

She stared, entranced, at the shiny metal instrument with its double line of holes. No one in the valley was very musical except Miss Gordon, the piano teacher, and Mariam knew of only one other person in the whole area who played a harmonica. "I suppose you could play at the River Bend," she said, speaking softly. "It's the only night spot in the whole valley, if you could call it that. They've got a big new stereo jukebox, and the kids go dancing there on weekends. But I don't know if they'd let you sleep there."

"Could you show me where it is?" he asked, picking up the battered suitcase once more. "If it's not too far."

She fell into step beside him. "It's not far."

He liked the girl from that first moment, liked the valley and the tiny village that seemed to form its core. She introduced him to her father, and to a big man named Hark who seemed to be the sheriff. Then she took him to the River Bend, where a few farmhands stood by a rough plank bar, drinking beer with a self-conscious air of guilt. It was early, not yet supper time, and perhaps they felt they should still have been in the fields.

The place itself was almost gloomy in the afternoon sun, and the odor of beer was heavy in the air. In the evening, when the lights came on and darkness settled outside, it would be better. Tuck knew these places. He'd seen so many of them in the past three years.

"The kids dance in here," the girl told him, leading the way to a bare back room where an unplugged juke box was the only adornment. "Not tonight, though. Just weekends," she apologized.

She introduced him then to an aproned bartender. His name was Smith, though it might have been anything else. Tuck had forgotten many faces like that in his travels. "Harmonica? Like Big Ben up in the hills, huh?"

"I don't know Big Ben," Tuck told him.

"Just as well. Hairy and mean." He wiped at the bar with a damp cloth. "I'm just managing the place. Don't know if I could hire you or not."

"All I'd want is food and a place to sleep. And any tips they throw me."

"They don't throw tips at the River Bend," Smith said with a chuckle. Then, "Let's hear you play, boy. Won't do no harm."

So he played for them, played as he had in a hundred other road-side places; head bent, eyes closed, making the only kind of music he knew how, cupping his hands around the silver harmonica and play-ing, playing. When he paused between songs he noticed that the farm-hands had moved in from the bar to listen, and he was not surprised. People had always listened to him when he played.

He ran through a shortened version of *Casey Jones,* and then did *Blue-Tail Fly.* He played some ballads of the Scottish border that a man in Carolina had taught him once, then finished with his favorite *Night Train* and a jazz version of *John Henry.* It was a lot of music to get out of a little harmonica.

"Never heard one played that good," the bartender admitted. "Guess I could take you on for a week anyway, till the boss gets back."

Tucker Baines nodded. He hadn't expected any other decision.

When the boss came back, he liked Tuck's playing too. Most of all he liked the crowds of kids who were coming every night now to the River Bend. They sat and listened and sometimes danced; and often toward the end of the evening they even threw dimes and quarters onto the little stage where Tuck sat and played his wonderful harmonica.

He saw the girl, Mariam, some nights after he finished, and once he sat for a long time with Sheriff Hark, talking about his travels and listen-ing to a history of the valley's residents. Hark was that sort of a man, big, talkative, interesting.

"You plan to stay around long, son?" he asked Tuck one night.

"Don't know, Sheriff. I'm a sort of a wanderer, I guess. But it's peace-ful here. Don't hardly see that there's any work for you."

"I try to keep it that way," Sheriff Hark said. "Sometimes I have to crack a few heads to do it, specially at harvest time."

Tucker Baines had been playing at the River Bend for two weeks when he finally met Big Ben. He'd heard a lot about the man, mostly from Mariam and the kids who came around. They'd all heard Ben and his harmonica, mostly at church suppers and family picnics. Tuck was better, they assured him, but Big Ben was pretty darned good.

One night when he was leaving the River Bend, figuring to stroll a while before bedtime, Tuck heard someone hail him from a parked car. "Come over here a minute, boy! Got a question for you!"

The Night My Friend

He walked over, squinting his eyes against glaring headlights, and saw at last a great mountain of a man stuffed behind the wheel of the ten-year-old sedan. "You want something?"

"I hear you play harmonica," the big man said, speaking through a bushy mustache that almost obscured his mouth.

"I play a little."

"One of these?" the man asked, holding out his hand. In it rested a silver-plated harmonica.

"Just like that." Tuck studied the man in the reflected headlights. "You must be that Big Ben they talk about."

"Ha! How did you figure that one out?" The man shifted uncomfortably, shoving his massive stomach around the steering wheel. "I'd like to hear you play, to play with you sometime. I was listening from here, and it sounded pretty good."

"Thanks."

"I got a cabin back in the hills. How about coming up?"

"Not tonight, thanks. I'm pretty bushed."

"Tomorrow, the next night. I'll pick you up when you finish."

Tuck didn't really want to go with the man, but there seemed no way out. He had a youthful sense of arrogance that told him he could best the mountain of a man in any contest, musical or physical, and perhaps that helped decide him to go. "Maybe tomorrow," he said.

"I'll be here."

The old car pulled away almost at once, and Tuck watched until its taillights had vanished around a distant curve in the old dirt road.

By the following night, Tuck had forgotten all about the odd invitation. He'd spent the afternoon with Mariam, swimming in an old quarry a few miles off, and then he'd come back to the River Bend to have a light supper with Sheriff Hark. He was growing to like the man, to like most everything about the village. He wondered if maybe, just maybe, it was time to settle down.

He played until midnight, giving the kids a solid hour of the newer folk songs and country tunes. He'd picked up a lot of them listening to the jukebox in the afternoons, and he played them well within the harmonica's limited range.

When he dropped the harmonica into his jacket pocket and stepped outside for some air, he saw the familiar car waiting across the street. All right, he decided, he would go with Big Ben. Certainly no harm could come from it. He went back inside for a quick beer, then went across and climbed into the old car.

"I was thinking you weren't coming," the big man said.

"I came, I came. I don't want to stay out all night, though. I gotta get some sleep." He'd had three or four beers all told, and he was feeling a bit drowsy.

Big Ben drove the old car over the rough dirt roads as if he knew them like the back of his hand. He probably did, since he'd had a long time to learn them. "I was just a kid during prohibition," he said, talking as he drove. "I used to make the runs with my older brother over these same roads."

Finally they reached the house, which was no more than a log cabin set a little ways off the road. Perhaps someone had built it for hunting or even for living, but that had been a long time before Big Ben moved in. It was probably no more disorganized than a bachelor's quarters in a city might be, but there was a difference. The canned goods, the piled newspapers, the jazz records—they all seemed slightly musty, maybe like Ben himself as he moved through the mess and motioned Tuck to a chair.

"The place isn't much," he said, not really apologizing but only explaining. "After my father and brother got killed, my mother sorta went to pieces. I've been here alone a long time."

"They were killed on the highway?"

Big Ben lowered himself carefully onto a chair. "Went through a roadblock with a trunkload of moonshine. Smashed themselves against a tree. I endured." He smiled and picked up his harmonica. In a moment he was running through *St. Louis Woman,* then switching in mid-refrain to *Gloomy Sunday* and the less familiar *Unquiet Grave.*

"That's good," Tuck told him when he paused to hit the harmonica against his palm. "Damn good."

"I used to play like you, till I put on all this weight. I used to do a lot of things." He squeezed himself out of the chair and brought out a half-full bottle of cheap rye whiskey. "Here, have a few gulps and then play for me."

Tuck accepted the bottle and passed his harmonica to Big Ben in turn. "Try mine."

The big man took it and started to play, then grimaced in pain. "Can't play it," he said, handing it back. "Damned mustache gets caught." He started playing again on his own instrument, then waved to Tuck to join in.

They played and drank like that for more than an hour, first singly and then together, until the room began to blur and spin Tuck's vision. "I have to get back," he mumbled at last.

"Hell, you don't need to ever get back. Them girls'll wait for you."

"Gotta—"

"That Mariam's pretty good, isn't she? I hear tell you go for her. I'd go for her myself if I was fifty pounds thinner. I'd even—"

"Shut up!"Tuck wobbled to his feet and struck out at the man. He shouldn't drink, man, how he shouldn't drink! But then why do people always say things to—

"You lookin' for a fight, boy? Big Ben could break you in two! Big Ben could fix your mouth so you'd never play a harmonica again."

Maybe that had been it, the reason for it all. Maybe the man had brought him here out of some twisted jealousy to maim or kill him. Tuck didn't wait to think, to reason any further. Suddenly the jackknife was in his hand, and it was no stranger there. He sank it up to the hilt in Big Ben's flabby stomach and watched the surprise spread over the man's face.

"What? What do you think you're doing, boy?"

The knife came out and in again, and Big Ben stumbled against the table, upsetting bottle and glasses and harmonicas. "Die!" Tuck breathed. "Can't you die!"

"I been trying all my life," Big Ben gasped. "Maybe you come just to help me along."

Tuck stabbed him three more times before the big man went to his knees and the blood began to bubble at his mouth. Then, desperate with drink and cold with fear, he slashed out at the offered throat and ended it.

For a long time Tucker Baines stood staring at the body, as if wishing it alive again. There had been other times, but nothing like this— he'd never really killed a man before, never taken a human life. The sight of it, the blood and the great bloated body, had sobered him almost at once, and now he wondered what to do.

In the past he had always run from trouble, but this was something different, something dangerous. To run away would be an admission of guilt. He began running over it in his mind. No one had seen him with Big Ben, no one knew he'd come here. He remembered touching nothing except the bottle and glass and harmonica, and perhaps the edge of the table. Now he quickly wiped these off, and wiped off the knife as well, dropping it into his pocket.

Still, he could not take chances. He found some fuel oil for the stove and emptied it onto a stack of newspapers in one corner. The place would burn like tinder, body and all. Let them think what they wanted, after that.

He tossed a match from the doorway and watched the papers catch and flare. Then, at the last possible instant, he remembered the harmonica. It was still there on the floor by the overturned table. He ran back toward the crackling flames and scooped it up, then retreated as the ceiling timbers caught the first glow of the fire.

He was halfway down the hill, traveling through the darkened fields, when it started to rain. No matter—behind him the flames had already broken through the log roof of the cabin. There would be very little left for Sheriff Hark to examine.

She saw him the very next morning, early, strolling up the hill to join the crowd. He looked almost as if he hadn't slept, and she wondered if he'd been up late practicing on his harmonica.

"Hi, Mariam," he said, stopping at her side in the trampled grass. "What's the excitement?"

"It's Ben's place—Big Ben's—it burned down during the night. They say he's dead inside."

He glanced past her head at the little knot of spectators, at the steaming remains of the cabin. The heavy rain had doused the fire before the destruction was total, but only blackened timbers were visible from where they stood. "That's too bad," Tuck told her. "I never did get to meet him."

"He was the only one I ever knew could play like you."

"Yeah." He moved a little away from her and seemed to be thinking. She wondered about what.

That night Tucker got to the River Bend early, and found Sheriff Hark already there waiting for him. He plugged in the jukebox to listen to a couple of folk tunes he was learning, then sat down at the sheriff's table.

"Too bad about Big Ben," he said, speaking first.

"Darned shame," Sheriff Hark agreed. "You ever meet him?"

"Never," Tuck told him, shaking his head in confirmation of the statement. "Heard tell he was pretty good on the harmonica, though."

"That he was." Sheriff Hark sighed. "There was a little basement storage room under the cabin, and when the floor burned away Ben's body dropped through. The harmonica was there too, with him till the end. Looked just like the one you play."

"Was he pretty badly burned?"

"Not too much. Like I say, he fell through the floor before the fire did too much damage. And then it started to rain." Sheriff Hark was staring down at his hands. "Funny thing—looks like somebody killed him."

"Killed?"

"Yeah. Five or six stab wounds in the stomach, and his throat cut. Fire couldn't have done all that."

The kids were beginning to drift in. It was almost time for Tuck to start playing. "Who'd want to kill him?" he asked, slipping the harmonica from his pocket.

The Night My Friend

The sheriff shrugged his rounded shoulders. "A wanderer, probably. Someone passing by. Ben never had any money."

"You'll have to excuse me. I gotta start playing."

The sheriff nodded. Then, almost casually, "Say, Tuck, could I see your harmonica for a minute?"

"Sure." He passed it across the table.

"You ever have a mustache?" Sheriff Hark asked, turning the shiny instrument over and over in his hands.

"No. Why?"

The harmonica caught at a stray beam of light and reflected it toward the ceiling. Sheriff Hark looked uncomfortable. "Hell, I'm not one of those storybook detectives. I'd be lost with a fingerprint or a footprint. But I know my people, here in the valley." He took another harmonica from his pocket and laid it on the table next to Tuck's. "You say you never met Big Ben?"

"That's what I said."

"Well . . ." He shifted uncomfortably. "This harmonica was the one I found by his body. I think it's yours."

"You're wrong," Tuck said, suddenly breaking into a sweat. "This here's mine."

"Look close at it, boy. You'll see a thin line of solder near the top, above the row of holes. It's a trick fellows with bushy mustaches use to keep from gettin' them caught between the body of the instrument and the silvery top piece." He paused, looking unhappy. "This was Ben's harmonica, boy. He couldn't play one without that soldered top piece. You musta picked up the wrong one after you killed him."

"It's time," Tuck said, wetting his lips. "I have to play." His hand hesitated over the twin instruments, and finally rested on Big Ben's harmonica.

"Play," the sheriff told him. "I'll be waiting."

Tucker Baines nodded, walked over to his stool, and began to play very softly an old mountain melody. Somewhere outside a hawk drifted slowly across the evening sky, and the breeze was soft in the valley that night.

The Ring with the Velvet Ropes

For the better part of his twenty-seven years, Jim Figg had been preparing for that night. He'd fought his way through a disheartening maze of amateur bouts before turning professional, then scored six knockouts in a row to attract the attention of even the most jaded pros. Under normal circumstances, he would have had a championship bout with Anger when he was twenty-five, but the delays and hassles over a contract and a site had effectively held things up for almost two years.

In the meantime, Big Dan Anger had easily disposed of three lesser heavyweights, and Jim knew from the moment of weigh-in that morning that the champion considered him another pushover. The gamblers and Vegas odds-makers thought a bit more of Jim Figg's record of knockouts and made him only a 2-1 underdog.

The dressing room before the fight was crowded with well-wishers and casual friends, and Jim had to listen to endless conversation before his trainer finally chased them all away. All, that is, except Connie Claus, sports editor of the city's leading morning paper.

Connie was a little man with white hair and a perpetual smile, who knew everything about sports and never stopped showing off his knowledge.

The Night My Friend

His column went out on syndication to twenty-two newspapers, so most people listened politely when he spoke.

Now, straddling a chair while he cleaned the crusted bowl of his pipe, Connie Claus asked, "What do you think, Jim? Can you take the Champ?"

"I can take him," Jim said.

"You're a good fighter, boy. You've got a great name to live up to, though. Jim Figg—the *first* Jim Figg—was the earliest of the bare knuckle heavyweight champions. He held the title in England from 1719 to 1734."

"I know," Jim replied. In fact, he'd first read it in Connie's column more than a year before.

"Imagine! That was even before Broughton's rules went into effect."

"Yes." Jim stepped into the shower and turned on the water, momentarily drowning out the columnist's words. All right, he decided. Two hours from now it would all be over. If he won the fight—as he knew he would—he'd be the heavyweight champion of the world. For that, he could listen to Connie Claus's ramblings a bit longer.

"How's your girl?" Connie asked him as he emerged from the shower. "You gonna marry her?"

"Sue? I just might ask her if I win tonight."

"Can I use that in the column?"

Jim gave him a grin. "Wait till after the fight."

The little columnist was silent while Jim's trainer taped his hands. But finally, thoughtfully, he drew on his pipe and asked, "Ever hear any talk about another champion, Jim? Someone besides Big Dan?"

"What do you mean?"

"I don't know. It's crazy, I suppose, but you hear things in my business."

Jim grunted and flexed the muscles of his right arm. He was feeling good. "If there's somebody else wants a crack at the title. . . ."

"You don't understand what I mean, Jim. Some people say Big Dan Anger's not the champ—that he never was the champ."

Jim snorted and held out his hands as the gloves were slipped on. "Who in hell is, then?" He was just making conversation. His mind was already in the ring with Anger.

"Have you heard the name Blanco? Roderick Blanco?"

"Wasn't there a lightweight named Blanco in Chicago a few years back?"

Connie Claus shook his head. "This is a different one."

"Well, who is he?"

The columnist shrugged. "No one knows. If I knew anything more about it, I'd do a column. The name was mentioned by a retired referee one night when he was drunk. He sobered up and wouldn't say a word about it. But stories get started."

"Let's go!" Max, the trainer, said. "Enough gabbing for now."

Connie stood up and waved a hand. "I'll be watching. Good luck—Champ."

"Thanks," Jim said with a smile and stepped into the dim outer corridor that led up to the arena. This was his night, his moment. Even Connie knew it.

There was a great roar from the unseen crowd, and Max put a hand on his shoulder. The seconds and others clustered around as they halted a moment at the arena entrance. Former champions were being introduced—Clay and Liston and Patterson and someone else—and each name brought a renewed roar from the crowd.

Then it was Jim Figg's turn. He walked steadily down the aisle as the crowd's approval built to a shattering ovation. Big Dan had never been a popular champion, and the people had come to see him lose. Jim climbed through the ring ropes, the sweaty male odor of the previous fighters assaulting his nostrils.

Big Dan Anger always entered the ring late, and the chanting and foot stamping had already begun when he strode into view, a towering hulk of a man who'd been the heavyweight champion of the world for 2½ years. He looked more like a wrestler than a boxer, with close-cropped black hair and deep-set eyes that seemed constantly sleepy outside the ring.

The referee spoke quickly to the two men, running over the rules they both knew by heart. Then, with a suddenness that never failed to surprise Jim, the bell sounded and the crowd hushed momentarily—only to explode into shouting again as Big Dan landed his first blow to Jim's shoulder.

The fight went well for two rounds, with Jim circling and dancing, getting in a few good blows for points. He figured the first round as a draw and the second round probably his. At the beginning of the third, the champion was sweating, and Jim managed to open a little cut over one eye. Then he took a hard right to the jaw that shook him, staggering him against the ropes as Anger moved in for the kill.

The lights were a blur for an instant as Jim slid along the ropes and waited for the blow that would finish him. Then, somehow, his vision cleared. He blocked Big Dan's descending right glove and followed through with a right and a left of his own. The champion, caught by surprise, staggered backward and started to topple. Jim landed one more blow to send him on his way and then retreated to a neutral corner.

Big Dan Anger tried to rise at the count of seven, but his legs wouldn't respond. The referee counted him out on his knees, and the crowd went wild.

Jim Figg was the heavyweight champion of the world.

Back in the dressing room, the shouts of admirers ringing in his ears, Jim stretched out on the rubbing table while Max and the others went to work on him. He felt tired but with the power of accomplishment growing somewhere within him. He had done it, for Sue and Max and Connie Claus and all the rest who had believed in him.

"Message for you, Champ," Max said, passing him an envelope from the door.

"Somebody else congratulating me." Jim ripped open the envelope and stared down at the message.

You are invited to meet Mr. Roderick Blanco, it said. *A car will call for you tomorrow evening.*

"What in hell's this?" Jim said, tossing it aside.

The corridor door opened under the pressure of the crowd and Big Dan Anger hurried in, already in his street clothes. He seemed somehow smaller, deflated, vulnerable. "It was a good fight, kid," he mumbled. "You deserved to win."

"Thanks, Dan."

"Can I sneak out your back door? Claus is after me for an interview."

"Sure. Go ahead." Then Jim's eye caught the message he'd discarded, and he remembered Connie Claus's earlier words. "'Dan, tell me something—who is Roderick Blanco?"

Anger's face seemed to freeze at the name. He stared down at Jim for a moment and then answered, "You'll find out, kid. You'll find out soon enough."

Jim Figg slept most of the following day, and when he finally awoke sometime after noon, it was to see the sports section of the newspaper propped up at the foot of the bed. FIGG FLOORS ANGER FOR CHAMPIONSHIP! the headline screamed, and there was a half-page picture of him landing his final blow to Big Dan's jaw. Jim smiled and rolled over in bed, feeling good all over. Maybe tonight he'd even ask Sue to marry him.

He made a few phone calls and talked to not a few reporters and began that afternoon to discover the price of sudden fame. A weekly television show wanted him to appear the following Sunday evening, a newsmagazine wanted a portrait for their cover; suddenly everybody wanted something from him.

He decided to eat alone and pick up Sue afterward. It was on the way to her house that the sleek black sedan appeared from somewhere and edged his car to the curb. He climbed out, fists balled, and faced two men he'd never seen before. They were young and well built, but he knew he could take them both with ease.

"You boys need some driving lessons," he told them.

"We have Mr. Blanco's car. You were forgetting your engagement with him."

Something—could it be fear?—ran down Jim's spine. "I don't know any Blanco. I have an appointment."

"You have one, all right. With Roderick Blanco."

Jim took a step forward, and the nearest one slipped a small re-volver from his pocket. They weren't kidding. Whatever this was, it was the real thing.

They drove for a long time, across the state line, coming finally to a walled estate somewhere near the ocean. Jim was led inside, to a high-ceilinged drawing room where a handsome young woman waited. She had long dark hair and was wearing an evening gown that sparkled when the light hit it.

"Good evening, Mr. Figg," she said, speaking the words clearly but with just the trace of an accent. "I'm so glad you could join us."

"It wasn't through choice. What is all this, anyway?"

She ignored the question. "I'm Sandra Blanco. My husband will be joining us shortly. Could I get you a drink in the meantime?"

"A little Scotch might taste good." He watched her walk to the side-board and found himself admiring her hips beneath the tight red hos-tess gown. "I hope you and your husband know the penalty for kidnapping," he said.

"Oh, come now! That's much too strong a word for it. You could walk out of this house right now if you wanted to."

"And walk all the way back to the city, too, I suppose. Anyway, peo-ple are going to notice I'm missing quickly enough. I'm sorta news-worthy these days, you know."

"I saw the fight on television," she said, returning with the drink. "You have a wonderfully developed body."

"I could probably say the same for you. Aren't you drinking?"

She smiled down at him. "I'll wait till my huband joins us." She lit a cigarette. "You know, you're very different from the others."

"Others?"

"Other fighters. Other champions. You seem quite . . . educated."

"I've been around. I started boxing in college, actually. Never graduated, though." The drink was good and Sandra Blanco was quite charming, but he was growing restless. "Just where is your husband, anyway?" he asked finally.

A deep, powerful voice behind him said, "Right here, Mr. Figg. Sorry for the delay."

Jim got to his feet and faced the newcomer. Roderick Blanco was a dark-haired young man of perhaps thirty. He had the broad shoulders and massive chest of a fighter, and for the first time Jim began to wonder if there was any thread of truth in what Connie Claus had been hinting at. "Maybe you can explain all this," Jim said, purposely not shaking hands.

"Didn't you get my message after the fight?" Blanco tilted his head a bit to one side as he spoke, almost as if listening to some far-off sound.

"I got it."

Blanco turned to his wife. "Leave us alone, please, Sandra." She left the room without a word, apparently used to being ordered about. Blanco watched her go and then turned back to Jim. "My invitation to you here was in the nature of a challenge," he said.

"A challenge?"

Roderick Blanco smiled thinly. "I am the heavyweight boxing champion of the world. The real champion."

"That's crazy. Counting television, probably twenty million people saw me beat Anger last night."

The smile didn't change. "For your information, Mr. Figg, I knocked out Big Dan Anger in thirty-five seconds of the fifth round. This happened more than two years ago—to be exact, on the fourth evening that he held the championship."

"You expect me to believe that? Where was the fight held? Who witnessed it?"

"It was held in this house, in the basement. The referee was a professional—now retired—who was well paid for his services. I can show you his signed statement, if you wish, and also a document signed by Anger after the fight." The broad shoulders moved beneath his smoking jacket. "I have defeated every heavyweight champion for the past ten years." There was a note of pride in his voice as he spoke, and somehow Jim knew it was true.

"But *why?* Why this secret business? Why kidnap me at gunpoint?"

Roderick Blanco walked the length of the room, then turned and started back. There was a strange sparkle in his eyes, like that of a small boy on his way to a ball game. "My father was the richest man in the state, Mr. Figg. Rich men's sons don't go in for professional boxing. When I tried a few fights in college, he almost threw me out of the house." He cocked his head a bit to one side. "Even today, his fortune is tied up in a trust fund until I'm thirty-five. If I should engage in professional boxing before that time, I lose everything."

"Fantastic!"

"My father was a fantastic man." Now he really seemed to be listening, perhaps to a voice only he could hear. "He died in an asylum. Cut his throat with a piece of chicken bone and died before the guards could reach him. But enough of my story—you must be anxious to see the ring!"

"I'm not going to fight you," Jim told him, not moving from his chair.

"But of course you are! Tomorrow evening! You'll be my guest until that time. You can even work out with one of the servants tomorrow if you wish, though I imagine you're still in condition from last night's fight."

"If I refuse?"

"None of them ever refused."

"I'm refusing."

The dark-haired man spread his arms in a gesture of resignation. "Why, then, I'll just have to keep you here until you change your mind."

"Hold me prisoner, you mean? At gunpoint?"

"But it needn't be that way! The others were all willing to fight me! And afterward they returned to the public as if nothing had happened." He smiled at Jim ever so slightly. "No one will ever know that I have beaten you."

"And what if I win?"

"That has never happened."

Jim sat silently for a moment, weighing the possibilities. It was something of a challenge, and he had never been one to run away from a fight. Besides, fighting the man seemed the simplest way of gaining his freedom. "All right," he decided. "I'll fight you."

"Ah!" It was almost a sigh.

"But I'm expected in town tonight. I'll have to make a phone call."

"All right. But no tricks, please."

"No tricks."

Jim was hoping that Connie Claus would still be at the paper, writing his morning column. He dialed the area code and then the familiar number, while Blanco stood at his side. "Claus, please," he tried to mumble into the receiver when the switchboard answered.

After a moment's buzzing, Connie was on the line. "Claus here," he answered tonelessly, sounding bored or busy.

"Jim Figg, Connie."

"How are you, Champ?"

The Night My Friend

"Look, I can't keep our date for tonight."

"Huh?"

"Will you tell Max and Sue?"

"What are you talking about?"

Jim glanced into Blanco's deep brown eyes. "I'm spending a couple of days at the shore. With Snow White."

"Huh? What you talking about, Champ?"

Roderick Blanco's hand came down, breaking the connection. "That was foolish," he said. "White for Blanco. I doubt if he even understood you."

"I doubt it, too," Jim agreed sadly.

"Don't try anything like that again."

"I only thought you might want somebody from the press here to witness the fight."

Blanco shook his head. "No one from the press."

"What about a referee?"

"That has been arranged. An older retired gentleman, no longer active in ring work, will be paid a good sum to referee the fight."

"And spectators?" Jim asked.

"Only my wife and my servants. As I said, it is a private affair. Now come, and I'll show you the ring."

He led Jim down a wide stairway to the basement, a surprisingly high-ceilinged room that was brilliantly lit by overhead fluorescent tubes. In the very center of the room was a regulation-size boxing ring, flanked by a single row of theatre-type seats for spectators.

"The ring ropes are black," Jim observed.

"My one concession to good taste. The ropes are regulation, but they are covered in velvet."

"I see."

"Do you find it to your liking?"

"Sure. At least I won't have to worry about a lot of the crowd mobbing me in the ring afterward."

"There are few seats, to be sure, but every one is at ringside."

"Yeah."

Roderick Blanco held out his hand. "Then, until tomorrow evening? At eight?"

Jim shook his hand and watched the man walk quickly away toward the stairs. He wondered where he would spend the night, but almost immediately one of the servants was at his elbow. "You will come this way to your room, sir."

"Sure." He wondered if the man was armed, if he would shoot Jim at the first hint of an escape attempt. But he decided not to find out. He was going to stay and fight Roderick Blanco, because he was certain he could defeat the man.

Sleep did not come easily in the strange bed, and Jim pushed his head into the downy softness of the pillow and tried to free his mind of all thought. He was just beginning to drift off when his muscles tensed with the soft click of his door opening and closing. Someone had come into his room.

His first thought was Blanco or one of his men, but as he rolled over about to spring at the intruder, a soft voice whispered, "Don't be alarmed. It's Sandra Blanco."

He sat up in bed, seeing her only vaguely in the near-total darkness. "Do you always visit men's rooms at midnight, Mrs. Blanco?"

"I had to talk to you before tomorrow. You . . . seem different from the others, somehow. I think you could beat him."

"I *know* I can beat him."

He felt the weight of her body suddenly sitting on the edge of his bed. "That's why I had to talk to you. *You must let him win!*"

"Why should I do that? Just so he can keep his foolish little secret championship?"

"You don't understand! I was afraid you wouldn't. My husband is . . . quite mad. If you win that fight tomorrow night, you'll never leave this house alive."

"Oh, come now!" Jim tried to snort in disbelief, but there was a cold shiver down his spine at her words.

"No, I'm serious! The others lost and they lived, because Roderick knew they'd never tell the story to anybody and thereby admit their defeat. But if you should win the fight tomorrow, he would have nothing to assure your silence. And if you told the newspapers about it he would not only be disgraced at losing, but he would lose his father's trust fund as well."

"But murder!"

"It would not be the first time. There was an old referee who worked the last fight—one with Anger. He got drunk one night and talked, enough to start some rumors around the city. Roderick had him . . . run over by a car."

"You can't be serious!"

"But I am. If you win that fight tomorrow, he'll kill you."

Then, as quickly as she'd come, Sandra Blanco stood up and moved to the door. It opened and closed behind her, leaving him alone with the echo of her words.

The Night My Friend

When morning came, and Jim went down to breakfast, Roderick Blanco was nowhere in sight. Sandra Blanco dined with him, but there was no hint on her face of their midnight conversation.

"Where's your husband?" Jim asked, munching on a piece of toast. "Will he be joining us?"

"You won't see him until tonight. He's working out, getting in condition for the fight."

"In just one day?"

"That's all he needs."

Jim sipped his orange juice, glancing out at the heavy autumn clouds that were drifting in over the beach. "How did you ever meet Blanco?" he asked.

She glanced at the servant hovering nearby and answered, "That's a long story, and I won't bore you with it. I always wanted security; you can see I have it here."

"Yes."

"He's very good to me, really." She stared down at the breakfast crumbs on her plate. "And who knows? There may not be another champion he has to fight for years. After tonight."

"After tonight," Jim repeated.

"Do you want to work out with a sparring partner or something?"

"I should get the feel of the ring," he said.

"I'll have one of the servants take care of you, show you the dressing room and things." She left the table and went off into the depths of the large house.

Left alone at the table, Jim gazed out the window at the sea and suddenly realized the impossibility of the situation. Here, in the basement of a seaside mansion, he was going to fight a rich man's deranged son for the secret championship of the world! And if he won, he would be killed!

Jim rose from the table and walked quickly to the front door. The whole charade was just too ridiculous in the light of morning. He opened the door and started down the wide, curving driveway to the distant street. He was almost to the half-open gates when a voice called out, "Just a moment, Mr. Figg!"

It was one of the men who'd brought him there, and the gun was back in his hand. "You weren't thinking of leaving us, were you, Mr. Figg?"

Jim spent the rest of the day in the basement, resignedly punching and skipping rope. He went two quick rounds in the velvet-roped ring with one of the Blanco servants, easily flooring the man four times before calling it quits. There was about the whole affair an overhanging of unreality, as if at any moment an unseen director might end the play and call the whole thing off. Even the servants of Roderick Blanco contributed to the sense of unreality, moving through the endless corridors of the big house with frozen faces and soft-soled shoes.

"Will you be having dinner?" Sandra Blanco asked him late in the day.

"I never eat before a fight," he said. "Afterward, maybe."

She paused by the ring, staring up at him, and he almost thought she was about to say something else. But the moment passed and she was gone.

At seven thirty some servants came to help him with the final preparations, and promptly at eight he was escorted into the big basement room with its velvet-roped ring. Sandra Blanco occupied one of the seats, and the various servants filled the others. There were perhaps twenty of them in all, including the two men who had brought him there.

He climbed between the ropes, feeling the increased beat of his heart. It was the old sense of chilly anticipation he'd known so many times before. Only this time it was a bit different. This time, in a way, the game was for keeps.

The room was silent with pause, waiting—and then all at once Roderick Blanco was striding across the floor to the ring, shedding his robe to a handler as he walked. His massive chest was matted with curly black hair, and he wore dark blue trunks over firm thighs. In that moment, he looked like a champion.

He nodded to Jim and said, "Our referee," indicating a small balding man who'd followed them into the ring. "His name is Walters, and he handled two championship fights in the forties. Before your time."

The referee ran quickly through the standard rules of the bout, averting his eyes uncertainly from the participants, as if somehow doubting his own part in this affair. Then they stepped apart, returned to their corners, and waited until one of the servants acting as timekeeper rang the bell for round one.

Blanco moved out of his corner fast, keeping low, looking for an opening. Jim danced back a few steps, trying to figure the man's style, and realizing for the first time how difficult it was to fight someone he'd never seen before in the ring. They clenched quickly, and the referee pulled them apart. Jim landed a glancing blow on Blanco's shoulder, but the round ended without any damage to either man.

During the second round, Jim began to be bothered by the silence. He was used to the roar of a crowd, to the sweat and excitement of spectators' reactions to each blow landed. Here, before twenty people—all apparently on Blanco's side—the roar had shrunken to an occasional murmur, the excitement to the level of a few people watching a dull motion picture travelogue. It was almost as if the end were known, and perhaps to them it was.

He landed a firm right to Blanco's jaw during the closing seconds of the round and took up where he left off in the third. But Roderick Blanco could take an amazing amount of punishment without seeming to tire. They traded punches through two more rounds, and Jim was distressingly aware that the fight was pretty even at this point.

It was midway through the sixth round when Blanco unleashed his big guns, a rapid-fire series of blows that staggered Jim for the first time and finally drove him to his knees. With bloodied eyes he stared through the ring ropes at Sandra Blanco, saw her lips move as she told him to stay down. This was the moment he could do it. Stay down for a ten count and nobody would ever know. He was still the champion—why not let this madman have his moment of glory?

But then he was up as the count reached eight, ready to go at it again. Blanco gave him no chance but moved in for another fistic battering. This time Jim went down flat. He was just wondering what the count was when he heard the bell ending the round.

At the beginning of the seventh, Jim knew it would take everything he had just to stay on his feet. Blanco was no phony. He was real championship material. They tussled evenly through the three minutes, and then Jim returned sagging to his stool. "How long did Dan Anger last against him?" Jim asked the second.

The man hesitated a moment and then replied. "Six rounds."

"Good, I'm lasting eight, anyway."

In the eighth, the end came quickly. Blanco moved in to finish Jim off, somehow deceived by his bloodied face. Jim still had one punch left, the punch he'd used on Anger two nights before. Blanco took it, went back against his velvet ropes, and came looking for more. Jim saw at once that the man's guard was down, his eyes dazed by the force of the punch. One, two, three more—and Roderick Blanco collapsed in the center of the ring, his face against the canvas. The referee had counted him out before he even began to stir.

Jim Figg was still the heavyweight champion of the world.

Later, after he'd taken off the gloves, showered, and dressed, Jim faced Blanco in the upstairs living room. There was a piece of tape over the dark man's left eye, and the right eye was blue with swelling. He stared hard at Jim and said quietly, "You're a good fighter."

"Thank you," Jim told him. "You were a strong opponent. Tougher than Anger, by far." He could afford to be generous with his words.

Blanco was wearing his dressing gown, and both hands were buried deep in the pockets. Sandra stood to one side, her face a pale mask of apprehension. "This is the first time I have ever lost," the darkhaired man said, almost sadly.

"Roderick . . ."

"Be quiet, Sandra," he told her. "Yes, the first time. And I bow to a superior boxer—a true champion."

Jim nodded uncertainly. "Then I'll be going now."

"Well," Blanco said slowly, "I'm afraid not. I'm afraid I can't allow you to leave this house and spread the word of your victory across every front page. No, no."

Sandra tried to step between them, but Blanco pushed her aside. His right hand appeared, holding a gun. *"Run!"* Sandra shouted to Jim.

But already the servants were blocking the door. Jim saw that there was no way out. He glared at the gun in Blanco's hand and wondered if it was all to end like this. "You'd kill me?"

"I must, to protect myself."

"I won't tell anyone."

"Not even your friend Claus?"

Sandra tried to run forward again, but one of the servants grabbed her and held her firm. Blanco's gun came up a fraction of an inch. Jim glanced at the window, wondering if he'd be fast enough to dive through it, knowing already that he wouldn't be.

"All right," he said. "Then shoot."

"I'm sorry," Blanco said, and his finger whitened on the trigger.

"One more thing," Jim said suddenly, talking fast.

"What is it?"

"Suppose I give you a return bout?"

Blanco hesitated, and his trigger finger relaxed ever so slightly. "When?"

"Before I fight anybody else."

Silence. Then Roderick Blanco nodded slightly. "Very well. Do I have your word as a gentleman?"

"You have my word as a gentleman."

"And you will say nothing to the papers in the meantime?"

"Nothing."

Another nod. "All right. But if you go back on either promise, my servants will kill you. Quite painfully."

Jim gave a little bow as Blanco returned the gun to his pocket. "Then shall I say, until we meet again? In the ring with the velvet ropes?"

He turned and walked out of the house.

Two days later, Connie Claus joined Jim at a little table in the back room of a downtown bar. He was smiling like a newsman who scents a scoop. "You look good, Champ. How you feeling?"

"Great, Connie. Great."

"You said you had an exclusive for me." The little man leaned forward, resting his palms on the table. "You gonna tell me where you were for a couple of days? You gonna tell me about this Roderick Blanco?"

Jim merely smiled at him across the table. "No, I'm going to tell you that Sue and I are finally getting married."

"You called me down here just for that?"

"That, and to tell you I'm retiring from the ring."

"*What!*" Connie Claus stared at him unbelieving.

"I always intended to, when I got married. I'm going to open a little sporting goods store, I think."

"You're going to retire undefeated?"

"I already have. I notified the boxing commission an hour ago. I'm no longer the heavyweight champion of the world. The title is open."

Connie ran for the telephone, and Jim smiled as he signaled the waiter for another drink.

The telephone woke him the next morning, early. He rolled out of bed and went to answer it, thinking perhaps it would be Sue or even Max.

"Jim? This is Sandra Blanco."

"Oh? Hello."

"He killed himself two hours ago. He heard about your retirement on the late news last night, and he killed himself a few hours later."

"I'm sorry."

"Did you know he'd do it?"

"No," he answered honestly.

"It was just that he could never win the title back from you now. Even if he forced you to fight again, you're no longer the champion. You outwitted him."

"I kept my word," Jim told her.

"Yes, but . . ." Her voice was almost a sob.

"I'm sorry he's dead. That's all I can say." Then, for no reason at all, he asked, "How did he do it?"

"Downstairs, in the basement. He hung himself with one of those velvet ropes."

Homecoming

I suppose we're the old boys now," Cottrell said, surveying the stretch of familiar campus before him. "I see they've made some changes here since our day."

Tom Gent hefted his overnight bag and started down the curving driveway. "Yes, that dorm is new, and so's the gym. I hear they have an NCAA regulation pool now."

"That's all since the war," Cottrell observed. "Swimming wasn't so important in our time. I doubt if more than five of our whole class could swim."

The class had been Aldon Prep, '44, returning now for its 25th reunion. For many of them, it was the first time since graduation that they'd returned to the old school; the first time in twenty-five years that they'd made the train trip up from New York or down from Boston, getting off at the old station in the suburbs of Providence, then catching the bus for the twenty-minute ride to the Aldon campus.

The buses, too, had changed, of course. Now they were slick, sleek things of chrome and glass, pausing silently along the roadway to discharge a passenger with a gentle whoosh of air brakes. Cottrell and Gent had come by bus, but now they were regretting their decision when they saw Mark

Wedmer pull up in a taxi. They recognized him at once, of course, even after all those years, because chubby, round-faced boys like Mark often grow into chubby, round-faced men.

"Mark! Mark Wedmer! Good to see you! I'm Charlie Cottrell—bet you don't remember."

Mark Wedmer nodded and extended his hand. "Of course I remember. Am I likely ever to forget? And this is . . . Tom . . . Tom Gent! Right?"

"Right you are," Gent acknowledged, pleased to be recognized after so many years. Somehow it made him feel that he hadn't really changed, despite the receding hairline and the beginning of a paunch.

"Nice day for it, anyway," Cottrell said. "How's the old place look to you, Mark?"

The round-faced man let his brown eyes wander over the landscape. "That building's new, isn't it?"

"Gym and swimming pool. Come on, we were just going to take a look."

A bell rang somewhere and almost at once the doors of the various buildings began disgorging flocks of neatly dressed teen-age boys, many of them wearing the familiar blue-and-white blazers of Aldon Prep. "Reminds one," Mark Wedmer commented.

"What do you do now, Mark?" Gent asked.

"I'm on Wall Street. Investment banking. How about you fellows?"

"Insurance," Gent mumbled. "Up in Vermont."

Charlie Cottrell hesitated, then said, "I work on a little weekly newspaper near Boston. Doesn't pay much, but I like the work. Relaxing. Only one deadline a week."

"I guess you made it big," Gent said to Wedmer. "Wall Street and all. Do you live in New York?"

"We have a duplex up near Central Park. Nice neighborhood. One of those co-ops, you know."

An aging man, with bushy eyebrows partly compensating for his bald head, had appeared from somewhere to greet them. "You must be some of the old boys, up for homecoming," he said. "Let's see . . . I'm not too good at names after twenty-five years, so maybe you'd better identify yourselves. I'm Dean Adams."

"Tom Gent."

"Charlie Cottrell."

"Mark Wedmer. We all remember you, sir. You haven't changed at all."

Dean Adams gave a low chuckle. "Looked just as old back in '44, didn't I? But tell me about yourselves. Were you all in the war? We lost so many boys in the war."

They strolled and chatted for nearly an hour, while Dean Adams showed them the new gym and the recently completed dorm. "Big change from those little cottages we used to have—right? We're a real Ivy League prep shool now. Big time; more than a hundred already accepted for next year's freshman class."

By this time others had arrived, but their numbers were proving surprisingly slim. Of the thirty-five boys in the graduating class of 1944, it developed that twelve had died in World War II. Another three had died since that time, and two had dropped completely out of sight. That left eighteen who had been invited to the reunion, but of these only fourteen had come. They could hardly be noticed among the present student body and faculty.

Charlie Cottrell was first to recognize the last of the arrivals, a tall, handsome man with a touch of gray about his temples. "There's Randy Maxwell, isn't it?"

Mark Wedmer turned, startled at the words. He had been Randy's roommate during their senior year, but it was obvious he'd seen little of the man in the intervening years.

"Randy! Randy, old boy! How the hell are you!"

Randy Maxwell had been president of the senior class and easily its most popular member. Tom Gent remembered hearing somewhere that he had stayed in the army for some time after the war. Now, though he still had his handsome features and ready smile, there was a certain weatherbeaten vagueness about his face, as if he'd been out in the rain just a little too long.

"Well," he said, "all the old buggers back again. I haven't seen some of your faces since graduation!"

"What you been doing with yourself, Randy?" Cottrell asked. "Probably got a wife and ten kids, huh?"

"Three wives and no kids," Randy answered with a chuckle. "I know how to live."

"How was the army, Randy?" someone else asked.

"Like any army, any time. Lots of loving and not much fighting. I get a pension from them now; not much, but enough so I can bum around when I want."

Mark Wedmer stepped in close. "Didn't make it big like you were always going to, huh?"

"Who . . ." Then he seemed to recognize the round face and chubby body. "I'll be damned! It's Wedmer! I thought you'd probably curled up and blown away by this time."

Tom Gent, remembering it all now, wondered how he could ever have forgotten. There were four of them—a loose-knit inner circle of schoolboys, smoking in the gym, sneaking out after hours, doing all the things that schoolboys did back in 1944; four of them—Cottrell and Gent and Maxwell and . . . Yes, Franklin, but he'd died somewhere along the road to Paris, in 1944. The four of them; and Mark Wedmer had been Randy's bunkmate, a natural object of ridicule and jokes. No wonder Mark was now gloating at his own success.

They spent the early hours being received by the faculty, sitting in on classes, watching a soccer game, all the usual things. The president was new, and so were many of the teachers. Only Dean Adams and a few others were remembered from the old days.

"Yours was an unlucky class," the Dean told them as they strolled in groups along the shaded walk that led out to the riding stables. "You'd all come from good homes, all expected to leave Aldon and go to college. It didn't work out that way, of course, because the war came along. Mark, you were lucky in a way. A few minor infirmities kept you out of the army and you completed your education. For the rest, well, you all know how many of your class died over there, in North Africa or France or the Pacific. Of course some of you went back to college, and you managed to make out pretty well. You probably married and raised a family and achieved almost all of the goals you set for yourself back here at Aldon. Almost . . . I sometimes think that is the saddest word in the entire English language."

They reached the stables, and Tom Gent remembered how it had been, riding on a Saturday afternoon along the trails that took them at one point high above the shoreline of Narragansett Bay, although the area was flat for the most part. He remembered other Saturdays; the bus excursion to Gilbert Stuart's birthplace; the boat trip to the Newport Naval War College.

He remembered the Saturday that Mark Wedmer had tagged along with the four of them, and how they'd made his horse buck and throw him. They were always doing things like that to Mark, tormenting him with the casual sadism of the very young. Funny now that he had come through it all and made something of himself, while they—the rest of them—were only successful failures living out their middle-aged lives.

"Remember that tree?" Charlie Cottrell asked, pointing to the old dead oak that still stood beyond the stables. "It was a great one for climbing when nobody caught you. Remember it, Mark? The time we threw your pants up there and you had to climb up after them?"

"I remember," Mark Wedmer said quietly. He was staring at Randy Maxwell, perhaps remembering that he had always been the ringleader in those scenes of childhood torment.

"Of course the stables are new since your time," Dean Adams was saying. "One of our 1945 graduates donated them. He's quite a successful oilman now."

Randy took the lead going back, keeping them laughing with a string of jokes about traveling salesmen and sailors' girls. It was much like the old days. They might never have left Aldon, except that now they were twenty-five years older and their steps were a little heavier along the path.

Dinner was a rousing affair, with the entire student body rising in a singing tribute to the old grads. The president gave a proper speech, and then Dean Adams took the microphone.

"We have the old boys back every year," he began, "and I suppose by now I should be over the emotions of the event. But I'll tell you it still moves me, still almost brings a tear to my eye. I like to think that we at Aldon have done something quietly great, that we've helped supply the leaders of this great land of ours. Not every class can be made up of one hundred percent winners, but every class has its share. The class of '44 graduated at a difficult time in life, for our country and for yourselves. There aren't many of you still alive, but those who are tell us that even at the brink of war Aldon could still turn out boys—and men—to excite our pride.

"This evening I'm especially pleased to be able to announce a memorial to your class, and to its brave members who died in battle. Your classmate Mark Wedmer has advised me of his intention to donate $100,000 to Aldon over the period of the next three years, to be used for a new science wing, something we've needed for far too long. I know you'll join me in offering heartfelt thanks for the generous gift, on behalf of the class of 1944."

There was a round of applause from the student body, and from the old boys, though Gent noticed that Randy Maxwell kept his hands in his lap. The old days were not so far gone after all. Perhaps Randy realized that this gesture was only Mark's way of revenging himself for all those afternoons of teenage cruelty so very long ago.

After the speeches there were more songs, and then a basketball game in the new gym. Gent realized as the evening wore on that he'd fallen into an easy companionship with Cottrell and Maxwell, almost as if they were back in those golden pre-war days. They cheered together at every basket, and at the end of the game they clustered around the bench, talking with the boys and the coach. It was like old times.

Oddly, Mark Wedmer had joined them. He did not hang back as had been his habit in those earlier days, but instead seemed almost to be leading the conversations. He addressed many of his remarks to Randy, something he'd never ventured to do when they were classmates. "What do you think, Randy? They're surely taller boys than in our day."

"Yeah," Randy agreed uncomfortably. "Sure are."

Charlie Cottrell put his arm on Mark's shoulder. "That was quite a thing, donating a hundred grand! I don't see that much in ten years on the newspaper."

"It was nothing," Mark said. "Just making up for the old days."

There was a strained silence, and Tom Gent leaped into it. "Randy, you haven't seen the new swimming pool, have you? It's right at the other end of this building.

The three of them strolled off in that direction, with Mark Wedmer bringing up the rear. It was obvious they were not to be rid of him that easily. They passed through a ceiling-high folding partition that separated the gym from the pool, and Gent began filling the awkward void with words. "Here it is, Randy. Great thing, isn't it? Dean Adams says it's NCAA regulation, just like all the colleges have."

They stood at the edge of the pool, watching the gentle movement of the water from some unseen source. The odor of chlorine was heavy in the still air of the building.

"Diving and everything!" Charlie Cottrell observed. "They never had anything like this in our day. If they had, I'd probably have been a swimming champ in college."

"You didn't go to college, remember?" Randy reminded him.

"I did for a year, until I was drafted. I was doing good, too. I was really doing good." He looked down at his hands. "I wonder where I'd have been today if the war hadn't come along."

Randy Maxwell gripped the tubular ladder that led into the pool at one end. "Probably you'd have been an investment banker, like Mark here. Right, Mark?"

"Maybe. Then again, maybe not." Randy moved over closer to him. "Remember the time we tied you to the bed and gave you a hotfoot? Remember when we dumped the pail of water on you from the window?"

"I remember," Mark Wedmer answered, tight-lipped.

"Those were the days. Things you can remember all your life."

Cottrell joined in, chuckling. "There was the time we sneaked into town and left you to take the blame. Remember that, Mark?"

"I remember," he repeated.

The crowd from the basketball game had departed now, and there was only silence from behind the big folding partition. The water, blue, clear, continued to ripple ever so slightly. Randy Maxwell chuckled too, and even Tom Gent joined in. They all remembered.

"But now we're just old boys," Randy said. "That was long ago."

Mark turned as if to walk away from them, and Randy pushed him, hard. Mark staggered to keep his balance on the edge of the tile pool, but then slipped and toppled in. The water splashed the others as they stood laughing on the edge.

"I can't swim," Mark shouted. "Help me!"

Randy Maxwell stood with legs spread and hands on hips, looking down at the struggling figure in the water. "There's the ladder, fatso. Grab hold of it."

Somehow, gasping and snorting for breath, Mark managed to fling out a hand and catch the metal ladder. "I . . . help me . . ."

They stood there a moment longer, watching Mark struggle, and then Charlie Cottrell stepped forward. He brought his foot down hard on the grasping fingers that clung to the ladder. "Swim around a bit longer, Mark," he said. "Swim around a bit."

"I . . . help me . . . I can't swim . . . Please . . ."

He tried to reach the edge of the pool one more time, but now they were all three on him. Gent grabbed Mark's hair and forced his head under the surface, holding it down.

Mark broke free and pushed out to the middle, away from his tormentors. He gave one last terrified cry against the clear blue water, and then went under.

For a long time the three men stood there at the pool's edge in silence, and Randy Maxwell slowly smoked a cigarette. He waited until the water again was perfectly smooth, with only the slight ripple they'd noticed before.

Then, finally, he turned to the others and said, "We'd better get some help for him. After all, he's one of the old boys, like us."

A Checklist of the Non-series Short Stories of Edward D. Hoch

This checklist covers the 264 short stories of Edward D. Hoch, first published between 1956 and 1990, that do not fall within any of the two dozen series he has created. The vast majority are non-series stories in the strict sense but a few feature famous series characters created by others, such as Sherlock Holmes, Philip Marlowe, Dick Tracy and Batman, in authorized continuations of those characters' exploits. The stories collected in THE NIGHT MY FRIEND are marked with an asterisk.

The material in this checklist is culled from a comprehensive checklist of all Hoch's work, prepared primarily by Hoch and myself, and distributed at the 1991 Anthony Boucher Memorial Mystery Convention at which Hoch was the guest of honor.

FRANCIS M. NEVINS, JR.

I. STORIES PUBLISHED IN MAGAZINES

Adventure

4/71   Blow-Up!

Alfred Hitchcock's Mystery Magazine

1/62   *Twilight Thunder. (*I Am Curious (Bloody)*, ed. Alfred Hitchcock. Dell pb, 1971.)

Checklist

3/62	Dial 120 for Survival.
3/63	*The Picnic People. (*Alfred Hitchcock's Anthology #3: Tales To Make Your Blood Run Cold,* ed. Eleanor Sullivan. Davis/Dial, 1978.)
1/64	*Shattered Rainbow. (*Alfred Hitchcock's Anthology #10: Tales To Make You Weak in the Knees,* ed. Eleanor Sullivan. Davis/Dial, 1981.)
5/64	*The Patient Waiter.
7/64	Walk with a Wizard.
10/64	*Too Long at the Fair. (*The Wickedest Show on Earth,* ed. Marcia Muller & Bill Pronzini. Morrow, 1985.)
11/64	Secret Ballot.
1/65	*Winter Run. (*Alfred Hitchcock's Anthology #1: Tales To Keep You Spellbound,* ed. Eleanor Sullivan. Davis/Dial, 1977. *Hitchcock in Prime Time,* ed. Francis M. Nevins, Jr. & Martin H. Greenberg. Avon pb, 1985. *Five Classic Stories,* ed. Cathleen Jordan. Davis pb, 1986.)
2/65	*The Long Way Down. (*Best Detective Stories of the Year,* ed. Anthony Boucher. Dutton, 1966. *The Locked Room Reader,* ed. Hans Stefan Santesson. Random House, 1968. *Death on Arrival,* ed. Alfred Hitchcock. Dell pb, 1979.)
3/65	*Dreaming Is a Lonely Thing. (*Alfred Hitchcock's Anthology #17: Mortal Errors,* ed. Cathleen Jordan. Davis/Dial, 1984.)
9/65	The Way of Justice.
2/66	*They Never Come Back.
1/67	A Gift of Myrrh.
5/67	Stop at Nothing.
6/67	The Girl with the Dragon Kite. (*Companion,* 10/71. *Alfred Hitchcock's Anthology #13: Deathreach,* ed. Cathleen Jordan. Davis/Dial, 1982.)
7/67	It Could Get Warmer.
8/67	Warrior's Farewell. (*Alfred Hitchcock's Anthology #4: Tales To Scare You Stiff,* ed. Eleanor Sullivan. Davis/Dial, 1978.)
10/67	The Eye of the Pigeon. (*Alive and Screaming,* ed. Alfred Hitchcock. Dell pb, 1980.)
12/67	Another War. (*Alfred Hitchcock's Anthology #5: Tales To Send Chills Down Your Spine,* ed. Eleanor Sullivan. Davis/Dial, 1979.)
3/68	After the Fact.
5/68	Cold Cognizance.
6/68	Something for the Dark. (*Alfred Hitchcock Presents: Stories That Go Bump in the Night.* Random House, 1977.)
8/68	*Hawk in the Valley.
10/68	A Certain Power. (*Alfred Hitchcock's Anthology #16: A Choice of Evils,* ed. Elana Lore. Davis/Dial, 1983.)
2/69	Poor Sport.
4/69	*Homecoming.
5/69	Emergency.
7/69	The Dictator's Double.
9/69	Arbiter of Uncertainties. (*Murderers' Row,* ed. Alfred Hitchcock. Dell pb, 1975. *Alfred Hitchcock's Anthology #11: Tales To Make You Quake And Quiver,* ed. Cathleen Jordan. Davis/Dial, 1982.)
10/69	The Secret Savant.
4/70	Flapdragon.
5/70	A Place To See the Dark.

12/71	Rubber Bullets.
2/72	The Man at the Top.
5/72	Burial Monuments Three. (*Best Detective Stories of the Year*, ed. Allen J. Hubin. Dutton, 1973. *The Arbor House Treasury of Mystery and Suspense*, ed. Bill Pronzini, Barry N. Malzberg & Martin H. Greenberg. Arbor House, 1981.)
11/72	Day of the Vampire. (*13 Horrors of Halloween*, ed. Carol-Lynn Rössel Waugh, Martin H. Greenberg & Isaac Asimov. Avon pb, 1983.)
2/73	Two Days in Organville. (*Speak of the Devil*, ed. Alfred Hitchcock. Dell pb, 1975.)
5/73	The Man Who Came Back. (*Alfred Hitchcock's Anthology #9: Tales To Make Your Hair Stand on End*, ed. Eleanor Sullivan. Davis/Dial, 1981. *Manhattan Mysteries*, ed. Bill Pronzini, Carol-Lynn Rössel Waugh & Martin H. Greenberg. Avenel, 1987.)
6/73	The Plastic Man.
10/73	The Day We Killed the Madman. (*Alfred Hitchcock's Anthology #26: Shrouds and Pockets*, ed. Cathleen Jordan. Davis pb, 1988.)
11/73	Snowsuit.
1/74	The Witch of Westwood.
9/74	The Choker. (*Alfred Hitchcock's Anthology #8: Tales To Make Your Teeth Chatter*, ed. Eleanor Sullivan. Davis/Dial, 1980.)
10/74	Story for an October Issue.
12/75	The Death of Lame Jack Lincoln.
1/76	The Basilisk Hunt.
5/76	The Diamond Frog.
5/76	Here Be Dragons (as by R. L. Stevens).
7/76	The Judas Kiss (as by Stephen Dentinger).
8/76	Plastique.
9/76	The Quest for Jason Stannis.
10/76	The Scorpion Girl.
11/76	The Melting Man. (*The Deadly Arts*, ed. Bill Pronzini & Marcia Muller. Arbor House, 1985.)
12/76	End of the Line. (*Alfred Hitchcock's Anthology #2: Tales To Take Your Breath Away*, ed. Eleanor Sullivan. Davis/Dial, 1977.)
2/77	Anniversary Gift.
3/77	Bread Upon the Waters. (*John Creasey's Crime Collection 1979*, ed. Herbert Harris. London: Gollancz, 1979.)
5/77	A Simple Little Thing.
7/77	Second Chance. (*Women's Wiles*, ed. Michele B. Slung. Harcourt Brace Jovanovich, 1979.)
8/77	All Knives Are Sharp.
11/77	The Lady Or the Lion? (*John Creasey's Crime Collection 1980*, ed. Herbert Harris. London: Gollancz, 1980.)
6/78	Home Is the Hunter.
8/78	The Pact of the Five.
10/78	Memory in the Dark.
11/78	The Obsession of Officer O'Rourke.
12/78	Three Weeks in a Spanish Town.
7/79	The Rattlesnake Man.
8/79	The Paris Strangler.

Checklist

12/79	Code of Honor.
4/23/80	The Nine Eels of Madame Wu. (*A Special Kind of Crime*, ed. Lawrence Treat. Doubleday, 1982. *Alfred Hitchcock's Mystery Magazine*, Winter 1989.)
10/27/80	Fiction.
8/19/81	Seven Billion Day.
12/9/81	The Bad Samaritan. (*John Creasey's Crime Collection 1989*. London: Gollancz, 1989.)
9/83	Deceptions. (*The Year's Best Mystery & Suspense Stories*, ed. Edward D. Hoch. Walker, 1984.)

Argosy

9/71	The League of Arthur.

Blazing Guns Western Story

4/57	The Graveyard on the Hill. (*The Lawmen*, ed. Bill Pronzini & Martin H. Greenberg. Fawcett pb, 1984.)

Charlie Chan Mystery Magazine

2/74	Dinner with the Boss.

Child Life Mystery & Science Fiction Magazine

2/79	The Thing in the Lake: Part I.
3/79	The Thing in the Lake: Part II.

Crack Detective and Mystery Stories

12/56	The Late Sports.

Crime and Justice

1/57	Inspector Fleming's Last Case. (*Mystery Digest*, 7/58, as "Fatal Decision.")

Crosscurrents

10/90	The Detective's Wife.

Dude

3/77	Web.

87th Precinct Mystery Magazine

8/75	One Eden Too Many.

Ellery Queen's Anthology

Spr-Sum/73   The Lot's Wife Caper (as by R. L. Stevens).
Fal-Wtr/74   The Serpent in the Sky.

Ellery Queen's Mystery Magazine

10/63   I'd Know You Anywhere. (*Ellery Queen's Double Dozen*, ed. Ellery Queen. Random House, 1964. *Alfred Hitchcock Presents: Stories To Be Read With the Lights On.* Random House, 1973. *Every Crime in the Book*, ed. Robert L. Fish. Putnam, 1975. *Masterpieces of Mystery, Volume 11*, ed. Ellery Queen. Meredith, 1978. *Short Story International*, 8/81. *A Treasury of World War II Stories*, ed. Bill Pronzini & Martin H. Greenberg. Bonanza, 1985.)

2/64   The Perfect Time for the Perfect Crime. (*Adventures for Today*, ed. Christ & Potell. Harcourt Brace, 1968. *Killers of the Mind*, ed. Lucy Freeman. Random House, 1974. *101 Mystery Stories*, ed. Bill Pronzini & Martin H. Greenberg. Avenel, 1986.)

10/64   The Crime of Avery Mann.

2/66   The Odor of Melting. (*Alfred Hitchcock Presents: Stories To Be Read with the Door Locked.* Random House, 1975. *101 Mystery Stories*, ed. Bill Pronzini & Martin H. Greenberg. Avenel, 1986.)

1/68   *First Offense (as by Stephen Dentinger).

4/68   The Impossible "Impossible Crime." (*Ellery Queen's Murder Menu*, ed. Ellery Queen. World, 1969. *Companion*, 9/71. *Ellery Queen's Mystery Stories #2.* Bonomo, 1979. *Cold Blood: Murder in Canada*, ed. Peter Sellers. Mosaic/Riverrun, 1987.)

1/69   Murder Offstage. (*Ellery Queen's Grand Slam*, ed. Ellery Queen. World, 1970.)

1/69   Every Fifth Man. (*Ellery Queen's Grand Slam*, ed. Ellery Queen. World, 1970. *Quickie Thrillers*, ed. Arthur Liebman. Pocket Books pb, 1975. *Miniature Mysteries*, ed. Isaac Asimov, Martin H. Greenberg & Joseph D. Olander. Taplinger, 1981. *101 Mystery Stories*, ed. Bill Pronzini & Martin H. Greenberg. Avenel, 1986.)

1/69   The Nile Cat. (*Ellery Queen's Grand Slam*, ed. Ellery Queen. World, 1970.)

3/70   The Seventh Assassin.

3/70   The Seventieth Number.

4/71   The Way Out. (*Ellery Queen's Anthology #46: Lost Ladies*, ed. Ellery Queen & Eleanor Sullivan. Davis/Dial, 1983.)

7/71   The Physician and the Opium Fiend (as by R. L. Stevens). (*Ellery Queen's Mystery Bag*, ed. Ellery Queen. World, 1972. *Miniature Mysteries*, ed. Isaac Asimov, Martin H. Greenberg & Joseph D. Olander. Taplinger, 1981.)

12/71   Thirteen (as by R. L. Stevens). (*Miniature Mysteries*, ed. Isaac Asimov, Martin H. Greenberg & Joseph D. Olander. Taplinger, 1981. *Ellery Queen's Anthology #47: Lost Men*, ed. Eleanor Sullivan. Davis/Dial, 1983.)

2/72   Just Something That Happened (as by R. L. Stevens).

Checklist

5/72	Lot 721/XY258 (as by R. L. Stevens). (*Miniature Mysteries*, ed. Isaac Asimov, Martin H. Greenberg & Joseph D. Olander. Taplinger, 1981.)
7/72	The Forbidden Word (as by R. L. Stevens). (*Mysterious Visions*, ed. Charles G. Waugh, Martin H. Greenberg & Joseph D. Olander. St. Martin's, 1979. *101 Science Fiction Stories*, ed. Martin H. Greenberg, Charles G. Waugh & Jenny-Lynn Waugh. Avenel, 1986.)
8/72	The Legacy (as by R. L. Stevens).
2/73	The Most Dangerous Man (as by R. L. Stevens). (*Ellery Queen's Murdercade*, ed. Ellery Queen. Random House, 1975. *Penguin Classic Crime Omnibus*, ed. Julian Symons. Penguin pb, 1984. *Last Laughs*, ed. Gregory Mcdonald. Mysterious Press, 1986.)
7/73	King's Knight's Gambit Declined (as by R. L. Stevens).
1/74	Nothing to Chance (as by R. L. Stevens).
4/75	The Great American Novel (as by R. L. Stevens). (*Chapter and Hearse*, ed. Marcia Muller & Bill Pronzini. Morrow, 1985. *Ellery Queen's Anthology #60: 11 Deadly Sins*, ed. Eleanor Sullivan. Davis pb, 1989.)
7/75	A Deal in Diamonds (as by R. L. Stevens). (*Miniature Mysteries*, ed. Isaac Asimov, Martin H. Greenberg & Joseph D. Olander. Taplinger, 1981. *More Surprises*, ed. Burton Goodman. Jamestown, 1990.)
1/76	The Three Travelers (as by R. L. Stevens). (*Crime at Christmas*, ed. Jack Adrian. Equation/Thorsons (England), 1988.)
7/76	Five Rings in Reno (as by R. L. Stevens). (*A Multitude of Sins*, ed. Ellery Queen. Davis, 1978.)
8/76	The Centennial Assassin. (*Best Detective Stories of the Year*, ed. Edward D. Hoch. Dutton, 1977.)
2/77	The Price of Wisdom (as by R. L. Stevens). (*Best Detective Stories of the Year*, ed. Edward D. Hoch. Dutton, 1978.)
3/77	EQMM Number 400 (as by R. L. Stevens).
8/77	The Crime of the Century (as by R. L. Stevens). (*The Big Apple Mysteries*, ed. Carol-Lynn Rössel Waugh, Martin H. Greenberg & Isaac Asimov. Avon pb, 1982. *Ellery Queen's Mystery Magazine*, 6/85. *Manhattan Mysteries*, ed. Bill Pronzini, Carol-Lynn Rössel Waugh & Martin H. Greenberg. Avenel, 1987.)
1/78	Innocent Victim (as by R. L. Stevens).
7/78	The Missing Money (as by R. L. Stevens).
10/6/80	Deduction, 1996 (as by R. L. Stevens).
5/82	Just Passing Through (as by R. L. Stevens). (*The Year's Best Mystery & Suspense Stories*, ed. Edward D. Hoch. Walker, 1983.)

Espionage

5/85	Cover Story.

The Executioner Mystery Magazine

4/75	Bodyguard.

Famous Science Fiction

Fall/67   The Times We Had.
Fall/68   The Maiden's Sacrifice. (*100 Great Fantasy Short Short Stories,* ed. Isaac Asimov, Terry Carr & Martin H. Greenberg. Doubleday, 1984.)

Fantastic Universe

6/57   Versus.
6/58   Zoo. (*Combo #402,* ed. John Cooper. Scott Foresman, 1971. *Nova,* ed. Arthur Daigon. Prentice-Hall, 1977. *100 Great Science-Fiction Short Short Stories,* ed. Isaac Asimov, Martin H. Greenberg & Joseph D. Olander. Doubleday, 1978.*Triple Action Short Stories,* ed. Jeri Schapiro. Scholastic, 1979. *Riverfronts,* ed. Louise Matteoni et al. Economy, 1980. *Orbits and Opportunities,* ed. Theodore Clymer. Ginn, 1980. *Wingspan,* ed. Robert B. Ruddell et al. Allyn & Bacon, 1981. *Weird World #7,* 2/81. *Chains of Light,* ed. Theodore Clymer. Ginn, 1982. *Language for Daily Use,* ed. Dorothy S. Strickland. Harcourt Brace, 1983. *Building English Skills,* ed. Kathleen L. Bell et al. McDougal, 1983. *Fantastic Reading,* ed. Isaac Asimov, Martin H. Greenberg & David Clark Yeager. Scott Foresman, 1984. *Strategies in Reading,* ed. Ethel Grodzins Romm. Harcourt Brace, 1984. *Beginnings in Literature,* ed. Alan L. Madsen et al. Scott Foresman, 1984. *Young Extraterrestrials,* ed. Isaac Asimov, Martin H. Greenberg & Charles G. Waugh. Harper & Row, 1984. *Prentice-Hall Literature: Bronze,* ed. Roger Babusci et al. Prentice-Hall, 1988. *Sudden Twists,* ed. Burton Goodman. Jamestown, 1988. *Isaac Asimov's Science Fiction & Fantasy Story-a-Month 1989 Calendar,* ed. Isaac Asimov & Martin H. Greenberg. Pomegranate, 1988. *Challenge Plus,* Spring/1990. *Read,* 2/16/90.)

Fast Action Detective and Mystery Stories

8/57   The Last Darkness.

Future Science Fiction

10/58   The Last Paradox. (*100 Great Science Fiction Short Short Stories,* ed. Isaac Asimov, Martin H. Greenberg & Joseph D. Olander. Doubleday, 1978. *Bananas #6.* Scholastic, 1981. *Fantastic Reading,* ed. Isaac Asimov, Martin H. Greenberg & David Clark Yeager. Scott Foresman, 1984.)

Guilty Detective Story Magazine

11/56   The Chippy (as by Irwin Booth).

Checklist

Magazine of Horror

8/63   The Maze and the Monster. (*Devils & Demons,* ed. Marvin Kaye. Double-day, 1987.)

11/63   The Faceless Thing. (*Fiends and Creatures,* ed. Marvin Kaye. Popular Library pb, 1975. *Bug-Eyed Monsters,* ed. Bill Pronzini & Barry N. Malzberg. Harcourt Brace pb, 1980. *Masterpieces of Terror and the Supernatural,* ed. Marvin Kaye. Doubleday, 1985.)

9/64   A Stranger Came to Reap (as by Stephen Dentinger).

11/65   The Empty Zoo.

Manhunt

3/57   The Man Who Was Everywhere. (*Alfred Hitchcock Presents: Stories My Mother Never Told Me.* Random House, 1963. *Diners' Club Magazine,* 1/64.)

Mike Shayne Mystery Magazine

6/69   The Tomb at the Top of the Tree.
10/69   Picnic at Midnight.
6/70   Zone.
9/70   The Afternoon Ear.
2/71   Die-Hard.
3/71   The Poison Man.
6/71   The Sugar Man.
9/71   Blood Money.
11/71   The Sound of Screaming.
11/71   Fifty Bucks by Monday (as by Stephen Dentinger).
12/71   The Zap Effect.
3/72   A Country Like the Sun.
8/72   Suicide.
9/72   The Holy Witch.
6/73   Home Movies.
1/74   The Infernal Machine.
1/75   The Neptune Fund.
8/75   Twine.
12/76   Day of Judgment.
2/77   A Touch of Red.
3/77   The Wooden Dove.
9/78   A Man Could Get Killed.
11/78   After Class.
1/79   In a Foreign City.
3/79   The Gun.
4/79   Three Hot Days.
6/79   Tough Cop's Girl.
8/79   The Golden Lady.
9/79   Where Is Danny Storm?
11/79   Stairway to Nowhere (with Joseph Commings).
1/80   Just Like the Old Days.

2/80	High Bid.
3/80	Vulcan's Widow.
4/80	Midsummer Night's Scream.
5/80	The Ides of April.
6/80	The Traveling Man.
7/80	A Passing Stranger.
8/80	Just One More. (*100 Great Fantasy Short Short Stories,* ed. Isaac Asimov, Terry Carr & Martin H. Greenberg. Doubleday, 1984.)
9/80	Cop Killer.
2/81	When the War Is Over.
4/81	Rubbish.
11/82	Terrorist.
8/83	Line of Succession.
2/84	Lottery.
5/85	Smothered Mate.

Murder!

9/56	Getaway.
3/57	Execution on Clover Street.

Mystery

3/81	The Vorpal Blade.

Mystery Digest

2/59	Journey to Death.

Mystery Monthly

6/78	The Bank Job.

New Black Mask

#8 (1987)	Spy for Sale.

Nugget

10/75	Man in Hiding.
2/76	The Man Who Knew the Method.

Off-Beat Detective Stories

5/60	The Passionate Phantom.
1/61	Don't Laugh at Murder.
7/61	Lust Loves the Dark.
9/61	Hell's Handmaiden.
5/62	Setup for Murder.
11/62	Madman's Hotel.

Checklist

Original Science Fiction Stories

9/56   Co-Incidence (as by Irwin Booth). (*Miniature Mysteries*, ed. Isaac Asimov, Martin H. Greenberg & Joseph D. Olander. Taplinger, 1981.)

2/59   The Last Unicorns. (*100 Great Fantasy Short Short Stories*, ed. Isaac Asimov, Terry Carr & Martin H. Greenberg. Doubleday, 1984.)

Real Western Stories

2/59   Who Rides with Santa Anna? (*Ghosts*, ed. Marvin Kaye. Doubleday, 1981. *100 Great Fantasy Short Short Stories*, ed. Isaac Asimov, Terry Carr & Martin H. Greenberg. Doubleday, 1984.)

The Saint Detective/Mystery Magazine

7/58   Traynor's Cipher.
1/60   The Long Count.
9/62   *The Suitcase (as by Pat McMahon).
11/63   *Day for a Picnic (as by Pat McMahon). (*Child's Ploy*, ed. Marcia Muller & Bill Pronzini. Macmillan, 1984.)
3/64   The Wolfram Hunters. (*Rulers of Men*, ed. Hans Stefan Santesson. Pyramid pb, 1965. *The Saint Magazine Reader*, ed. Leslie Charteris & Hans Stefan Santesson. Doubleday, 1966. *Gods for Tomorrow*, ed. Hans Stefan Santesson. Award pb, 1967. *Voices in Literature, Language and Composition 4*, ed. Cline, Williams, Mahoney & Dziuk. Ginn, 1969. *Horizons 6*, ed. Guthrie, Campbell & Pielmeier. Ginn, 1970. *Chronicles of a Comer*, ed. Roger Elwood. John Knox Press, 1974. *Dark Sins, Dark Dreams*, ed. Barry N. Malzberg & Bill Pronzini. Doubleday, 1978.)
8/65   *In Some Secret Place.
9/65   Uncle Max (as by Pat McMahon). (*Child's Ploy*, ed. Marcia Muller & Bill Pronzini. Macmillan, 1984.)
4/66   *It Happens, Sometimes (as by Stephen Dentinger).
5/66   The Authentic Death of Cotton Clark (as by Pat McMahon).
7/66   Ring the Bell Softly (as by Stephen Dentinger).
10/66   Children of Judas.
1/67   Fall of Zoo.
1/67   *What's It All About? (as by Stephen Dentinger).
10/67   Recruitment (as by Stephen Dentinger).

The Saint Mystery Magazine (British edition)

7/62   *The Night My Friend (as by Stephen Dentinger).
8/62   Festival in Black (as by Stephen Dentinger).

The Saint Mystery Magazine (Revival)

8/84   Prison Bus.

Shock Magazine

9/60   The Man Who Knew Everything.

Signature/The Diners' Club Magazine

2/66   *The Only Girl in His Life.
5/66   The Fifth Victim.
10/66   *A Girl Like Cathy.
6/67   The Dying Knight.

Special Reports: Fiction

11/88-1/89   Something Green.

Two-Fisted Detective Stories

8/60   A Blade for the Chicken.
1/61   Drive My Hearse, Darling.

Upstate

12/22/85   The Teddy Bear Mystery.

Web Detective Stories

6/60   Sisters of Slaughter.
8/60   Murder Is Eternal!
5/61   The Night People.
9/61   To Serve the Dead.

Woman's World

10/14/80   Common Factor.
5/18/82   Behind Closed Doors.
2/22/83   Violet Crime.
1/24/84   Taxi!
8/14/84   The Woman from Yesterday.

Women's Sports & Fitness

5/86   Mystery at Wimbledon. (The solution is printed in the 6/86 issue.)

II. STORIES NOT PUBLISHED IN MAGAZINES

1965   *To Slay an Eagle (as by Stephen Dentinger). (*The Award Espionage Reader*, ed. Hans Stefan Santesson. Award pb, 1965. Reprinted in *Cloak and Dagger*, ed. Bill Pronzini & Martin H. Greenberg. Avenel, 1988.)

Checklist

1967   God of the Playback (as by Stephen Dentinger). (*Gods for Tomorrow,* ed. Hans Stefan Santesson. Award pb, 1967.)

1968   Cassidy's Saucer. (*Flying Saucers in Fact and Fiction,* ed. Hans Stefan Santesson. Lancer pb, 1968.)

1968   *The Ring with the Velvet Ropes. (*With Malice Toward All,* ed. Robert L. Fish. Putnam, 1968. Reprinted in *Alfred Hitchcock's Anthology #7: Tales To Fill You with Fear and Trembling,* ed. Eleanor Sullivan. Davis/Dial, 1980. Also reprinted in *Rod Serling's Night Gallery Reader,* ed. Carol Serling, Charles G. Waugh & Martin H. Greenberg. Dembner, 1987.)

1969   Unnatural Act. (*Gentle Invaders,* ed. Hans Stefan Santesson. Belmont pb, 1969.)

1969   The Future Is Ours (as by Stephen Dentinger). (*Crime Prevention in the 30th Century,* ed. Hans Stefan Santesson. Walker, 1969.)

1973   Night of the Millenium. (*The Other Side of Tomorrow,* ed. Roger Elwood. Random House, 1973.)

1974   The Boy Who Brought Love. (*Crisis,* ed. Roger Elwood. Thomas Nelson, 1974. Reprinted in *Magical Wishes,* ed. Isaac Asimov, Martin H. Greenberg & Charles G. Waugh. Signet pb, 1986.)

1975   In the Straw. (*Beware More Beasts,* ed. Vic Ghidalia & Roger Elwood. Manor pb, 1975. Reprinted in *Creature!,* ed. Bill Pronzini. Arbor House, 1981.)

1980   Exú. (*Voodoo!,* ed. Bill Pronzini. Arbor House, 1980.)

1980   The Locked Room Cipher. (*Who Done It?,* ed. Alice Laurance & Isaac Asimov. Houghton Mifflin, 1980.)

1980   The Weekend Magus. (*Mummy!,* ed. Bill Pronzini. Arbor House, 1980. Reprinted in *Mummy Stories,* ed. Martin H. Greenberg. Ballantine pb, 1990.)

1984   Last Year's Murder. (*Ellery Queen's Anthology #51: Prime Crimes 2,* ed. Eleanor Sullivan & Karen A. Prince. Davis, 1984.)

1984   The Chicken Soup Kid (as by R. L. Stevens). (*Murder on the Menu,* ed. Carol-Lynn Rössel Waugh, Martin H. Greenberg & Isaac Asimov. Avon pb, 1984.)

1985   Bigfish. (*A Treasury of American Horror Stories,* ed. Frank D. McSherry, Jr., Charles G. Waugh & Martin H. Greenberg. Bonanza, 1985.)

1986   Centaur Fielder for the Yankees. (*Mythical Beasties,* ed. Isaac Asimov, Martin H. Greenberg & Charles G. Waugh. Signet pb, 1986.)

1986   Murder at Rose Cottage. (*The Agatha Christie Mystery Collection.* Bantam, 1986.)

1987   The Return of the Speckled Band. (*The New Adventures of Sherlock Holmes,* ed. Martin H. Greenberg & Carol-Lynn Rössel Waugh. Carroll & Graf, 1987.)

1988   Essence d'Orient. (*Raymond Chandler's Philip Marlowe: A Centennial Celebration,* ed. Byron Preiss. Knopf, 1988.)

1988   The Tragedy of 1799. (*Mr. President—Private Eye,* ed. Martin H. Greenberg & Francis M. Nevins, Jr. Ballantine pb, 1988.)

1988   The River of Doubt. (*Mr. President—Private Eye,* ed. Martin H. Greenberg & Francis M. Nevins, Jr. Ballantine pb, 1988.)

1989   Kansas in August. (*A Treasury of American Mystery Stories,* ed. Frank D.

	McSherry, Jr., Charles G. Waugh & Martin H. Greenberg. Avenel, 1989.)
1989	Bull and Bear (as by R. L. Stevens). (*A Treasury of American Mystery Stories,* ed. Frank D. McSherry, Jr., Charles G. Waugh & Martin H. Greenberg. Avenel, 1989.)
1989	The Pirate of Millionaire's Cove. (*The Further Adventures of Batman,* ed. Martin H. Greenberg. Bantam pb, 1989.)
1989	The Other Phantom. (*Phantoms,* ed. Martin H. Greenberg & Rosalind M. Greenberg. DAW pb, 1989.)
1989	The Overheard Conversation. (*Foundation's Friends,* ed. Martin H. Greenberg. Tor, 1989.)
1990	The Joker Is Mild. (*The Further Adventures of the Joker,* ed. Martin H. Greenberg. Bantam pb, 1990.)
1990	Chessboard's Last Gambit. (*Dick Tracy: The Secret Files,* ed. Max Allan Collins & Martin H. Greenberg. Tor pb, 1990.)
1990	Jordan's Stage. (*New Frontiers, Volume II,* ed. Martin H. Greenberg & Bill Pronzini. Tor pb, 1990.)
1990	Remember My Name. (*Eastern Ghosts,* ed. Frank D. McSherry, Jr., Charles G. Waugh & Martin H. Greenberg. Rutledge Hill pb, 1990.)
1990	Christmas Eve in San Augustine. (*Christmas Out West,* ed. Bill Pronzini & Martin H. Greenberg. Doubleday, 1990.)